FULL
CIRCLE

Books by Michael Thomas Ford

Last Summer

Looking for It

Tangled Sheets

Full Circle

Path of the Green Man

Masters of Midnight
(with William J. Mann, Sean Wolfe, and Jeff Mann)

Midnight Thirsts
(with Timothy Ridge, Greg Herren, and Sean Wolfe)

Published by Kensington Publishing Corporation

FULL CIRCLE

MICHAEL THOMAS FORD

KENSINGTON BOOKS
www.kensingtonbooks.com

For the men who served in Vietnam

Acknowledgments

As always, much gratitude and appreciation to Mitchell Waters and John Scognamiglio, who let me do it one more time. Also to David Berry, whose kind assistance made the writing of this novel much more interesting. And mostly to Patrick, Andy, Sam, and George, who make a house a home.

Author's Note

Although this is a work of fiction, numerous people, places, and events from real life make appearances in the story. As much as possible, I have drawn on personal recollection and firsthand accounts when writing about these things. In some instances, most notably in the speech given by Harvey Milk at the 1978 Gay Freedom Day rally, I have incorporated fictional dialogue with actual transcripts from the event in order to better convey the sense of what occurred.

PROLOGUE

"Ned, it's Jack."

I open my eyes and look up into the shadows that fill the ceiling over the bed. Rain is falling, drumming on the roof, and vaguely I make a mental reminder to clean the gutters before the storm promised by the weatherman on the evening news arrives in full force. Tomorrow, perhaps, after I finish grading the stack of freshman essays sitting on my desk in the next room. If I can find the ladder in the mess that is the barn.

Beside me, Thayer rolls onto his back and breathes deeply. As usual, he's somehow managed to pull most of the quilt around himself so that he's cocooned in warmth. I both admire and resent his ability to sleep so fully, like a child. Or a dog, I think, as on his smaller bed beside ours Sam imitates Thayer, stretching his big paws and sighing contentedly.

How old is Sam now? I count back, ticking off the years. Eleven? No, I correct myself. Twelve. Twelve years since Thayer and I returned from the Banesbury County Animal Shelter with him sitting between us on the seat of our pickup, nose raised hopefully as he sniffed the air for the scent of home. Even then his paws had been enormous, hinting at the great lumbering beast he was soon to become.

Twelve years. How did they slip by so quickly, turning the lively puppy we couldn't keep away from the pond behind the house into the gray-muzzled fellow who now spends most of the hours asleep in a pool of sun on the porch? What have they done, too, to Thayer and myself? Somewhere in that rush of days we've slipped from our forties into our fifties, our hair graying and our bodies beginning to betray us in small ways—eyesight that proves more and more unreliable, muscles that complain more than they used to about getting the chores done. My last birthday was number 56, and Thayer will catch up to me in less than a month's time.

We are, all of us—men and dog—growing old together. Older, Thayer says whenever I mention the unstoppable advancement of time. Not old. "We'll never be *old*," he says defiantly, kissing me on top of my head where my hair is thinning. "And you shouldn't worry so much," he tells me. "It's burning a hole in your head, like a crop circle."

This eternal optimism is one of the many things I love about this man, my partner for nearly fifteen years. He is the antidote to my suspicion that the world is forever on the brink of calamity, teetering perilously between salvation and destruction, ready to tumble headlong toward annihilation at the merest push. He saves me from myself on a daily basis. And he bakes the sweetest apple pie I have ever tasted. What he sees in me I don't know and am afraid to ask, in case thinking about the answer finally makes him see what a fool he's been to stick around.

And what of Jack? Has Jack aged along with the rest of us? I can't help but wonder. Although I'm trying desperately to distract myself from thinking about him, he intrudes, pushing his way in as he always has, as if he belongs in the room simply because he wants to be there. It's how he's always approached the world. I know from far too much past experience that now that he's settled in, he won't go away, so I give in and pull back the covers.

The wood floors of our old farmhouse are cool beneath my feet, and groan softly as I walk from the bedroom, down the hallway, and into my office. Sitting at my desk, I turn on the lamp and surround myself with a circle of light. Pushed back, the darkness retreats through the window. The rain seems to dilute the blackness, and through the thinning night I see the outline of the barn. Beyond it is the pond, and beyond that the blueberry bushes and, finally, the woods. This is the place I call home, the place where until Jack's phone call I believed that I was safe from the past.

"Ned, it's Jack." And just like that the ground fell away beneath my feet. Even now, hours later, I still feel as if I'm tumbling through the air, waiting to hit the ground.

I open one of the desk's drawers and remove an envelope. Yellowed with time, it's addressed to a house I no longer live in, on a street thousands of miles away, in a city I left long ago without looking back. Inside is a card decorated with a Christmas scene and signed with a hastily-scrawled signature. Tucked into the card are two photographs.

I don't know why I've kept either the card or the photos. I'm not by nature a sentimental man, a trait that confounds Thayer, a hopeless romantic who still has the flowers I gave him on our first date, dried and stored in a box somewhere in the attic. I don't believe in cataloging my past, surrounding myself with reminders of people and places. What I want to remember I keep in my head.

But I've held on to these, although until Jack's call I hadn't looked at them in a very long time, and had to unearth them from a box of old tax returns and unfiled articles in my closet. Now, seeing them for the first time in many years, I'm reminded of something a photographer friend once told me. "The only subjects that photograph completely naturally," she said, "are children and animals. The rest of us are afraid the camera will see us for who we really are."

In the first photograph, Jack and I are children, probably four or five years old. We're dressed in nearly identical outfits—cowboy costumes complete with hats and little pistols. Jack is waving his gun at the camera and beaming, while I look at the gun in my hand with a perplexed expression, as if concerned that at any moment it might go off.

As I look at the boys Jack and I once were, I can't recall the occasion for the cowboy getups. It's one of the many childhood moments that have disappeared from the files of my memory like scraps of recycled paper. Without the photographic evidence, I'd be unable to prove its existence at all. But there we are, the two of us, captured forever as we appeared in that one brief moment in time.

The occasion of the second photograph I remember more fully. It was a birthday party for a mutual acquaintance. This time Jack and I are men nearing forty. It was one of the last times I saw him. Once again, Jack is smiling for the camera while I look away, caught in profile. Gone are the cowboy outfits, and there are no guns in our hands, but something much more dangerous separates us. A man. Andy Kowalski.

Andy stands between Jack and me. We flank him, like guards, although neither of us touches him. Andy regards the photographer with disinterest, his handsome face perfectly composed as if he is alone in front of a mirror. Once again I think of animals and children and how they lack the fear of being betrayed by the camera. Andy Kowalski is something of both.

These two photographs, taken decades apart, roughly mark the beginning and the end of my relationship with Jack. With Andy, too, although our time together was only half as long. Both friendships were laid to rest when I came to Maine to start my life over again, when I left behind everything I knew and everything I was, to become something else.

But the past has apparently decided not to stay buried. Jack's call has opened a door I thought to be long shut and locked. Now it stands open, waiting for me to walk through. When I look beyond it, though, all I see is a room filled with dusty boxes, boxes best left unopened.

"Hey."

Thayer's voice, soft and sleepy as it is, startles me. He comes into the office and puts his hands on my shoulders.

"What are you doing up so early? When I woke up and you weren't there, I thought maybe my mama was right after all and the Rapture had come and Jesus had swept you into his bosom. I was afraid you'd left Sam and me to face the army of hell all on our own."

"Somehow I think I'm the last one Jesus would sweep into his bosom if he came back," I tell him. "And even if he did, I think you and Sam would do just fine against Satan and his hordes."

"Sam maybe," says Thayer, leaning over my shoulder. "He's a tough old boy. But I'd be the first one on my knees letting 'em brand me with the Number of the Beast."

He picks up the photographs. "Who are these handsome gentlemen?"

I sigh. Although he knows the basic outline of my life's story, Thayer has heard very few of the details. Not because I fear knowing them would change how he feels about me, but simply because I've never felt the need to tell them.

"That is a long and complicated tale," I answer.

"Well, apparently it's interesting enough that it got you out of bed. And now I'm up, too, so I think it's only fair that you tell me," Thayer says. "I'll go put the coffee on."

He leaves me alone with the photos and with the memories that are starting to push their way into my thoughts. Do I really want to tell him about Jack and Andy? Can I even remember it all and make some sense of it? I teach history to my students, but my own is one I'm not sure that I'm completely qualified to relate. I fear that given my role in the events, I'm an unreliable narrator. At best, my memories are tarnished by years spent trying to erase them, so that what remain are faded, possibly beyond recognition.

Still, I find that part of me wants to tell the story. Maybe, I think, it will help me decide what to do about what Jack has called to tell me. More likely, it will simply resurrect old ghosts. Either way, Thayer is waiting downstairs with coffee, and I find that I can no longer sit up here alone.

I leave the photos behind and descend the creaky staircase to the first floor. The smell of coffee scents the air, and the kitchen is comfortingly lit. The doorway glows, and through it I see Thayer setting two mugs on the table. Sam has followed him downstairs and has stretched himself out on the floor. His tail thumps against the worn planks as I enter and sit down, and then he closes his eyes and settles back into sleep.

"All right," Thayer says, sitting down across from me. "Start talking."

CHAPTER 1

For many reasons, August of 1950 was not a pleasant time to be nine months pregnant, particularly for my mother, Alice Brummel. The war in Korea, less than two months old, weighed heavily on the minds of Americans everywhere, and my mother was no exception. Worried that there might be rationing, she'd taken to buying large quantities of things like bread, sugar, and coffee, all of which she stored in the basement, along with bottles of water and extra blankets, which she fully expected to need when the North Koreans began running rampant through Pennsylvania and it became unsafe to venture outdoors unarmed.

When she wasn't stocking up on emergency supplies, she was contending with my father, Leonard Brummel. Unlike his wife, my father felt that the whole Korean business would be settled swiftly and efficiently by the superior war-waging power of the good old U.S. of A. Unconcerned for his own safety, he was therefore free to focus instead on the war raging between his beloved Philadelphia Phillies and everyone else in major league baseball.

The summer of 1950 belonged—as far as the entire baseball-loving population of Pennsylvania was concerned—to the team that had been dubbed the Whiz Kids. Young, cocky, and with the talent to back up their attitude, the Phillies had stormed to the front of the National League thanks to the work of guys like Andy Seminick, Granny Hamner, Dick Sisler, and Robin Roberts. These resident gods of Shibe Park were my father's sole interest during those hot, sticky days, and every evening he came home from his insurance salesman job, settled into his favorite chair with a bottle of Duke beer, and listened to the night's game on the radio.

My mother was not without a sympathetic ear, however. As luck would have it, her best friend and next-door neighbor, Patricia Grace, was also pregnant. Like my father, Patricia's husband, Clark, was also unavailable for support, but not because he was in love with a baseball team. Clark Grace, who didn't know an earned run average from a double play, was a scientist—a physicist—and suddenly much in de-mand by the military. He was currently spending most of his time in Washington, working on something he described vaguely to his wife and neighbors as "a possible new fuel source made from hydrogen."

With their husbands otherwise occupied, Alice and Patricia spent most of their time together. As their bellies swelled in tandem, they passed the mornings playing cards while lamenting their sleepless-ness, their hemorrhoids, and the utter unattractiveness of maternity clothes. Out of concern for the welfare of the country, they were care-ful to limit themselves to two cups of coffee and four Lucky Strikes apiece, not wanting to take more than their share. In the afternoon, they did their shopping at DiCostanza's grocery store and, if Clark was staying in Washington, made dinner together in Alice's kitchen, leaving a plate in the refrigerator for Leonard before going downtown to see a movie or sit in the park. If Clark was home, dinners would be made and eaten separately, but as soon as Leonard was ensconced in front of the radio and Clark in his study, the two women would be out the screen doors of their kitchens and on their way.

Given this closeness, it was no surprise when both Alice and Patricia went into labor within minutes of one another. On a particularly torpid Thursday afternoon, while searching for potential ingredients to put into the fruit salad recipe they'd clipped out of the *Ladies' Home Journal* earlier in the day, Patricia was in the process of thumping a honeydew melon to test its freshness when she felt a wetness on her legs and realized to her dismay that her water had broken right there in the produce section and that her good shoes were most likely soiled beyond repair. Turning to alert Alice, she discovered her friend looking at the apple in her hand with an astonished expression that suggested that she, too, was engaged in something more significant than simply admiring the quality of the fruit.

Moments later, they were on their way to Mercy Hospital, Alice at the wheel of the Nash Rambler Leonard had purchased for her use in

May, but which she'd rarely taken out of the driveway. Patricia, in the passenger seat, clutched the door handle and called out directions. By the time they reached the hospital, both women were breathing heavily and barely able to remember their names to give them to the attending nurse. It wasn't until they were installed in beds next to each other and receiving simultaneous injections of scopolamine that they realized they'd forgotten to inform their husbands of their impending fatherhood.

As it turned out, there was no immediate hurry. Both women would be in labor for some hours, giving Leonard and Clark time to arrive at the hospital and take up stations in the waiting room, where they sat nervously and passed the hours waiting to hear their names called. For Clark, the call came shortly before midnight, when a nurse arrived to tell him that he was the proud father of a healthy baby boy. He had hardly finished receiving congratulations from Leonard when an almost identical nurse appeared to announce that the second birth had occurred at exactly one minute after twelve.

And so it was that Jackson Howard Grace was born on August the 10th and I was born on August the 11th. As for my name, had it been up to my father it would have been Phillip, for obvious and unfortunate reasons. My mother, however, stood her ground and I became Edward Canton Brummel. My father's disappointment at this turn of events faded later in the year when the Phillies won the National League pennant for the first time since 1915 in a nail-biter that came down to the last game on the final day of the season and a 4 to 1 win against the favored but despised Brooklyn Dodgers. And although they subsequently lost the World Series to what my father referred to for the rest of his life only as "that other team from New York," he continued to view his Whiz Kids as the greatest team in baseball history.

The next several years passed quietly, as Jack and I did the requisite growing up and our parents duly noted every coo and giggle, every burp and bowel movement, each more glorious than the last. Our days were spent together, as were most holidays, our grandparents living far enough away that regular visits were difficult. Our mothers even dressed us alike, so that we were often mistaken for brothers, despite Jack's having his mother's fair hair and blue eyes and me having inherited my father's darker looks.

Thankfully, my mother's preoccupation with the North Korean army waned as it became apparent that although the war was not

going to end as quickly as my father had believed, it was highly unlikely that our small house was going to become the base of operations
for Kim Il Sung's militia. And once it did end, in the summer of 1953,
she and Patricia celebrated by throwing Jack and me a third birthday
party, complete with matching cakes and a pony upon whose back we
were posed for numerous photographs.

In an age where most of us move fairly frequently to accommodate
changes in schooling, employment, romantic involvement, or just plain
boredom, it seems inconceivable that both my family and Jack's remained in the same houses for more than fifty years. Yet they did, and
for the two of us it meant that neither knew a time without the other.
From the time I can remember, Jack was there, as present and as constant as the sun.

The differences between us first emerged when we were old enough
to begin talking. Jack discovered early on that adults found him charming and irresistible when he spoke, a trait he was quick to use to his advantage. I, on the other hand, preferred to remain quiet, observing the
world around me and trying desperately to find in it some sense of
order that would explain the reasons things happened the way they
did. Our mothers joked that while Jack's first word was "more," mine
was "why."

These contrasting personalities extended to the ways in which we
explored our surroundings, beginning with the shared lawn between
our two houses and extending in larger and larger circles to include
first our street, then the neighborhood, and eventually the whole
town. Where Jack threw himself headlong into life, expecting someone to be there should he happen to fall and assuming that everything
would be okay, I wavered before every step. Jack wouldn't hesitate to
climb a tree or attempt to ride a bike, and even when he fell or scraped
a knee, he laughed, delighted at the many ways in which the world
could surprise him. I was more likely to be the one encouraging cau-
tion, to which Jack's reply was always a playful, "You worry too much."

Our partnership had benefits for both of us that extended beyond
the simple joys of friendship. As we advanced in school, my studious-
ness meant that I was able to help Jack with his assignments, which
held little interest for him. He, in turn, was the buffer between myself
and the social world of public school. Shy and awkward around other
children, I dreaded the daily social interactions that Jack took for
granted, in fact looked forward to. Popularity came naturally to him,

where for me it was almost completely unimaginable. Yet due to my association with him, I was spared a number of humiliations that otherwise would have assuredly befallen me. In the cafeteria, I always had a place at his side, and when the time came for choosing teams for kickball, I was always Jack's first pick.

Whether Jack was aware of what he was doing for me, I don't know. I think for him it was simply a matter of my being his best friend, and he was doing for me what best friends did for one another. Certainly we never spoke of it, any more than we spoke about how I did his math problems and helped him cheat on the occasional test. It was just the way things were, and the way they continued to be as year followed year.

I recall having only one fight with Jack during this time, in the summer we turned nine. It was over superheros. We were in Jack's bedroom, sprawled on his bed reading the latest issues of our favorite comics, which we'd just picked up from the drugstore, along with an assortment of sour drops, bubble gum, and licorice. Turning the pages of his Superman comic, Jack posed the question of who would win in a battle between Superman and Batman. "I mean, if one of them was a bad guy," he clarified.

"Batman would win," I said without hesitation.

"Batman?" Jack asked, clearly ready to disagree.

"Sure," I said. "He's smarter. Superman is strong and all, but he's not as smart as Batman."

"You don't have to be smart to win a fight," Jack told me, shaking his head. "What a dope. Everyone knows it's more important to be strong than smart."

"What do you know?" I shot back, suddenly angry and not sure why.

"Don't get sore at me," said Jack, surprised by my outburst. "I just said Superman could beat up Batman."

"He could not!" I shouted. "Take it back."

I felt myself shaking. I stood up, hands balled at my sides. "Take it back!" I said again.

Jack sat up and looked at me as if I was some new creature he'd never encountered before.

"No," he said stubbornly. "I'm not taking it back."

I threw myself at him, all fists and anger. He fell back on the bed, momentarily caught off guard. I was on top of him, pinning him with my knees. I raised my hand to hit him, but stopped. He was looking at me with a confused expression, making no attempt to cover his face or otherwise protect himself. I felt my heart beating wildly in my chest as I struggled to understand what I was doing. Beneath me, Jack's body rose and fell as he breathed, waiting to see what I would do.

I scrambled off the bed and stood in the middle of the room, glaring at my friend. Jack didn't move. The comic book was crumpled at his side, the pages torn. At my feet, Batman's face looked up at me. My cheeks burned with shame and lingering rage.

"You go to hell!" I told Jack.

His mouth fell open. Although Jack was proficient at cussing, I'd never sworn before, and the shock of hearing it must have taken him by surprise as much as my attack had. I could sense that I'd grown some in his estimation, and the knowledge thrilled me.

I turned and ran from his room, unable to look at him. Back in my own room, I shut the door and threw myself on my bed. Tears came hot and thick as I sobbed, letting out the emotions that roiled inside of me. Suddenly I didn't know who I was or what I was feeling. The world had turned upside down, throwing me off balance in a way that at the same time filled me with both fear and excitement. In Jack's room, for just a moment, our roles had been reversed, and for the first time I'd seen that perhaps neither of us was exactly what we appeared to be.

Eventually I slept, and when I woke, it was to hear my mother calling me for supper. I went down and joined her and my father at the table, where I ate my meatloaf and green beans silently while my parents talked to one another about their days. When I was done, I asked to be excused and slipped out the screen door to the backyard.

Jack was there, as I'd known he would be, sitting on the back steps of his house. He was holding a Mason jar in his hands and looking at a firefly he'd caught. I went over and sat next to him.

"Hey," he said.

"Hey."

"Want to sleep over tonight?" he asked.

I nodded, watching the firefly blink on and off and wondering if its light would burn my fingers if I touched it.

"Sure," I told Jack.

CHAPTER 2

For those of us born at the dawn of a new decade, life can take on the feeling of being trapped in the ever-advancing undertow of an unstoppable time line. Tied inexorably to the zero year of whatever period we happen to have been born into, we enter (or are dragged kicking and screaming into) each successive stage of life just as the world around us discards one worn-out cycle of years for a shiny new one. While amusing when one is young (how exciting to be in one's twenties during the Roaring Twenties, say, or to turn 30 just as 1969 passes into 1970), this can quickly grow tiring, particularly in the later stages of life when many of us prefer not to be reminded that as civilization's weary past is exchanged for the thrilling potential of a new decade, our own journey is winding down to its inevitable conclusion. (I imagine it is particularly vexing for those unfortunate enough to be birthed along with a new century, as the obvious challenge to live at least into the first year of the next one must be overwhelming indeed.)

Still, it is a remarkable experience to accumulate years hand-in-hand with the society in which you live. And it's most interesting, I think, for those of us born, as Jack and I were, during a time when the world was on the verge of being completely upended. Born in the first year of the '50s, we, along with every other citizen of the planet, were about to be plunged headlong into a period of extraordinary change that none of us could have foreseen.

The year Jack and I left the single digits and reached the magical age of 10, the adult population of the world had its attention fixed first on Fidel Castro, the charismatic yet worrisome Cuban leader whose willingness to purchase oil from the U.S.S.R. was causing more than a few sleepless nights in Washington, and later the spectacle of a sickly Richard Nixon debating fresh-faced John F. Kennedy in the first televised presidential debate. For those of us just completing our first decade, the year's highlights were somewhat less historic, although to us just as memorable. For Jack and me, it culminated in meeting Chief Halftown, the star of our favorite daily television series, at the Buster Brown shoe store one perfect Saturday afternoon. After an hour's wait in line we came face-to-face with our hero and he presented each of us with a personally signed photo and made us honorary members of his tribe. For weeks, we went nowhere without the eagle feathers he'd given us as tokens of our brotherhood, and we talked endlessly of leaving our terminally boring neighborhood and joining the chief and his painted braves in their secret western encampment.

The world seemed to only get more and more fantastic, with each passing month bringing new adventures for two boys with few worries. We felt like Tom Swift, whose encounter with the Visitor from Planet X and battles with the Asteroid Pirates I read aloud to Jack in all their dramatic glory as soon as I could check each new book out from the library, the two of us safe inside the fort we constructed—badly but proudly—from scraps of lumber my father picked up for us. Jack, in turn, perfected his impersonation of Roland, the pale vampire host of Philadelphia's own *Shock Theater*, which we watched religiously during sleepovers in the family room of his house. "Good night, whatever you are," Jack would intone ghoulishly, imitating Roland's trademark line as the credits rolled for *The Creeping Hand* or whichever spine-tingling movie we'd just watched. A makeshift cape over his shoulders, he would advance upon me in my sleeping bag, eyes widened in a hypnotic stare. I obliged by feigning enchantment, maintaining my composure until Jack's teeth were almost grazing my neck, at which point we would both collapse in hysterical shrieks, pleased beyond words.

Those are the mile markers of that time for me, those seemingly small memories that have remained in the files of my mind while others have been discarded. The events more commonly noted on official time lines—the Bay of Pigs invasion and the resulting days of fear, the shooting of the first person trying to cross the Berlin Wall, the death of Marilyn Monroe—were things I heard my parents talk about. To me, they happened in another world, not the one I lived in, and therefore were of no consequence.

The exception, perhaps, was the launching of the first man into space. What boy—what child—isn't captivated by the magic of the stars? Who among us hasn't stood gazing up at bodies whose silver light reaches us from millions of miles away, and wondered what secrets are cloaked by the darkness of frozen, swirling galaxies? Even now, waiting for Sam to finish his last voiding of water before bed, I sometimes stand in the yard beneath the spreading arc of night and imagine the worlds beyond worlds waiting to be discovered.

In the summer and fall of 1960, Jack and I spent hours discussing, with the unparalleled wisdom of 10-year-olds, the possibilities that awaited the first men to penetrate the vastness of the cosmos. NASA, created only two years before, could have benefitted greatly from the rich science of our boyish imaginations, if only they'd known we were available to them. Sadly undiscovered, we nonetheless outlined the dangers, enumerated the possibilities, and created, based on our knowledge (gleaned primarily from comics and the aforementioned Tom Swift novels), the best course of action for the lucky pioneers of the last frontier. When, on April 12 of 1961, Soviet cosmonaut Yuri Gagarin became the first human in space, we celebrated his victory over gravity with Pepsi-Cola drunk from appropriately missile-shaped bottles and a recreation of the event in our very own *Vostok I* made from three O-Boy lettuce cartons and copious amounts of aluminum foil purloined from our mothers' kitchens. While our parents murmured unhappily about the Soviets' early lead in the space race, we knew only that Gagarin had fulfilled our dreams, and was therefore worthy of becoming our hero.

He held the position for less than three weeks, when we unceremoniously dethroned him for our country's very own Alan B. Shepard. This time our relieved parents threw a backyard cookout in celebration of America's success. Rechristening our ship *Freedom 7*, Jack and I gloried in the power that was NASA, lying side by side in the cramped confines of the boxes and soaring together toward the moon while our fathers drank beer and our mothers dished up potato salad and hot dogs. We dreamed of one day being chosen to lead the charge to Mars, or Venus, and promised one another that we would do it as a team. Afterward, we dashed around the yard holding sparklers bought for the Fourth of July but broken out early. Spinning them in crackling circles of silver and gold, we were two comets hurtling with carefree abandon on dizzying trajectories through the early spring evening.

The friendship of boys is a powerful and mysterious thing. To the observer looking in from the outside, it may appear little more than a social contract, and to some extent it is. Boys, especially when young, form friendships based on nothing more than the proximity of their houses, a mutual appreciation of a sporting team, or even a shared enemy. Ask an 11-year-old boy why his best friend is his best friend, and you'll likely receive a shrug and an "I don't know" in response. Ask the same question of an 11-year-old girl, and the reply will be not only heartfelt but built around an extensive list of thoroughly-explored reasons.

Despite the seeming simplicity of the bond between boys, the core of the relationship is as complex as any advanced mathematical proof. Even the boys themselves may not understand why it is they seek companionship with one another. "I don't know" is, in fact, an honest answer. Rare is the adolescent boy who will look at you and, with measured tones, say, "I guess he's my best friend because when I'm with him I forget about all of the millions of self-doubts and insecurities I have. Oh, and even though I don't really understand it, knowing that he likes me makes me feel good about who I am."

Jack and I were no different. We gave little thought to what we were to one another. We just knew that we were best friends, even if we had yet to define what that meant. And we were to have two more years of innocent bliss during which things just were, without reason or motivation. But a funny thing happens in the twilight time around 13. The skin of boyhood begins to feel a little too small, and the soul starts to itch as it expands and the body follows. As legs grow too long for the pants of youth and wrists extend beyond the cuffs of shirts that fit only a week before, the world takes on strange new shapes, as if only now are the eyes coming fully into focus. Seemingly overnight, what seemed safe and familiar is revealed as foreign and filled with perils.

We were no exceptions to this rule. As 11 turned to 12, and 12 to 13, the very molecules of our bodies rearranged themselves. Voices deepened, muscles thickened, hair and new scents burst forth from beneath skin suddenly teeming with mysteries. Changing for gym class, we and the other boys stole anxious glances at one another, searching for evidence that we were not alone. This, in turn, gave rise to new anxieties as we began to compare and contrast the shifting geographies hidden beneath our clothes. Seeing someone further along in the process of adulthood made us question our own progress, filling our minds with a host of doubts and imagined failures.

I say "we" because I have the benefit of looking back with the surety provided by more than half a century of life. Almost certainly we were, to a boy, in the throes of agony caused by the machinery of previously-dormant gonads thrown into production, of glands and ducts dripping intoxicating elixirs into our blood that turned us mad and betrayed us in terrible ways. It is the rare boy who escapes the deliciously malevolent torture of becoming a man, and although nearly unbearable at the time, the end results are almost always worth the hardships.

And so we suffered in 1963, alone but together, the boys of the seventh grade class of James Buchanan Junior High School. Even our grade level was symbolic of our position, sandwiched as it was between the relative safety of the sixth and the restless excitement of the eighth, the springboard into what we believed (wrongly, we would find out soon enough) the total freedom of high school. Trapped in this limbo, we wandered the halls of a school named for the only Pennsylvanian to hold the highest office in the land. Buchanan, incidentally, was also the only bachelor president, a fact which might have comforted a few of us had we understood its potential significance to our own lives. At the time, we were too preoccupied with being embarrassed about everything to care.

We were a group of little wolves, men disguised as boys, trying to both remain a pack and forge our own paths. We pretended to be ready to take on anything, all the while scared to death that we would fail. We staged mock battles in the guise of football games and science club experiments, fighting for the chance to be king, if only for a moment, the other boys our grudgingly worshipful subjects until it was their turn. Most of all, we rode the swells of our emotions up one side and down another, startled at the ferocity of our feelings.

In the midst of all this, on the afternoon of Friday, November 22, as we impatiently awaited the arrival of Thanksgiving vacation and the promise of pumpkin pie, the world came to a standstill with the assassination of President John F. Kennedy. People of my age are frequently asked if they remember what they were doing when they heard that Kennedy had been shot. I do, of course, for more than one reason. It was a little past two o'clock, and I was standing in the locker room of the school's gym. I was looking, but trying not to, at the penis belonging to a boy with the unfortunate name of William Williams. We called him, of course, Bill. Tall and beginning to fill out with the muscles that would make him the formidable man he eventually became, Bill was the current frontrunner in the race in which we were all feverishly participating.

I was pulling my T-shirt over my head, using the opportunity to peer from beneath its temporary shield for a lingering look at what hung between Bill's legs and comparing it, unfavorably, to what lay cradled in the cup of my jockstrap. It was the last class period of the day, the only thing standing between us and a week free from classes, textbooks, and tests. There were two new Hardy Boys novels awaiting me at home, and for that brief moment even the looming threat of dodgeball and the victory of Bill's superior penis over mine couldn't bring me down.

Then Coach Stellinger walked in, his ever-present clipboard held at his side, and asked for our attention. We listened as, tears flowing from his eyes, he informed us of the death of the man who had promised to bring about a brave new world. School, he said in a voice shaking with unconcealed sadness, was to be dismissed early so that we could return to our families for comfort. We were told to get dressed and report to our homerooms as quickly as possible.

I walked home with Jack through a world that seemed to have come to a standstill. The policeman who waved us across the street had cheeks wet with grief, and even the dogs in the yards were quiet as we passed, as if they knew that life had forever changed. We stopped first at Jack's house and, finding it empty, went on to mine, where we discovered our mothers in the kitchen, teacups untouched as they awaited further news—any news—that would reverse time and make everything all right again.

That night Jack was allowed to sleep over, and instead of our usual arrangement of sleeping bags downstairs, we shared my bed. In the darkness, the moonlight illuminating the model rocket ships that hung from the ceiling, we talked awkwardly of our feelings about the murder of a man we didn't know, but whose loss we understood to be great.

I don't recall the words we exchanged. What I remember is the feeling of Jack's body next to mine. We'd slept together before, but that night it felt like the first time. Perhaps, electrified by the nation's shared heartache, I was filled as with the Holy Ghost, my soul expanding beyond reason and amplifying every feeling. When Jack's leg brushed against mine as he shifted beneath the blanket, I held my breath, both wanting the moment to end and wanting it to go on forever. When he didn't move, the warmth of his skin seared itself into me. His words became meaningless, and mine back to him instantly forgotten. My head swam with feelings of loss coupled with a growing excitement I couldn't explain. Horrified, I felt myself growing hard, and was instantly ashamed. I shut my eyes and willed myself to think about the president, his head burst open and his blood spilling across the pink field of Jackie's lap as her screams rent the air. Like a martyr tempted and beseeching God for aid, I looked into her face and asked for forgiveness.

Beside me, Jack faded into sleep. As he did, his hand slipped from where it rested on his chest and fell atop mine. I let it stay there, the beat of his heart transferred to me through his fingertips, until eventually I was overcome by tiredness and confusion and my mind saved itself by rendering me unconscious. My sleep that night was filled with visions of many things, of gunshots and people running in blind panic, of Bill Williams gently soaping his chest beneath a spray of water, of rockets and falling angels. When I woke up, I knew that not only the world, but I had changed forever.

Next to me, Jack was on his side, turned away and snoring gently. I resisted an urge to put my arm around him and pull him close, my chest to his back. Instead, I turned away, pressing my hands against my belly as if in prayer. It was then I discovered that my pajamas were stained with the milkiness of dreams.

CHAPTER 3

I often tell my first-year students that when attempting to understand history, it's crucial to ask yourself what the defining moments are. They nod in agreement, as if this is something they themselves have stated repeatedly to their friends. Then I ask them to name some of these moments. Inevitably, they rattle off a predictable list of battles, or discoveries, or inventions, and label these the points at which civilization took the next great leap forward: the harnessing of electric power, the ascendance of George of Hanover to the throne of England, the bombing of Hiroshima. These, they tell me with confidence, are the pivots on which the course of history has turned.

I then inform them, gently but firmly, that they are wrong. I tell them that the examples that they've listed are the *manifestations* of the turning points. The actual points themselves occurred earlier, probably in unremarkable places and under mundane circumstances, and will in most cases never be publicly known. They occurred in laundries, on trains, and in the holds of ships. They occurred while someone was standing on a hilltop in winter looking at the falling snow and thinking that it might provide excellent cover for an early-morning assault on the camp of the enemy below, in a bed where one or the other of a pair of sated lovers suggested that life might be more agreeable if an inconvenient spouse were done away with, and during a tedious sermon when an uncomfortable congregant's attention turned from the glory of God to the problem of ill-fitting trousers.

These seemingly unimportant moments, noticed by none but those to whom they happen, are the real history of the world. The parts seen by the rest of us, the results documented in artworks, written about in poetry, and celebrated in songs and statues, are the outcome of individual decisions. The bombing of Hiroshima, although spectacular and dreadful, would not have occurred unless someone somewhere had decided that the best way to get the attention of Japan's leaders was to present them with a display so terrible as to wipe away every trace of hope they held of victory, regardless of the human loss. The instant that decision was made and steps were taken to realize it is the instant at which history was made, not the well-documented moment when bombardier Thomas Ferebee pulled the lever that released Little Boy from the belly of the *Enola Gay*.

My students, when I tell them these things, look at me in either surprise or anger. It has never occurred to them that their field of interest is based almost entirely on moments they can never truly be witness to. They resent this deeply. They are bitter over the fact that although they can read numerous and lively accounts of the French Revolution and the role of the sans-culottes in bringing the monarchy of Louis XVI to its bloody, headless end, they can't possibly know the exact moment when the first laborer decided enough was enough and chose to do something about it. They cannot, no matter how much they read, know what possessed the first person to eat an oyster to suck such a peculiar creature from its shell, or what sequence of events (the sudden desire to go for a walk to escape the tedium of a boring text? an invitation from a friend? an attempt to impress a love interest?) led to Tycho Brahe's observation of a solar eclipse in 1560 and inspired him to abandon his studies of philosophy and law for a journey through the heavens. They want what they call history to be comprised of things that can be measured, about which they can write theses and dissertations, about which there is proof.

But history is not really about such things. It's about the inner workings of the human heart and mind that steer individuals in new directions, resulting in action and reaction. Wars are not really about armies and guns and strategies so much as they are about the motivations and fears of the people who wage them. The rise and fall of civilizations, while of course affected by natural disaster, plague, and other tangibles, are ultimately brought about by the greed and honor, the dreams and neuroses, of the populace. Who really knows how many cities were razed because some ancient warlord, rebuffed by a pretty girl when he was 15, sought a direction for his shame and cloaked it in the glory of territorial expansion. Or how many symphonies were written when a composer, frustrated at a rival's accolades, was spurred to compose what he later claimed was an ode to joy instead of the teeth-gnashing expression of irritation at the fickleness of success it truly was.

What holds true for generals, kings, and countries holds true for or-dinary boys. That morning of November 23, 1963, was the first major turning point in my personal history, not because of any event that could be documented, photographed, or studied, but because I real-ized, for the first time, that something dangerous lived inside of me. I couldn't, of course, give it a name. I only knew that it frightened me with its power, and so I chose to pretend that it didn't exist. After half an hour, during which I thought doggedly about the tragedy of Kennedy's death and not about the mess in my pants, Jack woke up and went off to the bathroom. I quickly got out of bed, changed my pajamas, and went downstairs to the kitchen. When Jack joined me a few minutes later, I was deeply involved in a bowl of Rice Krispies. Jack, thinking it a morning like any other (excepting the president's death) poured himself a bowlful and, in imitation of the cereal's Chinese cartoon character spokesperson, So-Hi, said, "Prease pass the mirk!"

He laughed. I couldn't look at him. I pushed the milk toward him and stared into my bowl. Oblivious, Jack splashed milk onto his cereal and began crunching. "What do you want to do today?"

I shrugged. What I wanted was for him to go home so that I could be alone with the boy I'd become sometime during the night. I wanted to not have him sitting across from me, to not hear his voice, to not think about how badly I'd wanted to put my arm around him. I re-sented him for not seeing how much my perception of myself had been altered by his touch, although if he *had* noticed, and asked what was wrong, my heart would have stopped. Instead, I told myself that I resented him for his continued cheerfulness in the face of my growing misery.

I was rescued from further humiliation by my mother, who entered the kitchen and informed Jack that as soon as he was done with break-fast, his mother wanted him to come home and help her clean out the garage. Jack rolled his eyes and sighed, as if the entire weeklong break had just been co-opted. I prayed he wouldn't ask me if I wanted to help.

He didn't, and when he left not long after, I retreated to my bed, where I pulled the sheets up and tried to distract myself by helping

Frank and Joe Hardy unravel *The Viking Symbol Mystery*. Solving it long before the brave but maybe-not-as-clever-as-they-thought Hardys, I closed the book and looked under the bed for the Fantastic Four comic I'd secreted there a day or so earlier after defying my mother and using my allowance to buy it. When I did, I discovered that Jack had left behind a T-shirt, dropped the night before while getting ready for bed and forgotten in his haste to get home.

I picked the shirt up and held it to my face. The smell of Jack filled my nose, a mix of sweat, Ajax laundry soap, and his father's Bay Rum aftershave, which he'd recently begun applying from time to time. Shucking off my pajama top, I slipped the shirt over my head and let it fall around me. Then I pulled the sheet and blanket over my head and closed my eyes. I imagined Jack beside me, our legs touching. I slid my hand across the mattress in search of him, half expecting to feel him there. Instead, my fingers met cool, empty sheets, and suddenly I was crying.

Once started, I couldn't stop. I cried out of frustration and fear, out of anger and the deepest sadness I'd ever felt. My chest heaved as sobs poured from my mouth. The sheets seemed to trap all of the grief inside, my tears and unhappiness mingling with the scent of Ajax and aftershave until all the air had been used up and I was sure I couldn't breathe. Still I stayed there, hoping I might drown and be free of the new emotions I couldn't define but which filled my heart near to bursting.

Preoccupied with misery, I didn't hear my mother come into my room, and when the sheets were suddenly pulled back and I saw her looking down, I saw there an angry god demanding explanation. I cried harder, and covered my face with my arm. My mother sat on the edge of the bed and stroked my hair.

"We're all upset," she said. "This is a sad time for everyone."

I heard her words and didn't understand. How could she know what had happened to me? I wondered, especially when I didn't really know myself. Being my mother, had she sensed some change in me, some horrible defect that had somehow gone unnoticed all these years?

"Imagine how little John John must feel," she continued.

Then I remembered. The president. She was talking about Kennedy, not about me. She thought my sorrow was for a man I didn't even know. True, I was sad about that. But did she really believe my feelings were so strong as to result in uncontrolled weeping? For a moment, I was irritated that she would think me so sensitive. Then relief flooded me. She didn't, as I'd feared, sense something more alarming in me. I sniffled again, softly.

"Besides, they've caught that murderer Oswald, and I'm sure everything will be all right. Your father says Vice President Johnson is a good man. Not as good as Kennedy, but a good man."

She patted my arm. I wasn't sure if she was trying to reassure me or herself. Politics had never interested her, but I knew she'd loved John Kennedy, with his movie-star face and Boston accent. She'd seen him, as had most of America, as a symbol of hope after the frigid foreign policies of Eisenhower. Now, with his death, everything was once more uncertain. I feared she might start hoarding sugar again.

"It will be all right," she said, standing up. "Try not to worry so much. Thanksgiving is coming up."

She smiled and left, glancing at the comic book lying crumpled beneath my arm but saying nothing. She shut the door, and I breathed a sigh of relief. She had been witness to history but was completely unaware of it. What she thought she'd seen—a boy caught up in the emotion of loss and patriotic devotion—was nothing of the sort. Like so many before and after her, she saw one thing in place of another, and the real history was obscured by a more plausible scenario.

I don't tell my students this story. It would mean nothing to them, lacking, as it does intrigue, heroic figures, and a casualty count. A 13-year-old boy crying in his bed and being comforted by his well-intentioned mother, moving as it may be, does not make for vivid history. But it is history nonetheless, particularly as it changed the entire course of my relationship with Jack and, ultimately, my life.

Like the richest history, this unfolding of events did not occur all at once. The impact of that awakening of my desire would take many years to be fully realized. In fact, for some time I would do everything in my power to stop it from happening. My first attempt was simple. I tried to ignore it. I told myself that the feelings I'd had for Jack were momentary, caused by my dreams and by the treacherous machinations of my changing body. At 13, I had been acquainted for some time with the possibilities for self-pleasure. I was also, of course, sure that I was the only boy in Pennsylvania, if not the world, who indulged in such behavior. Alfred Kinsey's shocking news that 92% of all American men did so regularly had been delivered fifteen years before, but somehow its arrival in suburban Philadelphia had been greatly delayed.

It would, in fact, be another year before myself, Jack, and the rest of the eighth-grade boys were gathered in the gymnasium one rainy Wednesday when outdoor activity was impossible and informed by Coach Stellinger that we were becoming men. He told us that our penises might become engorged with blood from time to time, and that it was nothing to worry about. However, we should refrain from touching ourselves because it might lead to mental illness and infertility. Coming far too late for most of us, this news was deeply unsettling, and I'm sure more than one boy spent the next week or so desperately trying to keep his hands away from his crotch before inevitably giving in and risking insanity and sterility.

By then I was already familiar with the pattern of resistance followed by failure. It began in earnest that Thanksgiving week of 1963. I pledged then that, no matter how difficult it became, I would not give in to the thoughts that were beginning to crowd my mind, clamoring to be given voice. Instead, I would think of sports, or math, or even the Lone Ranger, who I was sure would never be so depraved as to have thoughts like the ones I had. Like him, I needed to be filled with moral resolve.

I lasted until November the 27th. Four days. During that time I kept busy, constantly volunteering to help my parents with one chore after another. I raked and bagged leaves until the lawn was bare. I polished the silver. I emptied the trash and assisted with the baking of cookies. What I didn't do was spend a lot of time with Jack. I saw him, of course, but as infrequently as I could manage, using my chores as excuses for my unavailability. Fortunately, he was also kept occupied by his mother, who saw my enthusiasm for household activity and willed it upon Jack.

"What's wrong with you?" Jack asked during a break in the day on Wednesday, when our mothers shooed us outside so that they could finalize the menu for the Thanksgiving feast.

I shrugged. "I don't know what you mean," I said.

Jack grunted. "Thanks to you, I've spent all week cleaning."

"I just thought I should help out," I said. "My mom's been all upset about the president and all that."

"Yeah," Jack said, brightening but clearly still unforgiving. "Did you see that news footage of Ruby shooting ol' Oswald? Bam! He walked right up to him. Man, I'd like to have been there."

I nodded. Everyone had seen the footage. It was played over and over on the evening news, as had the images of the funeral, which had taken place on Monday. Now it was the day before Thanksgiving. I wondered what Jackie, Caroline, and John John were doing. How could they sit down to a turkey dinner after what had happened? I thought about it while Jack continued to talk enthusiastically about Oswald's assassination.

"Hey, my mom said you can stay over tonight."

Jack's remark startled me from my thoughts. "What?"

"Tonight," Jack repeated. "My mom says you can stay over tonight."

It wasn't an invitation. It would never occur to Jack that I might say no. And I didn't. Besides, I was sure that whatever had happened to me during our last night together had passed. The feelings had faded quickly once I'd decided to turn my back on them, and despite purposely avoiding Jack for the week, I was almost certain that it was safe for me to be around him now.

CHAPTER 4

I arrived at his house in good spirits, excited to resume our friend-ship. Tomorrow we would watch the Macy's parade on TV and eat ourselves sick on turkey, mashed potatoes, and pumpkin pie. And we still had three more days after that before we had to return to school. All in all, it was a fine position to be in.

That night I felt normal again. After a dinner of macaroni and cheese, Jack and I settled into the family room for our usual Wednesday night TV lineup, starting with *The Virginian* at seven-thirty. For ninety minutes we immersed ourselves in the dramas of the Shiloh Ranch as faithful ranch hand Trampas battled the bad guys of the Wyoming Territory with the help of the man with no name. Then at nine it was *The Beverly Hillbillies*.

At this point, Mrs. Grace checked in on us and, finding us wanting for nothing, retired to her bedroom to read. She and my mother were working through Shirley Jackson's *We Have Always Lived in the Castle* after seeing the film version of her novel *The Haunting* during one of their outings a month earlier. Mr. Grace was already ensconced in his study, where he would stay late into the night, going over the reports he seemed to crank out like pies on an assembly line. Jack and I were convinced he was now employed by one of the espionage branches of the government, so secretive had he become about his work.

With the elder Graces out of the way, we were alone. We watched, laughing, as the Clampetts prepared to celebrate their first Thanksgiving in Beverly Hills, an occasion nearly marred by tragedy when Elly May developed a soft spot for the intended guest of honor and protested the bird's execution. When it was over, Jack turned off the television and looked at me, grinning.

"Want to see something?" he asked.

What boy could refuse such a request? I nodded. Jack reached under his sleeping bag and pulled out a magazine, which he held up. The cover was white, with a familiar golden, bow-tied rabbit's head looking out.

"You got a *Playboy*?" I said, shocked.

"Shh," Jack said, looking nervously at the stairs, as if any moment the thundering of his parents' footsteps would be heard. Then he sat down on his sleeping bag. "I found it in the garage when I was helping my mom clean. My dad must have bought it and hid it there."

I couldn't imagine Mr. Grace reading *Playboy*. Like masturbation, it was a temptation that I believed simply did not affect dads like mine and Jack's. But there it was, the December issue. And not just any issue. As luck would have it, December of 1963 was the magazine's tenth anniversary, a fact emblazoned on the cover beneath the jaunty rabbit logo.

"Did you look at it?" I asked Jack.

Jack shook his head. "Not yet," he said. "My mom walked in right when I found it. I stuck it down my pants, and haven't had a chance to open it until now."

Jack and I looked at each other for a long moment. Then, carefully, as if just touching the magazine's pages might have terrible consequences, he opened it to the middle.

Donna Michelle was the first naked woman I'd ever seen. Not that she was totally nude; the magazine wouldn't break that taboo for another six years. But she was most definitely topless, and the rest could easily be imagined. Lounging on some brightly-colored pillows, her blonde-brown hair artistically draped over her breasts so that a single nipple peered through, she smiled out at us coyly. We stared at her for a long minute or two, neither of us speaking.

"It says she's a dancer," said Jack finally, his voice hoarse. "She likes horses and swimming."

"And she doesn't like men who think they're God's gift to women," I added, looking at the list of Donna's turn-ons and turnoffs helpfully provided for us.

Jack flipped through the pages. We saw Donna standing behind a wicker screen, her hair piled on top of her head. We saw her again against the pillows, and looking out a window. There were other girls, too, but I don't remember much about them. I recall only more breasts and buttocks, more hair tossed over the eyes and mouths gently pouting. When we reached the last page, Jack shut the magazine.

"Why do you think your dad has that?" I asked Jack.

"I guess he likes to look at it," he answered.

"Do you?" I asked. "Like to look at it, I mean."

Jack shrugged. "Yeah, I guess. I mean, the girls are pretty. Don't you think so?"

"Oh, yeah," I said quickly, afraid that if I didn't show some enthusiasm, Jack might begin to suspect that something was wrong with me.

Jack slipped the *Playboy* under an armchair, turned off the light, and got back into his sleeping bag. A foot away from him, I stared into the darkness and thought about Donna Michelle's breasts. Looking at them *had* stirred something in me, and I was pleased about it. I felt a disruption inside me, a familiar quickening of the spirit that signaled arousal.

I tried to will it away. After all, I'd promised myself that I wouldn't do that anymore. My mind needed to remain pure, even if my eyes had been sullied by looking at the *Playboy*. I couldn't let Donna Michelle lead me where I'd determined not to go. I shut my eyes and began to count to one thousand by threes. It was a trick I'd learned from my father when I was seven and convinced that a terrible evil lived under my bed. Tired of having me appear at his bedside every time I woke up scared and looking for refuge, my father taught me to focus my thoughts on counting. Monsters, he said, hated counting, especially by threes. If I could keep my attention focused on counting as high as possible in triple steps, I would be safe. As I always fell asleep before getting past even one hundred, I quickly came to believe in the game's power. And long after the monster under the bed was vanquished, I continued to utilize it in times of stress. It calmed me.

I began counting quickly—3, 6, 9, 12, 15—and Donna Michelle's breasts became a dim memory. My blood slowed as my brain required more of it to process numbers, and my erection subsided as its powering agent ebbed. I kept going—18, 21, 24, 27—and soon fell into the familiar rhythm, like the chugging of a steam locomotive, passing through the thirties and into the forties.

Around 57, I heard something that interrupted my counting. It was a faint rasping sound, like the rustling of leaves, but sustained and more rapid. I stumbled, forgetting whether I'd reached 63 or 66, and came to a halt. The sound continued, more quickly and loudly, and now it was accompanied by something else, the sound of breath.

I lay quietly, the darkness thick around me. The sounds continued, and I realized that they were coming from Jack. I almost asked if he was all right, then suddenly understood what he was doing and clamped my mouth shut before I could embarrass us both. I listened as he continued, apparently assuming I was asleep and oblivious to what was taking place inside his sleeping bag.

Worse, I was once more becoming hard. I've since come to understand that desire is infectious, and that once the fire is lit, it spreads quickly to those in close proximity. Then, however, I knew only that I was about to break my vow.

I did it quietly, trying not to breathe. I matched the motion of my hand with Jack's, hoping that if he did hear a sound he would think it was his own. I wondered if he was thinking about Donna Michelle, with her rosy nipples and long hair. Maybe, I thought, he was imagining what he would do to her if she were there in the flesh. As I myself had no idea what one would do with a naked girl, I had to leave it at that.

Whatever his thoughts (later he would tell me that he was thinking of nothing, just acting on impulse), Jack soon reached climax. I heard a sharp intake of breath, then a muffled moan, as if he had turned and buried his face in the pillow to keep from crying out. I followed soon after, my hand filling with sticky heat. Almost immediately I sank into the cold blackness of guilt. Even before my flesh had softened in my hand, I was berating myself for having been so weak. The wetness on my fingers felt like blood, staining my skin. I wiped them hurriedly on my shorts, wanting to be rid of the evidence.

Within moments, Jack was snoring, apparently exhausted by his exertions. I, however, was more wide awake than before, tormented by the demons that leapt, monkeylike, from the cracks and fissures of my mind. They danced through my thoughts, poking me with accusing fingers and laughing meanly at my disappointment in myself. I suppose I could have taken solace in the moment, in realizing that I was not, after all, alone in my depravity. Jack, too, had felt its touch. But reaching that conclusion would have required the reasoning of my adult self and he, sadly, was years away from being able to offer his opinions and reassurance. Instead, I felt even worse, convinced that, somehow, my immorality had rubbed off on my best friend.

It was, of course, all terribly dramatic. But as I say, I was young, and inexperienced, and in the throes of first love, although *that* was something I couldn't even begin to recognize or understand. I knew only that I was unhappy again, and that alone was enough to keep me awake for most of the night. Finally, near dawn, I succumbed to exhaustion. Minutes later, or so it seemed to my weary self, Jack was waking me up so that we could watch the Macy's Thanksgiving Day Parade.

Our families alternated holding holiday dinners, and it was my mother's turn for Thanksgiving. (Mrs. Grace would get Christmas, and the following year they would reverse duties.) So everyone convened in our house for the day, mothers in the kitchen and fathers with Jack and I in the living room. Despite my exhaustion, I do remember the parade. Elsie the Cow led the way as the newest balloon to make the march to Herald Square. Although the floats were draped in black in honor of Kennedy's death, a festive air still surrounded the events, and I couldn't help but be thrilled by the sight of Felix the Cat, Bullwinkle, Mickey Mouse, and Charlie Brown bouncing through the streets of New York as their handlers navigated the turns with aplomb.

Dinner was the usual affair, everything cooked to perfection following recipes from *Good Housekeeping* and *The Joy of Cooking*. Jack and I ate heartily, piling our plates with corn pudding, oyster stuffing, green beans, mashed potatoes with gravy, cranberry sauce, and, of course, the ubiquitous roast bird. We grew probably two sizes in the course of an hour and a half, and when we finally pushed ourselves away from the table, it was to collapse onto the floor in front of the television, bloated and groaning. We stayed there for the rest of the afternoon, watching with our equally stuffed fathers the annual Lions versus Packers game, in which we were only marginally interested, but which was far preferable to actually trying to move. When the game ended in a disappointing tie (we didn't care who, but we wanted *someone* to win), we managed to roll over and sit up long enough to eat two pieces of pie apiece topped with whipped cream.

I was half asleep by then, lulled away by food and my restless night at Jack's. When he and his parents said good night, I was up the stairs to my room in a matter of minutes. Pajamas on and teeth brushed, I slipped beneath the covers, not even bothering to read a few pages of the Jules Verne book I'd picked up after finishing the last Hardy Boys mystery. I closed my eyes, and within minutes fell asleep.

Donna Michelle came to me like Dickens' Ghost of Christmas Future, wrapped in snowy fur and bedecked with a crown of holly and gently flickering candles. She smiled as she reached for the clasp of her robe and unfastened it, letting it fall open to reveal her perfect breasts and, below, the bright flash of hair she'd kept to herself in her centerfold shot. She held out her hand to me, waiting.

"Don't you want to see what I have to show you, Ned?" she asked.

Reluctantly, I reached out and took her hand in mine. Instantly, we were flying through the air, snow rushing past us as we sailed over a city twinkling with lights. Donna laughed, her voice sparkling like diamonds, and pointed to something far below. We descended, the city rushing up at us so that I had to cover my face with my arm. And then all was still.

I opened my eyes and saw that we were in a room. It was a hospital room. Someone was in the bed, tubes protruding from his arm and connected to bags of clear fluid hanging from poles. Lights flashed on machines behind the bed, their holiday red and green colors hideously ironic in a room that stank of sickness and death. From beyond the slightly open door to the room I heard the sound of carols sung by voices weak with pain.

"Is that Jack?" I asked Donna, looking at the figure in the bed. His face was thin, the eyes sunken, and the skin the color of ash. Ugly purple spatters stained his arms and exposed chest, the bones of which protruded menacingly.

"That can't be him," I said, looking away. But Donna nodded and pointed again.

"What's happened to him?" I asked her, but she turned away. I grabbed her hand and spun her around to face me. "What's wrong with him?" I demanded of her.

"He's dying," she said. Tears ran from her eyes and down her face.

"From what?" I asked.

"From love," said Donna. "He's dying from love."

I didn't understand her. How could Jack be dying from love? Love was something good. What was she talking about?

Before I could ask any further questions, the lights on the machine behind Jack's head flickered and turned solid red. A faint buzzing filled the air, and a moment later the door was pushed open and a worried-looking nurse ran in. She looked at the machine, quickly pulled a pair of gloves over her hands, and held Jack's wrist in her fingers. After a moment, she gently laid his arm down at his side, reached over, and silenced the machine with the push of a button.

"Merry Christmas," she said softly as she pulled the curtain around Jack's bed closed.

"He can't be dead," I said to Donna. "Can't I do something? Can't I help him?"

"I am only here to show you what might happen," she answered. "Nothing is for certain."

"But what can I do?" I asked. "Tell me what I have to do so he doesn't die like this."

"Love him," Donna replied. "You can love him."

She began to grow faint. Her skin paled and the candles in her crown slowly went out. I looked over at Jack and saw that he, too, was disappearing. The whole room was dissolving around me.

I woke up in my own bed, shaking and feverish. My body was on fire from within, and coupled with the strange and disturbing dream, I was sure I, not Jack, was the one who was dying. It would turn out that I merely had the flu. I stayed in bed for the next three days. My mother brought me aspirin, soup, and cold washcloths until I felt better, just in time for school to resume on Monday.

I spent the time reading, but mostly I thought about the dream. Donna had said that Jack was dying because of love, but also that I could save him by loving him. It didn't make any sense. How could the same thing be his killer and his salvation? It was a puzzle far too complex for my undeveloped powers of reasoning. While I could easily spot the villain in a Hardy Boys novel, I hadn't the first clue where to start solving the mystery of my own heart.

Jack was forbidden to visit me during my illness, which was just as well. I didn't want to see him, fearful that I would see in his face the gaunt expression of death. When I finally did see him, Monday morning, I was relieved to see that he was his usual healthy self.

"Hey," Jack said as we began the walk to school. "What a lousy vacation, huh?"

"The parade was cool," I suggested.

Jack nodded as he kicked at the leaves covering the sidewalk. "Yeah, I guess."

"And Christmas break is only a few weeks away," I reminded him.

"Right," said Jack, noticeably more upbeat. "And I bet it will snow soon. It's cold enough."

"Sure," I said. "Then we'll go sledding."

With something to look forward to, Jack's mood improved considerably. He began talking animatedly about our winter plans, of ice skating and snowball battles and, best of all, the imminent arrival of the annual Sear's Wish Book and its store of treasures. I listened as he chattered, happy to be walking with him. But I also felt that I had now somehow become his guardian, responsible for making sure that he escaped the terrible thing that was waiting for him in the years ahead. I hoped that, like the flu, this new affliction would pass for both of us. Until it did, I would be watchful, looking for signs of danger, searching for the thing that would prevent Jack's destruction.

CHAPTER 5

It is a dreadful thing to feel responsible for someone else's well-being, and worse when that person seemingly feels no reciprocal obligation. Not that Jack didn't care about me. He did. But as we got older, his idea of caring came to consist primarily of making sure I wasn't ostracized socially, and this he did mostly because he needed to be sure of his own position in teenage society.

If I sound bitter, perhaps I am. Whether this is justified or not I cannot say. I only know that I spent a great deal of my time during the next few years keeping a watchful eye on Jack. I was always on the lookout for danger, always suspicious that disaster waited behind every corner. I developed a wariness that manifested itself in almost pathological shyness and a tendency to walk around with my shoulders pulled up. A stiffness settled in my neck and refused to go away.

I realize that I'm making Jack sound like a first-class egomaniac. He wasn't. He was a teenage boy, with all the usual faults of teenage boys. If others existed for his convenience, it was only partially his fault. As I've said, people tended to orbit around Jack, anxious to either earn his notice or take care of him. Boys liked him. Girls swooned over him. Through the changing parade of friends and hangers-on, I was the one constant, always there, always waiting.

During this time I learned to more or less ignore the feelings I had for Jack, or at least to convince myself that what I felt was friendship on a level slightly more focused than usual. This I attributed to the fact that we'd been thrust together at birth. It was only natural, I rationalized, that I would be closer to him than I would be to other boys. If I happened to sometimes think about him while I touched myself (after repeated failure, I'd given up hope of ever remaining chaste), that was only because we were so often together that he came naturally to mind. And if I thought about other boys as well, and never about girls, well, that was something I didn't allow myself to examine too closely.

Besides, I had gotten good at feigning interest in girls. Largely this was accidental, as I still didn't quite realize that I had any real reason to pretend. My imaginings during masturbatory sessions were not overtly sexual, tending to focus more on vague daydreams about intense friendships. When I did allow myself to think about sex, it was in an off-hand way, based mostly on glimpses of other boys in the locker room and wondering what it would be like to kiss or touch them. Even then, I hadn't the faintest idea what two boys might do together, and my fantasies almost always stopped above the waist.

And anyway, I liked girls. I found them interesting, at least when they weren't giggling and whispering together in corners, as they seemed often to be doing. I found that, with some effort, I could even engage with the other boys in conversations about which girls were the most kissable, personable, or likely to put out if asked (not that I really knew what this meant). If I never quite got to the point of actually asking one of them to a school dance, or to a movie, that was attributed to my retiring nature.

Girls were no problem for Jack. The charm he'd evidenced since birth only grew brighter as he reached his mid-teens. Where most of us spent a year or two battling acne, awkward bodies, and the ravages of hormones, Jack went through all of it seemingly overnight, going to bed a boy and waking up the next just a moustache away from manhood. His hair, once flaxen, was now a deep gold, which perfectly suited his blue eyes. Tall and lean, he'd discarded his baby fat long ago, leaving only muscle behind. It never occurred to him to feel inadequate because he was always the one against whom other people measured themselves.

It was no surprise that girls wanted to be with him, and beginning in the spring of 1964, he was frequently booked for Friday and Saturday nights. Often I was dragged along, usually as the partner of Jack's date's less-attractive friend. As it didn't matter to me what a girl looked like, this would have been the perfect arrangement, at least if the girls I was paired up with didn't inevitably fall in love with me. Several times I found myself doggedly pursued by a girl in whom I'd shown only polite interest. This would usually involve a few weeks of telephone calls and invitations to future events, all of which I accepted out of fear of hurting the girl's feelings. But eventually whatever charm I initially possessed seemed to wear off, and after two or three get-togethers, the girls usually moved on. I was puzzled by this interest in me for some time, until on the night of September 2, 1964, I received an explanation.

In February of that year America was introduced to the music of the Beatles. Like just about everyone else under the age of 25, Jack and I embraced this new sound enthusiastically. We purchased *Meet the Beatles*, which we played over and over until our parents begged us to stop. Thankfully, the Fab Four released three more albums before the summer was over, giving us a regular supply of new material with which to irritate the adults in our lives, who eyed our growing hair with suspicion and longed for the days of Marty Robbins and Patti Page.

When it was announced that the Beatles would be playing a concert at Philadelphia's Convention Hall in September, we knew we had to be there. But with tickets to the show sold out in a matter of minutes, we had little hope of going. That is until Lorelei Pinkerton asked Jack if he wanted to go with her. Short, plump, and years behind her peers in the development department, Lorelei had the classic plain girl's advantage of cleverness. Sensing early on that John, Paul, George, and Ringo were something special, she had quickly volunteered to start the local chapter of their fan club. As president, she wielded enormous power, particularly when it came to tickets for the upcoming show. She had four of them, and because of this she was in much demand. She had already been asked by half a dozen boys and begged by five times that many girls, all of whom promised to love her unconditionally if she would allow them to accompany her.

She had turned down all of them for Jack. She sat near him in several classes at school, and although he'd never so much as said hello to her, she had fallen under his spell. Now she presented him with an invitation which, despite her lack of beauty, he could hardly decline. He did, however, demand a compromise. He would go with her as long as I was allowed to come as well. Lorelei countered with a demand of her own—I would have to be the date of her cousin Betty-Anne, who was coming into town from Baltimore for the event. Negotiating on my behalf, Jack agreed, and with the deal struck, we looked forward to the date.

That Wednesday night we walked to the Pinkertons' house to meet the girls and be driven by Lorelei's father to the show. When we arrived, we were met on the porch by a thin, pretty girl with blonde hair tied back in a ponytail. She smiled, cocked her head, and introduced herself as Betty-Anne. She beamed broadly at Jack, giving me the most cursory of glances. When she went inside to inform Lorelei of our arrival, Jack turned to me.

"Here's the plan," he said. "You're going to be nice to Lorelei, and I'm going to have a little fun with Betty-Anne. Got it?"

By then accustomed to doing whatever Jack said, I nodded without arguing. It was a stupid idea, I knew, but I also knew that once he'd settled upon a plan, Jack was determined to see it through regardless of the consequences it brought him or, more likely, me. Besides, Lorelei seemed like a nice enough girl, where Betty-Anne and her ponytail scared me. I didn't know what to say to a girl like that.

When the girls came back out, we saw that Betty-Anne had attempted a makeover on her cousin, with dubious results. Lorelei's hair, normally flat, had been curled into ridiculous ringlets. Her face had been powdered to hide the pimples on her chin, and makeup had been applied with abandon to her lips and eyes. The overall effect was startling, as if she'd had an accident of some kind.

"You look nice," I told her, knowing instinctively that she was aware of her predicament and needed reassuring.

"Thanks," said Lorelei. She looked to Jack for his appraisal, but he was already deep in conversation with Betty-Anne. I could tell by Lorelei's expression that she knew she'd lost already, and was trying to decide how much of a fight to put up.

"It was really great of you to invite us," I said quickly, attempting to distract her from her humiliation. "This is going to be cool."

Lorelei looked at me as if for the first time. She smiled, and for a moment she did look pretty, even under the gaudy makeup. She nodded. "Yeah," she said. "It will."

I wonder sometimes if Lorelei ever thinks about that night and, if so, how she remembers it. I remember a long drive into the city, where we were dropped outside Convention Hall by Mr. Pinkerton, who told us to be back in that exact spot at eight-thirty sharp to meet him. I remember pushing through what felt like the biggest, noisiest crowd in the world. Talking was an impossibility, as the air was filled with the screams of girls, all of whom wanted desperately to marry a Beatle.

And, of course, I remember the music. Although the constant screaming made it difficult to hear the band, there was no mistaking the sounds of "Can't Buy Me Love," "A Hard Day's Night," and the other songs that had been staples on radio stations all summer long. We sang along, danced as much as we could while pressed together by a sea of bodies, and reveled in the joy of being young. When John Lennon launched into "I Want to Hold Your Hand," I looked over to see Jack and Betty-Anne doing exactly that. In a burst of expansiveness, I reached for Lorelei's hand and took it in mine. She wrapped her fingers around mine and kept them there for the remainder of the show and during our exit from the hall. Only when we approached her father's waiting Wagonaire did she reluctantly withdraw, leaving me to wipe my sweaty palm on the leg of my pants.

Mr. Pinkerton had spent the two hours of the concert at a local watering hole, and was in a grand mood. He even allowed us to open the Wagonaire's peculiar rear hatch, designed so that tall objects could be transported easily. The fresh air cooled the heat generated by our excitement and the tight confines of the show, and gave Jack an excuse to put his arm around Betty-Anne. Mr. Pinkerton, his vigilance against hanky-panky dulled by half a dozen beers, pretended not to notice.

Lorelei scooted over on the seat and pressed her side meaningfully against mine. Having made the first move by holding her hand, I felt obligated to go on, and so dutifully placed my arm across her shoulders. She leaned her head to one side, so that her hair pressed against my cheek and tickled my nose. For the remainder of the ride, I tried to gently blow it away from my nostrils, all the while fearing that Lorelei would mistake my puffing for further attempts at lovemaking.

It was on the front porch that I had my revelation. While Jack and Betty-Anne snuck a few kisses away from the glare of the porch light, Lorelei sat on the steps beside me, her hands folded neatly on her lap.

"Thanks for coming with me," she said. "I had a good time."

"Me, too," I told her. "Thanks for asking me. I mean for asking Jack."

I hesitated, afraid I'd said the one thing that would ruin the evening. I hadn't meant to remind Lorelei that I hadn't been her intended date, and that the boy she *had* asked was now busily kissing her traitorous cousin not six feet away from where we sat.

"I'm sorry," I said, fumbling for words. "I didn't mean . . ."

"It's okay," Lorelei said. "Really. I had a better time with you anyway."

"You did?" I asked, genuinely surprised.

She nodded. "Jack is, well, Jack," she said cryptically. "You're different. You're nice."

"Nice," I repeated.

"Nice is good," said Lorelei, sensing that I might be disappointed by her choice of descriptive. "You make me feel like a real person, not some airhead like Betty-Anne."

"You think she's an airhead?" I asked her.

Lorelei snorted. "Have you *seen* my hair?" she said. "Whose idea do you think this was?"

I laughed. "It's not so bad," I said. "And you're pretty nice, too."

Lorelei paused, then said, "Can I ask you something?"

"Sure," I replied.

"Why are you friends with him?"

"Jack?" I said. "We've always been friends. Why?"

"You're just so different is all," said Lorelei.

"Maybe that's why we're friends," I suggested.

"Maybe," Lorelei said, not sounding convinced. "Anyway, I hope you and I can be friends."

"You mean go out again?" I said hesitantly, having been down this road before.

"No," she said. "Just friends. No offense, but I think you make a better friend than a boyfriend."

"Oh," I said, both surprised and relieved.

Lorelei, apparently taking my response for dejection, put her hand on mine. "Not that it wasn't fun holding hands and all that," she said.

"No, it's okay," I told her. "Friends is fine. I'd like that."

She kissed me on the cheek. "I couldn't go out with you anyway," she said as she stood up. "I'm saving myself for George."

"George?" I said. "What about Paul? He's a lot better looking."

"I'll see you in school next week," said Lorelei as she entered the house, letting the door bang loudly to alert Betty-Anne, who pulled herself away from Jack and reluctantly followed her cousin inside.

"She's some girl," Jack said as we walked home. "What a kisser! How'd you do with Lorelei?"

"I had fun," I said. "I like her."

Jack continued to talk about Betty-Anne and her assets. I tuned him out, thinking about what Lorelei had said about me making a better friend than a boyfriend. I didn't fully comprehend what she meant, but it made some things a lot clearer for me. Maybe the girls who fell for me did so not for any definable reason, but because they felt comfortable around me. Where Jack had looks and personality, perhaps I had something less tangible but equally powerful.

Maybe, I thought, that's why Jack, too, continued to befriend me. Was it really possible that with all the attention heaped upon him by so many people, what he really sought was someone who saw beyond his looks and charm to the person underneath? It was an intoxicating thought, and thinking that it might be true filled me with more joy than holding the hand of Lorelei, or any other girl, ever could.

CHAPTER 6

Now that I've almost certainly passed the halfway point in my climb up the mountain of this life and am coasting down the other side with a tailwind at my back, I sometimes wish I could slow time to a crawl. I think this is why many of us, as we age, require fewer and fewer hours of sleep. It's not that our bodies have become more efficient; it's that we're afraid we'll miss something by wasting precious hours in slumber when we could be eating ice cream, reading Shakespeare, or scanning the night sky for falling stars. How many times have I wished for just two or three more hours in a day, not in which to accomplish a task, but simply to enjoy being?

Contrast this to the teenage years, when time can't possibly move quickly enough and every second seems to arrive more slowly than the last in the plodding journey toward adulthood. Those days are all rushing and hurrying, leaping from one adventure to another, storing up experience and memories enough to last the rest of our lives. Like bees, we dart and gather, pausing only long enough to take from life whatever we can carry. Only later do we realize that we can't remember what color the flowers were, or how they smelled.

Many things happened in 1965. Malcolm X was assassinated just as Dr. Martin Luther King, Jr. and the civil rights movement he championed took center stage in American life. *Lost in Space* premiered on CBS and Quaker Oats introduced Quisp cereal to grocery shelves. In Detroit, 82-year-old Alice Herz poured a container of lighter fluid over her head and lit a match, immolating herself as a protest against the escalating violence in Vietnam. Willie Mays hit home run number 512, breaking the National League record, and the Rolling Stones released "Satisfaction."

For Jack and me, none of these was the major event of the year. That honor belonged to our two-week stay on Treasure Island. For several years we had been part of local Boy Scout troop 49, meeting once a week after school and learning the basics of camping, knot tying, and other skills that would come in handy should we ever find ourselves lost in the woods and needing to construct temporary shelter and a fire. We went primarily because we liked collecting merit badges, and together and separately we'd managed to amass a number of them.

That summer we were going for the rank of Second Class. We'd reached Tenderfoot the summer before, and were anxious to be rid of that embarrassing designation. In order to reach our goal, we had to, among other requirements, plan and execute a 10-mile hike, display proficiency in swimming, identify ten examples of local wildlife, outline the procedure for removing a foreign object from the eye, and, to quote the handbook, "demonstrate Scout spirit by living the Scout Oath and Scout Law in everyday life." Should we accomplish all of these things, we would be allowed to attend the annual Pennsylvania troop gathering at Treasure Island, held the week following our birthdays.

Inspired by the idea of two weeks away from our parents, we completed our tasks in record time, earning our Second Class patches and our places on the trip. And so a few days after turning 15, Jack and I found ourselves loading ourselves and our gear onto a bus with thirty-two other scouts and heading for the Avalon of local scouting.

Treasure Island is legendary in scout circles. Open as a camp since 1913, it sits in the middle of the Delaware river, connected to its sister island, Marshall, by a small footbridge which, because Treasure Island is part of New Jersey and Marshall Island belongs to Pennsylvania, is considered the smallest interstate bridge in the United States. While this is undoubtedly fascinating, of more interest to we scouts was the knowledge that the Unami Indians had once called the island home, and that arrowheads were still sometimes found there.

There were twelve campsites scattered around Treasure Island, named after animals or important figures from scout history, and which site your troop was assigned to was considered an unofficial measure of your rank in the scout hierarchy. Wolf and Eagle sites were the most prized, for obvious reasons, and those such as Baden-Powell (named for the founder of the British Boy Scout Association) and Edson (after the co-founder of the elite scout program the Order of the Arrow) were acceptable if unexciting, while the hardly-intimidating Beaver and Bok were not high on most scouts' list of desirable locations. For those of us from Pennsylvania, the greatest calamity was to be assigned to the site called Jersey.

When our group learned that we would be camping at Nip site, we were relieved. Although its name was hardly inspiring, its location at the southeast end of the island, close to the Unami ceremonial grounds, gave it a certain cachet among the other campers. Slightly removed from the center of camp life, it also afforded a little more privacy, and its proximity to the Jersey camp (which that year was indeed populated by scouts from nearby Frenchtown) assured us of some memorable nighttime raids.

Jack and I quickly set up our tent and rolled out our sleeping bags. Housekeeping thus accomplished, we joined our troop mates for the walk to the clearing at the island's center. There, gathered around the flag pole, we were welcomed to Treasure Island, informed of the rules of our island society, and given the day's schedule, which began with a mandatory health check and swim test and finished with a campfire.

The daily routine of a scout camp is interesting only to those who are in the midst of it, and so I will pass briefly over the mess hall meals, survival skills practices, archery competitions, leather craft classes, and canoe races. In these things our Treasure Island experience was no different from that of scouts throughout history. Where Jack and I diverged from our fellow scouts was in what occurred on the night of Saturday, August 21.

We were at the end of a perfect first week. The weather, sunny and clear, had turned our skins a golden brown. We'd racked up three new merit badges each, and Jack had led our troop to a Capture the Flag win over the previous year's champions, Troop 137 from Erie. Already there was talk of nominating him to the Order of the Arrow once he earned his First Class rank. This distinction, the only one in scouting voted on by one's peers, was bestowed upon only the most popular and accomplished campers. Jack, as a first-time visitor to Treasure Island, should have been far down the list of potential candidates. The fact that his name was mentioned for inclusion by both campers and

scout leaders was further proof of his natural ability to outshine everyone around him.

With still another week to go, we were at the pinnacle of happiness.
That night, we sat beside one another at the all-camp bonfire, lustily
singing the words to the camp song. Although I've been able to forget
many things in the intervening years, the words to that ode to Treasure
Island have remained stuck in my memory, and only partially because
they were sung to the tune of the familiar and oft-used "Annie Lisle."

"By the river that surrounds thee, rolling mile on mile, 'neath the
stars that shine above thee, dear ole' Treasure Isle. We who know thy
woodland treasures pause in thought awhile, calling back to mind thy
pleasures, dear ole' Treasure Isle."

It goes on in a similar vein for another two verses, charming in its
imagery and hideous in its outdated and ungrammatical wording. But
we noticed none of that then, lost as we were in the camaraderie created when 150 boys are brought together for a shared experience. Like
participants at a revival, we were filled with the spirit of the Boy
Scouts, lifted high on a wave of brotherhood and pride. At that moment we were invincible, unafraid of darkness, rain, or snakebite. We
were prepared for any emergency, sure that our scout resolve could
handle anything. Had our scoutmasters asked us to launch an offensive against the enemies of Scout Law, we would have done it, and
gladly.

As we arrived at the song's final verse, with its message of finding
warmth and hope in our fellow scouts, Jack leaned over and whispered in my ear, "Let's go swimming."

Swimming at night was not allowed, but before I could protest, Jack
had disappeared into the shadows. I went after him, following his
darkened form as he raced down the path, not toward our camp, but
toward the southernmost end of the island. As we darted through the
trees, I tried to get him to slow down. He simply laughed and ran
ahead, forcing me to keep up. The moon, in its waning quarter, provided little light, and Jack's shadow leapt from one patch of silvery
glow to the next like Peter Pan's running from its owner.

Finally the forest ended and I found myself standing beside Jack at
the edge of the river. He was already removing his shoes and socks.

"We can't swim in the river," I said. "It's against the rules. We're only
supposed to swim in the pool."

"Come on," Jack said. "It isn't flowing that fast, and we won't go far. Nobody will know."

He pulled his T-shirt over his head and shucked his shorts off. I saw a glimpse of his ass, pale above his tanned legs, as he waded into the water. He turned and waved at me.

"Come on. It's not that cold."

I reluctantly did as he said, placing my clothes beside his and walking to the water. I stuck one foot in. While not exactly warm, it wasn't as cold as I'd expected, and I followed after Jack until the water was up to our chests and we could swim.

"See," Jack said. "The current isn't bad at all."

He was right about that. There was a slight current, but as long as we swam against it, we weren't pushed away from the island. Confident that there would be no difficulty getting back, Jack ducked under the water. A moment later, I was pulled under with him.

We came up laughing and sputtering, our hair plastered against our heads so that we resembled seals. I returned Jack's ducking, pushing him down and under. He came up behind me, wrapping his arms around my waist as he rocketed up and out of the water. For a moment, before he pulled me back down with him, I felt him pressed against me. His penis was nestled in the cleft of my cheeks, and I felt the curly swirl of hair at its root against my skin.

Then I was underwater, looking up as bubbles swarmed around my face. Jack let go and I floated away from him. I turned and watched him surface, his arms and legs ghostly against the darkness. I reached for him, wanting to pull him back against me, then remembered that I couldn't breathe and swam toward air and light.

Jack was heading back to shore, his strong arms carrying him quickly. I started to follow, then realized that my cock had swelled to attention. I didn't want Jack to see it that way, for fear he would guess what had caused it, so I slowed my strokes and waited for it to go away. By the time I reached shallow water, Jack was putting his sneakers on and my erection had abated. It was helped by the shock of the night air which, despite the relative warmth of the water, caused gooseflesh to rise on my skin.

"Let's get back to camp," Jack urged as I dressed. "We don't want them to miss us."

I nodded, saying nothing. Then I followed Jack back down the path we'd taken until it joined the one leading away from the ceremonial grounds. When we came to Unami Lodge, we went right, past the Win campsite and on to our own. Although several of the tents were zipped up and lit from within, others were dark, indicating that their tenants were still out, perhaps brushing their teeth or engaged in earning their astronomy badges. We had not been missed, and we entered our tent with feelings of having accomplished something dangerous and forbidden.

"Boy, that was fun," said Jack, unzipping his sleeping bag.

"Yeah," I said.

"What's the matter?" Jack asked me. "You sound funny."

"I'm just cold," I told him. "I need to warm up."

"Here," Jack said, unzipping my bag and pulling it closer to his. "We learned this in survival class today."

"What are you doing?" I asked him.

"Putting our sleeping bags together," he answered as he fed the teeth of my zipper into the slider of his and joined them. "Now we both get in and our body heat warms us up. It's how you stay warm if you're trapped in the snow or whatever."

He slipped into the new, double bag. I hesitated, then got in beside him, turning so that my back was to him. Jack zipped the bag closed and turned on his side. I felt his arm go around my chest.

"Don't worry," he said. "I'm not going to feel you up or anything. I know you don't do that on the first date."

He laughed, and I felt his breath against my neck. I closed my eyes. The tent smelled of wood smoke and water and pine. I tried not to think about Jack pressed against my back, or his hand resting on my stomach. I tried not to feel the heat moving between us.

"Now, if you were Cheryl Kipe, I might feel you up," Jack continued. "I might even do more than that, if you know what I mean."

He thrust his hips against me. Again I felt the bulge between his legs brush against my ass. My dick jumped in response, and I cringed inwardly. No, I told myself. Don't.

"Man, I wonder what it would be like to be with her," said Jack. "Have you seen her boobs? Pete Lowry told me she let him touch them once after he took her to a basketball game."

He reached up and squeezed my chest as if he had one of Cheryl's breasts in his hand. "I bet they're soft," he said. "So, who would you want to do it with?"

I struggled to think of an answer. My penis, already half erect, was getting harder. Jack still held me to him, his hand cupping me as he thought about Cheryl.

"I don't know," I said, picking at random a girl from my biology class. "Maybe Sheila Mullally."

"A Catholic girl," Jack remarked. "Everyone says they're the easiest. I bet she'd let you go down her pants."

As he said it, he slid his hand down my stomach to my underwear, mimicking what I might be able to do to Sheila. I held my breath, waiting for the awful moment when he realized I had a hard-on and pushed away from me.

His fingers touched the head of my dick and stopped. For a moment, Jack said nothing. Then he playfully squeezed my penis. "Looks like you already thought about that," he teased.

He didn't let go. Instead, he slid his hand under the waistband of my shorts. His fingers closed around my cock and stayed there. I could feel him breathing behind me, but neither of us said anything. He began to move his hand up and down, slowly, still not saying a word. I felt the bulge at my back lengthen, and I knew he was getting hard as well.

"You can touch mine if you want to," he said hoarsely.

He rolled onto his back and I onto mine, so that we were lying side by side. My hand trembling, I reached over and felt him. His dick was shorter than mine but thicker. My fingers barely met around the shaft. Our hands moved together, stroking gently, and neither of us spoke.

I remember that Jack came first, but that even after his shuddering subsided he continued to pump me until I, too, had release. It was the first time that I can remember that he considered the needs of someone else once his own had been met. Neither of us said a word as we wiped our hands on whatever soiled clothing we had nearby, and neither suggested separating the sleeping bags. I remember falling asleep soon after, despite the thoughts racing through my mind, and waking up in the morning with Jack once again pressed against my back, arm around me, snoring gently.

That was how it began. Although I expected there to be awkwardness between us that next day, there was none. Jack acted as if nothing at all unusual had occurred in our tent the night before. He went through the day as usual, devouring his morning pancakes with relish, taking his first shots with a rifle on the Marshall Island shooting range, and orchestrating an evening attack on the Jersey camp during which we pelted our unprepared foes with toilet paper and shaving cream stolen from the older scouts. And that night, when we were once more alone, he asked if I wanted to fool around some more.

That's what we called it from then on—fooling around. It continued for the remainder of camp, and then when we returned home. Several times a week we would find ourselves jerking off, sometimes alone and watching each other and other times together, our hands moving in unison. We came to know each other's pattern of arousal, and were able to time our manipulations so that we reached orgasm at the same time, gripping one another tightly as we released in tandem.

Jack never spoke about what we did other than to ask if I was interested in doing it. I didn't say anything either, afraid that if I did it would disappear, like the gold coins in fairy tales that turn back into coal as soon as dawn arrives to break the enchantment. Like so many relationships, ours was one that went undiscussed, each of us believing it to be what we needed it to be.

But silence has a way of growing loud beyond bearing, and eventually this one became deafening.

CHAPTER 7

Ionce dated a man who blamed his lack of enthusiasm for Valentine's Day on the grounds that it is a made-up holiday invented by purveyors of greeting cards and confections. I now realize that his disdain was rooted more in his lack of enthusiasm for romance in general, and that the high-minded position he espoused for boycotting February the 14th was nothing more than a convenient excuse for not buying me flowers and taking me out to dinner. Sadly, at the time I was not armed with ammunition to counter what I believed to be a reasonable argument, and so spent the evening alone, watching *Now, Voyager*.

Thayer, the very definition of a romantic, needs no persuading when it comes to celebrating the feast of St. Valentine, and so I rarely get the opportunity to use what I have come to know about the day in response to those who shun it. Since the date figures heavily into the course of Jack's and my relationship, and since I find in its evolution parallels to our life together, I think its history worth mentioning here.

The creation of a day devoted to all things amorous cannot, as my unromantic former beau believed, be blamed on Hallmark or the entrepreneurial Quaker Stephen Whitman and his chocolate samplers. Rather, the fault—as it does for so many things—lies with the Romans. On this historians agree. Where they cannot come to an accord is on the precise evolution of the tradition.

Oh, to be a pagan in the days of the Caesars and their brethren, with gods and goddesses for every occasion and spirited rites to accompany their worship. In this instance, the deities in question are Juno Februata and Lupercus, the goddess of the "fever of love" and the god of the fields respectively. Both are named as the originators of what we now call Valentine's Day, and with good reason.

Juno Februata, patron of marriage and women. Lupercus, lusty avatar of Faunus, horned god of the woods. On the 14th day of the second month, Juno was remembered. On the 15th day fell the Lupercalia, a commemoration of the raising by a she-wolf of Romulus and Remus, twin sons of the war god Mars by his rape of the Vestal Virgin Rhea Silvia. Two dates, two deities, but one tradition shared by both. On this date (whichever you choose, it hardly matters) the names of unmarried young women were written on slips of paper and placed in a box. These slips were then drawn, one at a time, by unmarried young men. The resulting couples were symbolically joined for a period of one year, during which they could enjoy one another's company as they saw fit. Although these mock marriages sometimes resulted in the real thing, primarily it was a lovely excuse for sexual exploration of all kinds.

One can, without much effort, see the appeal of such an annual rite. One can also imagine its vexatious affect on Valentine, the Christian bishop of Interamna, who not only found the pagan gods troublesome, but who was further inconvenienced by the proclamation of mad emperor Claudius II abolishing marriage, which he believed made men unfit for battle. Undeterred, Valentine encouraged young lovers to come to him to be wed in secret, earning him a reputation as a defender of love and a visit to the court of Claudius in the year A.D. 270. A conversation between the men, both equally convinced of the rightness of their convictions, ended regrettably for Valentine when he was clubbed, stoned, and, finally, relieved of his head.

But all was not for naught. Legend has it that during his imprisonment prior to his martyrdom, Valentine fell in love with the blind daughter of his jailor, eventually using his divine powers to restore her sight. On the eve of his execution, he reportedly wrote a farewell message to the girl, signing it "from your Valentine." It is not recorded whether he also presented her with a box of sweets for her troubles, but for her sake we can only hope that he did, seeing as how the girl and her father were later executed for accepting Valentine's other gift, the redemptive love of Jesus Christ.

When, in A.D. 496, it was decided by Pope Gelasius that it was time to once and for all stamp out the lingering pagan customs of the land, a replacement for Juno Februata and Lupercus was sought. Gelasius was wise enough to know that the Romans would more readily accept a substitution than an abolition, as they had when their winter solstice celebrations calling for the return of the sun and its light were retooled as the birth of the Christ child. He found a ready candidate in Valentine, with whose feast day he replaced those of the Roman deities. He also attempted to replace the drawing of girls' names with the drawing of the names of saints, whose lives the selectors were urged to emulate for the following year. This proved unpopular, however, and eventually Gelasius settled once more for the choosing of names, albeit omitting the sexual overtones of the celebration.

The rest, as they say far too casually, is history. Valentine the saint became valentine the missive. The slips drawn from the box soon became love letters, usually in verse, sent to young ladies by their admirers. The first known valentine, preserved today in the British Museum (where Thayer and I saw it on our tenth anniversary trip to London), was sent by Charles, Duke of Orleans, to his wife, Bonne of Armangac, in 1415, while the duke was imprisoned in London's White Tower following the Battle of Agincourt. I would urge all those gentlemen who find purchasing a card for their true love a burden to consider the lengths to which poor Charles had to go to send his valentine, which ought to put a 10-minute trip to the drugstore in perspective.

Considering the Roman beginnings of the tradition, I like to think that Julius Caesar, once famously described by Curio as "every woman's man and every man's woman," received some small token of affection from his most well-known valentine, King Nicomedes of Bithynia. Sadly, the sending of valentines between men is a largely unexplored avenue of romantic history, so whether Caesar ever received one we will never know. My own experience with such things, I can recall with awful clarity, began with Valentine's Day of 1966.

I gave it, of course, to Jack. We had exchanged them before, but always they had been of the sort that had Mighty Mouse or Donald Duck on them, and they were given along with the others we brought for all of our third- and fourth-grade classmates, stuffing them into tissue-paper-heart-decorated shoeboxes before being rewarded with pink-iced cupcakes. That year, however, I took great pains to make Jack a card. I'd looked for one at Woolworth's, but they all had verses clearly written with girls in mind, and reading them made me blush with embarrassment. Jack wasn't my sweetie or my honey. I didn't even have a word to describe what he was. All I knew was that I felt something for him and wanted to let him know.

I ended up making a card from red construction paper. Inspired by our one real childhood fight, I glued to it images of Superman and Batman cut from my collection of comics. I positioned the two super-heros standing side by side on the moon, holding hands and looking at one another. Behind them I drew a galaxy, complete with stars and planets and a comet. Inside, I wrote "To my Superman. Happy Valentine's Day." I signed it "Bruce," as in Bruce Wayne, Batman's true identity.

I was sure that Jack would like the card. Although we had been playing our sexual games for almost six months and still hadn't given what we did a name, I knew he felt about me the way I felt about him. I saw the valentine as a way to finally put into words what was between us. I suppose what I really hoped was that it would encourage him to tell me what was in his heart.

I gave him the card on the way to school, handing it to him when we reached our first corner and had to wait for a passing car before crossing. He looked at the cover, opened it, and then looked at me. "What the hell is this?" he asked, his voice angry.

"What do you mean?" I said, startled at his reaction.

"What do you think I am, a girl?"

I shook my head. I didn't know what to say, so I said nothing.

"Look, I'm not a queer," Jack said, looking around to make sure that no one was listening to our conversation. "And neither are you. Got it?"

He thrust the valentine at my chest, letting it go so that it fell to the ground, where the snow smeared the ink and stained the ground red. Then he turned and started to cross the street. I looked at the card, crumpled at my feet, then bent to pick it up. Jack was already on the other side of the street, walking quickly away from me. He turned and looked back. "Are you coming or not?" he called out.

I tucked the valentine into my notebook and ran after him. Neither of us said another word as we finished the walk to school, and when we walked home that afternoon, Jack seemed to have forgotten all about the incident. Alone in my bedroom, I took the valentine out, tore it into as many pieces as I could, and deposited it in the waste-paper basket beside my desk.

A minute later the phone rang. When I answered it, it was Jack, telling me that he had asked Mary Shaughnessy to go to the movies that night, and that I was taking her friend Bernice Kepelwicz. He would pick up some cards and candy for the girls. All I had to do was be ready to go at six.

Defeated, I did as he told me. At the appointed time, I arrived at his house, where he handed me a red envelope and a small box tied with a pink ribbon. "You can give these to Bernice," he instructed me. He had slicked back his hair and applied aftershave. The smell, as it always did, reminded me of being next to him in bed. I felt my heart tremble, but was able to control myself as we walked downtown to the theater. It wasn't snowing, but the air was bitterly cold, mirroring the chill in my soul.

Mary and Bernice were waiting for us in the theater lobby. Jack handed Mary her card and candy, accompanying it with a kiss on the cheek. Bernice looked at me expectantly, and so I did the same, adding, "Happy Valentine's Day." The girls looked at one another, exchanging smiles, while Jack scanned the marquee to see what was playing.

"How about *Fantastic Voyage*?" he suggested. "I hear it has great special effects."

Mary screwed up her nose. "I don't like science fiction," she said. "Bernice and I want to see *The Singing Nun*, don't we, Bernice?"

"Debbie Reynolds is the best," Bernice agreed.

Jack rolled his eyes at me behind the girls' backs, but walked to the ticket window and plunked down two dollars for tickets for himself and Mary. I did the same, handing Bernice her ticket. Then Mary meaningfully suggested that popcorn and Cokes would be nice, so Jack and I waited in line at the concession stand while the girls went to find seats.

"Man, this movie is going to suck," Jack said.

"Why are you pretending to like Mary?" I asked him, suddenly angry.

"What do you mean?" he said. "I like Mary all right."

"Since when?" I demanded to know. "You just invited her this afternoon."

"So?" said Jack defensively. "Maybe I didn't think of it until then."

I bit my lip to keep from accusing him of anything else. I knew full well why he had suddenly decided to arrange Valentine's dates for us. He knew, too. But neither of us would say it, not in a crowded theater. Maybe, I thought, not ever.

We got our popcorn and sodas and joined the girls, who had artfully arranged themselves so that they were seated together and Jack and I had to sit on opposite sides, as far from one another as possible. Mercifully, the lights dimmed soon after, and we settled into silence as the movie began. It was, as Jack predicted, monumentally dull, despite the catchiness of the hit song on which it was based. Only Agnes Moorehead, who I recognized from my Thursday-night viewings of *Bewitched*, provided any amusement in her role as a cranky nun.

When, halfway through, I felt Bernice lean against me in an invitation of affection, I dutifully obliged. Upon placing my arm around her shoulders, I found my fingers come into contact with Jack's, who had his own arm around Mary. To my surprise, he left his hand where it was, even going so far as to hook one finger around mine, linking us together across the barrier of the girls. We remained like that through the rest of the film, none of which I can remember.

Afterward we said good night to the girls, who thanked us with actual kisses on the mouth. Bernice's lips tasted of salt and Coke, and I was relieved when we parted after a short time. I don't think I was her idea of a perfect Valentine's Day date, which was just as well. I had no intention of taking my performance any further, and was not looking forward to days or weeks of having to feign excitement at her presence.

Mary appeared more content with her experience, kissing Jack several times before being led away by Bernice. He and I then walked home through the cold, our hands stuffed deep into the pockets of our coats. When we reached his house, he stopped.

"That was one bad movie," he said.

"It sure was," I agreed.

"The girls had a good time, though."

"Sure," I said.

Jack stepped forward, and his lips met mine. It was only for a second, and then he moved away, his eyes on the ground. "I'll see you tomorrow," he said.

He ran up the steps to his house, the door shutting loudly behind him in the still night. I ran my tongue over my lips, trying to taste him, but all that remained was the lingering syrupy sweetness of Coca-Cola. I couldn't tell if it was from Bernice's kiss or Jack's, but I savored it until it grew faint. Then I walked up my own steps and into the house.

Many years later, I would discover that the real singing nun, Jeanine Deckers, left the convent after the success of her song "Dominique" and in 1985 committed suicide along with the woman believed to have been her lover for over a decade. But that night in 1966 all I knew was that, like her, my heart was singing.

CHAPTER 8

There are few things more defiant in the face of almost certain failure than a romance between young people. Despite the fact that a relationship begun when one is 14, 15, or 16 is highly unlikely to last the length of a school year, much less forever, millions of boys and girls blissfully ignore the statistical probability and pair up. When the inevitable breakup comes, they act surprised, as if the possibility had never occurred to them. And perhaps it didn't. The future, after all, is not something the young often consider, believing as they do that time is an endless commodity. They live in the moment, oblivious to the danger of heartache, even when it is all around them.

There are, of course, exceptions to the rule. We have all at one time or another met the couple who came together in high school, only to marry and thrive. Secretly, we hate these couples because they have managed to escape what most of us go through at least half a dozen times on the road to emotional maturity. We tell ourselves that avoiding this maturation is how they've managed to do it, and pity them their simplemindedness, much as we pity the former cheerleaders and quarterbacks who remember high school as the best times of their lives.

For the rest of us, high school dating was practice for later life. By dating, we were allowed to act out the dramas and comedies that are part of being creatures who love. We tried and failed, won and lost, and hopefully learned a thing or two before the stakes were raised. As the only real consequence at the time was pregnancy, we had free rein to do as we liked, or at least as far as we dared.

At least as long as we were heterosexual. Those among us who leaned in another direction were, with almost no exceptions, left to figure it out on our own. I maintain that this is why so many of us had—and continue to have—trouble when we finally did begin dating. We hadn't had the years of practice that our straight brothers and sisters had. We weren't given the opportunity to find out what we liked, and what we had to offer. As a result, we had to do it on the fly, all the while feeling that we really ought to know what we were doing.

I envy a bit the young queers of today, with their gay-straight alliances, their centers, and their freedoms. I'm sure it's every bit as difficult being outside the norm as it was when Jack and I were 15, but at least they have access to information. At least they, most of them, know that they are not alone in the world. For myself and Jack, it was like waking up and finding everyone else gone. We had no idea who or what we were, and had to find our way on our own.

We didn't call ourselves gay. We didn't call ourselves anything. We were just two boys who loved one another. We didn't have Elton John, Harvey Fierstein, or Rupert Everett to show us what we could be. We didn't have *Will & Grace* or *Queer as Folk* to reflect our lives (however one-sided those portrayals may be). We didn't have Falcon Video or *Honcho* to show us what men did with one another in bed. We had only one another.

The sex part we muddled through as best we could. Boys are nothing if not resourceful beasts, and we figured out quickly what felt good and did it often. Stroking turned to licking, and then to sucking. Hesitant at first, we quickly overcame our inhibitions about taking one another in our mouths. Because our lovemaking was done mostly late at night, with our parents asleep a room or two away, we were restrained in displaying our excitement, muffling our groans in pillows and coming with silent exaltation.

We turned 16 in August, spent our second summer on Treasure Island (where Jack was inducted into the Order of the Arrow and we celebrated by jacking off on top of the observation tower at Yoder's Lookout), and a month later returned to school as sophomores. Understanding that camouflaging ourselves was a necessary course of action, we continued to date girls. This was more important for Jack than it was for me, as his popularity had grown exponentially and he was now, among other things, captain of the football team and vice-president of the student body. While I was far from being on the lowest rung of high school society, my positions as newspaper editor and first trumpet in the band were not in the same league as Jack's.

Jack was better than I at mimicking enthusiasm for the fairer sex. Where my dates rarely went beyond kissing, with perhaps a hint of tongue or a hand on a breast, Jack felt that both keeping our cover and his reputation required more of him. Accordingly, he occasionally allowed a girl to go down on him, and several times went all the way when a girl was particularly insistent and he needed a good story to tell the guys in the locker room.

Rather than envy these girls, I was thankful to them. Not only did they help Jack and me keep our relationship a secret, they provided us with ideas for our own times together. We owed a particular debt to one Margaret Alice O'Leary, fourth daughter of our town's chief of police. Jack's time with Margaret Alice culminated at the school's annual Halloween Dance, to which Jack went dressed as Tarzan. Margaret Alice, showing little imagination, came attired as a nun in an actual habit that had once belonged to her aunt, Sister Patrick Theresa, a resident of the Convent of Divine Love in Philadelphia, where she spent day and night in prayer and adoration of the Holy Spirit, Christ, and the Virgin Mary.

All of the O'Leary girls were good Catholics, and Margaret Alice, being the second-to-youngest, had learned much from her older sisters. After the dance, while making out in the front seat of the car Jack had borrowed from his parents for the evening, she lifted her habit and suggested that Jack do something that had hitherto never occurred to him.

"She said if we did it that way, she would still be a virgin and it wouldn't be a sin," he explained to me later that night, after dropping Margaret Alice off and joining me in my bedroom.

"Did you do it?" I asked him, still doubtful about the feasibility of Margaret Alice's suggestion.

Jack shook his head. "I told her I had too much respect for her and wanted to wait."

"And she believed you?"

"I'm invited to her house for dinner on Sunday," said Jack. "After they go to mass. She says her mother will love me, even if I'm not Catholic. So, do you want to try it?"

"Try what?" I said.

"You know," Jack replied. "What Margaret Alice wanted to do."

"Do you think we can?" I asked. "I mean, can you actually put something up there?"

"Margaret Alice is a lot smaller than we are, and she was ready to do it."

"Yeah, but girls are built different," I countered. "Maybe they're, I don't know, bigger back there or something."

"Come on," Jack said, already taking his pants off. "We won't know until we try it."

Reluctantly, I got undressed. My parents were out for the evening and not expected home until late, so with the fear of discovery gone we could be less cautious. Soon we were both naked.

"How do we do it?" I asked Jack.

"Get on your stomach," Jack suggested.

"Me?" I said. "Why not you?"

"It was my idea," Jack answered. "You can go next. I promise."

Knowing it was useless to argue, I lay on the bed while Jack got on top of me. I felt him push his dick between the cheeks of my ass.

"I guess I just put it in," he said, thrusting forward.

Nothing happened.

"What's wrong?" I asked.

"It's really tight," said Jack. "I can't get it in. Maybe if I push harder."

He tried. My resulting cry caused him to make a hasty retreat.

"Did it hurt?" he inquired.

"I don't know about Catholic girls," I said, "but you're not getting that thing in me."

"Okay, okay," Jack said, trying to calm me down. "Let's try again. This time I'll do it really slowly. I know with girls sometimes you can't stick it in right away. You have to kind of loosen them up first."

"I'm not a girl," I shot back, using the line he'd once used on me.

"I know," said Jack. "But let's just try it again."

I turned over again and once more Jack positioned himself between my legs. Again I felt him prodding me. I held my breath as he entered me, a little at a time. It still hurt, but it wasn't the searing pain it had been the first time. Still, it burned.

"It's really dry," Jack said, pulling out. "We need something to make it wet."

He spit into his palm, and I heard him rub it into his skin. But when he tried to re-enter me, it hurt too much and I told him to stop.

"What about butter?" Jack suggested. "That's oily."

"We use Parkay," I said. "Besides, my mom would notice if that much was gone." I thought for a minute. "I know. What about Vaseline? There's some in the medicine chest in the bathroom. We hardly ever use it, so it won't matter if some is gone."

Jack hopped off the bed and ran down the hallway to the bathroom. He returned a moment later with the jar of Vaseline in his hand. Taking the lid off, he scooped some out and applied it to his dick.

"Man, this stuff is slippery," he said appreciatively. "If this doesn't work, nothing will."

It did work. Not perfectly, but it worked. After much pushing and pausing, advancing a little bit at a time as I told him it was okay, he managed to get himself all the way inside me.

"Are you okay?" he asked, lying on my back with his mouth beside my ear.

"Yeah," I said. "It feels weird, but it's okay, I guess."

"Weird how?" Jack asked as he tried pumping his hips. "Weird like it hurts?"

"No," I answered. "More like I'm going to . . ." I hesitated, not wanting to say what it felt like.

"Going to what?" Jack asked, his breath ragged.

"Going to go," I said.

"Go where?"

"You know. *Go*," I said, emphasizing the word.

Jack pulled out quickly and backed away.

"I didn't say I was going to," I said, turning to look at him. "I just said it kind of felt like it."

"You're sure?" he asked, looking doubtfully at my ass.

"Pretty sure," I said. "Just try it some more."

I guess the thrill of this new activity outweighed Jack's fears of an imminent explosion, because he mounted me again, and this time he kept pumping until he came. When he pulled out, he rolled onto his back and I turned over. Noticing my hardly-erect penis and the unstained state of the sheet, Jack asked, "Didn't it feel good?"

"It felt good," I said. "Just different. I think we need to do it some more." Truthfully, I really didn't see what the big deal was. It had felt good, but not as great as Jack seemed to think it did. Besides, my ass was gummy with Vaseline, which I knew from other experiences was almost impossible to get off.

"Why don't you try it now," Jack suggested, rolling over.

Having had the advantage of going first, I was slightly better prepared than Jack had been. I was not, however, prepared for how good it felt when I finally sank into Jack's behind. I know I gasped, and I know I didn't last long. I think Jack's experience with girls, limited as it was, had taught him at least a little about holding off climax. I, being new to intercourse, had no such advantage, and it wasn't long before I lay, shaking and sweaty, on Jack's back.

"Is it like that with girls?" I asked him.

"No," said Jack. "Not even close. This is a lot better."

"So we can do it again?" I said.

"Yep," Jack replied. "And guess what, you're not a virgin anymore."

"But I thought Margaret Alice said this didn't count," I objected.

"That's because Margaret Alice has two places to put it in," explained Jack. "We only have one. So now you're not a virgin."

Having lost my virginity to Jack, I felt I'd become a grown-up. And now that Jack and I had expanded our sexual repertoire, we went at it as often as possible. We became reckless, doing it in our bedrooms during the day, sometimes while our mothers were downstairs making us snacks of chocolate chip cookies and glasses of milk. We experimented with alternatives to the vile Vaseline, trying salad oil, shampoo, and even the stuff Jack used to condition his baseball glove before discovering that plain old Corn Huskers Lotion worked perfectly well and wasn't quite as difficult to wash off.

We never worried about who was the "man" and who was the "woman." It would be another five or six years before someone asked me if I was a top or a bottom (at which time I still wouldn't know what the question meant). Our roles, at least in bed, were interchangeable. One of the advantages to being almost completely ignorant about what it meant to be gay was that we were equally ignorant about many of the misconceptions others had about homosexuals. We knew that men who slept with men weren't well-liked, at least enough to keep what we did together between us, but the sometimes violent hostility that would later be directed at the gay community had not yet shown its face to us. The year before, three people had been arrested for staging a sit-in at Dewey's restaurant in Philadelphia after diners assumed to be homosexuals were denied service. But apart from a brief mention in the newspaper, the event resulted in little public notice.

In talking about this fairly remarkable absence of either pro or anti-gay activity with an historian friend years later, he remarked, "They still had the blacks to beat up. They just hadn't gotten around to us yet." True, the African-American community was taking more than a little abuse at the time. But history was about to change again, and it would take me and Jack with it.

CHAPTER 9

There used to be, at Knoebels Amusement Park in Elysburg, Pennsylvania, a ride called the Scrambler. It consisted of three arms extending out from a central hub. From each arm hung four individual cars. As the Scrambler turned, the cars spun independently in the opposite direction of the arms' rotation, so that the feeling of speed was intensified and riders were quickly disoriented. Disembarking from the car at the end of four or five minutes, walking was difficult, and the area around the Scrambler often appeared to be populated by drunkards as people struggled to regain their balance. Our family made at least one trip to Knoebels every summer when my father had a week off from work, and Jack and I were sure to take several turns on the Scrambler, reveling in the intoxicating effects.

In the waning years of the 1960s, living in America was like riding the Scrambler on a daily basis. Just as we would regain our footing from one startling event, another would come and send us reeling in the other direction. On the same day in 1967, January 10, Edward Brooke, a Republican from Massachusetts, became the first black man elected to the United States Senate by popular vote, while in Atlanta, vocal segregationist Lester Maddox, who in 1965 chose to close his popular Pickrick chicken restaurant rather than serve black customers after the signing of the Civil Rights Act, was inaugurated as the new Democratic Governor of Georgia. This peculiar dichotomy was emblematic of the social upheaval rocking the nation. As if the entire country had slipped down Alice's rabbit hole into Wonderland (appropriately, Jefferson Airplane's psychedelic "White Rabbit" was a staple on radio in 1967), we peered, bewildered, into the funhouse mirror of American culture.

In San Francisco, the Summer of Love was about to unleash its message of peace, love, and LSD. But in suburban Philadelphia, interest and concern was focused on the arrival of the first Marine combat troops in Vietnam and President Lyndon Johnson's announcement of plans to enact a draft lottery. Until then, the armed forces had operated under the old system of registering all men aged 19 to 26 and calling them as needed, from the oldest down. Although nearly one million men had already been drafted to fight in the conflict against the National Liberation Front, those of us approaching the age of eligibility more or less considered ourselves safe, assuming that it would take a very long time to work through all the men currently in their twenties. Under the newly-proposed system, we could be called much earlier, a proposition that thrilled no one.

Still, we believed the threat to be a distant one. We also believed that the ugliness in Southeast Asia would soon be over. Demonstrations, the burning of draft cards, and defections (or, as my father called them, "desertions") to Canada and Europe were increasing. The conflict in Vietnam had sharply divided America, and it seemed we would either have to end our involvement in what appeared to many to be a losing battle or risk humiliation both home and abroad.

Given the current debate over gay marriage, it's interesting to remember that it was only in June of 1967 that the Supreme Court struck down state laws banning interracial marriage. Little did I think, when that news made the front pages of every newspaper, that 35 years later Thayer and I would ourselves enter into civil union, first in neighboring Vermont and, more recently, in Canada. The idea of two men marrying seemed as remote then as that of a white woman marrying a black man must have in 1942. Yet the world had changed considerably since World War II, and now, in the midst of another war, it was changing again, moving forward one step at a time. (Is it coincidence that changes in social policy occur historically in the midst of war? And will we finally see gay marriage instituted nationwide only after the sacrifice of another million lives?)

It never occurred to me at 17 that I might one day marry Jack. Our identity as a couple was sketched only in the broadest of strokes, confined as it was to the privacy of our own bedrooms. We were not free to walk down the street holding hands. I could not wear the letterman jacket he received after his winning season or his class ring on a chain around my neck. Still we took girls to the movies and dances. I sat in the stands, holding hands with Melania Brewster, watching Jack carry a football down the field. Afterward, I kissed the sweat from his skin as we celebrated his victory. We were invisible to the world, which made it impossible to imagine a life together beyond the moment.

In 1968, the shock of John F. Kennedy's assassination repeated itself in the twin murders of Martin Luther King, Jr., and Robert Kennedy within two months of one another, further bringing into focus the divisions threatening to splinter America. That fall, Jack and I entered our final year of high school. For the first time, we were forced to think about what would happen when we graduated. As the country faced its own uncertain future, we looked forward and saw that we, too, could be torn apart.

It was my idea to apply to college. On the surface, this would seem like the perfect solution. There were, however, obstacles. First there was my father, who I discovered had been assuming that I would join him in the insurance industry. His plan was to get me a job at his office, where I could learn the business, and to then open our own shop, Brummel & Son. The fact that I'd never displayed the slightest interest in his profession apparently had passed him by, and my announcement that I intended to go to school was met with mute disappointment.

Jack's father, being a scientist, was more open to the idea of further education for his son. Unfortunately, Jack's academic success had been far eclipsed by his performance on the field of play. A fair student, he'd gotten by largely because of my assistance and his ability to win the affections of his teachers. As we investigated the possibilities for advanced study, however, it became apparent that he would need more than that to earn him acceptance at a university.

While I worried, Jack was as unconcerned as ever, telling me whenever I started to express my fears that "something would happen." This being Jack, of course it did. It came in the form of a baseball scholarship offered by Pennsylvania State University. My academic achievements were enough to get me a full ride, thereby negating my father's concerns over the cost and neatly settling our dilemma.

So as the final year of the decade dawned, Jack and I looked forward to our future. With the pressure off, we were free to enjoy the blissful last months of our high school lives, culminating in the spring formal, which we attended with two girls whose hearts we would break soon after when we told them that preparing for college would prevent us from dating on an ongoing basis. That night, though, we danced with them in the crepe-paper-bedecked gymnasium as the Fifth Dimension serenaded us with "Aquarius/Let the Sunshine In." Afterward, we took the girls to a party, where we made sure they drank enough strawberry wine that they wouldn't notice when we dropped them off at home far earlier than they had probably planned. Then Jack and I drove in his car to a spot we'd discovered in a nearby park, where we quickly shed our polyester prom tuxes and made love in the backseat.

We thought we were almost men. At 18, we certainly looked the part. Our bodies had filled out. We had both allowed our sideburns to grow long in imitation of Jim Morrison, whose brooding sexuality aroused us and whose songs were frequently the background music to our sexual encounters. We carried packets of Lucky Strike cigarettes in our jacket pockets (although we were careful to hide them from our parents) and had once or twice tried marijuana.

Graduation was a relief. As I tossed my cap into the air along with those of my classmates, I was overcome with a sense of having made it to the end of a very long, very tedious race. It occurred to me that I would no longer have to see the same faces every day of my life, or move robotlike through the routine of class upon class. There would be no more dreary sessions of calculus, with Mr. Larson droning on about implicit differentiations while the afternoon sun made me struggle to stay awake, no more essays to write for Mrs. Peabody about *Babbit* or *Of Mice and Men*. High school and its petty obsessions with rules and schedules was finally behind me, and the open road of college awaited.

Jack and I did not go to Treasure Island that final summer, having grown too old for tents and campfire songs. Instead, we took jobs to save some money for our first year at Penn State. Jack worked for a landscaping company, putting his muscles to use, while I, in a peace-making gesture to my father, toiled in air-conditioned boredom at the office of the Quaker State Insurance Company, filing claim forms and being flirted with by the middle-aged secretaries. At night we escaped, as our mothers before us, to the movie theater, where we saw a string of films seemingly designed to inflame our gay sensibilities. *Midnight Cowboy*, *Easy Rider*, and *Butch Cassidy and the Sundance Kid* all provided us with emotional kindling, and I still recall giving Jack a hand job in the balcony of the Milgram Theatre while watching Jon Voigt's Joe ply his trade on the streets of Manhattan.

While we found *Cowboy*'s Joe and his seamy sexuality erotic, we saw ourselves more as Butch and Sundance. We were living in our own buddy movie, an idyllic place where two 18-year-old boys could be in love with one another and it was okay. In a short time we would be off to the beautiful town of State College and the campus of Penn State. We would be far enough away from our families that we would have our freedom. What this meant, exactly, we didn't know. We knew only that we were about to fly.

We weren't the only ones ready for change. In the early morning hours of June 28, the patrons of New York's Stonewall Inn gay bar fought back after the latest in a series of raids by the city's police department. The resulting skirmishes, taking place over several days and since given the somewhat mythological name of the Stonewall Riots, signaled a change in attitude on the part of the gay community. In Philadelphia, however, demonstrations for gay rights had been going on since 1965 in the form of the Annual Reminder, a protest held in front of Independence Hall each Fourth of July. Less theatrical but arguably much more political, the Annual Reminder following the events of Stonewall was the largest yet. (It would also be the last, as in 1970 gay pride parades took center stage and became the event of choice for proclaiming gay power.)

Jack and I, in Philadelphia to see the fireworks, witnessed the 1969 Annual Reminder in person. We watched from across the street as protesters stood in front of Independence Hall holding signs proclaiming messages such as 15 MILLION U.S. HOMOSEXUALS ASK FOR EQUALITY, OPPORTUNITY, AND DIGNITY and HOMOSEXUALS ARE AMERICAN CITIZENS TOO. We had heard about the incidents in New York, but only through newspaper articles. This was real. The neatly-dressed men and women standing not 100 feet away from us were real. When they saw us watching them, some smiled. These were not faceless people; they were like us.

We watched them for a long time, listening to the speakers who talked of equal rights and the importance of community. When the crowd began to disperse, we followed several of the men as they made their way west through the city, finally coming to The Spot, a small bar on Chancellor Street. I don't know why we followed them, except that we were curious to know what real homosexuals did and where they went. For all we knew, they were ghosts, appearing for a moment to shock and frighten unsuspecting humans and then returning to some mystical place unknown to mortals. There they were, though, going into a very real place. Jack and I watched the door to The Spot for some time, watching men (and a few women) come and go as if it were the most natural thing in the world for homosexuals to gather in the middle of Philadelphia.

Neither of us suggested that we go in. We were still not quite gay, despite the fact that we regularly sodomized one another and thought nothing of it. To actually go into The Spot, though, to join the people inside, would have been to count ourselves among their numbers, and we were unprepared for that. Instead, we hurried back to Independence Hall to see the fireworks explode in all their patriotic glory, raining red, white, and blue stars down on our heads as we clapped and cheered.

In August, our parents threw us our annual birthday party. We toasted the end of our eighteenth years with the traditional barbeque, this time accompanied by bottles of Duke beer presented to us by our fathers like royal scepters being handed down to the next in line for the throne. We pretended they were our first ones, clinking them against our fathers' and manfully overseeing the grilling of the hamburgers. It had long been a sore point with Jack and myself that we had been born in August and not been allowed to start kindergarten until we were six, resulting in our always seeming to be a year older than everyone else in our class. Now, though, the additional year gave us a certain cachet, and we looked forward to perhaps being mistaken for sophomores at our new school.

It's no great revelation to say that it sometimes takes leaving a place to make you truly see it for the first time. In those last weeks of August, I felt that keenly. Not only did the people and places I'd known for nineteen years suddenly seem alien to me, but so did my life as a whole. I no longer fit, as if I'd grown too large for our house, our street, our town. Everything felt confining, designed to keep me trapped forever in that one, small place.

When the long-awaited day came, my bags and boxes were packed and ready. On Saturday, September 6, I packed it all into the 1966 Ford Fairlane station wagon Jack's father had given him as a graduation gift. All four of our parents stood on the porch of the Graces' house as we said our good-byes. Our mothers cried and our fathers shook our hands, telling us to drive carefully. We promised, hugging first our own mothers and then each other's. Then we got into the Ford, gave a final honk of the horn, and started the 200-mile journey to our new life.

CHAPTER 10

A college dorm on the first day of a new term resembles nothing so much as a sea lion rookery during the winter birthing season. Upperclassmen, appointed to oversee the operations, herd the newcomers with a practiced, weary air, while the freshmen pups tumble over one another in their hurry, all wide-eyed excitement mixed with fear of the unknown. An infectious madness surrounds the proceedings, and it's impossible not to be swept up in it. Soon things will settle into a more sedate routine, but those first few days are pure bedlam. If you are one of the fresh arrivals, you feel half-explorer, half-clown, vulnerable in your newness but determined to make your way in this unfamiliar world.

As Jack and I carried our belongings into Pinchot Hall and up to our room on the third floor, we passed through a circus of sights, sounds, and smells. The voices of the Grateful Dead mingled with Janis Joplin's as Jimi Hendrix's guitar wailed behind them. Men of all kinds moved in and out of doorways, enthusiastically greeting old friends and nodding curtly at new faces. Most had hair longer than that of Jack and myself, and it appeared that growing a beard would be one of our first priorities. Peace sign posters and images of Che Guevara graced many dorm room walls, and the scent of pot was ever-present, in bold defiance of the numerous warnings we'd received in our new-student packets about the university's no-tolerance policy on drugs.

Our room was number 308. It was a double, as we'd requested on our applications, and it was completely unremarkable in every way. To the left of the door was a closet, then a long L-shaped desk, the shorter leg of which extended into the room and separated the work space from the sleeping area, which featured a twin bed situated against the wall. The right-hand side of the room was a mirror image of the left, as if the entire building had been rolled from an assembly line. Not that we much cared what it looked like. Pinchot (named after two-time Pennsylvania governor and avid conservationist Gifford Pinchot) was the newest of what were called the East Halls, built in 1967 and therefore mostly free from the wear and tear inflicted by previous occupants. Rising ten stories above the green lawns, it felt to us like our very own castle.

As we unpacked, we discovered that our mothers had followed the packing list sent by the school's office of student housing to the letter. They had also apparently done their shopping together. Opening a box marked BEDDING, we found inside two corduroy bedspreads, both blue, as well as two sets of sheets in the same hue. Matching towels waited for us at the bottom of the carton. We stacked it all on our beds in two tidy little blue pyramids.

"Are you guys brothers or something?"

We turned around to see Andy Kowalski regarding us with an amused smile. We didn't know it was Andy, of course, never having seen him before. What we saw was a big, broad boy wearing bluejeans and no shirt. His light brown hair was shaggy but not overly long, his cheeks were covered in stubble, and around his neck was a leather thong on which were threaded three ceramic beads the color of fire. Against his tanned skin they shone like rubies. His chest was patterned with hair, which trickled down his stomach and disappeared into the top of his jeans. His feet were bare.

"I'm Andy," he said, giving us a name to put with his face. He then repeated the question, "So, are you two brothers? All your stuff matches. That's why I asked."

"No," Jack answered, as usual speaking for both of us. "Not really. I'm Jack, and this is Ned. We're neighbors. From back home, I mean. Philadelphia."

Andy nodded and smiled again, as if everything was now perfectly clear to him. "Got it," he said. "City boys. I'm from Crawford County."

The part he didn't say—and didn't need to—was that he was a farm boy. I could tell by his way of talking. Like many people from Western Pennsylvania, he identified himself by his county, not his city. It was a holdover from the days when farm boards, and not the government, were the principal holders of power in a region. Although that had changed, many in the farming communities still saw themselves as being united against the threat of bureaucracy. Since many small towns had similar or identical names, or had yet to even make it onto maps, a person's county of residence made for the most easily-recognized form of identification. To Andy, hailing from Crawford County was akin to being part of a clan.

"We don't live in Philly exactly," I said, correcting myself. "We live a little outside it."

I don't know why I felt the need to de-citify myself and Jack. I suppose I feared that Andy would think us snobs, and for some reason I wanted him to like us. He was the first person we'd met since arriving at Penn, the first person, really, we'd met outside of our old lives. I wanted it to go well.

"Well, how would you not-quite-city boys like to share a joint with me?" Andy asked.

I hesitated, but Jack immediately said, "Sure."

"Come on," Andy directed. "Let's go to my room."

His room was on Pinchot's seventh floor. A double like ours, the right side was Andy's space. The bed was covered with an actual quilt made of hand-pieced squares in the traditional Jacob's Ladder pattern favored by the Amish. On the desk was a photograph of Andy with two people I assumed to be his parents, although they seemed a little old to hold those positions in his life. A poster of Jane Fonda in her *Barbarella* getup was taped on the wall beside the bed, and a dog-eared copy of Timothy Leary's *The Psychedelic Experience* lay on the floor.

Andy shut the door and sat down on the edge of the bed. Reaching beneath it, he pulled out a wooden box about six inches long by four inches wide. Like the quilt, it too looked handmade, the wood rubbed to a soft glow. Andy removed the lid from the box and took from inside it a small bag of pot and some rolling papers. Taking a paper, he folded one edge over to form a vee, into which he poured some of the marijuana. Then, with what looked like practiced hands, he rolled the cigarette using his thumbs, gave the edge a quick lick, and sealed everything shut by running a finger along the resulting seam.

The whole process took less than a minute. It reminded me of a scene in *True Grit*, which Jack and I had seen back in June the weekend it opened, where Kim Darby as Mattie Ross, the feisty teenage tomboy hunting down her father's killer, rolled a cigarette for John

Wayne's sheriff Rooster Cogburn and placed it in his mouth. Mattie's brazen action said a lot about who she was—independent, free, and nobody's fool. Andy's said something similar. By inviting us to share a joint with him, he was welcoming us in. By showing us how well he could roll one, he was displaying a sophistication and bravado that set him apart as someone willing to court danger. It was his first attempt at seduction, as far as Jack and I were concerned, and it worked.

"What about your roommate?" I asked as Andy lit the joint and inhaled deeply.

He held the toke for a long time, finally releasing the smoke in a gentle stream. It curled up from his mouth, like the dying breath of a dragon. "What about him?" he asked, passing the cigarette to Jack.

"Will he mind?" I said. "About, you know, this?" I waved at the joint, which Jack was inexpertly sucking on.

Andy laughed. "Shit, no," he said. "He won't mind. He's a Negro." He laughed again, as if this explanation was complete in itself.

Jack held the joint out to me. I took it from him, pinching it between my thumb and forefinger. Andy was watching me, and I wanted him to think I knew what I was doing. Putting the joint to my lips, I inhaled deeply. My lungs inflated, filled with the acrid smoke. The burn was intense, much more than anything I'd experienced the few times Jack and I had smoked pot before. I wanted badly to cough, but I forced myself not to. I held the breath as long as I could, then let it out. My lungs, still afire, sucked in clean air.

"Good shit, isn't it?" said Andy as I returned the joint to him.

Already the potent THC was coursing through my blood. My mind was being tickled by teasing fingers, my thoughts slowing as I sank into the warm glow. Jack, too, was feeling it. He settled onto a chair and leaned back, grinning. I looked from him to Andy, suddenly happy beyond words.

"Hey, are you guys into Blind Faith?" asked Andy, jumping up and going to the record player that sat on a makeshift bookcase beneath the room's lone window. "Have you heard their album? It's fucking amazing."

He pulled an album out and showed it to us. The cover photo depicted a young girl, naked, holding some kind of phallic silver airplane in her hand, the head pointed suggestively toward her crotch. Andy laughed. "Fucking *amazing*!" he said again.

He removed the record from its sleeve, placed it on the turntable, and gently lowered the stylus. Music poured from the speakers placed on either side of the window, a bluesy rumble of guitar.

"Clapton is God, man. He's *God!*" said Andy, standing up and swaying as the song burst into life. He took another hit from the joint, shutting his eyes and tilting his head back.

We stayed in Andy's room all afternoon. When the joint had been smoked down, and even the roach was nothing but a charred nub, we made a quick trip to a grocery store for chips and beer, which Andy purchased without an ID by charming the teenage checkout girl. We went in his beat-up pickup truck, a red 1958 Mercury-100. It had a three-speed automatic transmission, and whenever it would reluctantly move into another gear, Andy would yell, "It's Merc-O-Matic!" Jack and I found this hysterical, and by the time we returned to Andy's dorm room, we were all shouting, "It's Merc-O-Matic!" about every fifteen seconds or so.

Andy's roommate was there when we got back, sitting at his desk and reading. As promised, he was black. Tall and thin, he wore his hair in an afro. Upon seeing him, Andy let out another whoop.

"Chaz, my man," he said. "What's going down? These are my buddies, Ned and Jack."

"Hey," Chaz said. He went back to his reading. Looking over his shoulder as I passed, I saw he was deep into Eldridge Cleaver's *Soul on Ice*.

"Chaz is one of them revolutionary Negroes," Andy said as he popped open a beer and handed it to me. "What's that group you were telling me about, Chaz? The Black Cougars?"

"Panthers," Chaz said, not taking his eyes away from the book. "The Black Panthers."

"Panthers," Andy repeated. "Chaz says they're going to take the power away from white people. Sounds good to me. Let someone else be in charge for a while."

Chaz turned to look at us. "Damn right someone else needs to be in charge. Do you know for every white man being drafted to fight in Vietnam, three black men are being drafted?"

"That's because someone needs to take the place of all those faggots running to Canada," Andy replied. He took another record out and dropped the needle to it. The Who's *Tommy* rocked the room. "Hell, those black boys should be proud they're over there shooting gooks."

Hearing Andy say the word *faggot*, I felt my sense of happiness fading. I had no real opinion about the war in Vietnam, and my feelings about the men who went north to avoid being drafted into the conflict were equally neutral. But through the cloudy haze of my high, I realized I was one of the faggots Andy had so casually dismissed, and I didn't want him to hate me. I looked at Jack, to see if he was having a similar reaction, and was both surprised and saddened to see that he was laughing along with Andy at the joke.

"You won't think it's so funny when you're over there trying not to get your white asses killed," said Chaz, returning to his reading.

"We can't get drafted," Jack said. "We're in college."

Chaz snorted derisively. "That's right. All you white boys are safe in college. How many black men do you think can go to college? Why do you think they're taking so many of us?"

"You're here," Andy pointed out.

"And I worked like hell to get here," said Chaz. "My momma and daddy worked like dogs to save enough money so I could come here. Didn't nobody hand me a scholarship or pay my way."

"Hey, I'm not here free either," Andy told him. "My grandfather's worked his farm for forty years and never asked anybody for a handout. Everything we have, he earned."

"What about your parents?" I asked, noticing he made no mention of them.

"Dead," Andy said. "Killed in a car accident when I was two. My grandparents raised me."

That explained the photograph on his desk. And, I thought, probably the hand-stitched quilt as well. I imagined his grandmother piecing the blocks together and quilting the open spaces with painstaking care. What would she think, I wondered, if she could see Andy sprawled across it with a beer in one hand and his dirty feet resting on the top.

I made a silent prayer that neither Chaz nor Andy would ask me and Jack if we were at Penn on scholarships. Already I feared Andy would end our friendship if he found out about what Jack and I did with one another. I didn't want to give him—or Chaz—another reason to view us with disdain.

Fortunately, the conversation waned as Andy became more and more drunk. Chaz accepted a few hits from the second joint to be rolled from Andy's stash, and soon he was laughing along with Andy and Jack as he tried to explain Eldridge Cleaver's argument for the rap-

ing of white women as a way of eroding the dominant power structure. I listened, growing more and more anxious, until finally I reminded
Jack that we had a lot to do before our first day of classes began the
next morning. Reluctantly, he said good-bye to our new friends and
the two of us returned to our room.

"Andy's great, huh?" Jack said as I made my bed and unpacked the
rest of my things.

"Yeah," I said. "He's a nice guy."

"I like Chaz, too," Jack continued. "I've never had a Negro friend before."

"I don't think they call themselves that," I said. "I think they're just
black."

"Oh," said Jack, halfheartedly putting away some clothes in his
closet. "Anyway, they're both cool."

I wanted to ask him why he'd laughed at Andy's remark about faggots. Before I could, he was behind me, sliding his hands around my
waist and pushing his crotch into my ass suggestively. "Want to fool
around?" he asked.

I almost said no. The combination of beer and pot had made me far
too relaxed. But Jack continued to grind himself against me, and
slowly my libido wrestled its way through the blanket of conflicting
emotions in which I was wrapped. I found myself growing hard, and
when Jack slipped his hand down the front of my pants and began
stroking me, I gave in. Moments later, we were on my bed, naked, our
limbs entwined as we celebrated our first night truly away from home.

We fell asleep in my bed, our joined bodies curled into a question
mark.

CHAPTER II

Many things have been called life's great equalizer: death, education, subway cars, hospital gowns. I would add to that list the first few weeks at college. It's during this time that high school students learn that who or what they were back home doesn't necessarily apply anymore. Now that I have students of my own, I see this every fall, when a new crop of faces appears on campus and the transformations and run-ins with reality begin. The ones who were popular—the athletes and prom queens, the comedians and the simply wealthy—arrive their first day expecting to be afforded the same level of attention they enjoyed just a few short months before. Coming from a place where their accomplishments, abilities, or families were widely known and respected, they see no reason why their privileged status should not be immediately granted in this new setting.

It's easy to spot these high school celebrities. They come to their first classes smiling and confident, sitting in the front rows so as to give me an up-close experience of their wonder. They smile and toss their hair. They look at one another, searching for proof of their superiority. They have almost never read anything from the assigned reading list sent to them upon their acceptance at the school.

In contrast, at the back of the room sit the outsiders. Quiet, sometimes even sullen, they arrive at college shell-shocked from their four or more years spent enduring the horrors of lower education. Kept from the upper ranks of teenage society by their appearance, habits, interests, or any multitude of sins against the code of acceptable adolescent behavior, they have learned to look on from the outside. Often they are bitter about this, although they would never admit it.

In between the front and the back, always squarely in the middle, are the rank and file. Seemingly ordinary, they neither excelled nor failed. They were usually invited to the parties, even if they were never the center of attention once there. They may have enjoyed one or two shining moments on their journey to freshman year, but they are, by and large, unremarkable as individuals. However, one never dislikes them for this. In fact, their presence is comforting, for they can always be counted upon to hand their assignments in on time and contribute to class discussions.

As the first weeks of the semester pass, an interesting thing happens. The students who arrived filled with the buoyancy of popularity often discover that their stock has plummeted dramatically. No longer are they the prettiest, funniest, or most physically gifted. They're now only one of many others who share the same gifts, hitherto thought to be completely their own. Struggling for attention, their belief in themselves falters. They lose their glow. Their eyes take on a bewildered look. This is a wholly new experience for them, and they have no idea how to regain their stature.

For their less-attractive peers, the process is reversed. What were once seen as flaws suddenly become useful tools. Thinking. Dissecting. Questioning. Once considered obstacles to conformity, these traits are forged into weapons of revenge and wielded with newfound skill. It quickly dawns on the dwellers in the back rows that life has changed. Generally they blossom, becoming more confident by the day as the selves that have lain dormant awaken and stretch their limbs. One by one, they move closer to the front, displacing their former tormentors and objects of jealousy and sending them into exile.

Now, this is not always true. Not every boy who bullied his way through school and girl whose lack of intellectual curiosity was pardoned due to her ample bosom and laxness of chastity is doomed to look back on the high school years as the golden ones of their lives. Nor does every student who ate lunch alone while thinking dark thoughts about the laughing clique nibbling their sandwiches two tables over enter an intellectual cocoon upon arrival at university and emerge three weeks late a golden-winged butterfly. However, it is not uncommon. College, unlike high school, is a wide-open playing field. Whereas before students lived in a closed community with a more or less immutable class structure (generally beginning with the jocks and descending through the uselessly beautiful before arriving at the merely smart), college is an entire world, with different continents and cultures and societies, some secret and some not. Success is attainable to all willing to put forth the effort, and it is this that ultimately distinguishes one student from another. If it is the formerly ignored who succeed more often than the formerly glorified, this is perhaps the universe's way of maintaining some balance.

Another truth is that those in the middle tend to stay in the middle. It is safe there, and usually those students who have experienced such safety for most of their lives feel no need to test its boundaries. I say this having been one of those for whom being in the middle had become a way of life. I neither stood out nor hid. I simply was. Because of this, I found my first weeks at Penn State to be mostly a matter of figuring out where my classes were and how to get to them on time.

For Jack, however, things were slightly more difficult. Used to being a star, he now found himself one among many others stars. He still shined, but now his light was mixed with that of others who shined just as brightly. Even among his baseball teammates he was only one of several boys who had arrived there due to their ability to field a ball or hit it an impressive distance. Also, he was a freshman, a fact the older players would not let him or any of the other first-year players forget.

"I probably won't even get to start," Jack complained to me after his first meeting with the team. "Not until I'm a sophomore."

I was only partially sympathetic. Although it had been only a few days, I was finding my classes to be exciting, and without Jack's shadow to obscure me from view, I was beginning to see myself as someone who existed apart from him. I still loved him, though, and I wanted him to be happy. I spent several hours that night reassuring him that he was someone special, neglecting my reading of *Beowulf* for Survey of English Literature so that I could get on my knees and show him how wonderful I thought he was. Jack sat on the edge of the bed, his fingers entwined in my hair, and slowly his old confidence returned.

Because it was our first semester, we had mostly introductory classes assigned to all incoming students: American History I, Composition, Introduction to Critical Thinking, and the like. But we were allowed two electives each, courses we could take as a way of helping us decide what we might want to major in when the time came to declare our futures. I'd chosen Intro to Eastern Philosophy and, because my father demanded it, Fundamentals of Business Administration. Jack had opted for Art Appreciation and, because he thought it suited him,

Public Speaking. As there were several sections of each of the basic classes, we found ourselves sharing only two. We each also had one class in common with Andy Kowalski, Jack his art appreciation class and me my course in philosophy.

As a result of these common threads, and also because he kept asking us, we found ourselves spending most of our free time with Andy in his room. Largely this was due to the fact that Andy's stereo, beer, and pot were in the room, and it was easier for Jack and I to go up there than it was for him to carry it all down four flights of stairs to our room. Also it was because Chaz was so seldom there. Having befriended some other black students on campus, he was devoting a lot of his energy and time to helping them organize protests against the school administration's allegedly racist policies. Still, he managed to find time to get high with us at least several times a week, during which he would chastise our lack of political awareness and we would ask if we could touch his afro, a request he always refused.

It was, I think, the third week of September when Andy first mentioned a girlfriend. "Her name is Linda, and she looks kind of like Linda McCartney, only with bigger tits," he said. "She likes it when I bang her in the ass. Have you guys ever done that?"

He and I were supposed to be reading about the life of Lao-Tzu and the development of Taoism. Jack was supposed to be writing an essay about the role of slavery in launching the Civil War. Instead, we were listening to the Flying Burrito Brothers' *The Gilded Palace of Sin* and smoking a joint. I'd never heard anything like the music of Gram Parsons and Chris Hillman, and was blown away by the sound. I was stretched out on Chaz's bed, while Andy sat on his with his back against the wall, and Jack sat cross-legged on the floor.

When Andy asked his question, Jack and I looked at one another and laughed. Andy looked at us. "What?" he said.

"We've done it," I said, feeling brave because of my high.

"You guys have girls back home?" asked Andy.

"Nothing steady," Jack said. "Just casual stuff."

Andy nodded approvingly. "Yeah, Linda said I could see other chicks if I want to," he said. "She's really cool like that. We don't tie each other down."

"So, she can see other guys?" I asked him.

Andy shrugged. "Guys. Girls. Whatever she wants."

"She likes girls?" said Jack.

"Who doesn't?" replied Andy, grinning and picking up another beer. "Sometimes she and I do it with other girls, yeah. It's no big deal."

I wanted to ask Andy if he'd ever done it with another guy, but I couldn't. For a boy from a small farm town, he was much more experienced than Jack and I. I was intimidated by what I thought of as his worldliness, so I sipped my beer and concentrated on Lao-Tzu. I was trying to understand the concept of "action through inaction" and was having a difficult time, and not only because the image of Andy, Linda, and another girl refused to leave my mind. I was being asked to think about things beyond my previous experience, and like most first attempts, it was somewhat painful. Even if I hadn't understood my world fully, I had at least not felt awed by it. Now I was being asked to consider points of view that not only had never occurred to me, but which stood in stark contrast to what I'd been taught was true.

Andy, apparently determined that if he wasn't going to study, no one was, insisted on continuing the discussion.

"Have you met any girls here you want to hang with?" he asked.

Jack shook his head. "I've got too much to think about," he said. "I don't have time."

It was a believable excuse, and one I used myself when Andy asked me the same question. But Andy was not to be put off so easily. "We should get some girls together and really party," he suggested. "You know, get down with some good hash. Maybe mushrooms. You guys ever do mushrooms?"

When we answered in the negative, he promised us that we would all have to do mushrooms, and soon. "You won't believe the stuff you see," he assured us. "Have you read Castaneda? *The Teachings of Don Juan?*" He didn't wait for an answer. "It's fucking powerful, man. It's all about expanding your consciousness. That's what we should be reading, not this bullshit." He closed his philosophy textbook and tossed it onto the floor. "Life isn't in there," he said, pointing at the book, then pointing to his head. "It's in here. You just have to let it out."

All of a sudden he leapt off the bed and jumped on top of me. Ripping the book from my hands, he pushed it aside and rapped on my forehead with his knuckles.

"Let it out!" he said. "Come on."

I had no idea what he wanted me to do. He was straddling me, looking down into my face and grinning. He looked like some kind of wildman, all shaggy hair and craziness. He tapped my forehead again, then leaned down and kissed it. Then he was on his feet again and changing the record, which had stopped.

It took me a minute before I realized that I had a hard-on. When I did, I was both surprised and frightened. Had Andy brought out that reaction in me? I wondered. Or was it coincidental? I hadn't been conscious of becoming aroused, but the evidence was against me. I looked at him, taking a record from its sleeve and examining it, and the image of him and Linda, naked and rutting, flashed across my vision. Andy's ass was moving up and down as he pumped away at Linda. I quickly willed the thought away.

On the floor, Jack was oblivious. He was attempting to roll a joint, and was failing. The pot was falling on the carpet like green snow. Andy, seeing it, sat beside Jack and started to show him how to do it properly while Led Zeppelin emerged from the stereo. I rolled onto my stomach and pressed myself into the quilt on Chaz's bed, picking up my book and trying to focus on the words in front of my face.

In that one minute, the comfort I'd felt in Andy's presence evaporated. Helplessly, my body had responded to his, and I felt that I had somehow betrayed Jack. Worse, I realized that I was excited. But why? I had found attraction in men besides Jack, but never had I considered what it would be like to be with them in any real way. Now, closing my eyes, I saw Andy once again, only this time he was pumping himself into me, and not Linda. Meanwhile, he sat beside the boy who had been my lover for more than four years, not two feet away from me, both of them oblivious to my infidelity.

I felt sick. My stomach began to rise, and I suddenly needed to be anywhere but in Andy's room. Getting up, I excused myself and left, running toward the bathrooms that were situated in the middle of the hall. I made it into a stall just in time, dropping to my knees and retching. My insides emptied themselves again and again as I relieved myself of the pain knotting my guts. The stale smell of vomit filled my nose, and I threw up some more. Miserable, I flushed the toilet, slumped onto the floor, and began to cry.

It didn't dawn on me—at least not then—that what I was feeling was the pain of outgrowing my old self, of taking those first steps away from the middle rows and toward the front of the classroom. I was cracking from the inside out, sloughing off old ways of thinking and being. The old me was dying, and the new one was trying to birth. That process, though, would take a long time. At that moment, the cool tile of the bathroom beneath my cheek, I only knew that my heart ached.

CHAPTER 12

As September became October, the cool weather of fall arrived, causing the trees to erupt in a riot of red, gold, and orange. Walking to class, my feet kicking at the fallen leaves, I felt that I, too, was experiencing a change of seasons. Ever since the night in Andy's room when he'd playfully tackled me, I had felt uneasy around him. I shied from his touch, fearing it would arouse me again. I avoided being alone with him, and started spending more time in my own room. Jack noticed my reluctance to make nightly visits with him to Andy's room, and asked me why I was reluctant to go.

"I just have a ton of work to do," I told him, gesturing to the mountain of textbooks piled on my desk.

It was true that I had a lot of work, far more than I'd ever had in high school. Jack, too, had a heavy load. The difference was that he ignored his. Used to having me write his papers for him, he was unaccustomed to setting deadlines for himself. Assignments meant little to him because he had never before been controlled by their demands. But now, because we were in mostly different classes and because I had more than my own amount of work to complete, he was largely on his own. Still, he didn't worry. My questions about term papers and upcoming test were met with, "I'll worry about it later." But later never seemed to come, and as we entered our sixth week at Penn, the effects of Jack's nightly parties with Andy became apparent.

The first indication of trouble was a D on an English test. Having read virtually none of the assigned work, Jack was lucky to do even that well. He fared even more poorly on our first American history exam, receiving an F to my A-. When we compared our results, he fell into a black mood.

"Why didn't you make me study?" he said, as if his failure were my fault.

"I asked you to," I reminded him. "You wanted to go hang out with Andy, remember?"

"Whatever," Jack said, crumpling his test paper up and tossing it into the trash. "History's all lies anyway."

"You sound like Chaz," I said, mocking him gently in an attempt to cheer him up.

"Chaz says everything we were taught as kids was made up by the government to make us think they know what they're doing," said Jack. "You should hear some of the stuff he's told me. It would blow your mind."

"Maybe Chaz should take your next history test for you," I commented.

"Why do you hate him and Andy so much?" Jack asked, surprising me with the question.

"What do you mean?" I said.

"You hardly go up there anymore. Don't think they haven't noticed. They think you don't like them."

"I like them!" I said. "I just can't hang around up there all the time like you do."

"Right," Jack said. "I forgot. You're the smart one. I'm the idiot."

"You're not an idiot," I said. "That's not what I said. I was making a joke."

"It's what you meant," Jack shot back. He picked up his jacket—the letterman one he'd gotten in high school—and walked to the door. "I'm going out for a while. I'll see you later."

He left. Shocked, I looked at the closed door for probably five or six minutes, expecting at any moment that it would open and Jack would come back in. I didn't understand why he'd sounded so angry. A failed test had never been a big deal to him before, so I couldn't imagine that was it. But if not that, then what? Everything had been fine until he'd brought up Andy and Chaz.

Was that it? I wondered, my chest tightening. Had he seen or sensed something that night in Andy's room? Did he know what I'd been thinking? He'd never really asked me why I had stopped hanging out with Andy so much. Maybe because he knew. The realization hit me like a punch to the stomach. The last thing I ever wanted to do was hurt Jack. He meant everything to me. He *was* everything to me. I just wanted us to be happy together.

I waited for over an hour for him to return, trying to read but unable to concentrate. The words on the page kept turning into ants that scurried around in confusing patterns, fleeing from my attempts to make meaning out of them. I read the same paragraph over and over, each time reaching the end without understanding a word of what I'd read. I checked the clock obsessively, thinking that surely hours had passed, but finding that it had been only two or three minutes since the last time I'd looked.

Unable to sit still another second, I got up and grabbed my coat from the hook in the closet. Pulling it on, I left the room and the building, heading out into the cold night air to look for Jack. I had no idea where he might be. I had yet to even familiarize myself with the entire campus, so spread out was it that I'd mapped only a small portion. I stood for a moment in the harsh light of a street lamp, trying to make up my mind.

I decided to try the athletic fields. Growing up, Jack had often worked out his frustrations by running, saying that the physical exertion cleared his head. Maybe, I thought, he was resorting to tried-and-true methods of dealing with the anger he'd expressed toward me. Getting my bearings, I walked down the path to the track. It was some distance from the dorm, and by the time I got there, I was quite cold. It was only the 7th of October, but already I could feel frost in the air. I shoved my hands in my pockets and stood at the top of the stairs going down to the track from the crest of the rise on which I was perched. I scanned the area for Jack, but it was deserted. There was no figure moving through the oval of lights, circling around as he tried to run away from the heat inside of him.

Disheartened, I turned and walked back the way I had come. As I retraced my steps, I thought about how I would apologize to Jack. I rehearsed the words, choosing them carefully. I played out the conversation in my head several times, until I was sure that it would bring about the desired result, which was the return of peace between Jack and me. I just wanted everything to be the way it had always been.

As I passed Pattee Library, it occurred to me to check inside. Perhaps, I thought, Jack had gone there looking for some quiet. It was unlike him, true, but not out of the realm of possibility. Besides, I told myself, maybe he'd been spurred into action by his poor test result. Maybe, while I'd been worrying and looking for him, he had been safely tucked into a carrel, catching up on his schoolwork.

I pushed open the door to the library and went inside. Past the check-out desk, rows of tables set with softly-glowing lamps were positioned before the forests of stacks. Most of the chairs were filled with students hunched over their books, scribbling in notebooks. One or two were asleep, their heads resting on their crossed arms. Again I looked for Jack, but he wasn't there. Suspecting it was fruitless, I nonetheless walked through the stacks, thinking I might come upon him searching for a particular book. I was not surprised to come up empty-handed. Jack's going to a library for refuge was unlikely, but I had no other ideas for where he might have gone.

Unless it was to the most obvious place of all. Feeling ridiculous for not having checked there first, I left Pattee and hurried back to Pinchot Hall. Too impatient to wait for the elevator, I took the stairs. As I climbed to the seventh floor, I again rehearsed what I would say. Probably Jack had told Andy at least something about our fight. If he had, Andy would be even more resentful of me for having avoided him. I wanted to defuse both situations at once, which I planned on doing by pretending nothing had happened. I would just walk in and pick up where we'd left off. I could deal with Jack later, when he'd worked through his initial anger.

In my haste to get to Jack I had hurried, and by the time I reached the seventh floor, I was panting heavily. I walked to Andy's room and paused there, catching my breath. From behind the door I heard the sound of the Zombies singing "Hung Up on a Dream." I also heard muted laughing, two voices, which made me sigh with relief. Andy was not alone, and it was likely Jack he was with.

I opened the door and walked in, a smile on my face and a cheery hello ready on my lips. But I stopped in my tracks when I saw what was going on. Andy was on his back on the bed, naked. Sitting on top of him, her back to me, was a girl I'd never seen before. She had long red hair, which was bouncing against her back as she rode Andy vigorously.

"Hey," I said, unable to stop myself before it came out.

Andy looked up, his eyes dreamy from smoking the joint he still held in his hand. When he saw me, he smiled as if having me show up while he was in the middle of making love was the best thing that had happened to him all day. The girl, too, turned around and looked at me. Her small breasts, the nipples red like her hair, jiggled softly as she continued what she was doing.

"Ned!" Andy said expansively. "Come on in. Tracy, this is Ned."

"Hi," Tracy said breathlessly, giving a little wave of her fingers. I could see Andy's balls between his spread legs, and every time Tracy raised herself up, several inches of his shaft slid out of her.

"I'm sorry," I said, trying not to look at Tracy's breasts. "I was looking for Jack. I thought he might be here."

"No," Andy said. "I haven't seen him. But, hey, why don't you stay? I bet Tracy wouldn't mind."

Tracy giggled and winked at me coyly. "I wouldn't mind," she confirmed.

Andy pumped himself up into her, making her cry out and giggle again.

"She's a wild one," he said slapping one of her ass cheeks with his free hand. "Want a ride?"

"Thanks," I said. "But I've got to find Jack. Sorry to interrupt."

I retreated from the room, shutting the door before I could see anything else. Inside, Andy slapped Tracy's ass again, the sharp smack followed by more laughing. I walked away quickly, before I heard anything further, and descended the stairs to the third floor as if I were running away from the scene of a crime.

When I got back to my room, Jack was there. Like Andy, he was stretched out on his bed, but instead of Tracy and her breasts, he had a book open on his chest.

"Where have you been?" he asked, looking at the clock. "It's almost eleven."

"I was looking for you," I said. "Where'd you go?"

"Just for a walk," he answered. "You know I like to get some exercise when I'm hot."

I nodded. "I went to the track," I said.

He laughed. "I should have guessed," he said. "Look, I'm sorry about earlier. I was just mad about the test. I didn't mean anything."

"I know," I told him.

"And I guess I should stop spending so much time with Andy, too. It hasn't exactly been helping my grades."

"I think Andy's found someone else to spend time with," I said as I took off my shoes and sat down. Then I told Jack about walking in on Andy and Tracy.

"You're kidding," Jack said. "She just kept right on riding him?"

"Like a merry-go-round horse," I said. "Up and down and up and down and . . ."

"I get the picture," said Jack. "That guy is just crazy. He's fun, but crazy. I guess I let myself get kind of carried away by him."

I didn't say anything. Jack was apologizing, and I was happy that we were on good terms again. But I knew that I had something to apologize for, too, and I wasn't doing it. I couldn't. I could never tell him that for a brief moment I'd actually considered joining Tracy and Andy on the bed, and not because I wanted to get my hands on Tracy. For the second time, I felt as if I'd chosen someone else over Jack, and for the second time that person was Andy.

I picked up my business class text and turned to the chapter we would be discussing in class the next day. Of all my courses, this was the most difficult for me to have any interest in. The material was dull, and the instructor even duller. I couldn't believe some of my classmates actually found the discussions of profit and loss, earning statements, and inventory control interesting. Worse, I couldn't believe my father had devoted his entire life to work that centered around these things. When I looked ahead and imagined myself at a desk, computing the week's accounts, I wanted to slam the book shut and never open it again. I'd already promised myself I would never take such a job, for any reason.

Over on his bed, Jack groaned and flipped the pages of his textbook in irritation. "Why can't this guy write in *English*?" he complained.

"What are you reading?" I asked.

"Chaucer," he said. "It's supposed to be a poem."

"Chaucer?" I repeated. "Chaucer does write in English."

"Well, it doesn't look like it to me," said Jack. "I don't get any of it."

I closed my business book and took Jack's from him. "It's Middle English," I explained. "It just sounds funny. Here, I'll read it to you."

For the next hour we went line by line through the first part of the prologue to *Canterbury Tales*. Having already covered it in my class the week before, I was able to help Jack cut through the arcane language. It was tedious work, especially as Jack kept insisting that Chaucer was making up words that didn't exist. But I kept on, feeling that it was my penance. I told myself that I owed it to Jack for what I'd been thinking of late. I'd let him down, and helping him with his translation seemed the least I could do.

When we reached the part where Chaucer begins to name the pilgrims, I stopped. "That's enough for one night," I told Jack, who gratefully took the book and set it on his desk.

"Is it all like that?" he asked.

I nodded. "Pretty much."

Jack groaned as if in pain, then took his toothbrush and toothpaste from its place on the closet shelf. "I'll be right back," he said. "I'm just going to the bathroom."

I undressed and got into bed, waiting for Jack to come back and thinking about what we'd just read. Like Chaucer's pilgrims, we were on a journey together. There was Jack, the handsome Knight, fair of face and beloved by all. Myself I cast as the Yeoman, faithful servant to the Knight, always by his side ready to do his bidding. Andy, too, was along for the ride, as bawdy and uninhibited as the Wife of Bath. We made for strange companions, the three of us, yet it seemed that, for better or for worse, we had cast our lots together.

What, I wondered, would our tales be when we were finished?

CHAPTER 13

Jack's renewed dedication to his studies lasted about a week, during which he managed a C+ on a speech about the origins of the Peace Corps and a 72 on an art history test in which he mistook Turner's painting of Norham Castle at sunrise for Monet's landscape portrait of Paris' Parc Manceau. As his enthusiasm for his classes waned, he returned to Andy's room more and more often. Apart from our shared classes, I had not seen much of Andy since interrupting his tryst with Tracy, but he continued to be friendly to me and in no way seemed offended by my decreased presence in his room.

I, however, was miserable because of him. To my annoyance, I'd discovered that I was fantasizing about him often. Even when I was with Jack, I would sometimes see Andy's face, or recall the glimpses I'd had of his dick. He became a distraction to my studying, an ever-present figure in my thoughts who demanded attention at inconvenient times. I resented him for it, and I hated myself for allowing it. I should, I believed, be able to control my thoughts and feelings.

Objectively, I understand that my growing infatuation with Andy makes little sense. Love seldom does. Its unreasonableness is what makes it so dangerous. It's what allows so many of us to make terrible decisions, decisions that can lay waste to lives (especially our own) and end with us sitting wounded and bleeding in the midst of ruin, wondering what happened. It also sometimes results in unimagined joy, although I suspect that's more true of movies and novels than it is of real life.

I can't, even now, fully explain what it was about Andy Kowalski that allowed the hooks of love to plant themselves in my heart. Partly it was his wildness, which I both admired and was jealous of. Partly it was his beauty, which was undeniable. And partly it was because he wasn't Jack. I can see that all these years later, although at the time I didn't allow the admission to enter my conscious thoughts.

Jack had been my best friend for nineteen years, my lover for four. Having taken place in secret, our relationship had therefore also been untested. Until our arrival at Penn, there had been no other possibilities for my romantic interest. Now, though, I was discovering that my feelings for Jack might not be exclusive to him, and that frightened me. Like so many people, I'd come to believe that love flowed only in one direction, its course as fixed as that of the Mississippi or any great river. That this river could have tributaries, that it could flood and overflow its banks, was a shock.

It was made worse by the knowledge that Andy was unavailable to me. His hunger for women had been made clear, and despite his invitation to join with him and Tracy, I could not imagine that he would have any interest in me as a solitary object of desire. This made my feelings for him all the more ridiculous, and deepened my misery. I retreated more and more into myself as a way to dampen my feelings, although admittedly it did little to stop me from weaving daydreams about being in Andy's bed.

Jack didn't notice. One of the advantages to self-absorption is that you're able to completely ignore any cracks in the foundations of your relationships. Being on top of the pedestal precludes having to view the base, so that by the time the marble has started to crumble, it's usually too late. Again, I'm being a bit harsh on Jack. He had no more experience of relationships or love than I did. Also, he had the disadvantage of never having lost. He had not learned to recognize the signs of impending trouble. Even if he had, he would expect someone else to divert the danger, leaving him safe. He had no reason to think that our relationship was beginning to shift in a perilous direction.

Halloween of 1969 fell, conveniently for those interested in celebrating it without the worry of having to attend class the following day, on a Friday. The campus was the scene of multiple parties, all of which began as soon as classes were out in the afternoon. I remember walking back to the dorm following my history class and passing through a crowd of ghosts and ghoulies, all of them in a festive mood. In particular, I recall a girl dressed all in green, with sequins sewn to her clothes like scales. A long tail extended from her backside, and she'd painted her face to match her costume. As I walked by, she exhaled a cloud of marijuana smoke into my face, exclaiming, "Happy Halloween from Puff, the magic dragon!"

That was only the beginning. The halls of Pinchot were filled with revelers. I walked past pirates and devils, hippies (probably uncostumed), and Gandalfs. On the second floor landing, I encountered two Richard Nixons sharing a joint. And in my own room I discovered Jack laying out some items he was pulling from a brown paper bag.

"What's that stuff?" I asked him, eyeing the goods warily.

"Our costumes," he said proudly. "We're going to a party."

"We are?"

He nodded. "Andy invited us. It's at the house of some friend of his. Off campus."

I didn't want to go to a Halloween party. Correction—I *did* want to go to a Halloween party. Just not one that Andy would be at. I couldn't tell Jack that, though, not after he'd gone to the trouble of actually buying us costumes.

"What are we going as?" I asked, resigned to spending a night dressed like who-knew-what.

Jack held up a cowboy hat. "Butch," he said.

"Let me guess," I said. "I'm . . ."

"Sundance," he said, holding up a second hat.

He'd also found some vests, chaps, and cheap plastic spurs, all of which we put on. When we were done, we looked like the world's worst cowboys. Jack handed me a toy pistol.

"Don't forget this," he said. "Now you look like the real thing."

The final step was to paint on moustaches. We'd been growing our own out since the beginning of the semester, but the results had been unimpressive. At least mine had. Jack's was thicker, but because it was blond, it looked a little scraggly. We fixed that with some greasepaint. We also painted on heavy beard growth, smearing our cheeks with the stuff. The combined effect of the makeup and the getups was presentable, if a little haphazard.

Andy had given Jack the address of the party, and we drove over there in Jack's Fairlane. Things were already in full swing, even though night had barely fallen. A grinning jack-o'-lantern greeted us on the front porch, a flickering candle lighting up its eyes and mouth. A paper skeleton hung on the front door, flanked on either side by arching black cats.

Our knock on the door was answered by a young woman dressed as a witch. When we told her that we were friends of Andy, she showed us in, saying, "Andy's over there talking to the milkmaid."

She pointed to a couch on one side of the room. We saw the milkmaid, all breasts and pigtails, and we saw Andy. He was shirtless, and his pants were covered in what looked like clumps of fur. On his head he wore what appeared to be a fur hat with pointed ears affixed to it. It wasn't immediately clear what he was supposed to be.

We worked our way through the crowd of people standing around with beer bottles and plastic cups in their hands. There were perhaps twenty people crowded into the house's living room, and the din of their voices, combined with the Cream album being played on an invisible stereo, made it difficult to hear anything. When we reached Andy and the girl, it was all we could do to say hello.

"Look at you two," Andy said. "Git along, little doggies. Who-hoo!"

"What are you?" I asked.

"What?" Andy mouthed.

"What are you?" I shouted.

Andy lifted his head and howled. "A-woooooooo. A-a-a-woooooooo."

"The Wolfman!" Jack exclaimed. "Cool."

"I hope you brought a silver bullet," Andy said to the girl, biting her neck. The girl laughed. Andy grinned. "Guys, this is Melanie. How do you like her milk pails?"

Melanie laughed again. I could tell she was high, or drunk, or probably both. Andy, too, seemed to be stoned. He squeezed one of Melanie's breasts and stood up.

"Come on," he said, putting an arm around each of us. "You guys need a drink."

He led us back through the crowd to the kitchen, where a table was piled with cookies, candy, and other assorted treats. Andy picked up two brownies and handed one to me and one to Jack.

"Try these," he said. "They'll start you off right."

While Jack and I ate the brownies, Andy procured three beers from the refrigerator. He popped the tops off and handed us each one.

"That's good shit," he said, nodding at the brownies, which we'd almost finished eating. "Premium California weed. I've had two already."

The pot *was* good shit. Within minutes, all my worries about Andy, the party, and Jack were gone. I was laughing at everything Andy said, and when we returned to the living room to see what was happening,

I even found myself in conversation with a mummy about the films of Franco Zeffirelli, none of which I'd actually seen. The mummy, most likely as high or higher than I was, didn't seem to notice. He (or she, I never saw the face behind the toilet paper wrappings) nodded a lot and said very little.

I know I went back for at least one more brownie, and possibly more. Having skipped dinner, I was easily wasted, and soon I had no idea of the time or much of anything else. When Andy came over and guided me back into the kitchen, I went willingly. He'd brought Jack as well.

"Here," he said, handing us each a small square piece of paper. "You've got to try this. Don't eat it. Jut put it on your tongue."

I didn't ask what it was. I placed the paper on my tongue and waited for something to happen. Nothing did. I looked at Jack. He, too, was holding his paper on his tongue, looking from me to Andy and back again.

"What's it supposed to do?" I asked.

"Just wait," Andy said. "It takes awhile to kick in." He put a tab on his own tongue, then motioned for us to follow him.

We went upstairs to the second floor, where Andy led us down a hallway and into a bedroom. The lights were off, but several lava lamps glowed in the corners, the purple, blue, and yellow blobs inside them bubbling thickly. In their glow I could see that the floor had been covered with several mattresses, on which nude bodies were writhing. Their moans mingled with the music of the Beatles as *Abbey Road* played in the background.

"Come on," Andy said, stepping over a pair of legs and heading for a bare mattress.

I hesitated, unsure of what was going on. I saw full well what was happening in the room, but I didn't know what we were doing there. But I was also high enough that it all suddenly seemed perfectly ordinary. I took Jack's hand and walked to where Andy had seated himself. He was stretched out in the middle of the mattress, arms behind his head. Jack and I took up positions on either side of him.

"Just listen to the music," Andy instructed us. "Let it talk to you."

I stared at the ceiling, where the light from the lava lamps swirled in slowly-changing patterns. I watched circles form and stretch, becoming ovals that eventually broke into two. It reminded me of viewing amoebas under a microscope in biology class. As George Harrison sang "Here Comes the Sun," the amoebas danced joyfully above me, changing shape and color. I became lost in them, following each one's birth, halving, and death with intense interest.

I don't know how long I lay there. I remember at one point looking to my left and seeing a man with his head between a woman's legs as another man pumped his penis between her breasts. I was sure I could see writing on the men's skin, and I was trying to read it when I felt someone take my hand.

"Do you feel it?" Andy asked.

I turned to look at him and saw the face of the Wolfman, all hair and teeth and dark eyes. But I wasn't afraid. I reached out and stroked the soft fur of his cheek. He leaned forward and kissed me with his lupine mouth, his tongue slipping inside and exploring as I ran my hands down his hairy chest. I paused at his stomach, but with a firm hand he pushed me lower.

I felt something hard and pulled away, looking down. Jack's face was buried in Andy's lap, moving up and down slowly. What I'd felt had been the crown of his head. I watched, not comprehending. Jack was naked, and I realized with surprise that I, too, had somehow lost my costume. We were all three of us bare.

I felt something grab hold of my cock and begin stroking me. It was Andy. I bent my mouth to his stomach and kissed it, feeling hair beneath my lips. Slowly, I worked my way up his abdomen to his chest, taking a nipple between my lips and sucking. I lay beside him and wrapped one leg around his. I could feel his heart beating beneath me, a steady pounding that seemed to be driving the music that played in my head.

Jack moved up on Andy's other side and the three of us lay entwined. I kissed Andy's mouth, then made way for Jack. I kissed Jack, our heads meeting over Andy's chest as he stroked us both. It felt as if the three of us were becoming one creature. I saw us joining, splitting apart, and coming back together until none of us were comprised of our original cells. We had melded into something new.

Hours seemed to pass, during which we changed our configuration many times. First, I would be between Jack's legs, feasting on him, and then I would be on my back, Andy's mouth drawing me in. Mouths, hands, and cocks came into contact with one another like colliding asteroids, connecting and going off in new directions, only to collide again. The whole time, a kaleidoscope turned in my mind, the images and colors shifting continuously. For a moment, a pattern would freeze and I would be looking as if through a stained-glass window in a church. Then it would melt away, becoming something new before I could make out what I had been looking at. At one point, I was turned onto my stomach and someone—I don't remember if it was Jack or Andy—entered me from behind. A burst of colors flashed across my vision like thousands of tiny butterflies, and I found myself laughing as I was fucked, reaching out to try to catch the fluttering insects in my hands.

I don't know how many times we came, or if we even came at all. At some point, I fell asleep, and when I woke up, it was with Andy on one side and Jack on the other. My head aching, I looked around the room and saw half a dozen other naked, snoring bodies scattered in various poses on the mattresses. The lava lamps continued to bubble, and somewhere nearby a record needle unable to lift itself from the final groove of an album repeatedly voiced its distress.

It took me a few minutes to remember where I was and what had happened. When I did, I wished I hadn't. I looked at Andy. His Wolfman hat had fallen off and was lying beside the mattress along with my vest, chaps, hat, and spurs. His face and chest were smeared with the grease-paint Jack and I had used to draw on our facial hair. Jack's costume was at the foot of the mattress, apparently where he'd taken it off. My ass hurt, and my nipples were raw.

I carefully stood up and tiptoed around the sleepers into the hall. Trying not to make any noise, I searched for the bathroom, which I found I badly needed. Fortunately, it was nearby. I went in, shut the door, and pissed forcefully and long into the toilet. Afterward, I looked at myself in the mirror over the sink. My makeup was smeared, making me look bruised, and there were two huge hickeys on my neck, one on either side, as if I had been the victim of twin vampires. I ran the water in the sink and cleaned myself up with a washcloth borrowed from the bathroom's owner. Feeling marginally better, I walked back to the room with the mattresses and retrieved my clothes.

As I was dressing, Jack woke up. Rubbing his eyes, he looked around and asked, "What happened?"

I couldn't think of a good answer to that, so I said nothing. Jack sat up, looked over at Andy, and then back at me. "You okay?" he asked, perhaps beginning to remember.

"Yeah," I said. "I'm fine."

Jack nodded.

"I'll be outside," I said, gathering up my costume and standing.

I went downstairs, where more sleeping bodies filled the couches and even some spots on the floor. Outside, I breathed in the fresh air of a bright, clear All Saints' Day and felt not the least bit better. My head was still cloudy, and the events of the previous night shrouded in mysteries I was almost sure would never be fully revealed. But one thing I knew for sure—things between Jack, Andy, and myself could never be the same again.

CHAPTER 14

The weeks between Halloween and Thanksgiving break were tense ones. Jack and I didn't talk about what had happened. We rode home the morning after in silence and spent the rest of the day at our desks working on term papers, our backs to each other and our thoughts private. I don't even know that Jack thought about it much at all. I, however, thought about everything, as I am wont to do. At least, as much as I could remember. The specifics were fuzzy, but I knew that both Jack and I had given ourselves to Andy during the course of the night, and that was really the bone I worried like a dog, gnawing at it until there was only gristle remaining.

I know there are couples on both sides of the sexual fence (I suppose I should also include those sitting in the middle) who advocate non-monogamy, or at least view it as a harmless diversion. At my age, I find the whole idea of it tiring. Who has the time or energy to deal with *one* lover, let alone a multitude? I'm afraid it's beyond me. I told Thayer on our first date that I was looking for one man to spend the rest of my life with, both in and out of bed, and that if he wanted to keep his options open, he should look elsewhere. I believe his answer was, "I'm going to look around for an hour or two. If I don't get a better offer, I'll take you up on yours."

I've heard it argued that men aren't physically wired to be with only one person. We have a built-in biological need to scatter our seed as far and as wide as possible. Something about survival of our gene strain. It doesn't matter if you're gay or straight, they say, you just can't help yourself. Perhaps not. If left to my own devices, though, I'd also eat Ben & Jerry's brownie batter ice cream until I weighed six hundred pounds, but somehow I manage to stop myself when my pants start to get a little tight around the middle. But to each his own. And if you're going to do something that might piss off your partner, you might as well have science on your side.

At 19, I hadn't even heard the term "non-monogamy." All I knew was that Jack and I had had sex with someone other than each other. At first I blamed the drugs. Without their influence, I told myself, nothing would have happened. Then I reminded myself that when Jack had slept with girls in high school I hadn't gotten upset about it. Finally, I tried arguing that because we'd done it together, it couldn't be cheating. But that ignored the fact that I would have done it whether Jack was there or not, and even if I hadn't been high, I knew that if Andy had asked I would have done anything he wanted me to. That left only myself and Jack to blame, and that was a no-win situation.

It didn't help when, on Monday, Andy sat next to me in our philosophy class. He seemed not the slightest bit uneasy about seeing me, acting as if the last time we'd seen each other I hadn't been kissing him while my boyfriend gave him a blow job. I sat through class trying to avoid looking at him, and when his knee accidentally brushed against mine, I gave such a start my books fell to the floor with a thunderous crash.

Afterward, he walked with me back to the dorm. Only when we were in the elevator, alone and as far apart as I could make us, did he bring up Halloween night.

"How'd you like acid?" he asked.

"Is that what that was?" I said. "Those little squares of paper?"

Andy nodded. "That's LSD, man," he said. "Did you see anything cool?"

"I don't really remember," I answered honestly. "I just remember feeling like I was, well, sort of melting."

Andy laughed. "That's *it*, man. That's what you're supposed to feel."

The elevator stopped at my floor and the doors opened. As I stepped out, Andy put his hand on the door to prevent it from closing. "I had fun," he said. "And you know, if you ever want to do it again, it's cool. I mean, I'm not queer or anything, but if you want to help me out sometime, I'd be up for it." He cupped his crotch with his hand and squeezed, showing me the outline of his cock.

I stood looking at him. I did want to. I wanted to do it right then, right there. I wanted to get back in the elevator, drop to my knees, and take him in my mouth. But I couldn't answer him. I could only stand there, trying to get my lips to form words, until finally the elevator began buzzing angrily and Andy had to let the door close.

I went to my room and tried to work. Jack was in class, so I had no distractions. Still, I couldn't concentrate. I kept thinking about Andy's words. He'd said he wasn't queer. Did that mean that he thought I was? That Jack was? Did it even matter? He'd extended the invitation. All I had to do was accept it.

I waited another half an hour before going up to his room, ostensibly to talk about our homework assignment. That we did, for all of fifteen minutes. But I couldn't stop thinking about Andy's earlier offer, and my eyes kept darting to his crotch. When he leaned back on his bed, putting his hands behind his head and cocking his head to the side, I hesitated only a moment before falling between his legs.

My fingers fumbled with the zipper of his jeans. As I slid it open, his erect dick sprang out from the V formed by the spreading teeth. I put my mouth over the head, sliding down the length of his shaft even before his pants were off. Anxious to have him inside of me, I pulled his jeans down only as far as his thighs, resting my body on his pinned left leg as I sucked him.

I held his heavy balls in one hand, caressing them while I attempted to force him all the way into my throat. When I hesitated, afraid I wouldn't be able to take his whole cock without gagging, Andy placed a hand on my head and pushed me down until my nose met the rough hair of his belly and I smelled the musky scent of his crotch. I rested there as long as I could, enjoying the way he filled me with his thickness, then had to come up for air, the taste and smell of him lingering along with a faint and not unpleasant soreness.

I resumed working him with my hand and mouth, and it wasn't long before he came, holding my head in both his hands as he released heavy blasts of bitter-tasting stickiness that coated my tongue and slipped down my throat. I kept him inside me until he softened, only reluctantly letting go after milking the last drops of cum from him. When we were done, Andy lit up a joint as I sat beside him on the bed. He didn't offer to get me off, and I didn't suggest it.

"Most gooks are Buddhists, right?" he said, taking a hit and then passing the joint to me.

"Yeah, I guess," I said. "Why?"

"Well, I was just thinking. If Buddhists are all about peace and love and shit, how come they're all fighting us?"

"The North Vietnamese are Communists," I said. "They don't believe in religion."

"What a bunch of assholes," said Andy, shaking his head.

I waited four days before visiting Andy again, then three, and finally I was going upstairs every other day. Each time, I went to his room pretending that I wanted to discuss philosophy. After some initial conversation, Andy would produce a joint and light up while I settled between his legs. Sometimes he would grab my hair, directing me, but mostly he laid back with his eyes closed, occasionally telling me how good it felt. He never warned me before he came, although I was soon able to recognize the signs: the quickening of his breath, the tightening of his balls, the stiffening of his cock. And always I took his cum in my mouth, waiting until he was drained before letting him pull out.

I timed my trips to the seventh floor to coincide with Jack's classes or his practices. In fall, the baseball team trained indoors for several hours in the afternoon, giving me plenty of time for my dalliances with Andy. I was always careful to be back before Jack returned, so that when he entered the room he would find me at my desk, studying or writing.

Our sex life together had slowed. We still made love, but far less frequently, and often we simply jerked one another off before bed. More and more I thought about Andy while touching Jack or being touched by him. That sex with Andy was almost entirely one-sided didn't much concern me. I could take care of my own needs, and I still had Jack for those times when I wanted more personal attention. My desire for Andy was centered around pleasing him and having him want me, not about what I might want.

As my encounters with Andy increased, my feelings of guilt about them did as well. I didn't like betraying Jack, and on some level I suppose I knew that things couldn't go on the way they were forever. But I couldn't help myself. Every visit with Andy made my hunger for him grow more intense. Like a drug, I needed him more with every taste. I was simply avoiding the inevitable. Someday, I knew, I would have to make a choice. I just wasn't ready to make it.

The morning of the day Jack and I were to return home for Thanksgiving break, I reached a point of unbearable anxiety. Knowing that I would be away for four days, with parents I hadn't seen in three months, filled me with dread. It had been only a short time since I'd left, but I had changed dramatically. I felt it, and couldn't believe that my parents, too, would not notice that I was a different boy than the one they'd known for nineteen years. Even if they couldn't sense it, I feared they would see it. My hair had grown longer and my beard, what there was of it, covered up the boyishness they were used to. My clothes were not the ones I had come to Penn with. I'd begun to dress like Andy, in faded jeans and loose-fitting shirts that were open to the chest. I'd acquired an army jacket from a surplus store and wore it constantly, a small peace button affixed to the lapel, and a Strawberry Alarm Clock patch sewn on the back.

I knew my appearance would be a surprise, if not a shock, to my parents. I also felt somehow that going home threatened the independence I'd achieved. I wanted to see my mother and father, but I didn't want our relationship to be what it had been. I wanted them to treat me like a man, and I knew they wouldn't. I would be forced to return to my childhood, sleeping in my old room with the model spaceships and the comic books, helping my mother with the dishes, listening to my father lecture me about the necessity of my business class.

Coupled with this was the dread I felt over being alone with Jack in the car. I knew that he, too, was worried about what his parents would think of his altered appearance. Worse, he worried what they would ask about his progress in the classroom. I feared our combined neuroses would combust from the tension, any little spark being capable of igniting that fire, and that I would reveal my secret unintentionally.

I told myself I was going to Andy's room to see if I could buy some pot from him to help keep me mellow during the weekend. Jack was at his final class before the holiday, and I wanted to get up to Andy's room and back before he returned. He would want to leave immediately, I knew, and I wanted to be ready. Maybe, I thought, I would smoke half a joint to calm my nerves.

I opened the door to Andy's room without knocking, and for the second time walked in on him in the midst of sex. Only this time his partner wasn't a giggling redhead with perky breasts. It was Jack. There he was, in my place between Andy's legs, his lips around the head of Andy's dick and his bare ass pointed toward me.

"Jack?" I said, as if perhaps it was someone who merely resembled him.

Jack looked back, his hand still clasped around Andy's shaft.

"You're supposed to be in class," I said stupidly.

Andy sat up and looked at me. "Hey," he said, "could you close the door? I'm not putting on a show here."

The ride home was worse than I could ever have imagined. For the first half hour, neither Jack nor I said a word. Finally, he said, "I'm really sorry. I didn't mean to . . ."

"Was this the first time?" I asked, interrupting his apology.

Jack was quiet.

"I didn't think so," I said. I had no right to be mad at him, but I was. Oddly, I was less upset about discovering that Jack, too, had been making trips to Andy's room than I was about how much guilt I'd felt about *my* indiscretions. All that time I'd been beating myself up, when Jack had been just as guilty as I was.

"Look," Jack said. "It's not a big deal. I mean, it's just a little fun."

I ignored him. It occurred to me that he must not know about Andy and me, otherwise he would have played that card. It occurred to me, too, that if I forbade him to see Andy anymore that I would also have to abide by the edict or risk further damage to our now-fragile relationship. Andy was apparently good at keeping secrets, but I suspected even he had his limits.

"Forget about it," I said.

Probably relieved to be off the hook, at least for the moment, Jack retreated into silence. I sat, stewing in my rapidly-multiplying feelings of anger mixed with shame. How, I wondered, had everything gone so horribly wrong? My trip to State College with Jack had been filled with laughter and bright hopes for the future. Our return home was about as happy as a death march. Worse, we had to pretend that everything was fine or risk a lot of unpleasant questions from our families.

Four hours and fewer words later, we pulled into the driveway of Jack's house just after ten o'clock. The lights were on, and I knew my parents would be sitting in the Graces' living room, waiting for us to arrive. I steeled myself for the onslaught of hugs and kisses and got out of the car.

The front door opened and both my mother and Jack's ran out. Immediately they grabbed us, crushing us to their chests and holding on tightly. I could feel my mother's body shaking, and realized that she was crying. Behind her, my father and Mr. Grace were standing quietly on the porch, their hands in their pockets.

"What's wrong?" I asked my father.

He cleared his throat. "On the news," he said, his voice halting. He cleared his throat. "On the news," he said again. "They just announced it. There's going to be a lottery."

"A lottery?" I repeated. "For what?"

My mother pulled away and looked into my face. Tears ran from her eyes as she ran her hand over my beard. "For the draft," she said.

CHAPTER 15

I've often wondered about the timing of the announcement of the 1969 draft. I picture Richard Nixon sitting in his office, trying to decide how best to inform a country of parents whose support for the war was waning rapidly that he was about to send their sons into the fray. What better time than on the eve of Thanksgiving, when families were sure to be together, when they would be surrounded by loved ones who could soften the coming blow with pats on the back and assurances that everything would be all right? Like Jack and myself, most young men who had recently gone off to college would be home when the news came. I'm sure he thought it was a brilliant tactical move.

The first order of business, once we pried our weeping mothers from us and got into the house, was to find out exactly what had happened. Fortunately, the news was still on, and we were able to hear for ourselves what had transpired that afternoon at the White House. According to Dan Rather, reporting live from Washington to Harry Reasoner in the CBS studio, Nixon had signed the draft bill after winning bipartisan support in both the House and Senate. In a complete turnaround from previous draft procedures, the new system would begin with men who were 19 years old, rather than putting all men aged 19 to 26 in one group and drawing from the oldest first. According to Nixon, this new system would be more fair, as potential draftees would have only one year, rather than a possible seven, to learn their fate.

After listening for a few more minutes, Jack's mother turned the TV off. "I can't listen to any more," she said. "This is outrageous. Just three weeks ago the president said he had a plan for getting our men out of there. Now he wants to send more?"

"Patty, don't get all worked up," Mr. Grace said, putting his arm around his wife's shoulder. "A draft doesn't mean every boy will be going to war."

"Right," Jack said. "Besides, Ned and I are in college. They can't draft us anyway."

A worried look passed between our parents before my father said, "There's talk of ending the deferments. The deputy attorney general, what's his name . . ."

"Kleindienst," Mr. Grace said.

"Right," my father continued. "He said the president is considering ending the deferments."

"Although the White House denies it," Jack's father added quickly as my mother and Mrs. Grace began to cry once more.

I went and put my arm around my mother. "Well, there's nothing we can do about it tonight," I said. "And tomorrow's Thanksgiving. I forget, whose year is it this year?"

"Ours," my mother answered weakly.

"And I bet there's a pumpkin pie waiting on the kitchen counter, isn't there?" I said, kissing her cheek.

"Right," Jack said. "And tomorrow we'll watch the Macy's parade and watch the game. Who is it this year?"

"Vikings and the Lions," my father answered. "Should be a good game."

After saying good night to the Graces, my parents and I returned to our house. I went upstairs and put my bag in my room. It seemed impossibly small, as if I'd outgrown it in the past thirteen weeks and was now in a house built for dolls. Everything seemed to be from a different time, to belong to another boy I knew once but had forgotten. Looking around at my books and posters, the models and toy cars, I both wanted to put them all in boxes and hide them in the basement and also to be the boy who had loved playing with them.

My mother came into the room and sat beside me on the bed. She reached over and ran her fingers lightly over what there was of my beard.

"You look like your father when he was your age," she said.

I laughed. "I bet his hair was a lot shorter than mine, though."

"A little," she said. "But you have his face."

"Don't worry about the draft," I told her, knowing it was still on her mind.

She put her hands in her lap and sighed. "Your father was a little too young for the Second World War and a little too old for Korea," she said. "I'm thankful for all the men who died in those wars, but I'm more thankful he wasn't one of them." She paused, then looked at me. "I don't want my son to be in a war, either."

"I'll be fine," I said. "Really."

"You don't know what it's like," she said. "You don't know how it feels to think you might lose your child. I don't know if I could live through that."

I didn't say anything. Her words were melodramatic, but I knew that she believed them. And she was right, I didn't know how it felt to fear losing my child. But I was afraid for myself, even if I didn't show it. The war had always seemed to be happening to other people. Now it was at my doorstep, and soon I might have to open the door and let it in.

"I was only nine when World War II began," said my mother. "I didn't understand it. But I was 15 when it ended. I remember hearing the men on the radio talking about what was happening. It all seemed so far away, like a play or a movie. I couldn't imagine that these terrible things were happening to real people. But then my mother's brother came home. He'd been part of the troops who liberated the concentration camps. I forget which one. Treblinka, maybe. He had some photographs another soldier had taken of him helping survivors walk out of the camp. I remember looking at them and not believing that the figure my uncle was holding up was a human being. I *couldn't* believe it. The idea that people would do something so awful to one another was too terrible."

My mother looked across the room and out the window. The moon, full a few days earlier, was still round. Its light streamed through the window and pooled on the floor. My mother stared at it as if looking into a crystal ball. I wondered what she saw there.

"It was too much for my uncle as well," she said, still staring into the light. "He stayed with us for several months. I remember he used to wake up screaming and my mother would sit with him for hours, whispering to him. I could hear their voices through my bedroom wall. Sometimes she would fall asleep and we'd find her in the morning, holding him like a child. Then he left us and moved into his own apartment. A few weeks later he shot himself in the head with his service revolver."

"How come you never told me about him?" I asked her.

"I don't know," she answered. "Maybe because it was so sad. I tried to forget about it. But forgetting is a mistake."

A dreamy quality had entered her voice, as if she was suddenly back in her girlhood. Unspoken emotions flashed across her face. I could see them in the lines of her eyes and the set of her mouth. For the first time, I imagined my mother as someone with a history. This is a fault of all children, I think, viewing their parents as creatures whose lives began only with the birth of their offspring. We forget that before us came years of loves and trials, pains and pleasures. Mostly, we never ask them about these things, too occupied with our own lives to think about it.

Sometime during every semester, I ask my students to interview their oldest living relative. Usually this is a grandparent, sometimes a parent and, very rarely, a great-grandmother or great-grandfather. Most of my students think they know everything there is to know about their subjects. They are always wrong. They return to class with wonderful stories, stories of heroics and crimes, of sacrifice and survival. They discover a grandmother who became pregnant by a secret lover while engaged to someone of her parents' choosing, a father who once hiked across Switzerland at the age of 18, a great-grandfather who sold his shoes in order to buy a ticket on a boat leaving Scotland for America.

That night in my room with my mother, I discovered a great-uncle I never knew about. I saw, too, that there was more to my mother than I'd ever imagined. I'd read about World War II, of course, but had never even thought to ask my mother or father what it had been like to be alive during it. It was in the past, and therefore uninteresting. Now, though, I saw that the past could reach into the future.

"What else do you remember?" I asked my mother.

She sighed, shaking her head. "Oh, lots of things. Ration books. Saving the foil from chewing gum. Victory bonds. Thinking the Germans were monsters waiting in the dark to kill us. I don't know. It was so long ago."

"How did you feel?" I asked.

"Sometimes I was afraid of what might happen," she said. "Sometimes I was proud of America. Mostly I didn't think about it. I had other things on my mind, like marrying Frank Sinatra."

She patted my leg and stood up. "Unfortunately for him, Bobby Genovese got to me first," she said. "He was my first sweetheart. We went steady for two whole weeks, until he dumped me for Francine Putty because I wouldn't let him get to second base."

I couldn't help laughing imagining my mother fending off the advances of Bobby Genovese. She put her hands on her hips. "Don't you make fun of me, Edward Brummel. You're not so old that I won't give you a spanking."

"I'm not laughing at you," I said. "I'm just wondering how far he got with Francine Putty."

"Let's just say she ended up marrying him," my mother said. "And not because she wanted to."

"Too bad," I said. "I kind of like the way Ned Genovese sounds."

"I won't tell your father you said that," my mother answered, pretending to be shocked. "Now good night."

"Good night," I said. "And Mom."

"Yes?" she said, turning around.

"I love you."

"I love you, too," she said softly, pulling the door shut.

I undressed and slipped into bed, turning off the light on the bedside table and pulling the blankets up. Listening to the house settle around me, I realized how quiet it was. I'd gotten used to the continuous hum of the dorm, and without it in the background every sound was amplified—the furnace going on in the basement, the light tapping of rain that had begun to fall on the roof, the creak of the stairs as my father walked up them. Also, Jack wasn't there, and I felt the absence of him with some relief. The anxiety I felt about him, and about Andy, was still there. But it had coiled itself into a ball and settled deep inside, where it could wait until I had time to attend to it.

The rain started to fall more heavily. I listened to it, aware of how much I'd missed it now that I lived seven floors beneath the roof. So many things had changed. So much about *me* had changed. The last time I'd slept in that room, my life had been uncomplicated, my biggest worry what to watch on television. Now I was bound with worries and complications: Jack, Andy, school, my life. And now the draft.

It occurred to me that, like Jack and myself, Andy would be eligible for the draft if deferments were suspended. I wondered if he knew and, if he did, how he felt about it. Many of the men in my class would be 19. I tried to imagine Penn State without us. How much would we be missed if we all left? I multiplied that by the number of 19-year-olds across the country. How many of us were there? I wondered as my eyes closed. A hundred thousand? A million? I had no idea.

I fell asleep and woke in the morning, having dreamed nothing. It was still raining. The sky was gray, and the wind drove spatters of rain against the windowpanes. I could hear my mother rattling pans in the kitchen, and remembered that it was Thanksgiving. I looked at the clock beside my bed and saw that it was after nine. Jack and his parents would be arriving shortly. Reluctantly, I got up and walked to the bathroom to shower.

Despite everything, or maybe because of it, the day went smoothly. Dinner was the usual success, and I won ten dollars from my father when Minnesota trounced Detroit 27 to nothing. No one mentioned the draft or the war, as if neither hovered over us like a specter. If there was any news about either, we didn't hear it, as the television stayed tuned to football and then *The Jim Nabors Hour*. It was as if, by mutual agreement, we all decided to pretend Vietnam didn't exist.

Jack and I, too, pretended. We pretended everything was fine between us. We pretended school was going well for us both. We pretended so well that I almost believed it, until I overheard Jack telling his mother about his new friend, Andy, and how nice he was. Then I remembered. I avoided being alone with Jack for the rest of the day, afraid of what I might say to him. When he left, we made no plans for the following day.

On Friday, the news came that the draft would be held on the following Monday, December 1. This was accompanied by an announcement from the White House that all men currently enrolled in college would be allowed to finish out their education. Upon hearing this news, my mother cried with relief. I, too, felt a sense of having narrowly escaped something, although I was also struck by the unfairness of the deferment. Why, I wondered, should those of us who could afford college or who had gotten there by other means get to stay, safe in the halls of academia, while men who either couldn't afford school or who had elected not to go for other reasons were conscripted? I imagined what Chaz would have to say when we returned to Penn. I could hear him already, his voice ripe with righteous indignation as he decried the burden being placed upon the backs of the poor and the uneducated.

With the threat of the impending draft gone, the remainder of the weekend was free to be enjoyed as much as possible. Jack and I extended our truce, joining together on Saturday to help our fathers clean the gutters and bag the final leaf fall of the year. It almost felt like before, when we had no reason to question one another's loyalty. Only when Sunday dawned did I feel the uneasiness in my stomach stir again, as I contemplated the ride back to school and what we would, or would not, talk about.

We left after lunch, so as to be there before dark. My mother loaded us down with Thanksgiving leftovers, our fathers with cash tucked into our pockets as we said our good-byes. We promised to call soon, then were on our way.

To my surprise, Jack was the one to speak first.

"That wasn't so bad," he said.

"No," I agreed. "It wasn't so bad." I said nothing else, deciding that if he wanted to discuss our relationship, it was up to him to do it.

"I've been thinking," he said after another ten miles had passed silently. "Maybe we should get different roommates."

Nothing he could say could have surprised me more. I stared at him, my mouth open.

"You know, next semester," he said, speaking quickly. "They let you switch around in January if you want to. I read it in the student book."

"You want to room with someone else," I said flatly.

"Maybe," said Jack. "I mean, yeah, I guess. I think it would be good for both of us."

"Just who do you have in mind?" I asked him.

He shrugged. "I hadn't really thought about it," he answered. "Nobody in particular."

"So not Andy," I said.

"Andy?" said Jack. "Why would I room with Andy?"

"I don't know," I said. "Maybe because he's so *nice*?" I emphasized the word so he'd know I'd overheard him talking to his mother. "Maybe because you like sucking his dick?"

Jack started to say something, then stopped. He looked straight ahead, as if it took all of his concentration to keep the car on the road.

"It's not like we're married," he said finally.

"No," I said. "It's not. So do whatever you want. You're right, it will be good for us."

Everything was unraveling. I couldn't think, and I couldn't breathe. The car felt suffocating. I rolled down the window and stuck my head out into the fresh air, letting it wash over me until my skin was numb and I could barely feel my fingers when I touched them to my face.

CHAPTER 16

No American man born in the years 1944 through 1950 will forget where he was on the date of Monday, December 1, 1969. Chances are, he was glued to a radio or television set, waiting to find out whether or not he might be headed for Vietnam. The lottery system proposed by Lyndon Johnson and championed by his predecessor, Richard Nixon, was about to be put into effect only five days after being signed into law, altering the lives of millions of young men.

Despite the promised deferment for college students, that day the campus of Penn State was eerily silent. Although the voices of a handful of protesters rang out, mostly we were hushed as we went from class to class, if we even bothered to attend. Most of us, unable to think about our studies, congregated in communal rooms or wherever there was a television. The lottery wouldn't be held until the late evening, but we began gathering early, to talk and share what rumors and gossip we'd heard.

Some of the men had brothers, uncles, or friends who were already in Southeast Asia. A number of these soldiers had returned with tales of atrocities committed on both sides and accusations of government propaganda being disseminated to mask miserable conditions, while others insisted the war was being won and that Communism was on the brink of collapse. Depending on their point of view, men were either excited or apprehensive about the coming draw, and most often were a mixture of both. Strangely, I remember no fighting between opposing camps. I think no matter what our political stance, we all simply wanted to know where we stood. Those of us in our first year would have three more of safety, while seniors would have only until graduation before becoming eligible.

I hadn't spoken to Jack since he'd informed me that he thought changing roommates would benefit our relationship. Upon arriving at Pinchot Hall the night before, I'd opened a book and pretended to study, while Jack had left, saying he was going for a walk. I'd eventually smoked a joint and gone to bed. When I woke up, Jack was in his bed, asleep with his back to me, and I'd left before he rose. I hadn't seen him all day.

As night fell and the hour of the lottery drew nearer, more and more guys filled the fifth-floor lounge, which housed Pinchot's lone television set. In open defiance of university rules, joints and bottles of beer were in abundance. Some students were already partaking, needing the narcotic effects of alcohol and marijuana to help calm jittery nerves. Others kept them nearby, ready for either celebration or consolation depending on the outcome of the draw.

Around half past nine, Andy appeared. He seemed relaxed and confident, as if he cared little one way or the other what transpired in the next hour or two. Drinking from a bottle, he sat down beside me on a couch and asked, "Anything going on yet?"

"No," I told him. "I think they're starting at ten."

"Cool," he replied. "How was your break?"

Again he was acting as if there was no cause for strain between us. He made no mention of Jack, or of how he'd been sleeping with both of us for who knew how long. He either assumed the matter had been decided between Jack and myself, or he didn't care. I wanted to hate him, both for what I saw as his two-timing of me, but more for his lack of concern. I'd even rehearsed what I would say when I saw him again. Now, though, the angry words died on my lips.

"It was good," I answered. "How about yours?"

"Great," he said, offering no further details.

Andy began a conversation with the boy next to him, and I settled into tense silence. Finally, shortly after ten o'clock, the lottery began. Jack still hadn't appeared as the television cameras, broadcasting direct from the Selective Service National Headquarters in Washington, showed us a room filled with people, both civilians and government officials. On a table in front of a podium sat a tall glass jar perhaps two feet high. It was filled with blue plastic capsules.

We watched as the ceremony began with an invocation in which God was asked to lend his wisdom to the proceedings. I couldn't help but feel that the organizers were invoking God as a way of assigning blame for the results to divine providence. I scanned the faces of the government and military representatives, most of them much older than the men whose lives they were playing with. Behind them sat a number of neatly-dressed young men and women, some of the 650 state delegates from the Youth Advisory Committees founded by President Nixon to provide a voice for America's next generation. I wondered what they were all thinking, or if, like those of us watching, they were simply waiting for it all to be over.

When the first capsule was drawn, by New York Congressman Alexander Pirnie of the Armed Services Committee, we waited anxiously as it was opened and the slip of paper inside removed.

"September 14," the announcer said. "Draft number one goes to September 14."

There was no sound from the men in Pinchot Hall, but a woman in the television audience screamed, whether because she was proud or terrified that her son would be one of the first ones drafted, we couldn't tell. None of us, it seemed, had the chosen birth date. Again we waited, as capsule after capsule was removed from the jar by a member of the Youth Advisory Committee and its contents revealed. The general consensus was that any number below 100 was a guaranteed ticket into the war, so the greatest reactions came from men in the 1 to 99 group. There were a number of them, and as their birthdays were called they cheered or groaned. For those of us who had yet to hear our dates called, the tension built with each successive pick.

Having the YAC representatives draw the capsules was another brilliant marketing ploy used to sell the draft, and the war it fed, to the American public. Young people choosing for their peers was the ultimate symbol of support for the action in Vietnam, particularly as some of them surely would be going to Southeast Asia themselves. What the cameras didn't show, however, were the delegates from Michigan, Alaska, and the District of Columbia who refused to draw, and were therefore excluded from the televised proceedings. Also unknown is how the years affected the consciences of those who chose early on, knowing that the men whose date of birth they drew from the jar would almost certainly encounter the risk of death.

At the time, I had other concerns, in particular listening for the an-

nouncement that August 11 had been drawn. The first dates to be chosen were taken heavily from the later months of the year (eight of the
first ten fell in September through October), and I knew that, statistically, my odds were increasing. Years later, it would be argued that the
lottery system, rather than providing an equal chance to all, was actually weighted against those born in the last quarter of the year, as the
capsules were placed into the jar chronologically and, even though
they were stirred up, those from the final four months remained
largely at the top, and therefore most easily reached by the choosers.

The first date in August to be selected corresponded to draft number 11. Hearing the month read, my heart stopped for a moment until
the date—the 31st—followed. I then had another respite until the
drawing of the 21st number. It was August 10. For a moment I congratulated myself on escaping by one day. Then I remembered that the
10th was Jack's birthday. He'd been chosen, and early. We'd always
joked about how he'd come into the world only a few minutes before
me. Now, those few minutes might mean much more than who got to
blow out the candles on our shared birthday cake first.

I wondered if Jack even knew, if he was watching or listening somewhere else or if he'd forgotten about, or decided not to witness, the
lottery. Momentarily forgetting my anger at him, I was tempted to go
find him. But I had to push this urge away and stay to hear my date
called. Jack would have to wait.

So would I. As the roll call continued, I heard many other birthdays
announced. One by one, the men in the room learned where they
stood in the luck of the draw. Some sat grim faced, comforted by those
around them. Others claimed excitement at the prospect of fighting,
declaring their solidarity with "the boys in Nam." Beer flowed freely,
and a cloud of pot smoke hovered above our heads.

As the number reached, then passed, 100, the mood of those of us
still waiting to hear lifted perceptibly. Knowing we were not likely to be
called, we relaxed a little. In sympathy for those already called, we
were not overly enthusiastic, but I sensed that I was not, by far, the
only one whose heart had slowed from its earlier thundering beat.
Free to consider the future, we did so with much more optimism than
we had an hour before.

Andy, his spirits bright as ever, continued to chat with whomever
was at hand. Then, as the date of October 24 was called, he let out a
whoop.

"What number am I?" he asked.

"Number 196," a boy closer to the TV told him.

"Right in the middle," declared Andy. "Maybe yes, maybe no."

He sounded pleased with his position. At any rate, he returned to enjoying himself and seemed to forget all about why we were all gathered in the room. I ignored him, continuing to wait as number after number was assigned to dates other than mine. I sat through the 200s, then the 300s, until finally I found myself drawn at number 324. By then I had stopped worrying. There was virtually no chance that men of my draft number would be called, even if education deferments were abolished. I could look forward to my sophomore year without worry.

Free now to remember that Jack hadn't been as fortunate in his draw, I left the few remaining guys to await the end of the lottery and went to my room. Jack wasn't there, so I donned my jacket and went outside, walking to the student center and using the pay phone there to call my house. My mother answered, and by the tone of her voice I knew that she, too, had watched the drawing. I asked her if Jack's mother was there as well.

"Clark took her home a few minutes ago," she answered. "Is Jack okay?"

"Yeah," I lied. "I mean, he's in college, so he doesn't have to worry."

My deception was based partly on wanting to reassure her, but more on the fact that I didn't want her to know that Jack and I had not watched the lottery together. She would find that suspicious, and I wasn't in a mood for answering the inevitable follow-up questions. So I allowed her to think that everything was fine, even though I was far from sure that it was.

I hung up and looked around, thinking I might see Jack among the students talking about the night's events. He wasn't there, though, and once more I walked outside. The night was clear, and the stars bright. Looking up at them, I tried to imagine a soldier on the other side of the world doing the same thing. What did he see in their patterns? Did he watch them and dream of home? Did he curse them for having directed his fate in an unexpected and unwelcome direction? It suddenly seemed so absurd, the decision to send all the men born on a certain day into battle together, as if somehow their all being Aries, or Capricorns, or Libras would provide them some kind of instant kinship with one another, and therefore an advantage over the enemy.

I was thinking this when I heard someone say, "What's your number?"

I looked behind me and saw Jack standing there. He had a bottle in his hand, and by the way he swayed I guessed he had already drained a few before it.

"Three twenty-four," I told him.

He raised his bottle. "Congratulations," he said.

"You should call home," I told him. "Your mother's worried."

He ignored me, taking a long swallow from the bottle and wiping his mouth on his sleeve. He sat down on a concrete bench beneath a lamppost and leaned back, looking at the sky. I hesitated a moment, then went to sit beside him.

"Don't worry about having a low number," I told him. "They won't take you if you're in school."

Jack reached into his jacket pocket, removed something, and handed it to me. It was an envelope.

"What is it?" I asked.

"Open it," he said.

I opened the envelope and removed the piece of paper inside. It was a letter on university stationery. I scanned the contents quickly, puzzled as to why Jack was showing it to me. It was a notice of academic probation. Jack's midterm grades were below what he needed to keep his scholarship, and he was being informed that unless he raised his grade point average, he would have to pay for his next semester himself.

"I guess this is where you tell me I told you so," said Jack as I folded the letter and returned it to its envelope.

"So you might have to pay for school," I said. "It's not the worst thing that could happen."

Jack looked at me. His eyes were glassy. "You don't get it," he said, anger in his voice. "It's not about the fucking money. It's about the grades." He took the letter from me and waved it in my face. "They only give you a deferment if your grade point is above two-point-oh."

I looked at him, unable to think of a response. Never having had to worry about my grades, I was unaware of the requirements for deferment. I didn't know where Jack had gotten his information, but I had no reason to doubt its accuracy.

"Now do you understand?" he asked. "Now do you fucking see why I'm so fucking screwed?"

He stood up and jammed the letter into the back pocket of his pants. I stared at his back, thinking.

"You still have time to get your average up," I said quietly. "Finals aren't until the end of the month, and term papers are almost half your grade anyway."

Jack turned around and looked at me. He shook his head. "The only way that's going to happen is if someone a whole lot smarter than me does my work for me," he said.

I understood what he was saying. He wanted me to help him. I looked away. Jack sat next to me.

"Come on," he said, his voice pleading. "It's just a few papers. Maybe some homework. Just help me out, Ned. You always have before."

I closed my eyes and breathed deep. I could smell Jack's stale breath as he waited for my answer. He was right. He *could* probably get his grade point up with a few spectacular term papers. And I could write them for him. I'd done it many times before. This would just be one more time.

"Please," Jack said. "I know I've been an asshole, but I still love you."

I opened my eyes and looked at him. He smiled the smile I'd always loved to see, the one that made me feel as if nobody else existed for him. How many times had he used that smile to get what he wanted? How many times had I given it to him?

I stood up, pulling my coat around me. "I'm sorry, Jack," I said, looking down at him. "I'm really sorry."

CHAPTER 17

Winter came early in 1969. By the end of the first week, we had experienced our first snowfall. The grounds were covered in a blanket of white, and across the campus groups of students staged snowball battles, pelting one another and unsuspecting passersby with frosty missiles. Inspired, a group of guys from Pinchot gathered outside one of the girls' dorms in the middle of the night for a secret mission. When the women woke up and looked out their windows the next morning, they were greeted by a snowman sporting a top hat, scarf, and an erection made from the largest carrot we could find.

With Christmas break, and the end of the fall semester, only three weeks away, we were all thrown into overdrive as we rushed to complete work we'd put off for too long. I myself had three papers due on my instructors' desks: a critical analysis of Keats' "Ode to Melancholy," a comparison and contrast of Mohism and Confucianism during China's Hundred Schools of Thought, and a business plan for a mock company whose product I was supposed to select based on its likelihood of earning a substantial return.

Of these, the last was giving me the most trouble. In response to the recent draft, I'd decided that my company would produce antiwar buttons to be sold at rallies, charging only enough to make a small profit, most of which would be donated to groups working for peace. It was a good idea, but it suffered from the fact that my instructor, an avid supporter of the military operations in Vietnam, hated it. After handing in my initial proposal, I'd been encouraged to develop a more "traditional" business whose purpose was to make money for investors. With two weeks left to go, I'd yet to think of an alternative product, and I was becoming slightly nervous.

Being around Jack didn't help. Since my refusal to do his work for him, he had, I suppose understandably, grown even more distant. I rarely saw him, partly because he was often out of the room, but also because I stopped seeking him out. Also, I'd returned to Andy. I told myself it was purely out of convenience. On December 4, Black Panther members Fred Hampton and Mark Clark had been drugged with seco-barbitol-laced Kool-Aid by an undercover operative and then killed in their sleep by Chicago police during a predawn raid on Hampton's apartment. The next day, Chaz and several other Black Panther supporters elected to drive to Illinois for the funeral and had yet to return. Andy had offered Chaz's bed to me on a temporary basis after I'd complained of not being able to work with Jack around.

I was foolish to accept the offer, and I knew it. But I did it anyway. Although Andy had yet to acknowledge his role in the dissolution of my relationship with Jack, he seemed to relish having me around him more often. I, in turn, elected to take this enthusiasm for growing interest in me. I began to view Andy's affections, such as they were, as a prize to be kept out of Jack's hands at any cost. Like the holder of a ball in a game, I was determined to retain control. What I wanted, of course, was to hurt Jack. What I believed I wanted was Andy.

I did everything I could to get him. He without hesitation allowed me to resume my role as provider of sexual favors, all the while continuing to talk freely about Tracy and the other girls with whom he had affairs. As I had with Jack in high school, I considered these relationships inconsequential. What mattered to me was that Andy accepted my advances, and therefore me. I wove a relationship from these meager threads, convincing myself that I was in love with him.

I suppose I *was* in love with him, although I now find it contradictory to logic that one would fall in love with someone who did not return the feelings. Become infatuated with, of course, but doesn't love need to see itself reflected back in order to truly flourish? In the absence of its mate, should it not wither and die, or at the very least reveal itself as the inferior impostor it really is? How can we go on truly loving another who doesn't share the emotion?

I know, I know. It happens all the time. Perhaps. But I maintain that what we call love is often something less. It's only our need to see it as love that allows us to be blinded. In the end, though, it makes no difference. The agony we feel is the same. In matters of the heart, a counterfeit can be as intoxicating, and as dangerous, as the real thing.

And so I believed that I was in love with Andy Kowalski. I proved it by demanding nothing of him, probably because I knew that he would be incapable of fulfilling any requirements I might impose. Wearing my love like a ring around my finger, I set out to humiliate Jack by making sure he knew that I held first place in Andy's attentions. In addition to regularly sleeping in his room, I was careful to be seen as often as possible in Andy's company. I took to wearing his clothes, which he found amusing, and I delighted in riding in his truck with him, particularly when he would put his arm along the back of the seat and, purely by accident of design, around my shoulder.

Jack refused to take my bait, which only made me try harder. When he failed to start arguments I laid out for him, or to show anger after discovering evidence (Andy's lighter, a borrowed T-shirt) I strategically left in our room as proof of my flourishing romance, I responded by asking him how his schoolwork was coming. This alone sparked a reaction in him, which was to tell me to fuck off and mind my own business. I considered the slam of the door on his way out a victory claimed.

I am not, by nature, a vindictive person. Like anyone, I hold certain grudges, and I resent deceit above all things. But I like to think that I am not unkind. During those final weeks of December, however, I was guilty of every imaginable hateful feeling toward Jack. I convinced myself that he had deserted me first, conveniently forgetting that long before his suggestion of different roommates, I had harbored feelings for Andy, and had, in fact, acted on them repeatedly. We were both guilty of the sin of omission, but I was the one who upped the ante by adding cruelty to my list of transgressions.

That I might have gone too far didn't occur to me until a few days before the commencement of our winter break. Having handed in my final paper (I'd swapped my peace buttons for 8-track cartridge players and turned a tidy profit), I was now faced with the realization that I was supposed to return home in two days' time and that my means of transportation was the one person I'd been tormenting mercilessly. Jack had no reason at all to allow me to come with him, and I had no other way of going.

I considered my options, which basically consisted of making up with Jack, at least for the duration of the holidays, or finding alternate transportation. I'd made a number of friends other than Andy, but none who lived near my town. I briefly considered trying to convince Andy to come home with me for Christmas, but I knew his grandparents were expecting him. Also, I feared I would not be able to hide my feelings for him from my mother, particularly were we to share my bed.

With no other option, I approached Jack as he was trying to finish one of his many overdue assignments. Adopting a neutral tone, I asked, "Are you almost done?"

"No," he said sharply.

"Do you want some help?" I tried.

Jack looked up at me. "Not really," he said. "Why?"

"I just thought you might want some help," I said. "That's all."

"Well, I don't," he said, returning to his work.

I saw nowhere else to go with the conversation, so I decided to leave him and see what Andy was doing. As I opened the door to go, Jack said, without looking at me, "I told my mother we'd be there on Saturday around three."

"Three," I repeated. "Okay."

As we had so many times in the recent past, we'd come to a compromise without having to discuss it. My worries about getting home out of the way, I returned to Andy. Also done with his classes, he was getting into the Christmas spirit, taking the lid off a bow-topped tin of what looked like cookies when I entered the room.

"Look," he said, taking out a cookie shaped like a reindeer and holding it up. "This chick in my bio class made these for me."

"What are they?" I asked. "Gingerbread?"

"Even better," Andy said, biting the head off the deer. "Hash."

A half dozen pot-infused Rudolphs, Dashers, and Vixens later, I decided that I would give Andy my present a few days early. I brought out from under the bed a package wrapped in cheery paper. I handed it to Andy and told him to open it, then watched as he pulled the paper off to reveal Jethro Tull's *Stand Up*.

"Thanks, man," he said, getting up and putting the album on the turntable. "This is great."

He sat down again and mimed playing guitar along with Ian Anderson. Feeling expansive, I got up and lit some sandalwood incense, which Andy kept on hand to cover the smell of pot. I also lit a candle, turning off the lights so that its glow turned the room into a rosy cocoon.

When I sat down again, it was next to Andy. He leaned against me, still strumming his invisible guitar, and sang along to the song.

"'Spent a long time looking for a game to play.'"

His voice was rough and out of tune, but the sound of it thrilled me.

He looked over at me and smiled, nodding in time with the music. In the candlelight, he looked so beautiful that I wanted to kiss him. I leaned toward him, my heart racing, hoping he wouldn't turn his face away.

"What are you dumb white-ass faggots doing in here?"

I jumped as the door crashed opened and Chaz walked in, two other black men behind him. Andy stopped singing.

"My brother," he said. "Where you been, man?"

"I'm not your brother, and where I've been is none of your damn business," Chaz replied, slapping Andy's outstretched hand in greeting. He noticed the tin of cookies and took three, handing one to each of the men with him. "These *here* are my brothers, Cornell and William J."

"Hey," Andy said. Cornell and William J. held their fists up in the black power salute, but said nothing.

"Who's been sleeping in my bed?" asked Chaz, looking at the rumpled sheets.

"Oh," I said nervously. "I have. I hope it's okay."

"Who the hell do you think you are, boy?" he replied. "Goldilocks? Sleep in your own damn bed and stop getting your white dirt all over my sheets."

"Sure," I said. "No problem, Chaz." I looked at Andy, who had started playing again. "I guess I'll go," I told him.

"See you," he said. "Thanks again for the album."

"Yeah," I said. "Merry Christmas."

I got up, nodding at Chaz and his friends, who parted to let me through. Reluctantly, I went downstairs to my room. Jack was still working, and barely looked up when I came in. With nothing else to do, I got into bed and picked up the book I was reading, Joyce Carol Oates's *Them*, which I'd recently checked out from the school library after hearing my literature teacher praise it as a masterpiece of American fiction. The bleak yet beautifully-written story of the Wendall family and their lives in Detroit had drawn me in from the first page, and in the novel's violence and turmoil I saw something of my own life. As only a young man in the grip of unrequited love can, I felt a connection with every soul who had ever longed for something and been unable to have it. Happily, I allowed myself to swim in self-pity until, twenty or thirty pages later, I found myself falling asleep.

Andy left the next day without saying good-bye. I found out when I went to his room to wish him a safe trip and found Chaz and his friends looking at a copy of *Penthouse* magazine. They were, surprisingly, not looking at the pictures, but arguing over an article suggesting that the man accused of killing Martin Luther King was a scapegoat.

"I *told* you Ray was just the fall guy," William J. said as I stood, listening. "Cracker's too stupid to shoot anybody."

"Bullshit," Chaz said. "This is just more government cover-up. Who do you think reads this magazine? Uptight white men whose wives won't give them any pussy, that's who. They just put these shit-crazy articles in here so they won't feel like perverts for looking at a little cooch."

"This cooch don't look so bad to me," remarked Cornell, taking the magazine and holding it open.

Chaz finally noticed me standing there. "You looking for Andy?" he said. "He left a couple of hours ago."

"Really?" I said, disappointed.

"Really," Chaz said, perusing the magazine spread.

Feeling stupid, I mumbled a confused thank-you, good-bye, and Merry Christmas and left them to their magazine. None of them responded.

The following morning, I made one more ride home with Jack. It had begun to snow during the night (the winter of 1969 would end up being Pennsylvania's snowiest on record) and we drove all the way through in a semi-blizzard. Forced to go more slowly than usual, the length of our trip was extended by almost two hours as we watched the taillights of the cars ahead of us blink like eyes through the flurries.

When we were about halfway there, Jack suddenly said, "I didn't do it."

"Do what?" I asked, not understanding.

"Get a two-point-oh," he answered.

"How do you know?" I asked. "We haven't gotten our grades yet."

"I just know," he said without elaborating.

"But you were working so hard," I protested. "All that studying, and writing, and—"

"It wasn't enough," Jack snapped, cutting me off. "It just wasn't enough, okay?"

I shut my mouth and sat silently for a minute, watching the wipers wage their vigilant battle against the snow. Jack, both hands on the wheel, stared straight ahead.

"What are you going to do?" I asked finally.

"I don't know," said Jack.

I didn't have any suggestions for him, at least not any that seemed reasonable. He could go to Canada, or hope for a medical deferment. Neither of those seemed likely, however. Maybe, I thought, he was wrong. Maybe he had managed to squeak by. But he seemed so certain of his failure. Never before had I seen him admit defeat.

"It's my fault," I heard myself say.

"It's not your fault," said Jack.

"Yes, it is," I argued. "I should have helped you."

"I can take care of myself," Jack said. "We're not kids anymore."

He was right about that. We weren't kids. We were men, men who after walking the same road together for many years were now at a crossroads, each of us looking in a different direction. Where the paths we chose would take us, I had no way of knowing.

"I'm sorry," I told him for the second time in our lives. This time, I meant it.

CHAPTER 18

Why is it that so many people who never otherwise step foot inside a church decide that they will make an exception on Christmas Eve? This is a rhetorical question. Yet it bears asking. To me, it's rather like making an annual birthday visit to a convalescent home so that a bilious elderly relative whose failing internal processes and yellow, thickened nails fill you with revulsion might be moved by your expression of devotion into leaving you something in her will. Do we really believe that God, if he is indeed keeping score, will forgive our general lack of attention simply because once a year we come to wish his son many happy returns? Perhaps the understanding God of the New Age might overlook such blatant attempts at currying favor, but he of the New Testament would surely not.

Still, even for those of us who find faith a challenge, there is something magical about a Christmas Eve service. Each December 24 for the past fifteen years, Thayer and I have become temporary members in the congregation of St. Gregory's Episcopal Church, our tenure lasting for exactly the length of that evening's service. We go because it is a tradition, and because we like the music. Also, we go because there is something undeniably beautiful about a church viewed through gently falling snow and lit from within by candles. Entering such a place, even a confirmed old pagan such as myself cannot helped but be moved by the eternal story of hope arriving on Earth in the form of a child.

On Christmas Eve of 1969, I was not feeling so hopeful. I was, in fact, filled with great sadness and agitation. Since learning of the almost certain loss of Jack's scholarship, I had been punishing myself for what I had determined was an obvious desire on my part to see him harmed in some way. Why, I asked myself, could I not have helped him? Why had I outright refused to do so? There was, in my mind, only one answer to that question: I was a terrible person.

In the days since arriving home, I had tried to lift my gloomy spirits by throwing myself headlong into the familiar holiday rituals. With my father I had selected and set up the tree, a full-figured spruce whose top reached almost to the ceiling. Together we had strung the lights, and together we had cursed when a single failed bulb caused the entire string to wink and go out, resulting in our having to replace every single one in the line until we found the troublemaker. Then came the decorations, an involved process during which my mother kept us supplied with a steady stream of hot chocolate and cookies while providing a running commentary on the origins of each painted wooden bird and jolly glass Santa. The house, filled with the cheerful voices of Mitch Miller and his gang, was near to bursting from all the Christmas spirit.

And still I was depressed. Even my parents' murmurings of a mystery gift of extraordinary wonder failed to lift my flagging mood. I feigned joy for their sakes, but alone in my room I lay on my bed and tried to think of some way to make it up to Jack. Because of me, he was perhaps going to end up fighting a war that had nothing to do with him.

Then came Christmas Eve and the annual rite of attending the Ebenezer Lutheran Church nativity pageant. We'd been coming for years, at my mother's insistence, although we were neither Lutheran nor religious, apart from the occasional saying of grace at meals. I think my mother chose the church because she liked the stained-glass windows, which as I recall were indeed remarkable. For whatever reasons she'd selected it, we'd come there since I was a baby, and if any of the regular attendees found our presence irritating, they were kind enough never to let on.

The program was the same every year. It began with a procession of tiny shepherds. These were followed by the three kings, Melchior, Balthasar, and Caspar, carrying their gifts for the baby Jesus. Jesus, along with his parents, was already ensconced in his manger at the front of the church. Once all those who wished to adore him had arrived, the angels appeared singing "Hallelujah!" and the rest of us joined in welcoming the Son of God into our midst.

How is it that the sight of a small shepherd boy stumbling over the belt of his father's bathrobe on the way to stand beside a doll lying in a box of straw can bring one to the point of tears? It does now, and it did then. I remember that night watching the children assemble, the angels holding their tinsel halos to prevent them from falling off, poor Joseph peering anxiously at a somber Mary, as if terrified she might at any moment yell at him to stop fidgeting. As I looked at them, I saw Jack and myself at their age. Like them, we'd never worried about being sent to war. We'd never imagined that the games of soldier that we waged in backyards and school playgrounds would one day be undertaken in foreign jungles with real weapons. Their innocence, and the loss of ours, was heartbreaking.

Together we sang "All My Heart this Night Rejoices," a hymn I have only ever heard sung in that church. "All my heart this night rejoices," goes the first line with its peculiar up-and-down meter, followed by the staccato second, "As I hear, far and near, sweetest angel voices." The cycle is then repeated, and the Nativity story advanced, with "Christ is born, their choirs are singing. Till the air, everywhere, now with joy is ringing."

Like so many of the songs written by Paul Gerhardt, the Lutheran church's prolific and beloved hymnist, this one has many verses. Fifteen, to be exact. With true Lutheran doggedness, we sang every one of them while the children held their poses as best they could, the wise men frozen on their knees before the baby Jesus and the shepherds restlessly swaying from side to side, ready for the cookies and cider awaiting them in the church's basement.

Nearly forty years later, I still recall the words to that hymn, although I will admit that I did require some assistance. Several years ago, wanting to share the song with Thayer, I sought out a Lutheran hymnal to refresh my memory. (Thayer would say that I stole it from a church in town while pretending to admire the architecture, but I argue that my need was pure and God forgiving.) At any rate, I did remember its place in the hymnal, number 77, and was pleased to see that my recall was only somewhat lacking.

Admittedly tedious in its repetitiveness, the song is nonetheless blessed with some lovely imagery. My favorite of the verses is number eight: "Come, then, banish all your sadness, one and all, great and small, come with songs of gladness. Love Him who with love is glowing, hail the Star, near and far, light and joy bestowing."

The message, unfortunately, was lost on my 19-year-old self. I sang the words without hearing, and certainly not feeling, any of the gladness contained in them. Although I wanted to be happy, I wouldn't allow myself to be. I was too sad, and too angry. I was angry at Jack for allowing himself to fall so far behind in his schoolwork. I was angry at myself for refusing to help him and then taking pleasure in his failure. I was even angry at the baby Jesus for daring to offer his gift of salvation while so many were dying or preparing to die, and at the angels for proclaiming his goodness. My Christmas wish, had I been asked, would have been to switch places with Jack so that I, not he, would be facing the possibility of going to Vietnam.

We did not join the congregation for cookies following the service, instead returning home for a supper of oyster stew, a tradition which originated within my mother's family. In 1879, her grandmother had brought with her from Dublin a recipe for fish soup, long served in Ireland on Christmas Eve. Finding ling cod, the primary ingredient, unavailable, the resourceful woman (and many of her Southside Chicago neighbors) had substituted oysters, considered a poor man's food in 18th century America and therefore plentiful and cheap. She had taught my mother to make it when she was a girl, and she still did it the same way Brigid O'Reilly had a century before, tumbling the oysters into a pan of warm cream and melted butter and heating them until the fluted sides curled up indignantly. Served hot in a bowl with tiny crackers, it was a perfect precursor to the more substantial Christmas feast we would have the next day.

Christmas Eve was one of the few days we did not share with Jack's family. In almost all other ways identical to us, on the point of religion they had declared their independence. While we went to Ebenezer Lutheran, they went across town to the Emanuel United Methodist Church. In recent years, they had also begun to go with much more regularity, to the point where Mr. Grace was now a deacon and Jack's mother occasionally found herself having to host lunches for the Ladies' Auxiliary. They also opened their presents on Christmas Eve, while our family waited until the morning. As children, this had presented Jack and I with an unusual dilemma. While he went to bed with his gifts revealed and often in his arms or within easy reach, I was forced to spend an anxious night wondering what Santa would leave for me. Both of us would have to wait until I was finished tearing the paper from the boxes beneath the tree the next morning before we could compare our bounty over our shared Christmas dinner. Our parents explained the difference in Mr. Claus' schedules for visiting our homes by telling us that our houses, though side by side, were on different delivery routes, a lie we accepted rather than accept the awful truth.

One of the great disappointments of adulthood is the diminished thrill one receives from the sight of a wrapped present, whether it's handed over directly or discovered beneath an ornament-laden tree. Not that the getting of gifts can't be a joy. I have certainly in my life been the recipient of many a fine and excellent present. But after about the age of 12 or 13, I think the fear of disappointment gradually wears away at the experience. There are expectations on both sides—on yours that the contents of the box will be what you are hoping for, and on the other that you will be pleased—and this places undue strain on everyone involved. Should the present in fact be of dubious merit, the energy required to reassure the giver that it is precisely what the occasion called for makes for a very long day.

At 19, I had already experienced this sea change. Until about my tenth year, my presents had generally been of the kind that are anticipated by boys: model airplanes, the occasional book, a bicycle. As adolescence dawned, these had been replaced, at first slowly and then in a steady stream, by more practical items, chiefly clothes of which I was deeply embarrassed. I had eventually accepted that this was to be my fate, and since then had spent Christmas mornings opening in tandem with my father boxes of underpants, socks, and sweaters.

After the oyster stew, consumed in relative silence by myself and my parents, I said good night and retired to my room. Lying in the darkness, I tried to remember what it had felt like to be excited on Christmas Eve. I could recall praying for sleep to come, restlessly tossing and turning as I tried to will my rushing thoughts to still. Every thump was the hoof of one of Santa's reindeer alighting on the roof, every scritch and scratch the sound of his girth scraping the chimney bricks as he descended to our living room. In my head, I would run through the list of items I had requested in the annual letter posted to the North Pole, and worry that perhaps, this year, I had not made it onto the "Nice" list. Hours seemed to pass as I struggled against wakefulness, until finally I woke up and discovered that I had slept and that it was time to go downstairs.

Although long past the days when the notion of Santa and his sack of toys had kept me up, that night I once again found it impossible to relax. My thoughts swirled, mimicking the snow outside my window, which had begun to fall in mid-afternoon and showed every intention of becoming a blizzard by morning. Also like the snow, they chilled me deeply, freezing my heart in my chest and making me long for any warmth, any spark of hope, that would ease the suffering.

I imagined Jack in his own bed, just across the yard from mine. Was he, like me, lying there thinking about the mess we'd made of our future, and of our friendship? Did he, as I did, regret anything that had happened, anything that had been said? Unable to sleep, I got up and went to my window. Through the snow, I saw the lighted square of Jack's window. For a moment I thought he was standing there looking back at me, and my heart skipped. Then the figure moved, and I saw that he was simply walking around the room, getting ready for sleep.

As boys, we had once tied two empty Green Giant Peas cans to a length of string and stretched it between our windows to make a telephone. Although the words spoken into the can on one end were certainly not audible on the other, reduced by the distance to the barest of vibrations, we pretended they were, and used the primitive device to exchange secret messages late at night. I wondered if Jack remembered that, or if he had forgotten it along with other things for which he no longer had any use.

If I could pick up the can and talk to him, I asked myself, what would I say? I'd said I was sorry, but was it even possible to be sorry enough for what I'd done? Was it possible that we could mend the rift that grew wider with every passing day? I still loved him. That much I knew to be true. But had that love changed so much, been altered so drastically by both our actions, that it had become something else, something impossible to return to its original state?

Standing there, watching Jack's shadow through the scrim of snow, I thought perhaps hope wasn't entirely dead. I thought of the words of the hymn I'd sung only a few hours before. "Love him who with love is glowing," I whispered in the darkness, looking at the light from Jack's bedroom. Its warmth shined through the winter cold. Maybe it wasn't too late, I thought. Maybe, despite everything, we could go back. Andy, school, the war—perhaps none of it had damaged us beyond repair.

I returned to my bed happier than I'd been in weeks. Tomorrow, I thought, I would talk to Jack and see if we couldn't start again. I would offer to help him with his grades. I would demand that we remain roommates. I would even, if he asked me, agree to give up Andy if that would allow us to be what we had been for so long. I could do that for him. I could do it because I loved him, had always loved him.

As I had years before, I waited for sleep to overtake me. Morning seemed impossibly far, and I too anxious for its arrival. I turned one way and then another, but my mind kept rehearsing the words I would say to Jack when I saw him. Over and over I spoke them to myself, searching for the perfect arrangement that would make him see how determined I was to make everything right.

CHAPTER 19

When I woke up, it was with the thought that it must still be the middle of the night. I was delighted to see that I was mistaken, and that the pale light of morning was in fact visible outside. Happily, I got up, pulled on my clothes, and went downstairs, ready to embrace what I hoped would be a day of reconciliation and renewal. My mother, always up early on Christmas morning, was busily setting out breakfast. My father was adding a log to the fireplace, poking at the embers and watching them intently, as if in their glow he could read the secrets of life.

"Ned," my mother said, coming to give me a kiss. "Merry Christmas."

"Merry Christmas," I said.

"Are you ready for your big surprise?" she asked.

I'd forgotten all about the gift about which she'd been dropping hints since my arrival. I had been buried under the avalanche of worry, unable to think of anything that might threaten my sorry state. Now, having dug myself out and into the fresh air, I found that I *was* excited. Feeling 10 years old again, I said, "You bet. Where is it?"

My father put his hand on my shoulder and turned me around, away from the Christmas tree. Marching me to the front door, he opened it. "Take a look," he said.

I stepped onto the porch. There, in front of the house, was a 1970 Ford Mustang. An enormous red bow sat on top, matching the car's red paint job. I stared at it for a full minute, wondering where my surprise was, before I realized that the car *was* the surprise. I couldn't believe it. I turned to my father, unable to speak.

"Vietnam has been hell on the economy, but it's been great for the insurance business," he said. "Merry Christmas, kid."

I couldn't wait to show the car to Jack. I knew he'd be even more excited about it than I was, and letting him drive it would be the first step on the road to mending our relationship. Maybe, I thought, I could even get him to drive to our favorite make-out spot. I hurried through the rest of the morning, anxious for him and his parents to arrive for dinner.

They came just before noon, Mr. Grace and Jack carrying armfuls of gifts that they'd saved for the traditional after-dinner swap and Mrs. Grace carrying a casserole dish I knew contained green beans mixed with cream of mushroom soup and French-fried onions. I welcomed them in and took some of the presents from Jack, who gestured his thumb toward the door and said, "Whose Mustang?"

"Mine," I answered, beaming.

Jack's eyes opened wide. "Yours?" he said.

I nodded. "Want to go for a ride in it?" I added, holding up the keys.

A minute later, after promising to be back in half an hour, Jack was sitting in the driver's seat of the car, running his hands over the steering wheel. "This is one hot piece of shit," he said.

In the passenger seat, I leaned back and let the happiness wash over me. Jack seemed his old self at last, full of excitement and the boyish wonder I'd always found so attractive. As he started the engine and laughed at the roar, I almost leaned over and kissed him. But that could wait, I told myself. I had some things to say to him first.

Because of the snow, he drove slowly, although Jack's slow was still faster than most people's idea of pushing the limits. The car handled beautifully, and when Jack finally stopped, in the almost-empty parking lot of a diner whose windows twinkled brightly and where a hand-lettered sign read SPEND X-MAS WITH US!, he shook his head appreciatively.

"You scored with this baby," he said.

I nodded. Suddenly, I was nervous, as if we were on a first date. I wanted to say so many things, but I couldn't remember a word of what I'd rehearsed the night before.

"I have something to . . ." Jack and I said simultaneously.

We both stopped, each waiting for the other to speak. I nodded at Jack. "Go ahead," I said.

"I've, um, been thinking a lot," he said. "You know, about stuff."

My heart raced, waiting for him to give me the lead-in I'd been looking for. I almost interrupted him, so anxious was I to get what I was feeling out into the open.

Jack looked out the window, seeming to scan the parking lot for an eternity before turning back. "I'm not going," he said.

Not going? I didn't understand. Then it dawned on me—he wasn't going to Vietnam. He'd decided to find a way out. This time I did lean over and kiss him. But it was awkward, his mouth hard and unyielding. When I pulled away, confused, he was staring at me with a puzzled expression.

"Why'd you do that?" he asked.

"You said you're not going," I answered. "You're staying."

He nodded. "Yeah," he said hesitantly. "So why are you all happy about it?"

"You're *staying*," I said. "In school. With me. You're not going to Vietnam."

Jack slumped in his seat, shaking his head.

"What?" I asked.

He looked at me and sighed deeply. "I'm not going back to Penn," he said. "I'm staying here."

"But you'll be drafted," I said, as if this would be news to him.

"There are other kinds of deferments," said Jack. "I'll get one."

"For what?" I asked. "What are you going to do, tell them you're queer? Shoot yourself in the foot? What?"

Jack looked down. "I'm going to seminary," he said.

He might as well have slapped me across the face. I couldn't believe I'd heard him correctly. "Seminary?" I repeated.

"Wesley Theological," he answered. "In Washington. My dad knows some people there through church, and . . ."

"Jack, you've been to church what, maybe twenty times in your life? And now you want to be a minister?" I laughed harshly.

"It's my way out," he snapped. "There's no way I can make it at Penn. This is a chance for me. My dad had to pull in a lot of favors to get me in there. I don't have a choice."

"You always have a choice," I shot back.

"No," said Jack. "*You* always have a choice, Ned. I don't. I have two, just two. I can get drafted and probably end up dead or lying in some piss hole with my legs blown off, or I can stay here and do this. Don't tell me I have a choice when all you have to worry about is writing some stupid fucking papers and reading a bunch of books!"

He was shouting. I put my hands over my ears to drown him out. I didn't want to hear it. I just wanted him to be quiet so that I could figure out what to do, figure out where I'd gone wrong and fix everything. A minute before I'd been at the top of the mountain; now I was slipping down the side, unable to grab hold and heading for the rocks at the bottom.

Jack stopped yelling. I took my hands from my ears and sat with them in my lap. I couldn't look at Jack, so I looked at my gloves, trying to count the stitches in the leather. I couldn't think about the fact that Jack, my Jack, was going to Methodist seminary while I went back to Penn State.

"I just wanted you to know," he said. "I guess it's a good thing you got a car, huh? Now you don't have to take the bus back."

I wiped my nose on my sleeve and asked, "Do you believe in God?"

"What?" Jack asked.

"God," I repeated. "Do you even believe in God?"

Jack shrugged. "Sure," he said. "Doesn't everyone?"

"The Communists don't, if you believe Nixon," I said. "Isn't that why we have to make sure they don't take over Vietnam?"

"I don't know," Jack mumbled, clearly confused by the turn the conversation had taken.

"It doesn't matter," I said. "I was just curious. You know, since you're going to be a minister now."

"Oh," said Jack. "Well, yeah, I guess I believe in God then."

"Good," I said. "That should help. Maybe you can convince me that he exists one of these days."

Jack looked at his watch. "We should be getting back," he said. "Your mom said half an hour. You want to drive?"

I shook my head. "You go ahead," I told him. "I'll get a lot of practice when I drive back next week."

We returned to my house. While we were gone, the Graces had filled my parents in on Jack's new career path. My mother congratulated him, while my father gave him what seemed a halfhearted handshake and wished him luck. Then we all sat down to dinner, which passed interminably as Mrs. Grace said every two or three minutes how pleased Reverend Plowman at their church was that Jack was showing an interest in the faith. Her voice, while light, also sounded a little strained, as if it was herself she was trying to convince, rather than the rest of us. Mr. Grace sat silently by, cutting his turkey into tiny bites and eating them one at a time.

After the exchanging of presents, the Graces went home, bearing with them several Tupperware containers of leftovers along with the blouse and earrings my mother had selected for Patricia from Boscov's, the bottle of Chivas Regal my father had given to Clark, and the scarf my mother had purchased for me to give to Jack. When they were gone, my mother turned to my father, the smile that had been plastered to her face all day wilting a bit.

"You weren't very nice to Jack," she said.

"I don't know what you mean," my father replied, dropping into his recliner and opening a *National Geographic*. "I was perfectly pleasant."

"I saw the way you shook his hand," my mother continued, not backing down. "Like a fish. I know you, Leonard Brummel. That's the handshake you use for customers you don't like."

My father shut the magazine and put it down. "Fine," he said. "Maybe I do think it stinks. That boy's no more a minister than I am. He's just doing this to get out of serving."

Fascinated, I leaned against the doorway to the living room and listened. My parents rarely fought, and my mother even more rarely expressed an opinion about anything even remotely political. I was curious to hear her defend Jack.

"That's easy for you to say," she said, angrily wiping the dining room table with a rag. "You never had to go."

"But I would have," my father said. "I would have if they'd needed me. It just so happened that the war was over by the time I was old enough."

"How lucky for you," my mother shot back. "But Jack isn't as fortunate."

"Neither are all the other boys who are over there," countered my father. "Now, because he won't go, some other kid will have to take his place. Is that right, Alice? Is that right?"

"What if it was our boy instead of Jack?" said my mother, stopping her cleaning and pointing at me. "What if Ned had drawn number 21, or 16, or 1? What would you think then?"

My father's face fell. His gaze moved to the *National Geographic* in his lap. I followed his eyes and looked at the cover. It showed astronaut Buzz Aldrin standing on the moon. My father stared at the image for a long time, then looked up at my mother.

"Jack has been a part of this family since the day he was born," he said. "I've watched him grow up right alongside Ned. He might as well be my own son. I don't want to see him hurt any more than I would want to see Ned hurt." He paused before continuing. "But I'd like to think that I raised my son not to run away from something just because he's scared."

He looked at me then, his eyes meeting mine. I knew he was speaking to me as much as to my mother. I nodded at him, as if agreeing to the unspoken question passing between us. No, I wouldn't run away. He picked up his magazine, opened it, and began reading.

My mother opened her mouth, as if to rebut him, then snapped it shut. Glancing at me, she went into the kitchen, and a moment later I heard the water running in the sink. I waited a moment, then went in to see her. She was scrubbing gravy from a plate, her hands encased to the elbow in yellow gloves.

"Men," she said, seeing me. "You're fools. Every last one of you."

"Dad was just . . ." I began.

"Don't," she said, throwing me a look. "Don't you say it. There's no reason that makes it all right for boys to die in a war that has nothing to do with them. None."

She returned to the dishes, her hand circling so violently that she splashed soapy water onto her dress. She ignored it, putting the plate down and picking up a fork.

"I drew a high number," I said, as if that should set her mind at ease.

She nodded but said nothing. I left her there, returning to the living room and my father, who was leafing through the *National Geographic*. I turned the television on and sat on the couch to watch *The Ghost and Mrs. Muir*. After a few minutes, my father said, "Is she okay?"

"She will be," I told him, taking my eyes away from the TV, where Captain Gregg and Carolyn were trapped in a dream version of *A Christmas Carol*. "She's just a little freaked out, I think."

"She loves Jack," he said.

So do I, I wanted to say. But talking politics with my father was not something I was going to do. Truthfully, I didn't know whether I agreed with him or not. I was angry at Jack, too, but our reasons were worlds apart. Could I really blame Jack for looking for any way out of a terrible situation? My father clearly did. But how could I, especially after I had help put him there? I understood that the lottery was a game of chance, and that I had won and Jack had lost. But I couldn't help wondering, if our situations were reversed, would he allow me any way out, or would he, like my father, expect me to face my fate without flinching? It was easy to be brave when there was little chance of encountering danger. But what if Jack had been the one looking on while I marched off to war? Would he do what he was asking me to do? Would he absolve me of any guilt I might feel at fearing for my life enough to ask another man to take my place? I didn't know if he would.

"Do you like the car?" my father asked unexpectedly.

"Yeah," I said. "I still can't believe you got it. It's fantastic."

He nodded approvingly and returned to his reading. As I went back to the TV show, I suddenly wondered, was the car a kind of apology from my father? Had he given it to me as a way of asking forgiveness for putting me in the path of danger by bringing me into the world at a time when the shadow of war was looming? Maybe, I thought, he felt guilty over escaping himself all those years before. Maybe his anger at Jack was really anger he could not direct at himself.

While he sought forgiveness from me and the other 19-year-olds of the world, I sought forgiveness from Jack. Yet it was Jack who was the focus of our combined rage, Jack who had to bear the brunt of our frustrations and fears because we could not turn them on ourselves. And because we could talk about none of these things, we remained silent, each of us trapped in a cell of our own creation, waiting for deliverance. My mother was right. Men are fools.

Unable to admit this to myself then, I retreated into the simpler world of television, where trouble seldom lasted past the next commercial and even the most difficult problem was solved by show's end.

CHAPTER 20

For reasons which will become clearer as this story continues, I've come to regard the New Year with suspicion. In addition to the usual perils provided by resolutions that are sure to be broken and hopes for the future that are almost certain not to pan out as expected, this particular time of year has, for myself, historically been one of unlooked-for upheaval. This is particularly true on the eve of a new decade. As previously noted, the years ending in 0 have a way of accumulating energy around them. Whether this is a result of some cosmic calendrical alignment or simply that humans as a species ascribe undue importance to the dawn of a new era and therefore create bother and worry where none need exist, who can say. The fact is, by the time that final year comes around, we are frequently only too eager to show the old decade the door and welcome the new one with bright smiles, conveniently forgetting that we did the same thing ten years earlier. This time, we hope, we will not end up disappointed.

As 1969 prepared to make way for 1970, I returned to Penn State and prepared to begin a new life without Jack. In the week following his announcement, I had seen little of him, as he'd been busy with readying himself for his new path. On December 31, our families had gathered for the traditional New Year's celebration, and we'd tried to be happy as midnight came and we toasted one another with hugs and best wishes. But things had changed for all of us, and the champagne Mr. Grace brought for the occasion could not make us forget, despite its bubbliness, that we were no longer the same happy family.

I said good-bye to Jack on January 2, got into the Mustang, and drove back to State College alone. Because the first day of the new year fell on Thursday, we wouldn't start the new semester until the following Monday. Those of us who arrived early therefore had the weekend in which to have a second New Year celebration. Pinchot was surprisingly full when I arrived, and I was relieved that I wouldn't have to endure the next two days in solitude. Although I sometimes resented the lack of privacy inherent in dorm living, I needed to not feel alone.

I spent Saturday morning packing up Jack's belongings, which I'd promised to mail back to him. I stacked the cardboard boxes against the wall on his side of the room, then sat on my bed and looked at them. Everything he had fit into a handful of boxes, and for some reason seeing that made me depressed, as if what he was amounted to very little. His side of the room was now bare, like a forest whose trees had lost their leaves and now stood empty and cold. I wondered if, when he notified the school of his leaving, I would get a new roommate, and what he might be like. Instantly I resented this newcomer. I didn't want him intruding on my life, trying to fill the void left by Jack's departure. Even more, I didn't want his presence to be a daily reminder of what I had lost.

My thoughts were interrupted by a knock on the door. Before I could answer, it opened, and Andy's face appeared. "Hey," he said. "You're back. Cool. Do you and Jack want to come to a Second Chance New Year's party tonight? This buddy of mine is having one."

I looked at Andy, trying to figure out who this man was who seemed to float effortlessly through the world, oblivious to almost everything but his own wants and needs. Did he not see the boxes, I wondered? Did he not notice that Jack's bed was stripped, his books gone from the desk, his jacket missing from its place on the back of his chair? I searched his face for some sign of recognition that things had changed in my life. He waited, saying nothing.

"Jack dropped out," I said. "He's going to become a minister."

Andy's eyebrows went up. "No shit?" he said.

"No shit," I answered. "He was failing, and he didn't want to get drafted."

Andy shook his head. I wasn't sure if he was expressing dismay over Jack's leaving, his desire to avoid the draft, or the war that was responsible for his having to make the choice at all. I noticed that he'd gotten a haircut. He looked more handsome than ever, I thought, and was immediately ashamed of myself.

"That really sucks, man," he said finally. "So, do you want to come to the party with me? It starts at ten."

I almost said no. I was *going* to say no. But I heard myself tell Andy that I would go with him. When he left and I was alone again, I berated myself for being so stupid. More than that, I berated myself for being so afraid to be alone that I would risk putting myself in a situation with Andy again. What was it about him, I asked myself, that I found so impossible to refuse?

There was no answer to that question, not then, so I pushed it from my mind and retreated into sleep. I awoke in darkness, and at first thought (not without some small sense of relief) that I had slept through the night and missed the party. But a look at the clock showed that only a few hours had passed, and I in fact had more than enough time to get ready. Dulled by the weariness that comes from having slept too early and too long, I slowly pulled myself off of the bed and turned on a light. It took another ten minutes before I could rouse energy enough to get dressed.

Andy tapped on my door a few minutes before ten. Still moving slowly, I followed him outside, where the cold air woke me up a bit. Having dumped several feet of snow across Pennsylvania, the Christmas storm had swept northward, leaving behind mountainous drifts and skies clear as ice. With only a sliver of moon remaining before the new one arrived, we were in a world lit only by stars and the watery electric light of the street lamps. I jammed my hands in my pockets, sorry that I had left my gloves back in the room.

I let Andy drive. For some reason, I didn't feel like letting him sit in the Mustang. Perhaps on some level I felt it was the one thing of mine he hadn't touched, the one remaining piece of my life I could say belonged only to me. Although it sat only a few spaces away, and I held the keys in my hand inside my coat pocket, I climbed into his pickup and shut the door. Andy started it up, clouds erupting from the rear and surrounding us like fog.

The house we went to was in the same neighborhood as the one where we'd attended the Halloween party, and for a moment I was afraid we were going back there. But Andy brought the truck to a stop in front of a different house, this one smaller than the other. I could see the lights of a Christmas tree flashing from behind the front window, and a path had been shoveled through the snow to the front door, on which hung an evergreen wreath tied with a red bow. Smoke trickled from the chimney, suggesting a fire in the hearth below.

"This is my buddy Ryan's place," Andy informed me as we walked to the door. "Actually, it's his parents' house, but they're out of town visiting family, so Ryan's got it to himself."

That, I thought as Andy knocked on the door, explained the cozy feel of the house. An actual family lived there, not just some random assortment of tenants or group of students who wanted a place of their own off campus. I hoped the crowd inside wouldn't alter too much the peaceful feelings the house aroused in me.

The door was opened by a young man about our own age. Seeing his red hair, worn in a crewcut, and his cheerful face with its pug nose, I realized that I'd seen him before around school, although whether he'd actually been in a class with me, I couldn't remember. He greeted us warmly and showed us inside.

"Hi," I said after Andy failed to introduce us. "I'm Ned."

"Ryan. I think we were in English lit together last semester."

"That's what it was," I said. "I knew I'd seen you before."

"I was the one who always showed up ten minutes late," said Ryan. "Those seven o'clock classes killed me. I didn't sign up for anything before nine this semester."

Ryan took our coats, disappearing into a hallway with them while Andy and I looked around. Unlike the Halloween party, this one was much more low key. Maybe fifteen or twenty people were there, spread throughout the living room, kitchen, and den. Crosby, Stills, and Nash played softly in the background, and although the smell of pot wafted through the rooms, the mood wasn't one of overindulgence. I found myself relaxing, pleased that I had come and wondering how it was that Andy knew someone like Ryan, who seemed the antithesis of most of his friends.

I knew no one at the party by name except for Andy, although I was fairly certain that I'd seen a number of the faces before. Mostly they were men, although here and there a girl's voice broke through the low murmur, like a bubble rising into the air. After exploring the rooms, I got a beer from the kitchen and returned to the living room. There I saw Andy sitting on the couch, talking to a man who looked remarkably like Ryan, only taller and less youthful. He was leaning forward, moving his hands animatedly while Andy nodded.

I walked over and took a seat in an empty armchair beside the couch. Andy tipped his beer at the man beside him. "This is Dylan," he told me as the man reached out to shake my hand. "He's Ryan's brother."

Now that I knew, the resemblance between Ryan and Dylan was remarkable. Like his brother, Dylan's hair was red and his skin pale and freckled. His green eyes surveyed me warily yet kindly, and he held himself in a way that suggested confidence and strength. The only detraction from his otherwise handsome face was a scar that ran from his right temple to his jaw, just touching the corner of his eye and mouth. Still pink, it seemed relatively recent, although Dylan showed no hint of self-consciousness about it.

"Dylan just got back from Nam," Andy informed me. "He got that scar from a gook bayonet."

Despite myself, I looked at the scar again.

"It's okay," said Dylan. "I'm proud of it."

"Dylan's in the 101st Airborne," said Andy.

"The Screaming Eagles," Dylan elaborated. "Best there is."

"Dylan was at Hamburger Hill," Andy said.

I didn't know what Hamburger Hill was. Dylan, noticing my lack of response, gave me a brief history lesson.

"Dong Ap Bia mountain," he told me. "Meanest motherfucking hill in Vietnam. Locals call it 'the mountain of the crouching beast.' Thing's so thick with jungle it's always nighttime under the canopy."

"Why Hamburger Hill?" I asked him, although his scar had given me some idea.

"Back in May," he said, "command decided it was time to clear the NVA out of the A Shau Valley once and for all. We thought we'd wiped 'em out after Tet, but while we weren't looking, they'd turned it into their very own staging area. Supply depots, spider holes, tunnels all through the place. We had to get rid of them."

As Dylan was telling the story, Ryan and a couple of other people came over to listen. Soon we had a small crowd around the couch, all of us quiet as Dylan talked.

"The 3/187th—the Rakkasans—drew Dong Ap Bia. Didn't think much about it. None of us did. You do what you're told, and they just knew they had to take it. What they didn't know was that it was impossible. But they found out soon enough. The VC were swarming all over that hill. They hit those bastards with everything they had, and they just wouldn't give up. Nine days they spent trying to get to the top of that mountain, sometimes fighting hand to hand, and every day more of 'em got themselves killed."

Dylan grew quiet, as if he was thinking about what his army buddies must have gone through. Somebody passed him a joint, which he took with a grateful nod. He inhaled, closing his eyes for a long moment. Then he exhaled and continued.

"Finally they called us in for reinforcement. The 2/506th. A Company. We got there at night. The next morning, we watched the jets fly over and drop shells, rockets, napalm, whatever they could find back at base camp. Just knocked the shit out of them. And for some reason, the stupid fuckers set off purple smoke grenades. We're looking up at that mountain, watching the shelling, and all of a sudden we see this purple smoke rolling down, like some kind of weird mist or something. Maybe they thought it would give them some cover. I don't know. But the boys just aimed for the grape and emptied their loads right on top of the VC hiding underneath."

He chuckled and grinned. Again his gaze went off into the distance, seeing something none of the rest of us could envision. When he spoke, something had crept into his voice, a sense of awe mixed with fear. The grin had disappeared, and his jaw had tightened. At that moment, I saw the soldier in him.

"At ten hundred hours we started up the mountain," he said. "The 3/187th A and C companies were on the right and in the center. We were on the left. We went slow, expecting fire. But we didn't get any. We made it to the first bunker line and kept going. We were closing in on the second line, maybe seventy-five yards from the top. That's when all hell broke loose. All of a sudden these NVA guys just pop out of the ground and start firing. They're rolling grenades down the hill at us. The guy to the right of me went down in pieces."

He took another hit from the joint, holding it for a long time, as if preparing for the climax of his story. I was surprised to find that I was anxious for him to finish. Despite the fact that he was sitting in front of me, and therefore alive, part of me feared for his life.

"I don't really know what happened after that," Dylan said. "I just knew we had to take that hill, so I kept moving forward, shooting everything that got in the way. I heard bullets, but none of them touched me. I felt like some kind of god, like there was this force around me or something. I could see the top of the hill, see guys going for it. I tried to run with them. Then something slashed across my face and I see this VC in front of me. I don't know where he came from. Just a little guy. Couldn't have been more than fourteen or fifteen years old. He's holding his rifle and screaming at me, jabbing this old bayonet toward me. And I realize he's got this big white patch pinned to the front of his jacket and it says KILL THE AMERICANS. I'm staring at that patch, and he's screaming something I don't understand, and I'm getting madder and madder. And all of this takes maybe a few seconds. Then I aim at that patch and I shoot."

He stopped there, letting us all imagine the path of his bullet and the inevitable conclusion of its flight. I imagined the body of the Vietnamese soldier as it crumpled to the ground. I saw the spreading stain as his blood poured out. I couldn't help wondering what his name was, how he had come to be a soldier, and what he'd left behind. Dylan saw him differently.

"We took the hill," he said proudly. "The NVA were all over it, but we cleaned it up. My face was bleeding pretty bad, but I had a medic patch it up until I could get it fixed up. It wasn't until later that I saw this."

He reached into the pocket of his shirt and drew out a playing card. It was the King of Spades. The card had been cut in half diagonally, the resulting scar on the king's face mirroring the one on Dylan's. Dylan flipped it over in his fingers, looking at it as if it were the world's most precious jewel.

"Spades represent the guys in the 506th," he said. "Most of us tuck one of these into our helmet bands for good luck. I guess it worked. That gook caught it with his bayonet, but he didn't kill me."

With the story over, a lot of the audience dispersed to find refreshment or more cheerful conversation. Andy, Ryan, and I stayed. Dylan's story had raised a lot of questions for me, and I wanted to ask him something.

"How do you feel about all the people protesting the war?" I asked him. "I heard there were more than 250,000 in D.C. last month, and a lot of them were veterans."

He shook his head. "They don't get it, man. They just don't get it. We're over there getting killed for a *reason*. We're there so those Commie bastards don't take over. Those Vietnamese, man, they *love* us. You go anywhere there and they're all, 'Thank you, Joe! Thank you for helping us!' They think America's the best place in the world. And the soldiers, we're happy to be there. It wasn't until new guys started coming in saying people back home were calling us baby-killers and shit that guys started getting down. If those hippies could hear the little kids tell us how great we are, man, they'd shut the hell up."

Andy and Ryan were nodding in agreement. I wasn't as convinced, although I had to admit to myself that there was something noble about wanting to help keep Vietnam free. Like most people my age, I'd been raised to see Communism as a mold, something that, once it took hold, spread quickly and invisibly until an entire house was brought down in ruins before you knew it. If we were in Vietnam because we were trying to stop the Communists from taking over, I reasoned, it couldn't be a bad thing, even if it was a terrible thing.

"I'm going in," Ryan said, and Andy and I looked at him. "Yeah," he said, as if we'd asked him a question. "I got a pretty high number in the lottery, and I just don't think it's fair that I get to stay out while some other guy goes in my place."

Dylan clapped his brother on the back. "Way to go," he said proudly. "If more guys had your balls, we'd win this thing next week."

I started to ask something else, but was interrupted by a girl calling out, "Come on, everybody! It's almost midnight."

We all got up and joined the others, who were in the den. As if it really were December 31, people had donned party hats and were holding noisemakers in their hands, ready to ring in the new year. From the happy looks on the faces around me, I saw that I wasn't the only one who was glad to have a second chance to start things off right. I pushed the memory of my failed New Year's Eve with Jack and our parents out of my mind, and as the last ten seconds of 1969 began to slip away, I counted them down along with everyone else.

At one, the room erupted in applause as we welcomed in 1970. I turned and looked for someone to kiss, but everyone around me was already partnered. Andy had his arms around a girl. Someone had given him a party hat, a cheap paper thing covered in glitter and feathers. He had it on his head, trying to hold it there while he kissed the girl. She was laughing, her arms around his neck.

Behind them, at the edge of the room, was Dylan. He was staring at the television, no expression on his face. Then he looked up and into my eyes. When he saw me, he held up his hand, the forefinger extended and the thumb raised. He pointed this gun at me and pretended to fire. His mouth opened in a silent "bang" and then he laughed.

CHAPTER 21

I was not assigned a new roommate, but nonetheless I was not alone in my room. Jack's presence haunted it more fully than if his flesh and bones had inhabited the space. Every morning I awoke to his empty bed, the desk with no books, and a closet whose hangers rattled accusingly whenever I walked by. Returning after class each day, I still opened the door and half expected to see him there. Twice I woke up, convinced he had called my name, only to find that I'd left the window open and the winter air was rattling the blind.

School was a welcome distraction. I found that with little effort I could easily lose myself in the multitude of tasks associated with higher education. The taking of notes, studying of texts, and writing of papers were my antidotes to loneliness, and I ingested my daily dose gladly. I looked forward to sitting in class, where I could focus my attention on the instructor and not on my increasingly-dark moods. I frequented Pattee Library so as to avoid being in my room, and made friends with the student workers, who sometimes let me stay in my carrel after hours while they performed their nocturnal duties.

I was particularly drawn to one of my new electives. Having enjoyed my philosophy class the previous semester, I'd signed up for another, this time focusing on existentialism. Immersing myself in the writings of Pascal, Sartre, Kierkegaard, Dostoyevsky, and the like, I began to question the value, the nature, the reality of my life. Every action and every human feeling became suspect, until ultimately I was left with one simple question: What was the point of anything?

My arrival at this most basic conundrum of philosophical reasoning took all of three weeks. With the surety and suppleness of youthful thought, I almost abandoned my previous beliefs overnight (such as they were) and threw in my lot with men who assured me that what I was feeling was simply man's inescapable desire to make sense of the insensible. The teachings of my Eastern muses were forgotten as, in my search for evidence that would lend value to my feelings of hopelessness, I clung to whatever "proof" I could unearth that none of it really mattered.

And proof was in abundance in the work of these philosophers and those they influenced. I read voraciously. I became enamored of Herman Hesse, Kafka, and especially Jack Kerouac, whose death the prior October I had barely noticed, but whose passing I now mourned deeply. Like so many of my generation, I found in Kerouac a kindred spirit, a relentless questioner on a search for something real and true. His brash, breathless prose got into my blood and made me drunk. After reading *On the Road*, I was more than half in love with him. In my daydreams I imagined myself traveling alongside him as we sought out the meaning of everything and discovered that it was, in the end, nothing.

In short, I traded one Jack for another. This new Jack, handsome, older, and wiser, was both the man I wanted to be and the man I wanted to be with. Unafraid of life, he'd plunged headlong into it, whereas I remained on the shore, timid and fearful, afraid to put even my toe into the water. Measured against him, I came up short, and this made me doubt myself. How could I become a man—a person—of any worth if I couldn't even embrace life? How could I find who I was when I viewed the world from the safety of my own mind?

In the tradition of all who worship artists, movie stars, and other idols and long to see them as divine, I ignored the fact that Kerouac's search ultimately led him into a life of chemical dependency, depression, and death from alcoholism. This I attributed to his sensitive nature and inability to live in a world that was ultimately doomed, thereby conveniently and usefully turning him into a martyr and deepening my affection for him. Years later, when it was revealed that Kerouac was, among other things, a closeted homosexual, or at the very least a frustrated bisexual, I would understand more fully our parallel lives and my attraction to him and his work. At 19, I simply saw him as my god.

One night toward the end of January, when yet another in what seemed to be an endless series of snowstorms had wrapped the campus in its arms, I sat in a corner of the library reading Sartre's *The Words*. While the wind howled outside, I made my way through Jean-Paul's autobiography of his first ten years of life. Fewer than fifty pages into it, already I felt myself an intellectual child. At an age when I had been unable even to tie my shoes on my own, Sartre had been making cognitive leaps and bounds, realizing even at five or six that his life was merely a series of events dictated by others, with himself playing a role based on what they needed from him. Reading this, I found myself relating to it, nodding my head in agreement every few pages.

I read into the night as, one by one, the students around me packed up their books and notepads and headed off to dinner, movies, and friends, until finally I was alone. Then, turning a page, I read something that made me stop. "But when lightning struck and left me blasted," Sartre wrote after describing his epiphany that his life was nothing but a play, and he an actor in it, "I realized that I had a 'false major role,' that though I had lines to speak and was often on stage, I had no 'scene of my own.'"

I reread the sentence again, then again, until it seemed that Sartre was speaking directly to me. In his description I recognized myself as the supporting actor in a drama that had been going on since my birth. While I'd believed myself to be the star of my own life, I now saw that I had been merely working in the shadows of others, first my parents and then Jack. Time and again, I'd become what I thought they wanted me to be, changing myself to fit their requirements. I'd been a son, friend, and lover, playing the parts as best I could. But I had never been entirely me, never been wholly Ned.

I shut the book and sat, slightly stunned, as I accepted the truth that I didn't know who I was. I had never, in my entire life, done something solely because it was what I wanted to do. Always I had viewed myself as less important, my wants as less in need of fulfilling as those of others. Suddenly, my feelings made sense. I wasn't mourning the loss of Jack; I was mourning my lack of wholeness. Having seen myself only in terms of him—of us—I'd had a huge part of what I perceived as my self amputated by his desertion. Now, left with only stunted pieces of a soul I'd long neglected, I was slowly dying. I needed to revive myself.

The question was how. The immediate and obvious answer was to, like Kerouac, take myself on an adventure. But I dismissed that as impractical and, worse, uninteresting. Many of my peers were already following the call of the counterculture, dropping out and going in search of the truth. I'd seen some of the results, and had been less than impressed. I wanted to go in a different direction from them, down a road where I would, for once, be required to expose who I really was as a man, and as a human. I needed a testing ground, free of safety nets and certainties, where my choices would really matter. In the outcome of those choices, I firmly believed, I would finally discover who I was.

When the answer came to me, I felt as Sartre had, blasted by lightning. I would go to Vietnam. I knew it was a ridiculous idea, but I knew also that it was what I would do. War had long been a place for young men to prove themselves, and I had much to prove. Also, I had been thinking a lot about the war, and what it meant, trying to see beyond the protests and flag-waving on both sides to what it was really about. If, as Dylan and so many others said, we were in Vietnam to save its people from the threat of Communism, wasn't that a noble thing? And if that was true, wasn't it my duty to aid in the fight?

I quickly turned my decision into a noble undertaking, brushing aside all reasonable arguments against its worthiness and latching on to the notion that I was doing something important. If nothing else, I argued, I would see the arguments of the philosophers played out in real life. There would be two sides, each believing itself to be correct, and the outcome would show who was right. Those of us engaged in the war of our own free will would be making choices based on these beliefs, living them on a daily basis instead of sitting in ivory towers debating them in hypothetical terms.

Energized and excited more than ever in my life, I gathered up my belongings and ran from the library out into the blizzard. Heedless of the cold, I dashed across campus to Pinchot Hall. I felt the need to tell somebody of my plans, to make them real by giving them voice. My parents were the obvious choice, but also the one I couldn't make. I knew that my mother at least would try to talk me out of it, and although I recognized that it was cowardice on my part, I'd decided not to tell my family until I'd already enlisted. There was Jack, but he, too, was not an option. For one thing, I didn't want him to think that I was doing this because of him. For another, I had only his address at

Wesley, and writing a letter would defeat the point of immediate action.

That left only Andy. Although our relationship had cooled somewhat, at least on my part, I still considered him a friend. I acknowledged, too, that I wanted to impress him, if only to use his admiration as further proof that I was doing the right thing, or perhaps as incentive to not back down should I later have doubts. He would, I knew, be in favor of my decision. I decided that he would be the first to know.

Chaz answered the door when I knocked, nodding brusquely and turning back to Andy, who was standing by his bed, stuffing clothes into a bag.

"And another thing," Chaz said, apparently taking up a conversation I'd interrupted with my visit, "Angela Davis says Vietnam is a war against poor people."

"Angela Davis is a Communist," said Andy. "Of course she'd be against Vietnam."

"She's also a professor of philosophy," Chaz countered.

"*Was,*" said Andy. "Didn't UCLA fire her ass last year when they found out she was a Red?"

"Yeah, but they had to rehire her," Chaz said. "They can't get away with trying to hide the truth."

"The truth," Andy said, snorting. "What the fuck does Angela Davis know about the truth?"

"A lot more than your motherfucking ass does," Chaz shot back. "But what the fuck do I care. Go on and get your white ass killed fighting for the man."

"What's going on?" I asked.

Chaz jerked his thumb at Andy. "Stupid motherfucker went and signed up," he told me.

"Signed up?" I repeated.

"For the army," Andy clarified. "I enlisted this afternoon. I'm not just going to sit "

I stared at him, speechless. I'd come there full of excitement, and now I just felt cold. Andy had trumped me. All I could do was say, "Me, too."

"You, too, what?" Andy said as he continued to pack his bag.

"Enlisted," I said. "I mean, I'm going to. Tomorrow."

"Yeah?" Andy said. "Cool. You should talk to the guy I talked to. Maybe we can get into basic together."

Chaz was shaking his head. "You guys think you're going to be heroes? Is that it? Well, guess what, you're not. You're just going to go fuck up the lives of a bunch of people who don't want you there. Probably end up dead while you're doing it."

He flopped onto his bed and picked up a book. I stood in the doorway, watching Andy and quickly losing my enthusiasm for the plan that had seemed so perfect only minutes before. He'd reacted to my news with only the slightest enthusiasm, nothing at all like the reception I'd expected. Chaz was simply dismissive. What I'd seen as a grand gesture, the beginning of my life as a person who was finally living for himself, was instead taking on an air of unimportance, as if I'd announced that I would be having spaghetti for dinner.

Still, I had to go through with it. I'd said out loud that I would. More important, I'd told myself that I would. I couldn't go back now. Not only would I look foolish to Andy and Chaz, I would look foolish to myself. If I didn't enlist, I knew that for the rest of my life I would feel the shame of not following through on the first major decision I'd made on my own.

"What's the name of the guy you talked to today?" I asked Andy.

He reached for a business card, which he handed to me. "Sergeant Vaughan," he said. "Nice guy."

"Thanks," I said.

"No problem," Andy said, as if he'd just loaned me a bar of soap or a quarter for the soda machine down the hall.

I put the card in the pocket of my jeans and turned to leave.

"Don't forget to ask if we can be in the same group," Andy reminded me.

"Right," I said. "I won't."

I left Andy to his packing and went back to my room, which now seemed colder than ever before. Sitting on my bed, I took out the recruiter's card and looked at it again. Would I really go talk to Sergeant Vaughan in the morning, or would I throw his card away and go about my normal schedule? Earlier in the evening, the choice had been clear. Now, with Andy already a step ahead of me on the path I thought I was blazing, I hesitated. Would the power of my action be diminished by his having gone first? Would I once more be assigning myself to a minor role while he assumed the spotlight?

I thought about something Camus had written, and which formed the basis of much of existentialist thought, about how we are the sum of the choices we make. I was facing a choice, and whichever way I decided to go, I would be affecting my sum, either increasing or decreasing it. In the end, I wondered, what would I add up to? And which choice would result in a positive tally?

I went to bed still undecided, hoping that I would wake up with an answer.

CHAPTER 22

A sign at the entrance to New Jersey's Fort Dix proudly proclaims it to be the HOME OF THE ULTIMATE WEAPON. New recruits and draftees, passing through the gate as they arrive for Basic Combat Training, cannot help but see it and realize that it is both a promise and a challenge. A soldier's performance during the next ten weeks will ultimately determine whether the prophesy is fulfilled, but the expectation, from that first glimpse of the base from a bus or car window, is that the men who enter will come out machines of war.

On the day that Andy and I passed that sign for the first time, February 4, 1970, it was covered in snow, the words obscured. All of Fort Dix was, in fact, hidden by the snow, which blew across the roads in sweeping sheets and covered the buildings, turning them into gingerbread cottages complete with smoke rising from their chimneys. The effect was deceiving, as our time there could hardly be considered a fairy tale. Any illusions we might have held about the army experience were wiped away the moment we stepped off the bus into a frozen world whose bitter cold instilled itself in our bones, where it would remain until the heat of Southeast Asia began, at last, to bring about a thaw some months later.

Our induction had been surprisingly swift, the army's relief at finding willing reinforcements on their doorstep greasing the notoriously slow-grinding gears of bureaucracy. I'd reported to the recruiting center on Friday, and by Monday the battery of required tests had been completed and everything was in order. Still reeling from my decision, I'd packed up my belongings, informed a surprised clerk in the student office that I was dropping out, and driven home to face my par-

ents before I could even entertain second thoughts about having
signed the forms the delighted recruiter had placed before me.

The reaction my news elicited from my mother was unsurprising,
but nonetheless difficult to take. At first disbelieving, she had accused
me of playing an elaborate practical joke on her, refusing to accept that
I had actually enlisted until I showed her the forms with their official-
looking stamps and seals and signatures. Then her mood had switched,
almost instantly, to one of anger and fear. Many tears were shed and accusations of familial disloyalty hurled, first at me and then at my father,
who stood mutely by, not knowing how to comfort a woman who was
convinced her son had just committed suicide. Finally, he had simply
let her cry herself out until, weary with unhappiness, she had con-
sented to being led to the bedroom, where she remained until
Tuesday evening. When she reappeared, she had the faraway look of
someone grieving for a lost loved one. And when she turned her eyes
in my direction, it seemed she looked through me, as through a ghost.

My father admitted to me that he had given her several Valium, prescribed to him by his physician as a sleep aid several months before
when he'd complained about insomnia. My mother would later develop a dependency on them and other pharmaceuticals provided to
soothe her steadily-unraveling nerves, sliding pill by pill into a dreary
suburban take on *Valley of the Dolls*, complete with bouts of hysteria
and paranoia. But for those few days I was thankful to have help in
dealing with her anxieties. I had enough of my own, not the least of
which was debating whether or not to tell Jack what I was doing.

Ultimately, I let the day run out without phoning him, and on
Wednesday morning rode with my parents to the recruiting center in
Philadelphia. There I met Andy and his grandparents, who had gotten
up well before dawn to make the six-hour drive across Pennsylvania.
They were inside, along with the other new recruits and their families,
enjoying the coffee and doughnuts set out by the army representatives
there to greet us. My father shook hands with Andy and his grandfather,
who nodded silently while his wife and my mother exchanged looks of
mutual commiseration.

Andy was ready and anxious to go, and when finally our names
were called out and our assigned bus indicated, he gave his grandparents
swift good-byes and headed for the door. I took a bit longer, embrac-
ing my mother and saying, "I love you. Don't worry, I'll be okay." She

smiled nervously and blinked back tears while my father, speaking for both of them, said, "We're proud of you, Ned."

I joined Andy in the line for the bus, looking back only once and waving as I stepped aboard. We took our seats, and I surveyed the other men as they filed on. Most seemed to be my age, and I wondered how many of them were there voluntarily and how many only because they'd been unfortunate enough to have been born on September the 14th or one of the other first-picked days. However they'd come to be there, we were now all heading for the same place, and by the pensive looks on the faces of those around me, we were all uneasy about what the future held.

Except for Andy, who tapped his hands on his knees and whistled, as if the rest of us were holding up his plans for the day. "Let's get this baby rolling," he said to no one in particular.

It took about an hour and a half to travel the forty miles between Philadelphia and Wrightstown, our progress slowed by the snow. The entire time, the bus was almost completely silent. Even seatmates refrained from conversation, as if we were in church and our voices would disturb the saints and God. Those seated beside windows looked out them, while those on the aisle looked straight ahead or down at the floor. A few slept, their heads cocked to one side or another, jerking awake whenever the bus lurched or they came near to tipping over.

No one can prepare you for your first encounter with the army. From the moment you step off the bus and your feet touch the ground, you're reminded that your life is no longer your own. The military's recent ad campaign highlighting the power of the individual notwithstanding, the army is by necessity one unit comprised of millions. Comparisons to an ant colony or a beehive are obvious, but appropriate. Designed for function, the army requires its working parts to operate smoothly, without deviation from their assigned purpose and with absolute devotion to the work of the whole.

From the outset, that which makes you unique is stripped away, beginning with your name. The first thing I learned during my initial minutes at Fort Dix was that I was no longer Edward Canton Brummel, nor even Ned. I was Private Brummel. Even my surname was unimportant, as I would be expected to answer to any order given to the generic "private," assuming myself at all times to be part of the group. All of this was explained to me, loudly, by a sergeant whose face, red when he began his introductions, grew progressively redder as both his voice and aura of menace increased.

Lined up in the snow, we did our best to act like the soldiers we were supposed to be as the sergeant moved from man to man, asking each of us why we were standing before him. Afraid to turn my head to see who was speaking, I heard only disembodied voices as men blurted out their reasons. "I was drafted, sir." "Because my father fought in Korea, sir." "It's my duty, sir."

I doubted that telling the sergeant that I was there because of a revelation received from a French existentialist philosopher would place me in high regard, either with him or my fellow recruits, so as I awaited my turn to answer, I tried to think of a more suitable reply. It did not occur to me to lie, and as my father had never served in the military, that was not an option. Nor could I honestly say that I felt it was my duty or obligation. Finding my options severely limited, I grew increasingly anxious as the men to my right grew fewer in number and my moment with the sergeant loomed.

He reached Andy, who stood to my right, and I heard my friend say, "I'm here to kill the Commie gooks, sir."

The sergeant paused, and I saw the corners of his mouth rise ever so slightly as he appraised Andy. I couldn't tell if he was pleased or disgusted by Andy's answer. A moment later, the smirk was gone and he was nose to nose with me.

"Why are *you* here, private?"

His breath was hot on my face. It melted the snowflakes that had come to rest on my eyelashes, and I felt water trickle into my eyes. Resisting the urge to blink, I blurted out, "I'm here to find out who I am, sir."

I regretted it instantly. I sensed the sergeant pause. His eyes bored into mine. He looked at me for a long moment before speaking. "I can answer that question for you right now, private. I can answer that question for every man standing here. Who you are—*what* you are—is a soldier in the United States Army. Nothing more and nothing less. So now that we've answered your question, maybe you can give me a *good* reason for taking up space in my camp."

I felt the tension as every man in line waited for me to deliver a satisfactory response. Already I'd made the mistake of standing out, and unless I corrected my error as quickly as possible, I ran the risk of becoming known as a liability, even before doing my first push-up. In a matter of seconds, I foresaw my failure and wished I could get back on the bus and go home.

"I'm here to protect freedom, sir," I said hastily.

The sergeant nodded, apparently satisfied, and moved on. I waited until he was five or six men beyond me before allowing myself the deep breath I needed. It was my first lesson in the art of camouflage, and one I would find useful in the coming years.

Introductions over, the process of rendering us into our most basic forms continued as we were sent to the base's processing center for physicals and testing. Hours later, our heads shaved, teeth checked, and arms smarting from a series of inoculations, our initial reduction was complete. In our freshly-issued uniforms, we were virtually indistinguishable from one another, a group of strangers whose first order of business was to bond based solely on the shared fact of our being thrown together.

Processing continued for several days, during which we discovered that we were now the men of Company D, one of three groups that would begin basic training the following week. We were further divided into four squads of twelve men each, using some unknown criteria assumably gleaned from the mental and physical tests we underwent throughout the days. I fell into A Squad. Andy was in C Squad, although it hardly mattered, as all four of our platoon's units would share a common barracks.

Training began in earnest the next week, when we were symbolically "shipped out" from our processing quarters to our home for the next nine weeks, a drafty barracks whose heat came from a smoky coal stove and whose wood plank walls—cheaply and hurriedly constructed sometime after World War II and little improved since then—had chinks large enough to permit snow to come in. There we were stacked in bunks and our gear stored in footlockers, everything ordered with the precision for which the army is famed.

The details of Army Basic Combat Training are only barely of interest to the soldiers themselves, and to those unfamiliar with military life, a recitation of the drills and classes is almost certain to result in a loss of attention. Anyway, the depiction of this initial period of combat training in films and television programs has more than adequately provided all but the most unimaginative with a rudimentary understanding of the specifics and a more thorough appreciation for the overall effect it has on the young men who experience it firsthand. In short, it is difficult, sometimes brutal, and generally demoralizing. It is meant to be. BCT was designed based on the notion that failure—at least in the early stages of training—forces a soldier to realize that he requires the assistance of his comrades in order to survive. By giving him tasks he can neither complete singlehandedly nor even in tandem with his unit perform to the demanded level of proficiency, he learns quickly that much more is required of him. The expectation is that in his desire to please he will rise to the occasion rather than let down his unit, his army, and his country.

In general, it works. Eager to be seen as worthy of wearing the uniform, most soldiers discover they can indeed give their all when called upon. And it is a self-correcting system. Although popular depictions of basic training generally portray the drill sergeant as the primary motivating force for underperforming recruits, this is not altogether accurate. Of more importance is the internal pressure. Those who cannot meet the standards are seldom released from duty. Instead, they are recycled into another company and forced to begin the process anew. Faced with the prospect of having to endure humiliation all over again, and in front of classmates who will be aware of their initial failure, most men will do anything to redeem themselves.

Objectively, the process is easily viewed as being cruel, and to some degree it is. But a military exists, ideally, for one reason only—to defend a country and its allies. Accordingly, it requires members who are equipped for that purpose, and with limited time available to prepare combatants for service, it is not surprising that a force whose very existence depends on the efficient utilization of resources would look for the quickest route to supplying itself with soldiers.

There were times during those nine weeks—many of them—when I wished wholeheartedly that I had never made the decision to enlist. There were times when I wanted to give up, or cry, or even turn a weapon on the shouting, finger-pointing source of my unhappiness. But I cannot deny that there was also something magical about going through it with a group of men who, like I did, simply wanted to see it through to the end. This, not the ability to handle a gun, scale a wall, or dig a trench, is the real reward of BCT. During those hours marching through the snow and mud, shivering and miserable, my body broken and my psyche bruised, I became part of something.

Perhaps I was more vulnerable to the experience, never having been on a sporting team, nor, with the exception of the Boy Scouts, belonging to a tribe of any kind. Whatever the reason, I came to love the camaraderie of my squad, and the platoon at large. The men with whom I shared these daily travails became my friends. I came to know who they were, and I came to love them. It was like having brothers for the first time in my life, and although I think somewhere in our minds we never stopped thinking about what might happen to us at the end of our training, for those two months we were strangely happy.

CHAPTER 23

People often ask about sex between soldiers, particularly in a time when women were a rare sight on military bases. They are often strangely disappointed when I tell them that, based on my experiences, such encounters are more the stuff of fantasy than of daily life. For one thing, we were too tired. For another, the effect of intimate companionship is not generally arousal but desensitization. After seeing another man's morning erection on a repeated basis, it becomes more a point of good-natured ribbing than of erotic fixation. Which is not to say that I didn't find some of my platoon mates attractive. I did. But these thoughts were fleeting, at the most resulting in masturbatory fantasies acted out at night, when the snoring of my neighbors would cover any squeaking of my indiscrete bedsprings.

It would be some time before I would have a physical relationship with another soldier. For the moment, I was more concerned with learning what I needed to know to stay alive in Vietnam. Although there was no guarantee that we would end up there (and ultimately only about one third of all soldiers serving during the Vietnam era did, and only a small percentage of those in combat), we all assumed that we would. After all, wasn't that why we had enlisted or been drafted, to continue the fight against the Communist followers of Ho Chi Minh? Although many of us feared what setting foot in Vietnam would mean, I think the majority of us would have been disappointed not to get there, especially after spending much of the winter on our bellies in the frozen mud.

I suppose this is difficult for those who weren't there to understand. The popular image today is of the Vietnam draft dodger running north to Canada or south to Mexico, burning his draft card, and moving from place to place, avoiding conscription at all costs. Largely, though, this is a figure whose mythology has been magnified well beyond his reality. Perhaps a hundred thousand young men out of the 2.2 million drafted (and an estimated five hundred thousand of the 24 million eligible but never called) avoided serving in this manner. Although often overlooked, the fact is that only about one third of the fighting force in Vietnam was comprised of men who were drafted, compared to two thirds in World War II and nearly one half in Korea. We were, by and large, a volunteer army, even if we had some reservations, and we did.

In discussions with my students about recent events in the Middle East, in particular the war in Iraq, I like to remind them that the Congress that voted to empower the president of the United States to use force against Saddam Hussein was comprised, by a vast majority, of lawmakers who never served in the armed forces, and who in many cases actively avoided serving. The president himself has a service record of questionable merit. In contrast, Vietnam was a war supported, at least initially, by men who had seen battle in Korea, just as Korea had been supported by men who had served in World War II. They understood, most of these men, what war was about. They understood what they were asking the young men of the country to do because they had been asked to do it before them.

For this reason, I believe the actions of those who opposed Vietnam—either by refusing conscription or by actively protesting against the war in other ways—were deeply wounding to a great many people of previous generations. Since the army was the only branch of the armed forces utilizing draftees in significant numbers, those fearing death in combat could greatly reduce their chances of bodily injury by voluntarily joining any of the other three. Although dodging the draft is often suggested as the only option for avoiding an early death, the fact is that there were alternatives beyond simple refusal.

Given these other possibilities, the question I ask my students to ponder is why someone would instead choose an action almost certain to result in stigmatization, if not prosecution and imprisonment? There are many perfectly acceptable answers to that, but chief among them is the argument that the majority of protesters nurtured the deep-seated conviction that war, for any reason, is wrong. This was a position the men of Company D found ourselves debating during basic training, not because our cadre asked it of us, but because it was at the heart of several incidents that changed, for some of us, our outlook on what we were doing.

It began only a week or so after our arrival, on the evening of Valentine's Day, when shortly before nine o'clock an explosion rocked the nearby Fort Dix Coffee House. A small brick building located not far from the camp, the coffeehouse was one of many organized near military installations around the country by antiwar activists. Its purpose was to provide not only a place for soldiers and their friends to congregate, but an opportunity to spread the truth about what was happening in Vietnam. Many of the coffeehouses were staffed by former military men, who were anxious to share their stories.

The Fort Dix Coffee House had been the target of violence for some time. Its large glass windows had been smashed only a few weeks before, and soldiers were unofficially discouraged by base command from frequenting it. Being in the early stages of our training, we were ineligible for off-base activity anyway, so for myself, Andy, and the others, staying away from the establishment was not an issue, regardless of our opinions of its mission, which were varied and largely undiscussed. On the night of the explosion, we were recovering from a long day of training. Sleep, not Valentine's Day or the Fort Dix Coffee House, was foremost on our minds.

We did, however, hear the explosion, which blew out the plywood that covered the coffeehouse's shattered windows. We heard, too, the sirens of the fire trucks that arrived minutes later. But it wasn't until the next day that we learned what had happened, that someone had tossed what appeared to be a "power bomb"—an army-issue training grenade—through the door of the coffee house. Packed as the place was with GIs and their dates, it was only sheer luck that no one was killed and only a few wounded.

New as we were to the army, many of us were still in the throes of first love. Andy, in particular, denounced the organizers of the coffeehouse as cowards and traitors. "I hope those fucking Commies learned a lesson," he said that night at mess, earning nods of agreement from many in both our and surrounding squads.

I feel the need to point out that we were not stupid. Yes, many of the draftees were there because they had been unable to attend college, either for financial or academic reasons. And we were young. But many of us—I would argue most—were capable of independent and at least somewhat nuanced thought, and for us the bombing raised questions, some of which we'd already considered and some which were new. This questioning was intensified a few weeks later, in early March, when there appeared around Fort Dix copies of *Shakedown*, an underground antiwar newspaper allegedly written and produced by soldiers from the base and nearby McGuire Air Force Base with the help of civilian sympathizers.

The cover of the March 6 issue, a typed-up and mimeographed affair, featured a photograph of the bombed-out coffeehouse with the headline FT. DIX COFFEE-HOUSE BOMBED . . . CLOSED BUT THE MOVEMENT GOES ON. The accompanying article decried the attack and provided additional details, including the charge that two men had been seen running from the scene and that rifle shots had been fired at patrons fleeing the explosion. Additional articles criticized the war in general, urging those of us still in training to recognize the barbarousness of what was happening in Vietnam and to protest our own treatment at the hands of the military establishment. Afraid to be seen reading the paper, I took a copy and hid it beneath my shirt. I read it later in the latrine, the only place I could get even a few minutes alone, then flushed it, page by page, down the toilet, lest I be discovered and accused of insubordination.

Years later, I came across that issue of *Shakedown* at a flea market in San Francisco, for sale by an old hippie who had collected all kinds of antiwar propaganda and now was making a living selling it off piece by piece. Today it hangs over the desk in my office at the college, where I frequently look at it and remember what it was like to sit in that freezing cold bathroom, wrestling with the philosophy of war while outside the stall door my platoon mates celebrated a successful run through the camp's obstacle course. If you had asked me then if I was prowar, I would have answered yes. Now, having had a few years during which to think about it, I might clarify and say that I was antiwar but pro-Vietnam, by which I mean that although I found the idea of warfare itself distasteful and inherently repellent, I believed that what we were doing in Vietnam was right inasmuch as we were trying to keep a hostile force from overcoming our allies. In addition to seeing my involvement in the war as an adventure and a quest, I quickly came to see it also as a mission of honor. Perhaps instinctively I needed to do so in order to spare myself some of the mental anguish I suspected was due to befall me. Or perhaps I was merely impressionable.

In any case, there was little time for doubting my purpose or anything else. I did what I was told, and by the middle of April and the end of BCT, I was ready to move forward. Having survived basic training, we were now ready for what the army refers to as "Advanced Individual Training." AIT is where soldiers learn the specialized skills needed for whatever job they or, more likely, their superiors think best suits them.

There was more than a little nervousness the day we learned what our AIT destinations were. For the unlucky, or those who for their own reasons volunteered, it meant more time at Fort Dix learning advanced infantry tactics. This was an almost guaranteed ticket straight to the battle zone, where a soldier's chances of coming home dead or damaged rose considerably. For the rest of us, our futures were less certain but probably safer. Many of us would eventually end up in Southeast Asia, but most likely in less hazardous positions than the infantrymen, who had earned their designation as cannon fodder by amassing more casualties than all other military units combined.

When I emerged from my company commander's office following my meeting, I found Andy waiting for me. "What'd you get?" he asked.

"Quartermaster training," I told him. "Fort Lee. How about you?"

"Helo mechanic," he told me. "I guess knowing how to fix all that farm machinery finally paid off."

"Congratulations," I said, knowing he'd been hoping for helicopter training all along. "Where?"

"Fort Eustis," he said.

"Right down the road from me," I said. "Maybe we'll see each other."

He nodded, clearly more interested in his AIT assignment than in our proximity to one another. I had mixed feelings about it myself. I was still undeniably attracted to Andy, although more and more I'd come to see him as someone who needed looking after. I'd had my fill of that with Jack. Plus, given Andy's apparent disinterest in continuing our sexual encounters (he hadn't approached me once in our ten weeks at Fort Dix, although admittedly this may have had more to do with the lack of both time and privacy than an abatement of desire), I saw no reason to encourage him. It was, I thought, a good time to make a clean break.

Graduation was attended by my parents. My mother looked drawn and tired, but she hugged me enthusiastically, and when she said she was proud of me, I believed her. My father actually saluted me, a gesture I returned before joking, "I expect you to call me 'sir' from now on."

As they were leaving, I broke a promise to myself and asked about Jack. My mother struck her forehead with her fingertips. "I almost forgot," she said, opening her purse. "He sent a letter for you."

I read it later, sitting alone on one of the massive log hurdles in the middle of the now-empty obstacle course. It was written in Jack's familiar, slanted scrawl on a single piece of lined paper, the edges ragged where he'd torn it from a notebook, as if he'd been in a hurry to send it and hadn't had time to find either a typewriter or stationery. I smoothed it out and read it as the spring sun was setting.

Dear Ned:

Congratulations on finishing basic training. I bet it was pretty tough. I still can't believe you're a soldier. Things are good here. Believe it or not, I like my classes, and the other guys are great.

I don't really know why you joined the Army. I hope it wasn't because you thought you had to take my place. I just couldn't go. I hope you understand that. I know you will, because you know me better than anyone else.

Take care of yourself, and don't get hurt or anything. I wouldn't be able to handle it if you did.

Jack

I folded the letter and stuck it in my jacket pocket. I wasn't sure what I was supposed to feel, or what Jack wanted me to feel. His letter seemed more like an excuse a child would bring to his teacher to explain a missed day of school than it did an apology or a simple goodluck wish. It was as if he wanted me to forgive him for a trespass he couldn't even name. His remark about not being able to go irked me. No, I didn't understand it. Being afraid, I could understand. Not facing that fear, I couldn't. Especially not from Jack. Our whole lives, he'd been the one to jump first, accept the dare, risk injury and embarrassment without hesitation. But now I was the one wearing a uniform and facing an uncertain future, while he remained safe behind the seminary walls.

I was angry at him, too, for thinking that I might have done what I'd done to make up for his actions. Did he really, I wondered, think we were seven years old and I was still covering his mistakes? Was it truly impossible for him to imagine that I might have made my choice based on *my* need to do something for myself? Despite his feeble attempt at expressing concern for my well-being, he had succeeded only in revealing further his own guilty conscience and his continuing belief that everything in the world was somehow concerned with him. He was the same old Jack.

I, however, had changed. During those ten weeks of training I had, bit by bit, discarded many of my old perceptions, allowing them to fall away as I marched doggedly through snow and rain and leaving them to be trampled into the mud by the boots of the men behind me. I still wasn't sure who I was, but I had started to know who I wasn't. I was no longer the boy who trailed along in Jack's shadow. I did not see him as a hero to be admired and defended. Even my physical desire for him had died, replaced by something more like pity, or perhaps disdain. His letter only served to prove to me that I was right in seeing him this way.

As I watched the sun go down, turning the muddy field a dirty orange, I said good-bye not only to Fort Dix, but also to Jack. In the morning I would board a bus for Virginia and Fort Lee. After that, I didn't know. What I did know was that I had bested Jack in the ultimate competition. I was, I told myself, a better man than he was, and that thought made me very happy.

CHAPTER 24

"Welcome to the Republic of South Vietnam, gentlemen." The voice that came through the Pan Am 707's speakers woke me from a restless sleep. Except for refueling stops in Anchorage and Tokyo, we'd been on the plane for almost twenty-two hours since taking off from Travis Air Force Base in California. Most of that time I'd been awake, my mind racing from one thought to another as I tried to prepare myself for actually being in-country. I'd spent the winter and spring getting ready, but the minute I'd received my orders to report to Vietnam, I'd felt as if I was back at my first day in basic.

After seven uneventful weeks of AIT at Fort Lee's Quartermaster school, I was now Private First Class Brummel, Military Occupation Specialty (MOS) 76Y, Unit Supply Specialist. All of that is a fancy way of saying that I was trained in the receipt, inspection, organization, and issue of supplies and equipment. But nothing is simple in the army, and so, like every other soldier, I'd been assigned a lengthy designation to explain the fairly straightforward work I was trained for. "What's your MOS?" was a frequently-asked first question when meeting another grunt, much like "What's your sign?" in a pickup bar. It's how we identified one another. Your MOS was a clue not only to your skills, but to your suitability for friendship and even your likelihood of survival. Finding out a man was 11B, for instance, the army's code for a generic rifle-toting infantryman, let you know not to get too close, as chances were high that he wouldn't see the end of the war.

There was nothing glamorous about being a 76Y, but we were an integral part of army life. Part of the Quartermaster Corps, we were the guys everyone came to when they wanted anything, from toilet paper to small arms and ammunition, blankets for their beds to dog food for the canine patrols. I'd been steered toward quartermaster training based on my above-average performance on memorization tests and demonstrations of organizational ability during BCT, and also, I suspected, because I'd scored near the bottom of my unit in marksmanship. As one drill instructor said after watching me barely pass my required shooting test, "Don't worry, Brummel. If you can't hit the enemy, at least you'll knock the leaves off the tree he's hiding behind."

As the plane descended, I looked out the window and tried to get a glimpse of Vietnam. It was early morning, dawn a blush of orange and pink, and the glare off the wing blinded me. Then we fell through a bank of clouds and I was looking at what seemed like a checkerboard of green, the ubiquitous rice paddies I'd seen in numerous photos. They stretched for miles on either side of a dirty-brown river winding lazily through the verdant squares like a snake moving through the grass. There was movement within them, tiny dots like pinpricks.

"Doesn't look like a country where a war is going on, does it?" said the man beside me. His name, I remember, was Camper. He was a 51E, a camouflage specialist. In civilian life he'd been an artist, a painter. Now he made things disappear against the backdrop of the jungle. It was, he'd told me earlier, his second tour of duty.

"It's beautiful," I answered. "I was expecting, well, I don't know what. Not this."

"Everybody says that on their first landing," Camper said. "It's surprising what you can cover up, isn't it?"

As the plane's wheels touched the runway at Bien Hoa Air Force Base, a cheer went up from the passengers. After months of waiting, we were finally in Nam, weary from traveling and anxious to be off the plane and moving.

When I stepped out the 707's door, my first inclination was to duck. I half expected to be the target of sniper fire. Instead, what I saw was a sea of military men standing on the tarmac around the base of the metal stairs that had been pushed up to the plane, all of them grinning ear to ear. For a moment I thought they were there to welcome us. Then I realized that they were simply waiting for us to get off so that they could get on. The plane bringing us in was soon to turn around and take them out. It was their Freedom Bird, and they looked at it as if it were taking them straight to paradise.

Many of them called out words of encouragement as we walked to the main terminal, but some stared with haunted eyes, saying nothing. Their faces frightened me, and I looked away, concentrating on the back of the man in front of me. I realized that although it was morning, I was already sweating. The air was hot and moist, and it smelled like a combination of growing things, piss, and diesel fuel. We'd been told to expect rain and heat, but still I wasn't ready for the overwhelming reality of being in a foreign land. There was something in its scent that brought to mind tangles of vines and the breath of wild animals. (Years later, while visiting the National Zoo in Washington with friends, I would open the door to the primate house and be hit with a blast of air from its central enclosure, and for a brief moment think that I had once again stepped off a plane in Bien Hoa.)

Once inside, we were directed to waiting buses, which carried us down Highway 1 to the 90th Replacement Battalion. Again I was surprised at the modernity of Vietnam. The highway had four lanes and traffic lights, a far cry from the narrow dirt roads I'd expected to find. Through the metal grates welded over the windows to prevent anyone from tossing a grenade into the bus (a popular VC pastime), I did see bicycle rickshaws and people wearing *no'n ba`i thos* and *ao dais*, the traditional conical hats and tunics of Vietnam, but there were also newer model cars and advertisements for "33" beer and Ruby Queen cigarettes. My notion of Vietnam as a land solely of barefoot farmers leading water buffalo and old women selling chickens on the streets was quickly disappearing.

A thirty-minute ride brought us to the 90th Replacement. Just about every serviceman coming in or out of South Vietnam passed through the 90th, usually spending a few days in each direction. Because it was the processing center for GIs both entering and leaving, it was a place with a strange, almost schizophrenic, atmosphere, simultaneously joyous and subdued. Those of us coming in for the first time eyed the veterans with curiosity, from their mud-caked and cracked boots to the assortment of patches and pins on their fatigues and the scars on their bodies. They, in turn, tried to see reflected in us any traces of the boys they'd arrived as months before and hoped perhaps to be once again. With only a few days before they got to go home, many of them moved about the camp warily, as if trying to avoid any injury that might jeopardize their impending departure.

I used to think it peculiar that the army would allow us to meet those outgoing soldiers, on the chance that we would listen to their stories and be made afraid of what was to happen to us. I understand now that they wanted us to see them, if only so we would believe that survival was possible. In those later years of the war, incoming soldiers had read and heard much about the mounting casualties and lack of success in pushing back the North Vietnamese Army, and morale was decidedly down from the time when it appeared that victory was imminent. Whereas the men leaving Nam were sometimes disillusioned by what they'd seen and experienced during their tours of duty, those of us just arriving were often already doubtful before even spending one day in the bush. This was especially true of the reluctant draftees among us, who were some of the first men called up following the December draft. The army could do little about what exiting soldiers thought, but I think they believed that by showing us men who had survived, they could send us into battle with at least some sense that what we were doing was worthwhile, or at least bearable.

The next few days were a classic army drill of hurry up and wait. After receiving my billeting assignment and dropping my gear off in the makeshift bunkhouse (really an open-sided canvas tent filled with rows of cots), I stood in a series of lines, each of which had a specific purpose, yet were indistinguishable from one another. One line allowed me to change some of my American dollars for Vietnamese piasters, which according to the handbook I'd been given I would use to pay for services, like laundry and haircuts, rendered by locals. My remaining currency I exchanged, after a wait in a second line, for MPCs, Military Payment Certificates we were supposed to use for all other purchases, the possession of greenbacks being against military code. Another line took me to an in-country briefing, where among other things I learned how to check myself for parasites and foot rot, was warned against frequenting prostitutes, and reminded that I was in Vietnam as a guest of the government, who had requested my assistance in freeing them from the threat of Communism. More welcome was the line for the showers, which I badly needed, and the mess hall, which satisfied the ache in my belly.

In between standing in lines, I filled out more forms, performed a few shifts of KP and guard duty, and tried to sleep. At this I was mostly unsuccessful, the sounds of mortar fire in the distance keeping me from ever fully shutting down. As a result, by my third day at the 90th, I was exhausted and more than ready for a change of scenery. To my relief, that afternoon my orders came down—I was being sent to join the 81st Quartermaster Platoon at Quan Loi. I had no idea where it was, but I was glad to be going somewhere else.

I and maybe thirty other soldiers boarded a C-123 Bookie Bird, strapping ourselves into the fold-down canvas seats on either side. When the engines started, the noise was deafening, and conversation impossible. So we sat, the roar of the engines humming in our ears, as we lifted off and flew to our new home. Closing my eyes, I tried to ignore the bone-jarring bouncing of the plane and thought about my last night in San Francisco, where several of us had gone for a pre-Vietnam celebration during our two-day layover at Travis Air Force Base.

All I knew about San Francisco, which wasn't much, I'd learned from news clips and articles depicting the city as one big hippie heaven. I'd expected nothing but bearded men smoking pot and shirtless girls handing out flowers and kisses. And there were some of those, but the streets weren't overrun with them, as I'd thought they might be. Instead, I discovered the most beautiful city I'd ever seen. I was thrilled by the elaborately-painted Victorian houses, the breathtaking span of the Golden Gate Bridge, and the trolley cars that trudged up streets so precipitous I was sure we would never reach the top. Even the summer weather—so oddly cold and foggy—couldn't dampen the city's spirit

After a day spent walking around and taking in the sights, we found ourselves in Chinatown at dinnertime. Choosing a restaurant at random from among the many available, we dined on food the likes of which I'd never tasted: gloriously plump dumplings filled with ground pork, noodles topped with crisp-skinned duck, and shrimp in black bean sauce. Afterward, we made our way to a bar on the waterfront, where we drank far too many beers until, dizzy with excitement, we stumbled into the night and walked through the foggy streets back to our waiting bus.

As we crossed the Bay Bridge, I told myself that one day I would live in San Francisco. The next morning, I hastily scribbled a postcard to Andy, still at Fort Eustis, and dropped it in a mailbox. Despite being stationed less than a hundred miles from one another, we hadn't seen each other at all during AIT. I'd sent Andy a couple of letters, and he'd sent back rushed replies, but that was it. I used my postcard—a photograph of twisting, turning Lombard Street—to inform him that I was shipping out. His training program ran longer than mine, so I knew he wouldn't receive his orders for another two months. I fully expected never to hear from him again. I did not write to Jack, who now occupied little of my thoughts.

I had, as much as possible, left my past behind to begin a new life as a new man in Vietnam. Now, as I felt the plane begin to descend, I wondered what kind of life it would be.

CHAPTER 25

If I'd been surprised by Vietnam, I was completely taken aback by Quan Loi. Once the site of the French Terre Rouge Rubber Plantation, which took its name from the red dirt out of which the forest sprouted, it was a strangely beautiful place, part stark military installation and part elegant colonial outpost, complete with a mansion, gardens, and what our French hosts told us was the most beautifully constructed swimming pool in Vietnam. Monkeys watched, curious and suspicious, from the safety of palm trees, the voices of birds provided a nonstop soundtrack, and the little flop-eared mongrel dogs adopted by the soldiers slept in the sun. Except for the machinery of war that had grown up like weeds where the rubber trees once stood, it would have been a paradise in the foothills. Enough of its grandeur remained, however, that I did feel as if I'd stepped into the remnants of the Garden of Eden, its perfection marred by sin but still evident beneath the dirt and scars of battle.

Located approximately fifty miles north of Saigon and ten miles from the Cambodian border on notorious "Thunder Road" (officially National Route 13), Quan Loi was used by a number of military units, including, at various times, the Big Red One, the 1st Cavalry, and the 11th Armored Cavalry. Its 3000-foot-long airstrip, carved out of the plantation's former golf course, served a constant stream of aircraft carrying troops and supplies, and helicopters darted over the trees like dragonflies.

I quickly fell into the routine of life there. My primary assignment was the inventorying and dispersion of stores, a tedious but easy job that kept me occupied most of the time. It also had the built-in benefit of making me popular with the other soldiers, as I was in a position to do favors for them. As a result, I soon made many new friends.

The general misconception of war is that it is a thing always in motion. The truth is, life as a soldier involves long stretches of boredom punctuated by sudden bursts of activity. Although the men of Quan Loi were most definitely at war, as evidenced by the frequent sound of gunfire, the occasional mortar explosion, and the flow of troops both going into and returning from battle, we also had many days when nothing happened. On such occasions, we were like any boys itching for distraction, which we found in cards, beer, and the swapping of stories.

I arrived at Quan Loi in the middle of the annual monsoon season. The daily rains quickly turned the red dirt into mud, which caked on everything it touched and turned soldiers into warrior braves with earth-painted faces. One day in July, after I'd been in Vietnam about a month, we had five straight days of downpours. At night we lay in our hootches and listened to the rat-a-tat-tat of drops on the corrugated metal walls, the sound reminiscent of gunfire and therefore anything but soothing. By day, we trudged through the soupy mud, performing our duties with mute resignation.

I was counting boxes of bootlaces when I was interrupted by the sound of helicopters cutting through the drone of rain. Shortly thereafter, the sergeant in charge of my platoon came in.

"Brummel, do you have any mortuary training?"

"No, sir."

"Well, you're about to get some. Come with me."

I put down my clipboard and followed him out into the rain. He walked toward a large building that had previously been used to store equipment for the plantation. It had since been turned into a Graves Registration Point, where the remains of soldiers killed in action were brought for identification and processing. Although we all knew what happened there, we seldom spoke about it, believing it to be bad luck.

"An infantry unit got into some fire with Charlie up around Loc Ninh," the sergeant told me as he pushed aside the plastic sheet covering the building's door and we stepped inside. "About two dozen of them went down."

The room was large, with a concrete floor and several metal tables against one wall. Three soldiers lay on the tables, their hands at their sides. Anyone glancing at them quickly would have thought them asleep, but a closer examination would have revealed the holes in their greens and the torn flesh where bullets had entered.

"Our refrig units can only accommodate ten bodies," said the sergeant as I tried not to look at the dead men. "With this rain and the heat, the guys we can't chill are going to turn ripe in no time. We've got to get them IDed, cleaned up, and out of here ASAP."

"But I don't know anything about . . ." I began to say.

"Watson here will show you everything you need to know," the sergeant said, interrupting me and nodding at a soldier who had just come in, a short, stocky man with red hair and a missing front tooth. "He's been doing this a long time. I'll leave you boys to get to work."

He left me alone with Watson, who said, "First time with GR?"

I nodded. He smiled grimly. "You'll get used to it," he said as he handed me an apron, gloves, and a surgical mask. "Besides, these boys need someone to look after them."

The care of the dead is an art, one I was introduced to that afternoon by a master. Lloyd "Digger" Watson was a third-generation mortician from Louisiana, a quiet man with a wry sense of humor and a love for death that at first frightened me, but which eventually I came to see not as an obsession but as a rare gift. He was on his second tour in Vietnam, having enlisted voluntarily after his only brother was killed during the Tet Offensive.

"When I saw the job they did on Bonner, I told my daddy I was going to make sure nobody else came home to their family looking like that," he told me as he prepared to lead me through my first experience with a dead body.

The soldier was a private, an infantryman whose dog tags revealed him to be Nicholas Betz, age 19. His clean-shaven face was perfectly intact, the eyes closed and the lips slightly parted. I helped Digger remove his clothing, at which point the single bullet hole in his chest was revealed. Digger ran his fingers over the ragged skin.

"They don't usually look this good," he told me. "This was a clean kill. He'll be a quick one."

He handed me a washcloth and together we cleaned the dirt and blood from Private Betz's body. It felt unnatural, bathing a corpse. The limbs were already stiffening, and Digger had to show me how to massage the lifeless muscles to loosen the grip of death. In order to calm the churning in my stomach, I told myself that the body wasn't real, that we were simply playacting. I couldn't accept that the young man whose body I tended was unable to feel any of our ministrations, that he would never again enjoy the touch of another human's hands.

The next step in the process required even more pretending on my part. Digger inserted two needles into the boy's neck, one into an artery for the insertion of embalming fluid and another into a vein for the draining of blood, which emptied into one of the big sinks behind the tables. As the crimson stream trickled out, Digger continued to massage the body, evenly distributing the fluids. I stood a few feet away, unable to bring myself to touch the corpse.

"You can't be afraid," he said, sensing my hesitation. "I think they know when you're scared of them. You have to tell them it's okay."

I thought he was crazy. The thing on the table was dead meat, I thought to myself, nothing but a collection of tissues and bones and now-useless organs. It couldn't hear, or feel, or understand what was happening to it. But if that was true, I argued, then why was I so afraid to touch it? Why did the sight of the dead soldier bother me so intensely?

"You've never been around the dead, have you?" Digger asked. He didn't wait for an answer, continuing to talk as he worked. "Maybe they don't speak out loud, but they still have a lot to say. It's our job to listen."

He turned to me. "Every body has a story. It's up to you to read it."

His strange pronouncements were making me even more upset. I felt like an intruder into a world where I had no business being. I wanted to be back with my boxes and lists, where all I had to do was count and record. Death was not something I wished to catalog or inventory. But Digger was unmoved by my discomfort. He indicated the body on the second table. "Why don't you start on him while I do this," he said. "You just collect their things and wash them. I'll handle the rest."

Grateful for at least not having to watch the draining and filling of Nicholas Betz, I moved to the middle table. Looking at the form on the clipboard Digger gave to me, I began filling in what I could: name (Hector Means), age (23), serial number (US67762419), and religion (Catholic). Then I began to remove his clothing, searching the pockets for personal items before folding the garments neatly and setting them on a chair beside the table. Every item was noted on the form, and soon I felt more at ease as I fell into the familiar rhythm of making lists.

I put into a plastic bag a wristwatch, Zippo lighter, and wallet containing sixty dollars in military scrip and a photo of Hector standing with his arm around a young Asian woman.

"Looks like he had himself a girlfriend," said Digger, coming over to check on my progress and seeing the photo in my hand. He then looked at the form. "He's one of McNamara's boys."

"One of his what?" I asked.

Digger pointed at the serial number. "He's a US67. They only give that designation to guys drafted under Project 100,000. It's this program McNamara set up to draft guys who couldn't pass the military's intelligence test. This guy must have really wanted to fight."

I looked at Hector's face. Part of it was missing, a big chunk just below his right eye. The bones of his cheek were exposed, some shards of teeth visible through the tangle of skin. Below his navel was another wound, this one uglier and rawer, probably the one from which he'd died. I looked back at Digger, who had inserted a trocar into Private Betz's abdominal cavity and was (I would learn this later, when my ability to stomach the process was more certain) puncturing the soft organs to be sucked out and replaced with more embalming fluid.

"You mean he was basically too stupid to join?" I asked.

"More or less," Digger answered. "McNamara says it's a way for the less-fortunate to still contribute to the fight. If you ask me, I say it's more like a good way to get a lot of boys who don't know any better to get themselves killed. I bet you at least half a dozen of the guys stacked out there are US67s."

He was right. As the day progressed into night and we made our way through the bodies waiting to be tended to, I counted seven men whose serial numbers began with the US67 designation. Each time I saw it, I looked at the soldier's face and wondered what it was that had driven him to enter the army. I couldn't imagine wanting so badly to fight that you would do anything to be given the chance. Even more, I couldn't imagine allowing these men to go to war.

We finished in the early hours of the morning. When we were done, twenty-six bodies were ready for transport to the main mortuary at Tan Son Nhut, ten of them in the refrigeration units and sixteen lined up on the floor in an adjoining room. We'd placed bags of ice over the ones too destroyed for proper embalming, covering them as much as possible to prevent decomposition. They would have to be seen to at the much more fully-staffed central collection facility. We'd done the best we could.

"Not bad for your first time," Digger said as we removed our blood-ied gloves and aprons. "Sorry to drag you in here. My assistant shipped out last week and they haven't lined up a replacement yet."

"It's okay," I told him. "I got used to it. Well, sort of used to it."

Digger laughed. "Enough to come back?"

I looked at him as he took a cigarette from a pack in his pocket, lit it, and took a drag. He blew a perfect smoke ring and watched it dissi-pate before continuing. "I could use you here," he said.

I hesitated. One day of GR duty was one thing, but doing it full time was something else. I didn't know if I could handle it.

"It's not like it's every day," Digger said. "Only when the war heats up and we get a delivery."

"Just like fucking Christmas," I said.

"Think about it," said Digger. "Let me know. If you can do it, I'll get your assignment rearranged."

I promised to think about it and said good night. When I walked outside, I discovered that the rain had slowed to a light drizzle. The sun, barely visible, had already heated up the air so that the com-pound was shrouded in a slow-crawling mist that rose to knee height. Walking through it, I felt like Charon crossing the river Styx, ferrying the dead to the other side.

After a quick shower to wash the stink of formaldehyde from my skin and a shot of Scotch to get the taste of blood out of my throat, I threw myself into my bunk for some much-needed rest. Around me, some men were getting ready for the day, while others, returning from night patrol or other graveyard shift duties, were just coming in. Ignoring the conversations around me, I closed my eyes.

Sleep didn't come. Instead, I was visited by the dead. One by one they appeared, standing naked before me, holding the plastic bags containing their belongings in their hands. Their wounds were cleaned, the bullet holes stitched closed, and the ends of missing limbs wrapped in gauze. The violence done to them was, as much as possible, erased, so that when their loved ones received them they would see as little of it as possible. That much we could do for them.

The last one to come was Hector Means. He stood there mutely, his bag held over his genitals. He looked like an overgrown child, shy and uncertain. The terrible head wound was bound up, the hole in his abdomen sutured together with Digger's careful stitches. Looking at him, I imagined him at home, before the war. Had he been loved? Would someone be waiting for him when his plane landed? I thought about the girl in the photograph. It was likely she would never even know he was dead. Had he loved her? Had he told her so, and had she responded in kind?

The stories of Hector Means and the other twenty-five men Digger and I had processed (I hated that word, with its connotations of canning and rendering) were now ended. We had helped write the final chapter. It was, I realized, a weighty responsibility, the gathering up and readying of the dead. I'd begun the job seeing those soldiers as lifeless remains. Now I saw them as sacrifices worthy of remembrance. More than just names and serial numbers on dog tags, they were brothers and husbands, fathers and lovers. Their deaths would, I hoped, mean something to someone beyond being mere casualty statistics. They were men, and they were soldiers, and they needed someone to see them home.

I knew that I would tell Digger yes. I'd come to Vietnam looking for something to change me, and I'd found it in a most unexpected place. The dead, I believed, had much to teach me, if only I would listen.

CHAPTER 26

"How did he die?" It seems a simple enough question. And often the given answer is equally simple. "He was shot." "He had a heart attack." "He fell from a great height."

But those are not true answers; they are merely shorthand for the truth. "He had a heart attack," for instance, doesn't begin to describe the process by which the cells of one of the heart muscles, deprived of oxygen due most often to the presence of a thrombus in the coronary artery, die, forcing the remaining muscles to overcompensate and, ultimately, fail. Similarly, death from a "broken neck" is an inadequate but perhaps less distressing way of explaining that when injury occurs to any of the eight cervical vertebrae that comprise the top of the spinal column, resulting in damage to the delicate cord they surround and protect, death may occur either by asphyxiation (if the injury occurs at the fifth vertebrae or above, resulting in loss of breath control), or (if the spinal cord is severely injured or transected at any point) a sudden and severe drop in blood pressure as the nervous system is rendered inoperable.

While this shorthand allows us to ignore the less pleasant physical aspects of death and dying, it also fails to acknowledge the surprising number of ways in which human life can be extinguished. As I spent more and more time with Digger, learning what there was to know about the preservation of bodies, I also learned much about how those bodies came to be dead. Die is, after all, a verb, and therefore an action. To die is to be a participant in a series of changes, some of them amazingly complex, that bring about an interruption of the normal processes of life. That this action results in total inaction is possibly the ultimate example of linguistic irony.

There was on the form we filled out for each body a place where we were asked to list the cause of death. We dutifully filled in these blanks with the requested answers—mortar fire, gunshot, bayonet wound—but between us we discussed the more precise reasons. Although he had only basic medical training, Digger was a deeply-knowledgeable student of thanatology. He understood death's methods and means, and his careful attention to the bodies that passed through our doors was due in equal parts to his firm belief that every man deserved to be treated respectfully and to his constant desire to learn more. The arrival of an 18-year-old with fatal shrapnel wounds caused by the faulty placement of a Claymore mine (a tragedy made even more absurd by the fact that the mines are clearly labeled FRONT TOWARD ENEMY) presented him with an opportunity to observe firsthand the effects of uniformly-sized lead shot tearing through human flesh and bone at high speed. A body fished from a river two days after death was a lesson in the ability of water and the native fishes to transform a man's face into something unrecognizable.

Digger was less interested in the cataloging of the personal effects that were found on the bodies, and so we often worked in tandem. While he attended to the corpses, I attended to what remained of their lives. More often than not, though, Digger talked as he worked, describing his discoveries and outlining his theories about them in detail. I, in turn, told him what I found in the pockets and rucksacks of the men whose wounds he was exploring. As a result, we often assembled quite a full—if not entirely verifiable—picture of the soldiers whose remains had been delivered into our hands.

The things men carry into war say much about who they are. There are the obvious: photos of loved ones, religious talismans, love letters from girlfriends and wives. I removed dozens of these items from pockets and wallets, so many that I was more surprised on the occasions when I did not find them. More interesting were the objects that appeared unexpectedly. One soldier had tucked into a pants pocket a PEZ dispenser featuring the head of Bullwinkle the Moose, the chamber still half full of candy. Another wore around his wrist a bracelet made of the metal pieces taken from a Monopoly game: the tiny shoe, dog, wheelbarrow, cannon, and others linked together on a length of plain white string. A third had in his chest pocket a small envelope containing a lock of coarse dark hair tied with a pink ribbon and a picture of the soldier standing beside a chestnut-colored horse.

I wondered about these things, these charms and tokens. Were they simply reminders of lives left behind, small beacons of light meant to guide the soldiers back? Or did the men ascribe to them some level of magical power, some supernatural ability to grant protection against harm? If so, what did it mean that they had failed? Was it the fault of the magic, or had the faith of the makers or wearers in their potency been lacking? As I put these items into the bags, along with the eyeglasses, watches, and wedding bands, I marveled at the ways in which men put their faith in something apart from their guns and their fellow soldiers. The army had taught us all to depend only on our skills and on our teamwork, but here was evidence that most of us needed something more.

I wondered what the North Vietnamese soldiers carried with them, if they, too, had pockets filled with letters and photographs and small gifts pressed into their hands by loved ones in the hopes that they would bring luck and protection. I imagined my NVA counterpart checking the clothes of his fallen comrades and sorting the bits and pieces of their lives into bags and envelopes to be delivered to grieving families. We were both, it seemed to me, the historians of death.

In August my 20th birthday passed, but I didn't remember until three days after, when I was checking an inventory sheet and realized that it was the 14th and that I had left my teenage years behind without celebrating. That night, Digger and some of my other buddies threw me a makeshift party in an underground bunker, complete with Carling Black Label beer on ice and the Rolling Stones on the turntable. My present was a pack of Marlboros that contained not regular cigarettes but enormous joints filled with Hanoi Gold. Each one was exactly the size and shape of a normal cigarette, but the pot inside was more potent than any North Carolina burley tobacco could ever hope to be. After just three hits I was gone, and the rest of the evening was a hazy dream of laughing, drinking, and swapping dirty jokes with my friends. A far cry from the cozy birthday parties I used to share with Jack. It was a celebration of men, and I felt very grown-up indeed.

I felt less so the next morning, when I woke up in my own hootch with a pounding headache and a mouth tasting of stale beer and ash.

Slowly I realized that some of the drumming was actually the sound of rain hitting the walls and roof, and the prospect of another wet, muddy day did nothing to improve my mood. I rolled over, tried to go back to sleep, then gave up when I heard the roar of a plane coming in for a landing. Groaning and trying not to move my head too much, I got up and pulled on my clothes.

When I reached the GR building, Digger was already at work on a body. Even from the door, I could tell that there was something unusual about it. The skin was discolored, and the smell in the air was stronger than usual. I coughed, and Digger looked back at me.

"You've got to see this," he said as I walked toward the table. "But you're going to want the Vicks."

I stopped and took the jar of Vicks VapoRub from the table on which we stored some of our tools. Opening it, I used my finger to scoop some out and dab it under my nose. Instantly the menthol-camphor scent filled my head, opening my sinuses and erasing not only the peculiar stench in the air but the remaining scent of beer and hash. Normally I hated the stuff, as I associated it with having to do particularly unpleasant work, but that morning it was a welcome relief.

My nose girded, I approached Digger and the body he was peering at intently. He moved aside, and I saw that it was a fairly small man. His skin, what there was left of it, was covered in a viscous black substance that looked like tar or burned sugar. I'd never seen anything like it before, and looked questioningly at Digger.

"Napalm," he said.

"Holy shit," I said. "Is he one of our guys?"

Digger shook his head. "Vietnamese," he answered. "But he's a local. Used to help our guys out as a guide."

I'd seen napalm used before, and had been impressed by its ability to burn down everything it touched. I'd witnessed huge chunks of forest reduced to blackened stumps in a matter of minutes. But I'd never seen its effects on a human body before. Looking at the charred corpse in front of me, I couldn't even imagine what his death must have been like.

"You know all those saints and martyrs and witches and whatnot they burned at the stake back in the Middle Ages?" asked Digger as he scraped at some of the black substance on the man's abdomen. It fell away, revealing a raw window of a hole, the view through which made my stomach lurch.

"Yeah," I answered, not understanding what the question had to do with anything.

"If they were lucky, they had themselves a big roaring fire," Digger continued, examining an area on the man's left thigh. "A big fire with lots of smoke. That way, the carbon monoxide knocked them out right away and they died before the fire did too much damage."

"And if they weren't lucky?"

"Then they ended up like this guy," he said. "A small fire and a slow death. Lots of pain." He stopped prodding the man's skin and stepped back so that I could view the full extent of the damage done to his body.

"Steel melts at 2400 degrees," Digger told me. "Napalm burns at something between 1800 and 3600 degrees, depending on what you use to ignite it. It sticks to everything, so once it's on you, you can't get away from it. It only stops once it's burned itself out."

"And by then you're dead," I said.

"That's the kicker," said Digger. "Usually, you're not. You're just burned. It hurts like a son of a bitch, but you think maybe you'll live. Burns are funny like that. Unless they're really bad, you don't die right away. But what happens is, over the next couple of days you lose a lot of blood mass while your body tries to heal itself. And if you still don't die, then it starts eating up the infected parts and putting it all back into your blood, so you die that way."

"You think he lived a few days?" I asked.

Digger sighed. "I know he did. He and his buddy were out in the jungle doing God knows what, got surprised by a napalm burn the boys were doing around a place they thought the NVA might be using as a camp. He got splashed, but his buddy didn't. His friend got him away from the smoke, but he couldn't do anything about the burns. He held out four days. If you ask me, his buddy would have done him a favor to leave him in there."

"What can we do for him?"

"Not much. Clean him up a little. Get the worst of the gunk off. It's more to show his wife and kids that he was a kind of hero than anything else."

I looked around the room for any other bodies. "What else have we got?" I asked Digger.

"He's it for now," he answered. "You want to skip this one? It's okay."

I looked at the dead man. I did want to leave. The savagery done to him by the napalm was terrible to see, worse somehow than the usual gunshot wounds and even the grisly results of a mine or mortar hit. His body was simply blackened, the skin cracked like the skin of a roasted animal. I imagined him praying for death and wondering why it wouldn't come.

"I'll stay," I told Digger.

Together we washed the body, careful not to do further damage to the skin. Digger was right that there wasn't much we could do, but still I felt better as we cleaned away at least some of the napalm's black kisses. No one looking at the body would ever believe the man had died of anything other than unnatural causes, but in some small way I felt we were giving him back at least a little of his humanity by treating him as more than just a burned husk.

Digger was showing me how to stitch up the worst of the open wounds when I heard a voice behind us say, "They told me I'd find you in here. When did you turn into Doctor Frankenstein?"

Hearing something familiar in the voice, I turned around. Andy stood just inside the door, shit-eating grin on his face.

"What?" he said. "Aren't you glad to see me?"

"What are you doing here?" I asked him, still not really believing it was him and not some hallucination brought about by the combination of hash, beer, Vicks, and scent of burned flesh coursing through my blood.

"Reporting for duty," Andy said. "They needed a helo mechanic, and I'm the best one around."

He walked closer, peering at the body on the table. "What's that, lunch?" he joked, laughing heartily. I saw Digger turn away and busy himself with something on the table. I was embarrassed by Andy's lack of compassion, and made a note to apologize to Digger later.

"Why don't I show you around when I'm done," I suggested to Andy.

"Great," he said. "I just got in an hour or so ago. When I heard you were here, I came to look you up. I haven't even found my hootch yet."

I remembered the sound of the plane that had woken me up. Andy must have been on it, I realized. If I'd known, would I have been there to meet him?

"I'll finish up here," Digger said before I could answer that question. "You introduce your buddy to Hotel Frenchie."

"Thanks, Dig," I said. "I'll see you later."

Andy and I walked out into a steamy soup of a morning. The rain had stopped, but the air was still heavy and wet. Andy gamely marched through the mud like a kid after a rainstorm, looking around at everything.

"You guys see a lot of action?" he asked me.

"Enough," I told him.

"Good," he said. "The last thing I want to do is sit around on my ass all day. I didn't sign up for that."

"You'll be busy," I assured him. "A lot of slicks come in and out of here."

"I'm putting my name in for door gunner," said Andy. "I like fixing the birds, but I'd rather be shooting at Charlie. You had any kills yet?"

I shook my head. "I'm mainly in the GR or stores," I said. "I do my share of patrols, but so far they've been clean."

"Too bad," said Andy, sounding genuinely sorry for me. Then he asked, "So, what's the pussy situation up here?"

"The what?" I said.

"You know," said Andy, grabbing his crotch and squeezing. "Me love you long time."

"Oh," I replied. "There's not much of that as far as I can tell. Guys usually wait 'til they've got R&R."

"Shit," he said. "I'm fucking horny as hell. I had this hot little grunt groupie while I was at Eustis, but she up and married some jarhead last month. I haven't had any since."

I knew what he was asking. He wouldn't come out and say it, but I could tell he was thinking about our times at Penn. I knew I should just ignore him, let him think I had no idea what he was hinting around at. But the truth was, I hadn't had any in a long time either. I'd more or less buried those feelings in the red mud of Quan Loi. But Andy's reappearance had stirred them up again.

"You want to see my hootch?" I asked him after calculating the chances of my bunkmates being on duty and finding them high enough to chance it.

Andy grinned. "Lead the way," he said.

As I'd suspected, the hootch was empty. It didn't take long before Andy's pants were around his ankles and I was on my knees, taking him into my throat. My back was to the door, and I knew that at any moment, one of my roomies could walk in and find me sucking Andy's cock. It was a foolish risk to take, but I was driven by a need more intense than the fear of discovery. I needed to claim Andy once more, and this was the only way I knew how to do it. I told myself, as I had so many times before, that his pretense of casualness was a distraction for the feelings he couldn't express. What was important was that he'd come back to me.

He came quickly, and as I felt his dick throb with the heavy pulse of release, I was surprised to find myself coming as well. I hadn't even touched my cock, yet I was emptying a load into my pants. With nowhere else to go, the stickiness slid down my shaft, coating it with wet heat. Unexpectedly, my thoughts flashed back to the night seven years before when I'd come in my pajamas while sleeping next to Jack.

Andy pulled out of my mouth and zipped himself up. Still slightly dazed by both my orgasm and the conflicting memories it brought with it, I was slower in getting to my feet. I had just stood when the door to the hootch opened and two soldiers entered.

"Hey, Ned," one of them said. "Who's your buddy?"

"Oh," I said. "This is Ja—, um, Andy. We were in basic together."

Andy nodded. My bunkmates welcomed him as they would any new arrival, oblivious to my disorientation. Andy, too, seemed unaware of my momentary confusion. He clapped me on the shoulder and said, "I should go check in. I'll see you later, okay?"

"Sure," I said. "Later."

After he left, I sat down on my bunk, listening to my roommates talk but hearing nothing. The warmth in my pants quickly turned to an uncomfortable coldness as the cum dried and glued my cock to the hair of my legs. When I moved, tiny fingers of pain pinched and scratched at me as the matted hair separated from my skin. But the taste of Andy was still in my mouth, and that made me forget everything else.

CHAPTER 27

There is a phenomenon familiar to anyone who works with the dead in which a corpse will arrive with, or depending on how much time has elapsed since death, develop during examination, an erection. This can be unsettling to the uninitiated. You do not, after all, generally expect the deceased to display an inclination toward the erotic. But they sometimes do. The cause has no supernatural origins; it is simply the result of pooling blood settling in the genitals. Morticians, in a wonderful display of black humor, call it angel lust.

This is the effect that Andy had on me. Having buried my desires out of necessity, I found them resurrected again, against my will, by his presence. I was at first a reluctant participant in my own delusion, stubbornly refusing to admit that I wanted him. Once roused, however, my need grew in strength until I was thinking about him almost constantly. He, of course, responded by pretending to be completely unaware of my love for him. As he had in college, he came to me when he needed release, but withheld any real affection.

He was quickly welcomed into base life, becoming a favorite almost immediately and making friends with anyone who came into contact with him. His work on the slicks was first rate, and did not go unnoticed by his superiors. After a month, he got his wish and began training to be a door gunner, and a few weeks later he flew his first mission. When he returned, he had the elated, almost frightening, glow of a hunter whose foray into the woods has been most successful.

"You should have seen it, Ned," he told me that night over a beer in the enlisted men's club. "Those chinks were running like roaches, man, and I was just firing away. It was like one of those games at a carnival. Bam. Bam. Bam. We've got a winner, here's your teddy bear."

"They're not chinks," I told him.

"Gooks. Chinks. Slants. It's all the same to me," he said, missing my dig at his geographic misstep. "If it's yellow, I shoot it."

The door opened and a couple of Andy's new chopper buddies came in. They sat down at our table and immediately started talking about their day. I listened, nursing my beer, and wondered how I could want a man like Andy, who didn't seem to see that I was in love with him and, worse, who seemed to have become a man who derived pleasure from killing. Was this the same man I'd talked philosophy with only nine months earlier? It hardly seemed possible.

And what was wrong with me that I wanted to be with him? As I listened to him talk, I tried to pinpoint it, but the best I could come up with was that I wanted to save him. I was convinced that underneath the cocky, self-absorbed exterior there was a man of real merit. The bravado was an act, one many men in the army employed to cover up their more vulnerable selves. Andy, I told myself, was one of them. If I could just reach him, he might become the man he needed to be. What I meant, of course, was that he might become the man that I needed him to be. But it would take me many years to realize that, and in the meantime I was fated to long for something that was just out of reach.

A soldier is a natural object of attraction. Strong, confident, and masculine, he's easy fodder for the imagination. The possibility of death only sweetens the deal. Those of us attracted to tragedy (and I believe many gay men are included in this group, as evidenced by our fondness for the likes of Judy, Marilyn, and other stars whose lives ended badly and with whom we are so intimate that we call them by their first names) find in the soldier the romantic ideal. If he finds it difficult to love us in return, we forgive him and ascribe it to his need to protect us from the eventuality of his death.

That night of his first kill, Andy committed another first, making love to me in the deserted storeroom housing boxes of ammunition and cartons of oil. He was brutal, quick, and hungry, pumping into me while his dog tags jangled against his chest and his hands gripped my waist. After he emptied himself inside me, he zipped up and left, using as an excuse an early-morning flight time. When he was gone, I jerked off furiously, telling myself that he'd taken one step closer to admitting his love for me.

What is it about the unobtainable that we find so irresistible? You might as well ask why we think if we just try hard enough, we can pluck the moon from the sky. We know the effort is futile, yet we put it forth anyway, without the smallest shred of evidence that we have a hope of succeeding. Like religion, we believe in it with absolutely no hard proof.

St. Clare of Assisi, founder of the ascetic order of Poor Clare nuns, refused marriage and, at 18, entered a convent. Devoting herself to the eternal adoration of the Divine, she wrote what can only be considered love poems to God. In one of her four celebrated letters to Blessed Agnes of Prague (the former Princess Agnes of Bohemia, and Clare's patroness) she described her most fervent desire, to be one with Christ:

> *Draw me after You!*
> *We will run in the fragrance of Your perfumes,*
> *O heavenly Spouse!*
> *I will run and not tire,*
> *until You bring me into the wine-cellar,*
> *until Your left hand is under my head*
> *and Your right hand will embrace me happily*
> *and You will kiss me with the happiest kiss of Your mouth.*

Clare's infatuation with what she could never truly have may indeed be purely metaphoric (although her clearly-imagined fantasy rivals that of any letter written by a 14-year-old fan to her favorite pop star), but her passion is unmistakable. And whether God or man is the focus of such fierce faith, nothing is as strong or as torturous. I saw past Andy's faults to the man I believed existed behind them. I projected onto him everything I wanted, but hadn't yet fully articulated to myself.

As the days passed and we reached the latter part of the year, the rains ended and the sun returned, drying the mud into rock-hard brick. The temperatures fell, although they remained much higher than anything I was used to experiencing in the fall, and warm enough that we spent many of the afternoons cooling off in Frenchman's Pool. Watching the men jump from the high dive into the water and splash one another in good-natured games, I was reminded of Treasure Island and the three summers Jack and I had spent there. I hadn't had a word from him since his letter in June, which I hadn't responded to, and bit by bit I was coming to accept that our friendship was over.

In October, following a week of intense skirmishes with the NVA during which Digger and I spent long hours in the GR, we celebrated Halloween with an impromptu party. The most popular costume, unsurprisingly, was a Viet Cong soldier, complete with actual items taken from the bodies of the downed enemy. These items, taken as souvenirs by men who mostly didn't know any better, lent an unintentionally macabre touch to the night, which was made even more sinister when a grenade, hurled out of the darkness, hit a hootch, sending dirt and metal into the air and causing all of us to fall on our faces, hands over our heads as we'd been taught in basic training.

When the rain of earth stopped, we got up to survey the damage. Fortunately, the hootch's occupants had not been inside, and the only casualty was the building itself. But we took the attack personally, and moments later, weapons in hand, we were looking for the perpetrators. We found them—a group of sappers—still making their way through the field of concertina wire on the camp's southeast perimeter. The grenade had been thrown by an antsy scout as a distraction, but he'd thrown too early, and we caught the enemy soldiers with fifteen yards left to go.

They were sitting targets. Trapped beneath the razor-sharp wire, the harsh lights of the guard tower turned on them, they had nowhere to go. All they could do was return fire and hope we missed. The air was filled with the sounds of a hundred M16s firing at once, the angry cries of soldiers wreaking revenge, and the muted sounds of bodies being pierced by bullets. Not one of the sappers screamed; they died silently, just as they'd come.

Beside me, Andy was firing repeatedly. I saw him take aim at a soldier attempting to turn around in the nest of wire. A moment later, the man's head exploded in a spray of blood.

"Pink mist, baby!" Andy shouted, pumping his fist. "Pink mist. That's what it's all about." He high-fived the man next to him and looked for another target.

It was over quickly. Afterward, a call went out for volunteers to drag the dead out. In general, the handling of North Vietnamese casualties was avoided as much as possible. Although officially we were supposed to collect any recoverable bodies and deliver them to Vietnamese officials, in reality we usually left them where they fell. Exceptions were made when their presence would result in inconvenience to U.S. troops. Faced with the prospect of a yard full of rotting NVA, we had no choice but to retrieve them.

I stepped forward, along with a handful of other men, and we began the tricky process of removing the bodies from their wire coffins. It was difficult work. The wire, designed to trap anything foolish enough to walk into it, was hardly a hindrance to the sappers, who had made an art out of learning how to crawl through it both unheard and uncut, but for us it required patience and care. Even then, we frequently felt the sting of the sharp-edged wire as we parted it with gloved hands.

I pulled out two men and went back for a third. Positioned toward the rear of the group, he was lying on his stomach. Blood had pooled around him, suggesting a belly wound, and his gun was a foot or two from his body. Stepping on the concertina wire to flatten it down, I made it to him and knelt down. I didn't want to drag him face-first over the wire, so I grabbed his wrists and flipped him over.

"Chieu hoi," he said, looking up at me with pleading eyes. *"Chieu hoi."*

"I surrender." It was a phrase seldom heard, as the soldiers of the NVA were trained to fight to the death. But American forces had been blanketing the country with leaflets promising amnesty for those who surrendered voluntarily, and occasionally someone took us up on the offer.

I looked into the man's face. He was young, just a man, and he was frightened. The bullet he'd taken had opened him up, and the front of his shirt carried a wide, wet stain. Still, I thought there might be a chance for him. We had any number of trained medics in camp, and with a little luck, the soldier might live to see his family again. I turned around and shouted for help getting him out as quickly as possible.

Two men answered my call, one a newly-arrived private and one a sergeant on his third tour of duty.

"He's still alive," I said. "Help me get him out."

The younger man knelt and started to help me lift the wounded soldier. The sergeant, however, said, "Put him down, boys."

I looked up at him. "But he's alive," I said.

"Put him down," the sergeant repeated.

I exchanged a glance with the young man, and we did as we'd been ordered. The sergeant nodded at me. "You found him. He's yours."

I didn't understand what he meant. Then he pointed at the rifle still slung across my back, and I knew. "He surrendered," I said, thinking perhaps the sergeant didn't realize what the situation was.

"*Chieu hoi,*" the man said weakly, reinforcing my statement.

"He's a VC sapper," the sergeant countered. "They don't surrender."

By then a small group of soldiers had gathered around us to see what was going on. Andy was among them, and I saw him watching me as I argued with the sergeant. "But . . ." I said, trying again.

"They *don't* surrender," the sergeant repeated. "Now take your kill, soldier."

I could feel the eyes of my fellow soldiers on me, their collective desire to bring the moment to an end forging itself into a red-hot fire. I knew I wasn't going to win. Also, I wasn't entirely sure the sergeant was wrong. The man was an enemy. My enemy. *Our* enemy. He'd come there to kill, and only accident had turned him from hunter to hunted. If our roles were reversed, I told myself, he would show me no mercy.

I lifted my rifle and pressed the tip of the barrel to the injured man's forehead. As I looked into his face, I saw his eyelids flutter. At first I thought it was his reaction to what he must know was imminent death. Then I realized that he truly was dying at that moment. His lips parted and his chest fell one final time as his wound took its toll.

Focused on me, nobody else noticed that he was gone. I hesitated for an instant, then pulled the trigger, firing a bullet into the man's brain. His body jumped and then was still. The sergeant clapped me on the back.

"Now get him out of here," he said.

I searched for Andy and found him. He was looking at me with an expression of approval and respect. I nodded once at him, then bent to pick up the soldier's body, my heart a bird in flight.

CHAPTER 28

After the death of the Vietnamese soldier, Andy treated me differently, as if the man had been a sacrifice I made to the gods in exchange for his attentions. I was now included in conversations about his missions, which increased as his prowess with the gun was proven time and again. His friends became my friends, and soon soldiers who'd barely spoken to me before that October night were calling me by name. I'd become a member of their fraternity, a society of brothers united not simply because we were soldiers, but because we'd seen combat.

That it was all based on a lie bothered me, mostly at night, when the soldier's face came to me and I heard his voice, soft and begging in my ear. Then I couldn't hide from the fact that I had shot a dead man. Would I have pulled the trigger if he had still been alive? I told myself I would have, but that was hardly better. I'd killed, twice, a man with no means of defending himself. The fact that he was an enemy changed nothing.

But the mind has a way of saving us from our devils, and mine rescued me by slowly changing the story, until after repeated tellings I convinced myself that I'd done my duty as a U.S. Army soldier and nothing more. When I reached a point where I could believe that without effort, I stopped thinking about it at all and simply enjoyed the status the incident earned me with Andy. We were spending more and more time together, much of it in bed when we could manage it and in any available spot when we couldn't. We made love inside bunkers, behind sandbags, and, once, in the belly of Andy's chopper while the rest of the crew slept off the weariness of a retrieval mission that had ended in five casualties.

The holidays came and went. We had a turkey dinner at Thanks-giving, and at Christmas we decorated a palm tree with shell casings painted red and green. On Christmas morning, before the slicks took off on their assignments, one of the sergeants dressed up as Santa and handed out presents. Andy and I each received a week of R&R in Vung Tau, which we took three weeks later.

Located on the southeast coast of Vietnam, Vung Tau is a beautiful seaside resort, a crooked finger of land dipping into the warm waters of the South China Sea. Once the base for Malay pirates who roamed the coastline in search of prey, it was given to the soldiers who liber-ated it from the bandits and became a destination for the wealthy fam-ilies of Saigon. In 1971, at the time of our visit, it was the base of operations for both the U.S. and the Royal Australian Army support units, and as such was a popular location for in-country R&R.

Anything you wanted could be had in Vung Tau. A thriving industry had sprung up to service the troops, and the many shops and bars that lined the streets served up everything from hash to pho, whiskey to women. As we walked downtown on our first day, one little boy after another came up to us with an offer, mostly for drugs or sex with a sis-ter, each one of whom was described as a "number-one cherry girl." We declined, until finally one young fellow, not more than nine years old, was so persistent in his offers of assistance that we agreed to hire him as a guide for the day at the exorbitant rate of two dollars.

His name, he told us in surprisingly good English, was Duc, and Andy immediately decided to call him Donny, which the boy accepted with good humor. "Mickey Mouse's friend," he said. "Quack-quack."

Duc proved to be a fine guide. He suggested we rent a scooter, even haggling over the price for us. With Andy driving, me seated be-hind him, and Duc standing on the running board, we took the grand tour. Duc provided running commentary all the way, pointing out the various temples and shrines for which Vung Tau was known, and throwing in a bit of history while he was at it.

"That is Bach Dinh, the White Mansion," he informed us as we drove by an imposing house. "Than Thai, the crazy emperor, he locked up there by the French long time ago. And there is Lighthouse Moun-tain. An American lives there. Two kids my age. Sometimes we play in the tunnels under the mountain and sit on the big guns on top."

We drove the long, winding road around the peninsula, coming to stop at one of the city's famous beaches, where we bought *bate gan* from a roadside stall. As we ate the pork-filled dumplings, Duc pointed to the mountain rising behind us.

"Nui Long," he said, his mouth full of pork. "Large Mountain. After we eat we go up and see Thich Ca Phat Dai pagoda."

"What's that, Donny?" asked Andy. "And why do we want to see it?"

"Shrine to Buddha," Duc explained. "Very famous statue of Buddha sitting on lotus. And over there," he said, pointing in the opposite direction, "Nui Nho. Small Mountain."

"What's that on top?" I asked, looking at a peculiar shape rising from the mountain's summit. It looked like the lower half of a standing figure.

"Jesus," Duc said, his voice harsh. "The Catholics build big statue, bigger than Buddha. It not done yet. Going to be thirty meters high. Buddha only seven meters."

"Sounds like religious persecution to me," Andy said, winking at me over Duc's head. "Maybe you should use those guns up on Lighthouse Mountain to take old Christ there out."

Duc looked thoughtfully in the direction of the old cannons, which probably hadn't worked since the end of World War II, and then at the feet and legs of Jesus. "Maybe you right," he said. "I look into it. Now we finish tour."

We continued on the road, which looped around the tip of the peninsula and ended back in town. By the time we arrived, it was late afternoon. Being winter, it was growing dark, and Vung Tau was coming to life as lights were turned on. The windows of the bars flashed with neon advertising beer and cigarettes, while the girls walking down the street were decked out in short skirts and high heels. A group of them eyed us brazenly, speaking to each other and laughing.

"You looking for boom boom?" Duc asked, noticing the exchange.

"No," I said. "No boom boom."

"Why not?" he said. "You want boy instead? I can get for you if you want."

"No, Donny, no boys," Andy said quickly. "What other kind of boom boom you got?"

Duc grinned. "Number-one cherry," he said. "You come with me."

He started to walk away, and Andy began to follow him. I grabbed his arm. "What are you doing?" I said. "Let's just go back to the hotel."

"Come on," Andy answered. "How many times are you going to get a chance at a Vietnamese whore?"

"I don't want a Vietnamese whore," I said.

"You've got to learn to live a little," said Andy. "You can go back to the hotel if you want, but I'm going. It's up to you."

Behind him, Duc called out, "Come on. This way."

"You heard the man," Andy said. "You can't keep Donny waiting all night."

"All right," I said. "All right. Let's go."

As we followed Duc through the streets, I kept telling myself nothing would happen. Probably we'd end up at some bar, Andy would have too much to drink, and I'd have to carry him back to the hotel. Maybe I would even make sure he drank too much.

"In here," Duc said after we'd been walking for five minutes. "This good place."

We were standing in front of what looked like a small hotel. I looked up at the sign above the entrance. "Cherry Blossom House," I read.

"What I tell you?" said Duc. "Number-one cherry girls. You go in."

Andy fished some coins out of his pocket and handed them to Duc. "Here you go, Donald Duck. Don't wait up for us. Maybe we'll see you tomorrow."

"Okay," Duc said, counting his money. "Tomorrow."

We pushed aside the strings of pink and red beads that covered the doorway and went inside. True to its name, the Cherry Blossom House was painted all in pink. The big main room was set up as a bar with tables and, in one corner, a jukebox that was currently playing Frank Sinatra. The tables were filled with soldiers, and girls moved from man to man, offering drinks or stopping to talk. Some sat on the men's laps, rubbing their heads and whispering in their ears.

We found seats at an empty table and were immediately descended upon by a girl wearing a pink negligee. "You want some beers?" she asked. "Pabst Blue Ribbon?"

"Sure thing," said Andy.

She disappeared, returning a moment later with two cans, which she set on the table. "How much?" Andy asked her, taking out his wallet.

The girl sat on his lap and put her arms around his neck. "No charge," she said. "I like GIs."

"I bet you do," Andy told her, picking up his can and tapping it against mine. "Here's to . . . what's your name, honey?"

"Mai," said the girl. "It mean 'cherry blossom.'"

"Of course it does," I said, taking a long sip from my beer in anticipation of what I felt certain was going to be a long night.

"You like cherry?" she asked.

"We love cherry," Andy said, and Mai laughed.

I drank my beer and watched while Mai flirted. I found it interesting that no girl came to talk to me, but was secretly relieved to be left alone. I didn't know what Andy expected me to do. He knew I wasn't looking for that kind of fun. Or did he? It occurred to me that maybe he thought I only had sex with him because it was easy. But he'd known about me and Jack. Had he forgotten already? I couldn't imagine he had, but watching him get more and more cozy with Mai, I began to suspect he had.

Three beers later, Mai got down to business. "You want to go upstairs?" she asked. She was still sitting on Andy's lap. His hand was on her thigh, and she was pressing her breasts against him.

"I don't know," Andy said, clearly toying with her. "Will you make it worth my time?"

"Sure, sure," Mai said. "We do everything." She looked over at me. "Your friend, too. If you want."

Half drunk as I was, I now understood why I'd been left alone. It was all part of the marketing plan. If Mai could get both of us to go with her, it doubled her profit and freed up another girl. It seemed that even when it came to sex, the Vietnamese were shrewd business-people.

"What do you say, friend?" Andy asked, looking at me over Mai's shoulder as she kissed his neck. "You want?"

No, I didn't want, at least not with Mai. But I also didn't want Andy to be alone with her while I waited downstairs thinking about what they were doing and probably being stuck with a hefty tab after drinking the bar's beer and not paying for a girl. If I couldn't have him to myself, I figured I'd take the next best thing.

"Why not?" I said, draining my beer for every drop of courage I could get.

Mai got up and led us through a doorway and up a flight of stairs that smelled like disinfectant and some overly flowery air freshener. At the top, we passed a shrine with a statue of Buddha, three oranges and a burning stick of incense resting at his feet. The hallway we were in was carpeted, the same bright pink as the rest of the place, and the doors were painted red. Mai stopped at one halfway down the hall and opened it.

Inside was a small bedroom, filled almost wall-to-wall by the bed, which was covered, I was surprised to see, not in pink, but white sheets. A cheap paper lantern covered the lone lightbulb hanging from the ceiling, and a noisy fan whirred from its place on top of a battered dresser. Next to it was a framed photograph of an old woman standing awkwardly in front of a nondescript house of the sort seen all over the Vietnamese countryside, her hands folded in front of her. As we filed in and Mai shut the door behind us, I found myself wondering if she actually lived there, and if the woman in the photograph was her mother.

When I turned around, she was already naked. Without her negligee, she looked much younger. Her skin was taut over her ribs and hip bones, and her small breasts sat high on her chest. A thin patch of dark hair peeked from between her legs.

"Okay," she said as she sat on the edge of the bed. "Who goes first?"

"How about we go together?" said Andy, already removing his shirt.

"No problem," said Mai as she slid backwards and stretched her arms over her head.

Trying not to think, I stripped down to my boxers. Andy was naked, his cock half hard and rising up from his body as he got on the bed. I looked at Mai, who was gazing toward the window, and realized that I'd never been naked in front of a woman before. Suddenly shy, I hesitated in taking off my shorts.

Andy was kneeling on the bed and Mai had drawn herself up and taken the head of his dick between her lips. She held it there while her hand pumped Andy's shaft, getting him hard. She did it with all the sensuality of someone inflating a bicycle tire, although every few seconds she let out the slightest of moans, as if she had to remind herself to do it.

Andy looked back at me and cocked his head, motioning me onto the bed next to him. Steeling myself, I shucked my boxers off and crawled across the mattress until I was beside him on my knees. Almost immediately, Mai's free hand gripped my penis and began to tug me in time with her other one. Then her mouth was on me, hot and wet, and her tongue flicked against my skin.

"Oh, yeah," Andy said, looking down at Mai. I closed my eyes, unable to watch. I concentrated on the feeling, trying to forget that it was

Mai whose mouth I was in and not Andy's. Unsure of what to do with my hands, I tentatively put one around his shoulders. He moved next to me and placed one of his on my ass, squeezing tightly.

Mai alternated between us, sucking first one and then the other. I stayed hard mainly by concentrating on Andy's hand on my ass. I wanted badly to kiss him, but was afraid of his reaction if I went any further. So I waited for him to do something.

Apparently deciding it was time for a change, Mai stopped and got onto her hands and knees. "Fuck me," she said. "One at each end."

Andy moved behind the girl while Mai indicated that I should face her. I felt her take me in her mouth again as Andy slid himself into her. I kept my eyes on his face as he began to pump in and out. Again, I felt awkward with my hands just hanging at my sides, so I tentatively put them on Mai's head. Her hair was unexpectedly soft.

Each time Andy's stomach slapped against Mai's ass, she was driven into me. Through her, I felt the power of his thrusts, and I imagined that it was me he was fucking. I never looked down, never at the girl whose mouth was the substitute for Andy and what I really wanted, which was to be her. I looked only at Andy's face, which was a mask of lust. I wanted him to desire me the way he seemed to desire Mai, not just as a source of release, but as something he couldn't resist.

I was surprised when I came. I hadn't expected to, or even been thinking about it. At the first spasm, I felt Mai pull away. My eruption spattered against the sheets. Across from me, Andy let out a loud groan and held himself still, his body tensing several times before he leaned back and Mai rolled over, sitting on the side of the bed and reaching for her discarded clothing. She paid no attention to us as we clambered off the bed and got dressed.

"You good fuckers," she said when we were ready to go, running her fingers through her hair and applying new lipstick in a cracked mirror. "Twenty bucks."

Andy handed her two bills, which she folded and secreted somewhere on her person. "Each," she said, looking at me.

I paid her and we left, going down the stairs and out the front door, where we were immediately accosted by more girls offering us their number-one cherries. We ignored them and walked the few blocks to our hotel. Back in our room, Andy threw himself onto his bed and laughed. "Man, that was something else," he said. "I just hope my dick doesn't turn yellow. You don't think she had anything, do you?"

"I don't know," I said. "Probably not."

"Yeah," Andy said, yawning. "Probably not."

We got into our separate beds and Andy turned out the light. Within minutes, he was snoring. I waited until I was sure he was fast asleep. Then I went into the bathroom and took a shower, running the water as hot as I could bear it and scrubbing my skin until it was raw.

CHAPTER 29

"The following program is in living color, and has been rated X by the Vietnam Academy of Magic."

The female voice coming from the radio sitting on the table in the GR building was Midwestern in its flatness, although the woman it belonged to called herself "Nguyen." It was early evening on a Wednesday in March 1971, about six weeks after Andy and I returned from our week in Vung Tao. Digger and I were working on some boys who had been brought in that afternoon after their supply truck was ambushed by NVA soldiers on Thunder Road. Such attacks were common, but had been more frequent in recent weeks. The attackers left the men dead on the road, but took the truck and its cargo of medical supplies.

"This is Radio First Termer," Nguyen continued. "The purpose of this program is to bring vital news, information, and hard acid-rock music to the first termers and non-reenlistees in the Republic of Vietnam. Radio First Termer operates under no air force regulations or manuals. In the event of a vice squad raid, this program will automatically self-destruct. Your host tonight is Dave Rabbit."

"Do you think they'll ever catch him?" Digger asked me as he finished closing the wound on the corpse he was cleaning up.

"I hope not," I answered as I cataloged the dead soldier's belongings. His VC killers had taken almost everything off him, leaving only a St. Christopher medal around his neck and, tucked into his boot, a condom in a well-worn wrapper suggesting it had been there for some time. "Rabbit keeps a lot of these guys going."

Dave Rabbit was, and still is, one of the lasting mysteries of Vietnam.

Allegedly a sergeant in the air force, he took to the airwaves every night from twenty hundred to thirteen hundred hours, broadcasting his show from a pirate station somewhere in the south of the country. A staunch opponent of the war, he specialized in taunting the lifers, the military men who made the armed forces their home, and who Rabbit blamed for dragging the war on for far too long. His irreverent message of sex, drugs, and rock and roll infuriated the brass and made him a hero with enlisted men.

To this day, Rabbit's real identity is unknown. Various guesses have pointed to everyone from government conspiracy theorist and radio commentator Art Bell to *Wheel of Fortune* host Pat Sajak, who during the time Rabbit's Radio First Termer aired was one of the military's in-country DJs. But no one has ever claimed responsibility for being the voice of Dave Rabbit, and except for some scratchy recordings of his shows, nothing else is known about him or his sidekicks, Pete Sadler and Nguyen.

Digger and I had been listening to Rabbit for several months. His anti-military tirades and crude but spot-on humor often had us laughing while we performed our grim work, and the music he played was first rate. He specialized in acid rock, which he encouraged us to listen to while getting high. Occasionally, we accommodated him, lighting up and getting into the Hendrix and Creedence Clearwater Revival tunes he sent our way.

"During the night," Rabbit informed us, "we're going to be reading some of the things we've found written on latrine walls across the Republic of Vietnam. Here's one. 'While I'm home, my wife is my right hand. While I'm here, my right hand is my wife.'"

Digger howled. "Ain't that the truth," he said. "I've whacked off so much since I got here, I've got calluses the size of cowpeas."

I chuckled. Digger rarely spoke about sex, a rarity for a grunt. It's one of the things I liked about him, especially since sex was a sore point for me. I hadn't quite forgiven Andy—or myself—for what had happened in Vung Tau. This didn't stop me from continuing to let him fuck me whenever he wanted, however, and that only added to my feelings of anger and guilt.

"Here's another quickie from the latrine walls," Rabbit continued. "This joker writes, 'Eighteen days until I can go home to picket and protest this fucking waste of human lives that lifers and the government call a war.'"

"Sounds like me," remarked Digger.

"How many days is it now?" I asked him.

"Twelve," he said, then looked at his watch. "Actually, eleven days, thirteen hours, and forty-five minutes."

Digger's second year in-country was just about up, as were his three years of service to the U.S. Army. Disillusioned by what he'd seen during the previous twelve months, he'd decided against re-upping, and would be heading back to Louisiana and his family's funeral home. That would leave me as the primary GR guy, but not for long. My own year was up in June, and then there would be a new crew coming in to handle the bodies. Unless I decided to do a second tour. I'd been thinking about that recently, but had yet to come to a decision.

There was certainly enough work to keep me busy if I did decide to stay. A year earlier, in April of 1970, reportedly after viewing the film *Patton* the night before, President Richard Nixon ordered U.S. troops into Cambodia, which up to that point had been considered a neutral country and therefore off limits to military forces fighting in Vietnam. The basis for his decision was assumed to be the need for intervention in the civil war raging in that country, a result of the overthrow in March of Cambodian Crown Prince Sihanouk's government while the prince was in Moscow receiving treatment for cancer. Angered by what they saw as the prince's capitulation to North Vietnamese forces who had invaded both Cambodia and Laos in February, the National Assembly voted to oust Sihanouk, replacing him with the country's former defense minister and acting prime minister, Lon Nol. Nol, an American ally, now found himself involved in a bloody fight against pro-Sihanouk forces led by the Khmer Rouge.

The day after Nixon's televised announcement of the invasion (made four days after troops had already crossed the border), opponents of the war staged protests across the United States. At Ohio's Kent State University, a four-day clash between students and police ended with the shooting deaths of four young people by the National Guard. To a populace already weary of the prolonged war and sickened by the recent revelation of the massacre of five hundred Vietnamese villagers by a U.S. Army company at My Lai, the Kent State shootings were further proof that things were going horribly wrong.

What they didn't yet know was that Nixon had ordered secret bombing raids on Cambodia beginning in early 1969 in an attempt at halting North Vietnamese use of the Ho Chi Minh Trail, which was the main supply route for the NVA. Quan Loi, located only ten miles from the Cambodian border, had long been used as a base of operations for these unofficial missions. With the official launch of attacks on NVA forces in Cambodia, we became even busier, so that by early 1971, most of the choppers flying out were headed west.

On February 8, South Vietnamese forces, aided by U.S. soldiers, invaded Laos and made another attempt to close down the Ho Chi Minh Trail for good. The attempt failed, and back home, Nixon's repeated assertions that the army of South Vietnam had been sufficiently trained so as to make the withdrawal of American troops imminent were met with disbelief and increased demands to bring an end to the war.

Those of us actually in Vietnam didn't know what to make of our situation. The number of bodies that Digger and I processed was steadily increasing. Making it worse, the soldiers who were coming in to take over for the dead and those of us at the end of our year-long tours seemed to resent not only the war itself, but the men they were replacing. They sometimes made us feel as if the fact that we weren't winning the war was our fault, that they were in Vietnam only because we couldn't take care of business. In many places, morale was low and tempers short.

Still, part of me loved Vietnam and the men I served with there. Although getting out seemed like it would be a relief, part of me was afraid that I would feel lost without the war. I'd joined the army to find myself, and what I'd discovered was that I still wasn't entirely sure who I was. Being a soldier gave me an identity, one that I was proud of, that made me something. Going back would mean giving it up, at least in part, and I wasn't certain I was ready to do that.

I worried, too, about Andy. Now that he was flying into Cambodia, his missions were becoming riskier. Twice his chopper had sustained damage from NVA rockets, once just making it back to Quan Loi. So far he and his team had managed to avoid serious injury, and they'd developed an attitude of invincibility because of it, an attitude I was certain would get them all killed one of these days. I knew I couldn't keep him safe by staying in Vietnam, but at least I would be there to know how he was.

"Here's a dedication to the new troops who have just recently come into the Republic of Vietnam and every day sit and watch those Freedom Birds fly back to the world again." Rabbit's voice interrupted my thoughts as he began playing Led Zeppelin's "Heartbreaker."

"You gotta come see me down south when you get home," said Digger. "We'll hit New Orleans. Listen to some jazz. Drink some beers. You ever had Jax?" He began singing before I could tell him I hadn't. "Hello, mellow Ja-ax, little darlin'. You're the beer for me. Yesireee."

"It's a date," I told him as we each took an end of the corpse he'd just finished and carried him to the cooler. "But you're buying."

A few hours later, I sank wearily onto my cot, looking forward to sleep. I hoped we wouldn't get any incoming casualties the next day, and not just because I didn't want to see any more soldiers killed. The sad truth was, I was getting used to death. Too used to it. I counted it a good day when "only" two or three bodies came in. Although I still treated each soldier with as much care as I could, I'd stopped grieving for every man who passed through the GR. Like so many military men before me, I'd begun to see the loss of life as the price of winning.

I fell asleep, but only moments later it seemed I was awakened by the sound of someone yelling outside the hootch. Groggy and half asleep, I staggered to the door, afraid maybe we were being attacked. When I looked out, I saw medics running toward the airstrip.

"What's going on?" I called out.

"Some of our guys got hit on a border run," a medic yelled back. "We've got wounded."

I turned and went back to my bed. Wounded men weren't my problem. I hoped none of them died, but if they did, someone would come let me know. I pulled the blanket up and started to go back to sleep, when suddenly a thought hit me like ice water: The wounded men had been on a mission to Cambodia. What if one of them was Andy?

I was up again in a moment, pulling my fatigues on and stumbling over my boots. Cursing, I managed to get them on and tie them, although my fingers refused to work properly and I fought to make a simple bow knot. Finally I was dressed, then out the door and headed for the airfield.

Unless you're intimately familiar with them, it's difficult to tell one chopper from another. To make it easier, crews often painted names and images on their birds to distinguish them from the other ones in the fleet. Andy's team had dubbed themselves the "War Cocks," a childish but appropriate name for a group of men who prided themselves not only on being the best, but also on being the rowdiest while doing it. Their logo, naturally, was a rooster whose oversized comb and impressive beak looked down menacingly on the enemy below.

I saw the rooster before I saw anything else. It was badly burned, only the tip of the beak and part of the name intact. It had apparently taken a direct hit. I could only wonder what had become of the men inside. I could see stretchers on the ground, with medics hunched over them. There was much shouting as soldiers were directed what to do with the wounded men.

I ran up and peered over the bowed backs of the medics. I saw Andy at once. He was lying on a stretcher, his body covered by a blanket. As far as I could tell, he was alive, but I saw blood seeping through the blanket where it draped over his legs. Before I could talk to him, two soldiers picked him up and carried him toward the medical building. I could only watch as he was taken away.

"What happened to him?" I asked one of the medics who had been attending to him.

"Bullet wounds," he said brusquely as he moved to another man.

"He'll be all right?"

"They tore through his femoral artery," the man answered. "He lost a lot of blood on the way back here. If he's lucky, he'll just lose a leg."

My heart sank as I realized my worst fear was coming true. Compounding it was the fact that I could do absolutely nothing but wait. Andy's life was in the hands of the men in the operating room. All I could do was go back to my hootch, sit on my cot, and prepare myself for the possibility that Andy would die.

Like so many people in my position, I thought with regret about how angry I'd been at him recently. I chastised myself for trying to turn him into something he wasn't, and not just accepting him as he was. Although flawed, I was certain that he cared for me. Maybe he wasn't in love with me, but he was undeniably my lover, and that was close enough. Could he help it if he wasn't ready to acknowledge that we meant more to one another than we ever spoke about?

I immediately forgave him everything—the irresponsibility, the aloofness, the inability to recognize his capacity for love. I swore that I would let him come to me on his own terms, without pushing for more than he could give or demanding that he accept more from me that he could handle. I would love him even more than I already did, and better.

I did something else then that is typical of those facing the loss of a loved one. I made a deal with God. We hadn't been on speaking terms for many years, God and I, but in tried-and-true human fashion, I suddenly found an infinite capacity for belief in his ability to save Andy's life. If he did, I promised, I would stay in Vietnam another year and pay him back by sending soldiers to him in the best condition I possibly could.

When I was done, I sat and waited for his answer.

CHAPTER 30

In April of 1972, giant pandas Hsing Hsing and Ling Ling arrived at the National Zoo in Washington, D.C., a gift from China's Chairman Mao to commemorate the recent diplomatic thaw between our two countries after a visit by President Nixon in February. Excited zoo-goers waited hours in line for a glimpse of the black-and-white bears, while Hsing Hsing and Ling Ling, oblivious to their role as goodwill ambassadors, sat in their bamboo-filled enclosure and peered back at their visitors with the inscrutability for which their countrymen are famed.

The same week the pandas came to Washington, I left Vietnam bound for San Francisco. I was a few months shy of both my second anniversary at Quan Loi and my twenty-second birthday. I felt much older than I was, because of what I'd seen during the past twenty-two months, but also because of my health. In January, I'd contracted a gastrointestinal parasite, and ever since I'd been fighting a running battle with my bowels. It was this that had earned me a premature release from duty and a seat on the Continental Airlines Freedom Bird that lifted me from the airstrip at Bien Hoa and carried me across the Pacific Ocean.

My new assignment was to be at the Presidio, the military base on San Francisco Bay. Built by the Spanish in 1776, it had subsequently been a Mexican garrison until it was taken over yet again in 1846, this time by U.S. Army troops, who repaired the fort's adobe walls, which had gradually washed away during years of winter rains, and established it as a key military outpost on the West Coast. It would remain so for the next 148 years, changing and growing continuously as army soldiers used it first as a base of operations in campaigns against the Modoc and Apache Indians in the U.S. and Pancho Villa in Mexico, then as a coastal defense site in World War I, and later as a point of embarkation for the Pacific Theater during World War II.

It was also home to Letterman Hospital, which had cared for sick and injured soldiers during every military conflict since the Spanish American War. The largest facility of its kind, Letterman had seen many cases of men returning home from tours abroad with all manner of exotic flora and fauna inhabiting their innards, and it was to be my first stop upon arrival. Following the eradication of the bacteria currently using my intestines as a Slip 'N' Slide, I was to report for duty in the quartermaster unit, where I would serve out the remaining months of my enlistment.

I was thrilled to be in San Francisco. My enthusiasm for the city hadn't died since I'd first seen it during my layover on the way to Vietnam, and I'd specifically requested to be stationed there. But I wasn't excited about the city just because it was beautiful. I was excited because Andy was there.

He'd survived the surgery and had, in fact, been far luckier than the pessimistic medic had supposed he might be. Despite serious damage to the nerves and muscles, it had not been necessary to amputate his leg. It was, however, the end of his military career. A few weeks after the shooting, he'd been shipped home for further treatment and ongoing physical therapy at Letterman. Keeping up my end of the bargain with God, I'd signed on for another tour.

During the intervening year, Andy had corresponded with surprising and welcome regularity, beginning with a letter every month and progressing to one or sometimes two a week. It was as if in letters he was able to say many of the things he'd been unable to when we were face to face. He thanked me for my friendship, and revealed his frustration with not being able to fight the war that had come to mean so much to him. He was, he wrote, proud of me for staying. He stopped short of saying that he loved me, but by then I was used to his detachment and hardly noticed.

After my arrival in California, it was four long days before I saw him. During that time I submitted to numerous tests and to the inspection of my colon by various doctors wielding a succession of increasingly unpleasant instruments, all of which seemed to have been placed in a freezer for several days before being inserted into my rectum. At the end of this orgy of prying, during which the effluents of my system were collected daily and examined in minute detail with frightening enthusiasm, I was prescribed a program of antibiotics and pronounced fit enough to venture out into the world, albeit with a warning to avoid the consumption of raw eggs or undercooked meat.

That night, I met Andy for dinner at the Sausage Factory, an Italian restaurant in the Castro. Emerging from the cab that brought me from the Presidio, I was stunned by what I saw. The sidewalk in both directions was lined with men, almost all of them in Levi's so tight that their packages were clearly outlined. They leaned seductively against buildings and over apartment balconies, and paraded by singly and in groups, laughing and talking in the warm spring evening. A first exposure to the city's—and perhaps the country's—gayest neighborhood has often been likened to Dorothy's first glimpse of Oz after the drabness of Kansas, and while the comparison is admittedly overused, I can think of none that captures the moment more fittingly. Never having seen anything like it, I found myself staring.

"Hey, soldier. You looking for some action?"

I turned to see Andy standing behind me. He, too, was wearing jeans, his damaged leg hidden beneath the faded, well-worn fabric. He also had on a red-and-black-checkered flannel shirt, the sleeves rolled up to the elbows, and a battered pair of combat boots.

"You saved them," I said, pointing at his feet.

He looked down. "Actually, no," he said. "Would you believe I bought them? I should have saved mine. Everybody wants these now."

I walked over and gave him a hug. Holding him in my arms, I almost started to cry. It had been so long since I'd seen him. He felt thinner, harder, as if he had been purified and all the excess burned away. To my surprise, he kissed me, briefly, on the mouth.

"You've got a moustache now," I observed.

He ran his fingers over the hair on his lip and smiled. "Like it?"

"It suits you," I said. "Let me guess—everybody wants one now."

He laughed. "Hey, it never hurts to look good. Speaking of which, it's time for you to grow your hair out. You're not in Nam anymore."

"But I'm still in the army," I reminded him as he opened the door to the restaurant and we went inside. I noticed that he was limping as we followed the host to our table. When we sat down, I asked him how his physical therapy was going.

"Not bad," he said. "I don't use a cane anymore. The doc says by this time next year I might be pretty much normal. At least until you see me naked."

"I can't wait," I said.

He ignored my intended come-on, looking intently at the menu. I wasn't sure he'd heard my comment, but I felt that repeating it would look like I was trying too hard. I wanted our reunion to be a good one, so I didn't say anything. Finally the waiter came and took our order. When he had gone, Andy asked, "So, how are things at Quan Loi?"

"The same," I said. "A lot of the guys we knew are gone. Now it's mostly helo jockeys and special ops. I don't know where things are headed. They're talking about a pullout."

Andy shook his head in disgust. "They're just giving up, man. They're letting those VC bastards win."

I didn't want to talk about Vietnam. I'd left it behind me, and I wanted to look ahead. Andy, however, wanted to go back and relive it all over again. I knew if I didn't find a way to change the subject, we'd be talking about the same old guys and telling the same old stories the entire night.

"What are you doing these days?" I asked him. "For work, I mean."

"Different shit," he said. "Mostly I bartend at this place not far from here."

"Bartend?" I said. "The army didn't set you up with anything?"

He gave a derisive snort. "Fuck no, they didn't," he answered. "I mean, they tried. They had me working goddamned carpentry with this guy who fought in Korea and runs a construction business. His whole crew is vets. But he was kind of an asshole, and with my leg and all, it just didn't work out. Besides, I make more bartending."

"Great," I said. "Where do you work?"

"Just down the street," he said. "Place called Toad Hall. It's a queer bar. We can go over there afterward if you want."

"A queer bar," I repeated, the word uncomfortable on my tongue. "This whole neighborhood seems to be kind of, you know, like that."

"The Castro?" said Andy. "Yeah, it is. Used to be all Irish and German families. They're the ones who built all the painted ladies. I don't think they're too crazy about all the gays moving in, but there's not much they can do about it."

"And the bar you work at is gay," I said. I wanted to ask him if he counted himself among the gay population, but I just couldn't. I hoped he would say it himself. I wanted to see how far he'd come in talking about who he was.

"Gays tip the best," he said. "Especially if they think it'll get them into your pants. I can take home a hundred bucks a night easy."

"Wow," I said, impressed. "I can't wait to see the place you've got with that kind of money coming in."

"It's okay," he said. "I share a flat with a buddy. It's the second floor of a house over on Diamond. The stairs are a bitch, but it's big."

This was the first I'd heard of a roommate. Andy had never mentioned one in any of his letters. I found myself getting a little jealous, especially as I still didn't know whether or not Andy had thrown himself into the city's apparently thriving gay world.

Our food came and we began to eat. Used to dinners in mess halls, where time was often of the essence, I put my head down and ate quickly. It was only after I'd put away half my bowl of spaghetti that I realized Andy was watching me. I put my fork down and wiped my mouth. "Sorry," I said. "I guess I'm still not used to being back in the real world."

"This isn't the real world," Andy said. "This is Never-Never Land, and we're the Lost Boys. The real world is back there." He jerked his head toward the window and, eight thousand miles beyond it, Vietnam.

"Tell me what's new these days," I suggested. "Movies. Music. Television. That kind of stuff. I've really been out of it."

Andy shrugged. "I saw *The Godfather* last week. It's pretty good. Music, I don't know. They play that 'American Pie' song every five minutes. You must have heard that one. I don't really pay a lot of attention to that shit."

"What do you do for fun?"

"Fun?" Andy repeated. "You know what I do for fun, Ned? I get high and I think about killing VC. I think about being in a chopper with an M60 blasting away at whatever the fuck gets in my way. That's what I do for fun."

Taken aback by the anger in his voice, I concentrated on twirling spaghetti around my fork. I hadn't realized how much Andy resented being taken away from Vietnam, and I didn't know what to say to him.

"Look, man, I'm sorry," Andy said, sounding less upset. "I just get worked up sometimes. It's not easy being back. People don't get it unless they were there. I have to listen to them talking about how we fucked everything up, especially after Calley and his boys went on trial for blowing the shit out of those people at My Lai. I try to explain what was really going on, but it all comes out wrong and they just look at me like I'm fucking nuts."

"I didn't know it was so hard," I said.

"You'll find out," he said. "We get vets coming into the bar. One of these guys—an old fag who was in World War II—he found out I was in Nam. You know what he said? He told me we should have fought harder, like he did. It's not just the civies who think we didn't take care of business, it's our own guys."

"Like you said, they weren't there," I told him. "You can't let it bother you."

"Tell me that after you've been back a year," said Andy.

Things weren't going well, and I was starting to think that I should go back to the base and see Andy another night, after he'd calmed down a little. But I had a feeling his anger was always with him, hiding just below the surface. Worse, I was beginning to think that seeing me just made it worse. I was his connection to Quan Loi, to the war, and I thought maybe having me there to bring back a lot of old memories was hurting him more than it was helping.

"I should probably get back soon," I said, laying the groundwork for an exit.

"No," Andy said. "Look, don't mind me. I'm just spouting off. Come on, I want you to see the bar."

We finished up dinner, I paid, and we left. Andy walked slowly, and several times I reached out to steady him when I thought he was going to fall. But he never did, and a few minutes later we reached Toad Hall. A crowd of men stood outside, smoking and holding animated discussions. More than a few of them called out greetings to Andy as we passed through them.

"My fan club," Andy joked as we went inside. Indoors, it was even more packed with men. The walls were painted black, and on one of them someone had painted a mural of the characters from Kenneth Grahame's *The Wind in the Willows*, from which the bar had taken its name. Music was pounding out of the speakers, and behind the bar a huge mound of old candle wax formed a kind of pyre, on top of which a row of votives burned, adding themselves to the landscape as they slowly melted.

A thin man with long hair, a moustache, and worried eyes came up to us. Andy greeted him enthusiastically, then turned to me. "Ned, this is Stan, the manager. He's the guy who saved me from construction."

"He was in here all the time anyway," Stan said, shaking my hand. "He tipped for shit, so I figured I either had to hire him or kick him out."

"Nice to meet you, sir," I said.

"Sir?" said Stan. "You must be one of Andy's army buddies."

"That's right," I said. "I guess you can't teach an old soldier new tricks."

"Maybe not," Stan said. "But I bet there are some guys in here who'd like to *be* your new tricks."

He and Andy laughed while I tried to figure out what Stan meant. Then Stan excused himself and left us alone. Andy went to the bar and returned with two Budweisers. He handed me one and drained a third of his own in one long swallow.

"Stan seems like a good guy," I said, raising my voice to be heard above the music and the conversations going on around us.

"He is," said Andy. He was staring past me at the door, as if looking for someone.

"Is it always this crowded?" I asked, marveling at the throng of men crammed into the bar.

"This is nothing," Andy said. "Wait 'til you see it on a Friday or Saturday night."

I couldn't imagine Toad Hall holding any more people than it was right then. For a guy who had never been inside a gay bar, it was a little disconcerting. I was used to hiding who I was, and now I was literally surrounded by men celebrating their sexual identity. I found myself excited but also a little scared. I drank some more of my beer, hoping it would relax my nerves.

I was also working up my courage to ask Andy if I would be going home with him that night. Watching the men in the bar, many of whom had removed their shirts and some of whom were kissing one another, I was suddenly very aware of the fact that apart from jerking off, I hadn't had any contact with a man in a very long time. Even though Andy had been so casual about our relationship in the past, I hoped that now that he was out of the army and surrounding himself with gay men that he might be ready to be more open about himself, and about us.

"So," I said, my heart beginning to race as I thought about touching Andy's naked skin. "I was wondering if . . ."

I stopped when I saw him look behind me and wave. "Hold on," he said. "My roommate's here."

I turned around, anxious to see what kind of man Andy had found to live with. Since he'd said nothing about him in any of his letters, I had no idea what to expect. I looked at the man coming toward us and felt my heart stop.

"Hello, Ned," said Jack.

CHAPTER 31

Since its opening in 1937, 1,218 people have committed suicide by jumping off the Golden Gate Bridge. The first was Harold Wobber, a World War I veteran who, while walking across the bridge on August 7, less than three months after the grand opening, turned to a stranger, said, "This is as far as I go," and stepped off into the air. Since then, roughly every two weeks another person has gone over the side and into the cold waters of San Francisco Bay. It has been called a monument to death, a soaring structure whose beauty is irresistible to those looking for a symbolic and almost surefire (only 26 jumpers have survived the 250-foot fall) means of ending their lives. When in 1973 the bridge's death toll neared 500, there was fierce competition among would-be suicides for the privilege of assuming that dubious honor, and when that number came close to being doubled in 1995, the official count was halted in the hopes of preventing a similar frenzy.

I never seriously considered a leap from the bridge. I went there because I needed to walk, and because standing on the span at night, you feel as if you're floating in space. The lights of San Francisco to the south and the Marin Headlands to the north form parallel galaxies, the Golden Gate a bridge of stars linking them together. Standing there, the water a sheet of black silk ripping with unseen currents beneath me, I understood why so many found it impossible to resist the urge to climb onto the narrow ledge beyond the waist-high railing. I imagined standing there, enchanted by the dizzying height and the whispering fog that caressed with ghostly tendrils and promised dreamless sleep. It would be difficult to say no, to turn and grasp once more the hard steel of the railing and pull oneself back into the real world. So much easier to just let go and fly.

As I say, I felt no real impulse to kill myself, although I am not convinced that there is not some magic in the steel of the bridge that plants such thoughts in the mind if you linger too long while crossing. In me it simply magnified the feelings of loneliness with which I was struggling since seeing Jack again. I was, to put it lightly, taken aback. At first, I had even refused to believe it was really him, and not simply someone of remarkable resemblance. I'd gotten used to thinking of him as someone from my past, and to encounter him in my present required a shifting of focus, one I was reluctant to allow.

We went to a coffee shop to talk, leaving Andy at Toad Hall surrounded by his many friends. Seated at a table, our cups untouched in front of us, Jack nervously straightened his silverware while I waited for him to speak. I didn't want to say anything, and wasn't sure what I would say even if I did. Although it had been only slightly more than two years since our last meeting, I felt as though a lifetime now separated us.

"I bet you're surprised to see me," he said finally.

I picked up my coffee and sipped it, my only response a slight nod. Jack opened a packet of sugar—his fifth since we'd sat down—and added it to his cup, stirring quickly. "Don't be mad at Andy," he said. "I told him not to say anything about me in his letters."

"Why?" I asked.

Jack leaned back in his chair. "I thought it might be too weird for you," he answered.

I couldn't help laughing. "Too weird," I said. "Why? Because the last time either of us heard from you was before we went to Nam, and then—poof—all of a sudden you're back? Yeah, Jack, you might say that's a little weird."

He lowered his eyes from my glare. "I know you think I took the easy way out," he said. "And maybe I did. But I can't change that now."

"Is that why you're here?" I said. "You want me to forgive you?"

"No," Jack said. "I don't expect you to forgive me. But come on, Ned, we were best friends for nineteen years."

"I was *your* friend," I said. "I'm not sure you were much of one back."

He looked up, hurt reflected in his expression. "You can't really believe that," he said.

"You were always the golden boy, Jack," I told him. "I was the one who always got the leftovers you didn't want. And then when I finally found something I did want, you went and took that, too."

"Andy?" Jack said. "Are you talking about Andy?"

I didn't answer. I was growing more agitated by the moment, and it was taking all of my military training to keep my cool with Jack sitting across from me pretending he didn't know what he was doing.

"Are you two lovers?" I asked.

Jack leaned forward and touched my hand. I pulled it away.

"I didn't even know he was in San Francisco," Jack said.

"Oh, so you just happened to move here and end up as his room-mate?" I countered.

Jack shook his head. "I was already here," he said. "I was only at Wesley for about a year. Then I decided that whole minister thing wasn't for me, and I decided to go to school for psychology."

"Psychology," I said. "Since when are you interested in psychology?"

"I'm not a total moron," Jack said. "I had a couple of classes in psych at Wesley, pastoral counseling kind of stuff. They were interesting."

"Why'd you decide to leave?"

Jack smiled. "They kind of asked me to after they found out I was sleeping with one of the theology profs. Well, he was only a TA, but the actual instructor was about a thousand years old and let James teach most of his classes. Anyway, someone found out and told the dean. Next thing you know, I'm in his office and they're telling me that homosexuality is 'incompatible with scriptural teachings.'" He said the last part in a gruff voice, knitting up his eyebrows and pointing a finger. "He said I had two choices. I could repent and go for therapy, or I could leave. I told him I was perfectly happy the way I was and walked out."

"What about your parents?" I asked. "What did you tell them?"

"Nothing," said Jack. "I just said I wanted to try something else. Then I found a school as far away from them as I could get, and here I am. I'm in the psych program at SF State. I was able to transfer a lot of my credits, so it's not like I'm starting over."

I drank more coffee to buy myself some time. I felt as if I'd stepped through Alice's looking glass. Jack was actually in college. Plus, he was talking openly about being gay. Had he really become such a different person while I'd been away? Part of me didn't believe it, but I could sense no trace of deception in his words. Maybe he had really changed, I thought. Then I remembered Andy, and the anger resurfaced.

"You never answered my question," I said. "About you and Andy."

Jack reached for the sugar again. "Like I said, I didn't even know he was here. I hadn't heard from him since Penn. Really, I'd pretty much forgotten about him. Then one day he just showed up at this clinic where I was doing some fieldwork for a class."

"He just showed up," I said, suspecting there was more to the story.

Jack nodded. "Yeah," he said. "He was there for a counseling session. Something the VA sent him in for. I saw him in the waiting room. At first I didn't recognize him. But when he saw me, he broke out that stupid grin, and then I knew right away."

"And then you moved in together?"

"Not right away. I wasn't sure what his deal was. A lot of those guys come back from Vietnam totally fucked up and . . ." He stopped, looking at me nervously. "Sorry," he said. "I forgot for a minute."

"It's okay," I told him, although inside I wanted to grab him by the neck and pound his face into the table for speaking so glibly about something of which he knew nothing.

"So we had dinner and started hanging out a little bit," he continued. "I could tell he was still dealing with what happened to him, but he seemed more or less okay. At the end of the school year, I decided I didn't want to live in student housing anymore, so I looked for a place. I couldn't afford one on my own, and Andy suggested we room together. That was just about a year ago now."

"And why didn't either of you tell me again?"

"I don't know," Jack answered. "I guess it was pretty stupid. I just didn't think you'd want to hear from me or hear anything about me, so I asked Andy not to mention it."

We were both quiet for a while, sipping from our mugs while people came in and out of the shop. I was trying to process everything Jack had told me, and I was getting hung up on one thing—the fact that he still hadn't answered my question. Twice he'd sidestepped it, which led me to believe that he didn't want me to get even more upset than I already was.

"Are you okay?" he asked, bringing me back to the moment.

"Yeah," I said. "I'm fine. Just thinking about all of this."

"I don't expect you to be all happy about seeing me," he said. "At least not right away. But I hope we can be friends again. We have a lot of history together."

I nodded. I couldn't deny that he was right about that. The difference between us was that I wasn't sure whether or not I wanted that history to keep going. I'd put a lot of effort into divorcing myself from my relationship with Jack. Now here he was wanting to pick up where we'd left off.

"I know I wasn't always the best friend," Jack said. "But I've learned a lot about myself, Ned. I'm not so afraid of who I am anymore."

"You mean of being gay?" I said, half hoping the word might wound him somehow.

"That's part of it," he said. "I couldn't have even said the word *gay* two years ago."

"I remember," I said cruelly. "Is that something else your TA taught you?"

"James was about as closeted as you can get," Jack replied. "He told the dean that I was the one who seduced him. He somehow forgot that he was the one who invited me to his room for a personal tutoring session on the Articles of Religion and then couldn't wait to get my clothes off. No, it was more living here in San Francisco that helped me get over the whole gay thing. It's hard to be here without loosening up. It's funny how fast people change when they move here. You'll see."

"I didn't know I needed to change," I said.

"Lighten up," said Jack. "I just mean your attitude will probably change. Some of that uptightness will go away."

"I'm not uptight," I said, annoyed that he somehow thought he was more enlightened, or evolved, or whatever than I was. "Just because I don't have hair down to my shoulders and jeans that haven't been washed in a month, don't think you can sit there lecturing me."

"I'm not lecturing you," Jack said. "Man, you really do need to mellow out. We should go back to our place and smoke some weed. Andy knows this guy who has the best shit."

"No thanks," I said, reaching for my wallet and taking out some ones. "I think I should go."

"Ned," Jack said. "Come on. Let's just talk some more."

"I don't want to talk," I said, standing up. "I've got a lot to do tomorrow."

"Maybe another night?" asked Jack.

"Maybe," I told him. "'Bye, Jack."

I walked out before he could say anything else. I hurried down Castro street, avoiding looking at the men around me. At 18th Street I managed to get a cab and surprised myself by telling the driver to take me to the Golden Gate Bridge. He looked at me suspiciously for a moment, as if checking for signs that I might be planning something he would read about the next day in the morning paper. Apparently finding nothing amiss, he started driving.

I didn't arrive at the bridge with any plan. It had just popped into my head to go there. I vaguely thought maybe I would walk to the other side, although there was nothing waiting there for me. It was purely for lack of any better alternative that I ended up standing in the center, looking out at the night.

Watching the lights of ships passing underneath the bridge, I was reminded of a story I'd heard from a World War II navy man—now a doctor at Letterman—while in the hospital. To distract me from the pain of one of the endless tests, he had, while peering into my bowels, regaled me with stories about the Presidio. Concerned more with trying not to soil myself than with listening, I forgot most of them instantly, but one stuck in my mind, a tale about a ghost ship that haunted San Francisco Bay. Its name was the *SS Tennessee*, and it had gone down in 1853.

While serving on the destroyer *USS Kennison*, escorting convoys and submarines to various California bases during the war, the good doctor was on deck one night in November of 1942 when the ship passed beneath the Golden Gate Bridge on its way back to port. As the fog parted, he saw another ship passing alongside, heading in the opposite direction.

"She was old," he said. "Not from our century. She didn't make a sound, but I heard the water moving, and she left a wake. And there were men on board, pale men who didn't say anything. They just stood there, looking back at us. Then I saw her name painted on the side—*Tennessee*. I thought I was dreaming, but later on I snuck a peek at the ship's log and there it was. I looked that name up later in the library and found out a lot of sailors have seen her over the years."

I'd written the doctor's story off as just another legend that someone wanted to be true and so had convinced himself that it was. But looking down from the top of the bridge, I suddenly believed him. I could easily imagine a ghost ship passing through those dark waters, attempting to carry her crew back to the land of the living. It made sense, in that place of so many deaths, that souls would congregate beneath the mighty arc of metal that so many had said could never be built. It was a place of impossibilities, the least of which was that it might be a crossroads between earth and heaven and hell.

Jack had appeared like a ghost, out of nowhere and without warning. Like the doctor staring at the foggy image of the past, I was looking over my shoulder at who and what I had once been. My choice now was whether I would run from that ghost or embrace it.

CHAPTER 32

"You come here to pray?"

I looked at the man standing beside me. Tall and blonde, with curly hair and rugged good looks, he resembled Ben Murphy, my current romantic crush as outlaw Kid Curry on *Alias Smith and Jones*. His blue work shirt was open, revealing the smooth skin of his chest beneath, and he leaned against the bar with a casual air that suggested he was very much at home there. I couldn't recall having seen him before, but I'd only been to the Stud a handful of times.

"Why would I come here to pray?" I asked him.

He smiled, and I saw from the way his eyes moved slowly from my face to my crotch that he was drunk or high. Probably both. "This is a church," he said. "You didn't know that?"

I shook my head no and took a pull on my bottle of beer. If he hadn't looked like Ben Murphy, I might have left him standing there and gone in search of someone with a better line. But his cleft chin and full lips kept me rooted to the spot.

"You're standing in the sanctuary of an official Universalist Life Church," he said, raising his arms and indicating the whole of the bar. "In about an hour, this becomes a place of worship." He looked at me, shaking my head, and said, "What? You don't believe me?"

"Sure, I believe you," I told him. "I believe that in about an hour, half of these guys *will* be on their knees, and the other half will be shouting hallelujah."

He laughed, a rich, deep sound that made my stomach tingle. Then he leaned in, his leg touching my thigh and his face hovering only a few inches away from my mine. "You're funny," he said. "But I'm dead serious. They had this place declared a church so it can stay open past two."

I didn't know whether to believe him or not (I learned later that he was right), but at that point I really didn't care if he was lying. I was picturing my fantasies about Kid Curry holding up my railroad car at gunpoint coming true. When, a long moment later, he asked me if I wanted to get out of there, I set my beer on the bar and followed him out the door.

Don't judge me too harshly. Remember, this was 1973. We did this kind of thing then. We still do, I know, but in those beautiful days when everything seemed too perfect to be true, we made a life of it. And, as I said, he very closely resembled Ben Murphy. You can tut-tut all you like, but I wasn't the first man to take a stranger up on an offer simply because he looked like someone else, and I'm sure I won't be the last.

We walked down Folsom, the infamous "Miracle Mile" of bars that existed to fulfill the dreams of San Francisco's gay men. It was July, the weather sultry, and many of the men we passed were wearing almost nothing. It wasn't unusual then to see someone giving head in a darkened doorway, or two, three, or more men engaged in foreplay outside a bar door, hands and mouths wandering over naked skin as they negotiated what might come next. The stale smell of the bars leaked out onto the streets, mingling with the scents of pot, sweat, and cooking meat emanating from Hamburger Mary's.

"By the way, I'm Art," my new friend said as we stopped to wait for a light.

"Ned," I told him.

"Well, Ned, where's your place?" Art asked me.

"I'd rather go to yours, if you don't mind," I said. "Mine's kind of crowded."

"Mine, too," Art said. "My wife is there."

Again he smiled at me, and I didn't know if I should take him seriously or not. He put his arm around my shoulder and started walking down 12th Street toward Market.

"Where are we going?" I asked.

"You ever been to The Club?" he replied.

"Which club?" I said.

"*The* Club," Art said. "That's the name."

"I've never even heard of it."

"Well, then, you're in for a real special treat," he said, holding out his hand to hail a taxi.

The cab took us downtown, into the Tenderloin, a neighborhood even seedier than SOMA and its bars. Girls in garish, tight clothes plied their trade under the harsh lights, and their customers lurked in the shadows, waiting and looking. I had no idea where we were going, and when the driver stopped in front of an address on Turk Street, I got out, still not understanding where we were. A sign over a black door said THE CLUB, but there was nothing to indicate what kind of place it was.

"You're gonna love this," Art said as he steered me inside, where he handed over some money to a man behind a window and received back two towels.

It quickly became clear, even to my naive eyes, what The Club was. Dimly lit, slightly damp, and reeking of sex, it was a bathhouse. I'd heard about them, but had never been in one, mostly because I found the idea of them slightly vulgar. Still affected by my conservative up-bringing, I preferred the bars, where I could at least pretend I was there for something other than sex. A bathhouse, to my mind, was too brazen, or maybe desperate. I didn't mind looking for sex; I just didn't want to be so obvious about it.

As Art led me down a corridor, I tried to avert my eyes from the naked men leaning against the walls and standing in doorways. Although I was far from being a virgin, I felt like some kind of unspoiled bride being led to her wedding night chamber. I sensed eyes on me, and was suddenly afflicted with almost paralyzing shyness. The idea that Art expected me to come back through that gauntlet wearing nothing but a towel terrified me, and I considered just turning around and leaving.

But I was horny, and curious, and so I went into a room where I removed my clothes and put them inside a locker with Art's. He kept the key, which he wore on a band around his wrist, like a charm. Before I could wrap my towel around my waist, Art grabbed my cock and held it while he kissed me. I responded despite my nervousness, and he squeezed me tightly. My hand went between his legs and found him to be equally aroused and impressively large.

After making out for a few minutes, he took me by the hand and led me back down the hallway. I tried to hold my towel around my waist to cover myself, but it wasn't quite big enough to circle me easily (probably by design) and my erection bobbed conspicuously in the gap. More than one hand reached out and gave it a tug, but in the darkness I saw only fingers, never faces.

On the second floor there was a large room covered with mats. As Art led me to an empty space, I remembered the night Jack and I had spent with Andy years before. This room, though, was filled only with men, men doing every conceivable thing to one another involving mouths, hands, cocks, and assholes. It was a constantly-changing tableau punctuated by moans, slaps, and the occasional volley of filthy words. Everywhere I looked a different carnal act was being played out in living stereo.

Art pulled me down onto the floor and tossed my towel aside. He began kissing me again while he played with my dick. After a while, he moved down and I felt the heat of his mouth as he took me in. I lay back and let him work up and down my shaft, focusing on not getting too excited too soon. Although I'd had a few encounters during the preceding months, the fact was, Art was the first in some time. I knew I could easily pop if I didn't distract myself, so I focused my mind on trying to remember the army's codes for small weapons ammunition.

I was jerked from my task by the feeling of something warm and wet pushing between the cheeks of my ass. I looked up and saw the top of Art's head. He'd pushed my legs back and was burrowing his face into me. Before I knew it, his tongue was inside of me, teasing me open. It was followed soon after by a finger.

"Hold on," I said, reaching down and drawing him up.

"What?" he asked, falling between my legs and pumping his cock against mine. "I want to fuck you."

"It's just that . . ." I began.

"Here," Art said, reaching over and picking up a small, dark bottle. "This will loosen you up."

He uncapped the bottle and held it under my nose. I'd used poppers once or twice before, so I knew what they were and what to do. I inhaled, feeling the rush as the amyl nitrate invaded my brain and exploded. Art took a hit as well, shutting his eyes as the buzz began, then opening them and smiling wickedly. "That should open you up like one of those doors on the *Enterprise*," he said, putting his hands behind my knees.

I let him do it. The amyl made everything okay. Not just okay— great. Now we know all the horrible things that can happen when you overdo that stuff, but I tell you, I'm not sure it isn't worth it. All right, when I'm being sensible I know it isn't, just like I know Thayer is right when he tells me three cups of coffee a day is enough. But lust is seldom sensible, and I know why so many guys still take whiffs out of those tiny bottles when they want to get things going. For that minute or however long it lasts, you feel like everything has opened up and that every electrical current in the universe is running right through your heart and out your dick. Everything is magnified a million times, and you don't ever want it to end.

I looked at Art and saw the most beautiful man in the world. He *was* Ben Murphy, my fantasy cowboy. I didn't know what I was to him, but I didn't care. All I cared about was the way he filled me up and made me want more of him, of anyone, of everyone. I found myself reaching out to the bodies around us, trying to draw them in. Some of them found their way, and we were a tangle of limbs. I felt tongues and fingers moving here, touching there, sometimes fleeting, sometimes lingering, and I didn't care who they belonged to. My face was buried between furry thighs, and I sucked eagerly at a musky pucker while somewhere below an invisible mouth coaxed an orgasm from my swollen erection.

I felt Art come inside me. I was certain that I couldn't contain it, that somewhere inside a dam was about to break, cracks in its walls widening and splitting me open. I tried to hold back, wanting to hang forever in that delicate space between desire and completion. Then someone's hand tightened around my balls, pulling gently, and I couldn't stop myself. I cried out as my balls were emptied, my jism flying out like silk from a spider. My body shuddered, and for perhaps a quarter of a minute I was orbiting the sun.

"Fuck, that was hot."

Art's voice brought me back to earth. He had pulled out of me and was lying on his back beside me. His cock had softened, and he played with it idly, as if petting a sleepy puppy. The men who had joined us had rolled away, becoming parts of other puzzles, and I couldn't tell which ones had participated in our orgy. I was sticky, and I reached for my towel.

"Want to go again?" asked Art as I cleaned myself up. "I can usually get it up after half an hour or so."

"Thanks," I said. "But I've got to get home."

"Okay," said Art, already looking around the room for potential replacements. "I think I'm going to stay."

"I need the key," I said, standing up and holding the towel in front of me.

Art looked at me, not comprehending.

"For the locker," I explained. "To get my clothes."

"Oh, right," he said, taking the key from around his wrist and handing it to me. "Just leave it at the front. I'll pick it up later."

I hesitated, waiting for him to ask me for my number, say he had a good time, or basically do anything that would suggest what we'd done meant something beyond just getting off. When he didn't, I turned and left him there, trying to get his flaccid dick to come to life.

This is the problem—or at least *my* problem—with the kind of sex I had in those days, that, actually, I had for a very long time. The spell seldom lasted long. It was as if orgasm shattered whatever fragile magic had maintained the illusion that what I was doing was worth the time and energy. And as soon as the enchantment was gone, I became unhappy. My partners and I turned from handsome, huge-cocked princes into warty little toads who hopped away, self-conscious and spent, into the mud.

Of course, at the time I just thought I was doing it wrong somehow. I told myself that if I did it enough, eventually I'd figure it out and be able to make the feeling I grasped in those moments before coming last an eternity. Like a singer training to hold a perfect note, I believed that if I could extend it each time, even by just a second, that one day I would be strong enough to sustain it forever.

That, however, was not to be my night. I was sated, but already I could feel the hunger beginning to gnaw at me. I needed to leave, and so I retrieved my clothes, dressed, and managed with only a minimum of trouble to find a cab to take me back to my apartment.

Actually, our apartment. Yes, I'd moved in with Jack and Andy. Not right away. After that night on the bridge, I returned to the Presidio determined not to have anything more to do with either of the men who had altered the course of my life. And I didn't, for about two months. Then, after repeated calls from Jack, I relented and went to their place for dinner. It was awkward at first. Jack and I were tentative with one another, and Andy was overly loud, as if he could break down the walls separating us by shouting at them. But I'd at last discovered that they were not lovers, although I suspected Andy allowed Jack to perform whatever services he might wish to when it suited Andy to receive them.

For the next eight months I remained on base, seeing Andy and Jack from time to time as Jack and I reforged the bonds of our friendship and I completed my duty to the United States Army. I was discharged in February of 1973, and accepted the invitation to move into the third bedroom of the spacious flat Andy and Jack had gotten for a ridiculously low rent because the owner of the house, a married Irish Catholic father of six, wanted tenants who would not be put off by his use of the uppermost apartment for the purpose of entertaining the teenage boys he paid to let him masturbate at their feet. The war had officially ended in March, and I was completely free to go about my life.

As for Andy, I'd slowly accepted that he was not going to be my lover, that he had, in fact, probably never been my lover. I still wasn't sure what he was to me, but I had settled into an uneasy truce with my heart regarding the matter, and was more or less able to live in the same house with him without running the risk of daily emotional upheaval. By unspoken agreement, Jack and I still never spoke of our various entanglements with him.

I left The Club and went back to this home I'd created. To my surprise, both Jack and Andy were there when I arrived. They were in the living room, listening to Joni Mitchell's *Blue* and getting stoned on grass and red wine. They were already well gone when I walked in, and greeted me with subdued enthusiasm.

"Where've you been?" Jack asked, stretched out on the worn oriental carpet that covered the floor while Andy lay crosswise to him, his head on Jack's bare stomach.

"I just went out for a drink," I said.

"You mean you got laid," Andy said, smirking. "Didn't you?"

"No," I said defensively.

"That means he did," said Jack, and he and Andy started laughing. "All right," I said. "I did."

"Didn't he want you to stay over?" asked Andy, rolling onto his side and sitting up on one elbow.

"We didn't go to his place," I admitted, flopping down in the armchair across from them.

"Where'd you do it?" said Andy. "In an alley?"

"We went to this place called The Club," I said, figuring I might as well tell them everything.

"The Club?" Andy exclaimed. "That place is a hole. You could have at least gone to the Ritch Street Baths. Shit, The Club."

"It was his idea," I said. "How was I supposed to know?"

"He better have been one good fuck," Andy remarked.

"It was fine," I said. "I don't want to talk about it."

"Come here," said Andy, waving me over.

I shook my head. "I'm just going to go to bed," I said.

"Come on," Andy insisted. "Get over here."

I joined him and Jack on the floor. I rested my head on Andy's stomach, while Jack laid his on mine, so that we formed a triangle of bodies. Andy handed me the joint and I took a hit.

"If you're driving into town with a dark cloud above you," Joni sang in her too-sweet voice, "dial in the number, who's bound to love you."

"See," Andy said as I closed my eyes and felt the rise and fall of his breathing. "It doesn't matter. Nothing matters."

I closed my eyes as Joni sang us her lullaby. "If your head says forget it but your heart's still smoking, call me at the station, the lines are open."

No, I thought. It didn't matter. Nothing mattered.

CHAPTER 33

"The SLA want Hearst to cough up four million more to feed the poor," Burt announced as I entered the office. "He says he doesn't have it."

"Bullshit," I said, taking off my coat and hanging it on the hook behind the door.

"If he wants little Patty back, he'll come up with it," said Burt, turning the page of the magazine in his hands.

"What've we got today?" I asked him, sitting down and looking at the stack of folders forming a Tower of Pisa on the corner of my desk.

"Same old, same old," he said.

I leaned back and stared out the window. It was raining. Still raining. It felt like it had been raining for months, although probably it had only been three or four days. But rain in San Francisco in February seems to last forever, turning life into one long, gray chill. Our office's antiquated heating system rarely came to life, and when it did, it let out only occasional burps of heat, which were quickly devoured by the dampness.

In early 1974, I was working for the Veterans Administration in the medical center on the site of the old Fort Miley base. I'd tried to distance myself from the military, but without a college degree, my options had been limited. After a year in low-paying jobs at coffee shops and bookstores, I'd returned to the army in search of better employment. They'd obliged by assigning me to the VA hospital, where I was in charge of following up on claims filed by Vietnam vets, who since returning from Southeast Asia were suddenly coming down with all kinds of ailments, both physical and mental. Concerned that something might be going on, the government had established an office specifically to look into these claims and keep track of the soldiers filing them.

That duty fell to me and Burt. Another veteran of the war in Southeast Asia, Burt had been a Marine chaplain stationed near Da Nang during some of the fiercest fighting. A few years older than myself, he was short, overweight, and possessed of a caustic wit, which he turned mostly on the government and any affiliated group. He also happened to be gay, as I'd been pleased to discover many of the VA staff were. Burt said it was because we were all anal-retentive and that made us good administrators.

"Why Patty Hearst?" Burt mused out loud. "I mean, if you're going to kidnap someone, it should at least be someone people care about, like Tricia Nixon."

"Too much trouble," I said as I took the first folder from the top of the stack. "Besides, then it would be a federal crime."

I opened the folder and read the patient's bio. PFC Trevor M. Headly. 27. Suffering from chronic headaches and unexplained neurological problems. After only a month on the job, I could predict with astonishing accuracy what I would find in the reports. Most of the soldiers were, like Trevor, young, and most were experiencing unusual symptoms not consistent with anything the army had ever seen in its soldiers. Private Headly had undergone several rounds of tests at the VA hospital, none of which had found anything out of the ordinary. It was my responsibility to telephone Trevor and inform him that there was nothing more we could do for him.

"Oh, my lord, you should see Gloria Vanderbilt's little boys," said Burt. "I swear that Anderson Cooper's going to be a big fairy when he grows up. Have you ever seen a gayer six-year-old?"

"What are you reading?" I asked him.

He held up his magazine. There was a picture of Mia Farrow on the cover.

"*People*?" I said, reading the title. "What's that?"

"It's new," he said, flipping through the pages. "This is their first issue. You've got to read it when I'm done. Did you know Lance Loud used to write to Andy Warhol when he was a kid? And he has a rock band? They're called the Mumps."

"Do people really care about that stuff?" I asked. "It sounds like a bunch of celebrity gossip."

"Please, Mary," Burt replied, slipping into the tone he usually re-served for conversations outside the office. "What do you think we do when we all get together at the Café on Sunday morning and dish about who did what to who on Saturday night? It's what we *live* for. This is the same thing, just on a bigger scale."

"Yeah, but they'll need more than the gay male population of San Francisco to buy that rag if it's going to stick around," I argued.

"You're forgetting housewives," said Burt. "They're basically gay men in curlers and slippers, and there are *millions* of them. They'll eat this shit right up. Look, it says here that Frank Sinatra served Mia Farrow divorce papers in front of the cast and crew of *Rosemary's Baby*. I always thought he was an asshole. Hot, but an asshole."

It was at times like these that I had a difficult time imagining Burt attending to the injured and dying while battle raged around him. I knew he had. I'd heard the stories of his bravery from a number of men who had served with him. He himself rarely talked about his three tours of duty, and he never mentioned any of his heroics. Some days I would have sworn he must have a twin somewhere, a much butcher version of himself who had gone to Vietnam while Burt stayed home and watched soap operas.

"Speaking of hot assholes," Burt said, closing the magazine and putting it down. "How's that roommate of yours?"

"I assume you mean Andy," I said, suppressing a smile. Burt had a well-known crush on him, which Andy had so far managed to com-pletely avoid noticing.

"That would be the one," said Burt.

"You should have come out with us last night," I told him. "You could have seen for yourself."

"Sorry, but I don't need the frustration of watching him flirt with everyone else at the Midnight Sun while I drink myself stupid," Burt said. "I had a perfectly good time at home watching *Mannix* and beat-ing off, thank you very much."

I had to laugh at his dramatics. Burt was a sweet man, and would have made anyone an excellent lover, but his physical type wasn't ex-actly prime meat in the bar market, a problem compounded by his preference for men with muscle and attitude. I kept telling him he should show up wearing his Marine uniform, a suggestion that was met with rolled eyes and a prim shake of a finger. "I only do drag on Halloween," he always said, immediately changing the subject.

I sometimes wished Andy *would* take an interest in Burt. He'd given up pretending he might still be interested in women, but since I'd come to live with him, he hadn't had anything even resembling a boyfriend. Instead, there had been a string of one-night stands, men whose faces I'd see once in the morning as they stumbled from Andy's bedroom to the bathroom, then would disappear back into the ever-swelling ranks of homosexuals flocking to the city and extending the boundaries of the Castro block by block. He never discussed these tricks, and on the rare occasions when Jack or I would comment about one of them, Andy always pretended not to know who we were talking about.

It was very clear by that point that whatever sexual relationships had once existed between myself and Jack, myself and Andy, and Andy and Jack had become something else. Friendship, yes, but more than that. It oversimplifies it to say that we had become a family. Families stay together out of obligations based on blood and sense of duty. We stayed together because we were all pieces of the same machine. Each of us had a different function. Jack was the engine. Andy was the fuel. And I, well, I suppose I was the brake that prevented everything from crashing.

Gay men are not unique in our ability to create lasting friendships with former lovers, but I do think that we've perfected it. At least, I know that I have never heard a straight person answer, "I blew him in the washroom of the San Francisco Hilton," when asked how he first met the friend of fifteen years that has been brought along as a dinner guest. It's a rare ability, being able to see sex as a perfectly acceptable form of social introduction, an even rarer one to move beyond an initial, perhaps fleeting, sexual attraction to something more without embarrassment. As a friend once remarked to me upon receiving news of his younger sister's engagement, "Straight people get married so that they can have sex. Gay men have sex so that they can get friends."

I have been with Thayer, and only Thayer, for many years now, and so have not acquired any new friends through carnal means. However, I continue to be connected to a number of men whom I did first meet because we bedded one another. In most cases, it's been so long since the original encounter that I don't even remember it. In others, I do remember, and now can't imagine what I was thinking at the time. Sometimes in conversation these friends and I refer to our early couplings, usually in disbelief followed by laughter, but by and large we leave the experiences in the past. As you age, I've found, even the most spectacular highlights of one's sexual history pale in comparison to the other connections made during a lifetime.

Although I still regretted not being able to make more of my feelings for him, I was nonetheless able to worry about things like wishing Andy could find a suitable man. I did still love him, and would have jumped into his bed if he'd asked me. But he didn't. Neither did Jack, who was so immersed in his schoolwork that he had little time for chasing cock. With his degree in sight, he was looking forward to graduation and what would come after. I teased him sometimes that his dick was going to shrivel up and fall off from lack of use, to which he would half-jokingly tell me I was welcome to lend him a hand in that department.

I did sometimes look at him and see the boy who had made my heart ache. But that boy was mostly gone, replaced by a man who resembled him only in appearance. The dewy magic that had surrounded us as children had evaporated in the sun of adulthood, and now I rarely thought about Jack in that way. When I did, I took care of it quickly and with a vague sense of irritation, so that when I saw him later I wouldn't be tempted to try and go back.

It was, I admit, an unusual arrangement, but not terribly so, at least for the time. After years of being secretive about our lives, we were now free to live them any way we chose. The multitude of options was dizzying, as if we'd been handed a menu featuring every possible delight and told to order freely and without worry as to cost or consequence. Because everything was so new to all of us, we were figuring it out as we went along. It would take many years before we realized what had truly worked and what hadn't, what choices we'd made that were perhaps not the best ones. For the moment, though, we were doing the best that we could.

"Do you want to go to a movie tonight?" Burt asked, drawing my attention away from the rain. He'd traded his *People* for the newspaper, which he had spread open on his desk.

"What are the options?"

"Let's see," he said, running his finger down the page. "Well, we've got *The Way We Were* at the Coliseum, *Sleuth* at the Castro, *Touch of Class* at the Four Star or . . ." He looked up and raised an eyebrow. "We can head over to the Nob Hill Cinema for a Jim Cassidy triple bill. *All Night Service*, *Manpower*, and *Desires of the Devil*."

"Hmmm," I said, tapping my finger on my chin. "Oscar nominees or your favorite porn star. That's a tough one."

"I wouldn't say Cassidy's my *favorite*," said Burt. "Anyway, I think I'd rather see Glenda Jackson. Interested?"

"Jack and I saw *Touch of Class*," I said. "But go. You'll like it. George Segal will make you forget Jim Cassidy."

"Really?" said Burt. "Is George Segal hung like a mule, too?"

"You'll have to ask Mrs. Segal," I said. "Because I'm not telling. Now, if you'll excuse me, I've got work to do."

For the rest of the morning I went through folder after folder, each holding the story of another man searching for answers to what had happened to him. It was fairly clear to me that the cause lay some-where in the one thing they all shared—time spent in Vietnam—but I had no idea where to begin looking. I hadn't the skills to unravel the mysteries of either the body or the mind. I could only record and archive the growing phenomenon and hope that someone would eventually figure out what, if anything, was going on. I'd heard rumors that the doctors believed the various complaints to be psychosomatic, physical manifestations of feelings that soldiers couldn't process. This was disturbing, but not unbelievable. I myself hadn't experienced any-thing to worry me, but as the files in my office had begun to pile up, I sometimes wondered if it was just a matter of time.

By three o'clock, I had worked the stack down to only a handful and was feeling slightly better, although a day of making phone calls to people whom you must inform that you have nothing more to offer them is hardly uplifting. I was considering taking Burt up on his offer of a movie, thinking it might boost my spirits sufficiently that I could come back the next day less inclined to moodiness. I wondered if I might be able to talk him into *The Sting*, which I'd yet to see. Watching Paul Newman and Robert Redford, together for the first time since they'd thrilled me as Butch and Sundance, was exactly what I needed to shake the winter blues.

I was about to ask him if he was interested when my phone rang. I picked it up, expecting the caller to be an unhappy client upset by my delivery of bad news.

"Ned?" a woman said.

"Yes," I answered, trying to place the voice, which sounded familiar but not immediately identifiable.

"It's Patricia Grace," she said. "Jack's mother."

"Mrs. Grace," I said, understanding now why I'd recognized her voice. "How are you?"

"I'm fine, dear. I'm actually calling for your mother."

"Mom?" I said. "Is she all right?"

She didn't respond right away. During the pause, I had time to realize that her calling me was probably not a good thing. Both Jack and I spoke with our parents regularly. If Mrs. Grace was phoning me, it had to be because my mother was unable to do it herself.

"Your mother is fine," she said, calming me down. "It's your father."

"Dad? What about him?"

I heard her voice falter, as if she was holding back a sob. "Oh, Ned," she said. "I'm so sorry. Your father is dead."

CHAPTER 34

Winter is a lousy time for funerals, and of the winter months, I think February must be the worst. My father's service was held on February 28, a day so bitterly cold that even had burial been an option, I don't think the living could have endured the weather for the time it would have taken to lower his casket into the frosty ground. As it was, only a handful of people were scattered around the sanctuary of Ebenezer Lutheran Church, which I'd last visited seven years before during that bittersweet Christmas Eve service. The warmth that had filled the church on that night was gone now, extinguished by the icy breath of death. Sleet lashed the stained-glass windows and the sun was swallowed up by dirty gray clouds as we gathered to mourn the passing of a man only 50 years old when an aneurysm in his brain burst, resulting in a cerebral hemorrhage. My father had died at his desk, just after witnessing the signatures of Garth and Claudette Perkins on their newly-purchased life insurance policies.

Among those in attendance at the funeral were my paternal grandparents, Canton and Wilma Brummel, who had flown in from Arizona, where they'd retired some years before. Now in their late seventies, they were not in the best of health themselves, but it had never occurred to them that they might one day have to bury their son, and so they were unprepared for the occasion. My grandmother sobbed silently while my grandfather, never one for displays of emotion, glared fixedly at a spot halfway up the rear wall of the chancel, as if his stare was the only thing preventing it from crashing down. Seated next to them was my mother, and I was beside her. We were a quartet of grief, each playing the song of mourning in our own manner. My grandmother's *stac-*

cato heavings were countered by the *largo* of my grandfather's stolidity, while my mother had opted for a kind of *legato sostenuto*, as if the middle pedal of her heart had been depressed and she was holding a long, low note of infinite sadness.

My own mood was difficult to define, as it changed frequently. The overarching feeling, naturally, was of loss. But also there was fear mixed with confusion. Always before I had believed that my father would be around to take care of everything, everything being my mother, our house, and the details associated with money and responsibility. With his death, these things had suddenly been thrust upon me. I had spent the previous day in the office of my parents' lawyer, who had informed me that while my mother would be well taken care of due to my father's life insurance policy (he'd apparently been his own best customer), there were matters that would require ongoing attention. We both agreed that my mother was in no condition to take them on herself, and so the burden fell upon me.

Given that I rarely had more than a couple hundred dollars in my bank account, this was not welcome news. I felt I was being asked to grow up in the space of a day, and while I was saddened by my father's death, I resented being asked to take over his role in my mother's life. As I sat in the pew, only partially listening to the pastor's words of consolation, I thought about the changes that might be wrought by this turn of events.

At home following the funeral, visitors came and went, bringing with them condolences and casseroles. Every other person who entered the front door seemed to carry a dish, as if the making of tuna noodle surprise and angel food cake was the natural antidote to death. Needing to get away from the constant stream of sad faces and lowered voices, I escaped into the quiet of the kitchen on the pretense of putting into the refrigerator the latest offering in a Fiestaware bowl. When I went in, I found someone was already there, bent over and peering into the icebox.

"Where's the beer?" Jack asked, looking back at me. "If this is going to go on all afternoon, I need at least two."

"In the back," I told him. "Behind the roast chicken from Mrs. Cousins."

He fished around for the beer, then reached for the bowl in my hands. "What's this one?" he asked, lifting the aluminum foil that covered the top.

"Pea torture salad," I said.

He laughed. "I haven't heard that one in a long time."

"Pea torture salad" was a term he and I had coined to describe the ubiquitous potluck dish consisting of pasta shells to which cold peas (and often mayonnaise) have been added. It seemed to be a favorite of suburban Philadelphia housewives, although I'm sure its existence is universal. The peas were always a nasty surprise, hard and unpleasantly bland, and we'd developed an aversion to it early on. Jack took the bowl and placed it in the very back of the refrigerator.

"I'm so glad you came," I told him after he'd shut the door and we both had a beer in hand. "This would have been an even bigger nightmare by myself."

"No problem," said Jack. "He was kind of my dad, too, in a way, plus, it was time for me to come see the folks. Can you imagine what kind of shit I'd get if my dad kicked off and I hadn't seen him in two years?"

"Yeah," I said. "I can. I'm waiting for my mom to blame this on me not coming home for Christmas."

"How do you think she's doing?"

I shook my head. "She's on so many tranquilizers, who knows? I can't tell what she's feeling, if she feels anything. She just gives that sad little smile whenever anyone asks her anything."

"My mom will take care of her," said Jack. "Don't worry."

"I don't know," I told him. "I'm thinking I might have to move back."

"You're not serious?"

"She can't live alone, Jack. What if something happens to her? My dad took care of everything."

"She'll learn," Jack said. "Look, one of the things we learn in grief counseling is that people are a lot more capable than we think they are. Right now you want to take care of her the way she took care of you when you were a kid. But she's a grown woman. You have to let her do this herself. You can help, but you can't do it for her."

"I think I liked you better when you were stupid," I said.

Jack tipped his beer at me. "I still am," he said. "I just know the right things to say. That's something else they teach you."

We finished our beers and returned to the living room, where my mother was ensconced on the couch. She looked drained and weary, nodding politely as people took her hand and mumbled words of comfort. Beside her, Jack's mother was perched like a bird, doing what my mother couldn't and thanking everyone for coming. She kept glancing at my mother, and from time to time she put her hand on her back, as if reassuring a child of her protective presence. Watching them, I saw how much they meant to one another, and it occurred to me that if it were Patricia's death we were marking and not my father's, my mother's level of sorrow might have been even greater. No one, I thought, knew her as well as her best friend, not even her husband. Seeing Jack across the room, talking to his high school baseball coach, who had also been a friend of my father's, I felt a great affection for him, and for everything we had been through together.

By early evening, everyone had left, gently herded out of the house by Patricia and myself. Only my grandparents, Jack, and his mother remained, his father having gone home earlier with the excuse that he had a report to finish before the next day. Finally alone, we ate a subdued supper pulled together from the many dishes in the kitchen. My mother picked numbly at a piece of fried chicken, while Patricia encouraged her to try the ambrosia whose donor's name had been forgotten but was believed to be a secretary from my father's office. "It has mandarin oranges and Cool Whip in it," Jack's mother said encouragingly.

With dinner over, my grandparents settled into the living room with my mother, while Patricia and I did the dishes. Jack hovered in the background, putting things away as his mother handed them to him. As we worked, I could hear the sounds of *The Waltons* coming from the television.

"When do you have to go back?" Mrs. Grace asked.

"My ticket is for Monday," I said. "But I'm thinking of staying."

"I told him he doesn't have to," Jack said. "I said you'd look after his mom."

Patricia handed me a wet plate, which I dried as she talked. "Of course I'll look after Alice," she said. "She can stay in our guest room as long as she wants to if she doesn't want to be alone here."

"Thanks," I said. "That makes me feel better."

Mrs. Grace was quiet as she washed a glass. "You know, when you decided to join the army, she would have done anything to have you here with her," she said. "She was so worried about you."

"So much for feeling better," I said.

She smiled. "But," she said, "she realized that you had to have your own life, even if it was one that made her afraid for you."

She handed me the glass and our eyes met. I nodded, understanding what she was saying to me. "I'll talk to her," I said. "And thanks."

Jack and his mother left soon after. My grandparents weren't far behind them, excusing themselves midway through *Ironside* and retiring to their room upstairs. My mother and I sat in silence, watching the television but not speaking. I had planned on waiting until the next day to talk to her about anything serious, but all of a sudden she turned to me and said, "I'm not going to fall apart."

"Who said you were?" I asked.

"I can tell what you're thinking," she answered. "You never did hide things very well."

"Well, you caught me," I said, humoring her but also surprised that she was so aware, especially given the number of pills I knew she'd been taking. I'd looked at her latest prescription. The bottle was half empty, despite being filled only a week before.

"Don't tease me, Ned," she said. "I'm serious."

I took her hand and held it. "I'm not teasing you," I said. "You're right. I am worried. And if you want me to stay, I will."

She shook her head. "No. Go back to San Francisco. Go home."

I was struck by her choice of words. *Home.* She considered San Francisco my home. Until she said it, even I hadn't thought of the city as my true home. That was a position held by the house we were currently sitting in, the one that had always been home to me. But she was right. That house was no longer my home. It was hers. Mine was the apartment on Diamond, with its creaky floors and high ceilings, its big bay window, and the fireplace that coughed smoke back in our faces when we tried to use it. Home was also the whole city, and the people in it.

"Are you happy there?" my mother asked.

"Yes," I said. "I am."

"And are you happy being . . ." She hesitated, turning her attention back to Raymond Burr and Barbara Anderson.

"Being what?" I prodded.

She squeezed my hand. "Nothing," she said.

"You were going to say something," I said. "What was it? Am I happy being what? An employee of the United States government? A college dropout? A veteran? What?"

"A homosexual," she said.

I froze. I wasn't sure I'd heard her correctly. Well, actually, I *was* sure I'd heard her correctly. She'd said it slowly and clearly. *Homosexual*. Like it was a nationality.

"I don't know what you mean," I said, trying to sound convincing.

"What did I tell you about not being able to lie?" she said. "It's all right, Ned. I've known for some time. Well, I've suspected."

"Why?" I asked, wondering what particularly nelly trait had given me away, and when.

"A mother knows these things," she answered. "I can't tell you how, but we do. Patricia knows about Jack, of course."

"She does?" I said, genuinely shocked.

"Don't sound so surprised," my mother said. "It's not like your generation invented it. I knew a few queer boys when I was growing up. Girls, too, although I think we girls do that sort of thing more naturally than you boys. Most of the girls I knew experimented with their girlfriends at least once or twice. For heaven's sake, Becky Zawitski and I learned how to French kiss by practicing on each other."

I was dumbfounded. My mother had never even said the word *sex* in my presence. Now she was talking about her foray into teenage lesbianism. For a moment I forgot that my father was dead, looking over at his recliner to see if he was overhearing anything she was saying. Then I remembered that he was gone, his chair sitting empty in the glow of the television.

"Well, are you happy?" my mother asked again.

"Yes," I said uncomfortably. "I'm happy." Maybe, I told myself, it was the tranquilizers that had put her in a sharing mood. If so, maybe she would forget the conversation when they wore off.

"Good," she said. "You should be."

I waited a minute before asking her my next question. "Did Dad know?"

"I don't think so," my mother answered. "But men never talk about those things, do they?"

"What do you think he would have thought about it?"

"I don't think he would have understood it," she said. "But he would have loved you no matter what."

I fought back the tears that formed in my eyes. I was supposed to be comforting my mother, but now she had comforted me. I didn't know what to say to her.

"Are you and Jack lovers?" she asked. "Patricia thinks so."

"Well, I guess she'll be disappointed to hear we aren't," I said. I stopped short of relating our long, complicated history. I was still reeling from the sudden shift in our relationship, and wasn't ready to go into detail about my sex life. "I'm not really seeing anyone. Neither is Jack," I added, hoping to head her off before she dug any deeper.

"She probably will be disappointed," my mother said. "But I'm glad. I love Jack dearly, but I think you can do better."

I almost laughed. Under different circumstances, I would have. Instead, I leaned over and gave my mother a kiss on the cheek. "I love you," I said.

"And I love you," she told me. "Now, can we agree not to worry about each other?"

"Agreed," I said. "At least not too much."

"I'm tired," she said. "I think it's time to go to bed." She stood up, letting go of my hand. "Do you know Monday night was the first one I've spent without your father in twenty-six years?" she told me.

"Do you want to sleep in my room?" I asked her. "I can sleep on the couch."

"No," she answered. "Your father and I shared that room since the night we were married. I've been Alice Brummel since I was seventeen years old, and whether he's in that bed with me or not, your father is still a part of who I am. I can live with a ghost if I have to."

She turned and walked down the hallway, leaving me alone. I looked again at my father's recliner, thinking about how many nights he had sat in it while I lay on the floor, watching a favorite program. I stood up and went to it. I could see the indentation where his body had worn its shape into the cracked genuine-artificial-leather vinyl. I reached out and ran my fingers over the arm, thinking for a moment that it might still be warm from the heat of him. But it was cold, and I pulled my hand away.

I couldn't bring myself to sit in it. My mother might have been able to share her bed with a ghost, but I'd had enough of haunted places. On Monday, I would get on an airplane, leaving my mother with her memories. I would go home. I didn't belong here. It was my father's house, not mine, and I would leave him to look after my mother.

I clicked the television off. "Good night, Dad," I said, thinking about everything my mother had said. Tranquilizers or not, I knew she meant every word. "I love you, too."

CHAPTER 35

"Happy birthday, old men."

Burt had to yell to be heard over the din. Buzzby's, as it almost always was, was packed. On that Saturday night—a warm one in the summer of 1975—it was overflowing with handsome men. Adding to the noise was the throbbing disco music pouring from the sound system. "You got me where you want me." The voices of the three women who called themselves the Ritchie Family sang the one line of their hit song "Brazil," which we'd been hearing in the bars for the past few weeks and which had been stuck in my head like a crazed bee.

Burt kissed me, then Jack. "Twenty-five," Burt said. "Do you guys feel old?"

"We're still younger than you are," I teased. To my relief, the Ritchie Family faded out and the unmistakable first notes of "Jive Talkin'" began. I'd developed a huge crush on Barry Gibb, whose beard and bedroom eyes I found enormously and embarrassingly attractive, and I tapped my foot in time with the music.

"Where's Andy?" Jack asked. "We're going to be late."

"Relax," I told him. "The show doesn't start for another forty-five minutes."

"Here," Burt said, handing me what was obviously a record album that had been hurriedly wrapped.

I pulled the paper off, revealing a copy of Shirley & Company's *Shame, Shame, Shame*, the cover of which featured a painting of Shirley shaking a disapproving finger at a cringing Richard Nixon.

"I thought it was appropriate," said Burt.

I had to laugh. I loved the song, and I appreciated Burt's humor even more. We'd both felt betrayed following the revelations of Nixon's lying about what was happening in Southeast Asia, and were even more disgusted by his involvement in the Watergate scandal. His resignation the previous year to avoid impeachment seemed to us to be the worst kind of cowardice, and our anger was only inflamed when Tricky Dick received a pardon from former Vice President Gerald Ford a month later.

"What do I get?" Jack asked Burt, pulling a wounded expression.

"You get to have your way with me," Burt told him, running his hands over Jack's chest and extending his tongue. "I'll do anything you want."

Jack pretended to think for a moment. "All right, then," he said, pulling Burt close. "I want you to drop your pants, bend over, and . . ."

"And what?" Burt said breathlessly.

Jack leaned into him, his mouth almost touching Burt's. "Tie. My. Shoe," Jack said, breathing each word into Burt's face.

"You bitch," said Burt, laughing as Jack tried to kiss him. "Get away from me."

"But you said you'd do anything," Jack replied. "What kind of sex slave are you?"

"Did I hear someone say 'sex slave?'" Andy materialized from out of the crowd, interrupting the game between Jack and Burt. He was holding a rolled-up magazine in his hand, which he dropped onto the bar. I picked it up.

"*Blueboy*," I read as Jack and Burt looked on. "'The national magazine about men.'"

"Open it," Andy said. "Page thirty-six."

I thumbed through the pages until I came to the one he'd told me to look at. When I reached it, Burt let out an audible gasp. "Is that you?" he asked, looking from the magazine to Andy, then back again.

"It sure is," Jack said.

"Every last inch," I added.

"What do you think?" asked Andy. "Aren't the pics great? They shot me so you don't see the scars on my leg."

I tried flipping through the rest of the magazine, still unsure what exactly it was, but Burt grabbed it from me and turned back to Andy's pictures.

"It's porn," Andy said, seeing my puzzled expression. "For gays."

"How'd you end up in it?" I asked him.

"This guy came into the bar last month," he said as he motioned for the bartender to bring him a beer. "Said he was a photographer and asked if he could take some shots of me sometime. I thought he was just looking for some action, but I figured why not? So I went over to his studio a couple of days later, and he turned out to be the real thing. He shot Cheryl Tiegs once."

"I don't think Cheryl Tiegs ever looked like this," Burt said, still admiring Andy's spread.

"Who's Brad Majors?" asked Jack.

"Oh, that's me," Andy answered. "I thought I should come up with something sexier than Andy Kowalski. Gene—that's the photographer—suggested Stanley Kowalski, but I didn't really get that."

Burt and I exchanged glances while Andy, oblivious to both the literary reference and his strong resemblance to Tennessee Williams's butch antihero, took a handful of peanuts and popped them into his mouth before continuing.

"Anyway, he thought I kind of look like Lee Majors. You know, from the *Six Million Dollar Man*. So Brad Majors. Brad was my idea. I think it sounds cool."

"Why use any name?" Burt said.

"For when I do films," Andy told him.

"Films?" Jack said. "You're going to do films?"

"Maybe," said Andy. "Gene says the money's good. Better than I make bartending. He knows some guy who directs, and he's going to tell him about me."

"I assume we're not talking about Francois Truffaut or John Schlesinger," Burt remarked.

"I don't know his name," said Andy. "Could be. But I thought Gene said it was Tony or Tommy or something."

"Well, congratulations, I guess," I said. "The pictures are great."

"The issue just came out," said Andy. "I stopped and picked one up on the way over here."

"I don't think you're the only one," Jack said, nodding.

We looked over and saw a group of men watching us. When they saw Andy looking back, they smiled and waved. I turned to Andy. "Well, Brad, I think you have some fans. We should leave before there's a riot."

We walked out onto the street and headed for the main event of the evening, a performance of *Beach Blanket Babylon* at Club Fugazi.

Although it had been running for over a year, I'd yet to see it, and I couldn't wait. Word had quickly spread about Steve Silver's bizarrely fabulous revue featuring campy songs and impossibly huge hats, and it seemed like the perfect way to celebrate Jack's and my birthdays.

"I can't believe we're living with a porn star," Jack said to me as we walked to California Street to catch the cable car. Andy, ahead of us with Burt hanging on his every word, was too far away to hear.

"I can't believe we *slept* with a porn star," I added.

Jack put his arm around my shoulder. "That was a long time ago," he said. "We can tell everyone we knew him when."

"What are you two talking about back there?" Andy called back to us.

"You!" I shouted back.

He and Burt waited for us to catch up. "What were you saying about me?" asked Andy.

"We were talking about how they'll need to put Vaseline on the lens when they shoot you," I said. "To make you look younger."

"I think it's more likely to be Crisco," Burt remarked, as Andy shook his head.

The cable car arrived a few minutes later and we boarded. As it began the climb up Cathedral Hill, we sat alongside tourists with cameras around their necks and street maps in their hands. Many of them had made the common out-of-towners' mistake of wearing shorts and T-shirts, believing that because San Francisco is in California, it must therefore always be warm. Now, with the sun going down, they were hugging themselves to stay warm. But still they were happy, as were we. We were, after all, in the most beautiful city in the world, chilly summers notwithstanding.

Where California crossed Powell Street, we jumped off and transferred to the trolley going north toward Chinatown, taking it as far as Jackson Street before getting off. The walk into North Beach toward Washington Square was not a long one, and we arrived at Club Fugazi with time to spare. We were seated at one of the tables for four in the front cabaret section near the stage, and minutes later we each had a drink in hand. By the time the lights dimmed, we were on our second ones and in a festive mood.

"Ladies and gentlemen, welcome to Beach Blanket Babylon Goes Bananas!" the announcer called out.

For the next ninety minutes we were treated to a spectacle. The cast, dressed as everything from apes to Carmen Miranda, Glinda the Good to French maids, performed skits and wowed us with their singing. One woman in particular, a petite brunette, brought the house down with her bluesy rendition of the torch standard "Am I Blue?" As she sang the final line, "Was I gay, 'til today, now he's gone and we're through, am I blue," the mostly male audience broke out in thunderous applause.

"She's fantastic," I said, whistling loudly along with everyone else. "Not only can she sing, she can do it wearing an eighty-pound hat covered in four-foot-high bananas."

When the show was over, we returned to the Castro, where we hung out at Twin Peaks until it closed. Herded onto the street, Andy, Jack, and I said good-bye to Burt and walked—not entirely steadily— back to our flat. Not ready for bed, the three of us opened a bottle of white wine and sat in the living room. I put Burt's birthday gift on the turntable, and Shirley & Company serenaded us while we talked.

"We should make a pact," Jack said, his words slurred slightly by all the alcohol we'd consumed in the past seven hours.

"What kind of pact?" I asked him.

"If we don't have lovers when we're thirty," he said, "we'll buy a house somewhere up in Russian River and all grow old together."

"Thirty?" I said. "That doesn't give us much time."

Jack knitted up his brow, as if he was trying to figure out a problem. "Five years," he said, sounding pleased to have arrived at an answer. "In five years, if we're not with anyone else, we're moving to Russian River."

"Sure," I told him, feeling expansive. "That sounds good."

"Not me," Andy said, rolling a joint between his fingers. "I don't want a lover."

"You don't?" Jack said, frowning.

Andy grinned. "Nope," he said, lighting the joint. "I want *lots* of lovers."

"You're going to be a big-time porn star," I reminded him. "You'll have more lovers than you know what to do with."

"Yeah, Mr . . . Mr. . . . What's your name again?" asked Jack.

"Brad," Andy said. "Brad Majors."

"Well, Brad Majors," said Jack. "You and all of your lovers can come visit Ned and I up in Russian River. Some of them might have to share our beds, though. Right, Ned?"

"Absolutely," I concurred.

Andy shook his head. "I don't get why anyone would want just one lover," he said. "There are too many good-looking men out there. Why not have them all?"

"Not all of us can get them all," I reminded him.

"This is San Francisco," he said. "If you can't get laid here, you just can't get laid. I bet I could look out the window and find at least half a dozen guys ready to come up here right now."

"Let's see it," I said, motioning toward the window. "I'll bet you ten bucks."

"You're on," Andy said as he got up and went to the big bay window, stripping off his shirt as he did. Leaning out, he surveyed the street below while Jack and I drank our wine and shook our heads at each other. Not a minute passed before Andy called out, "Hey! Where are you going?"

A man's voice answered back, but I couldn't hear what he said. I did hear Andy's response, though, which was, "Want to come up for a while?"

As he walked past us to the door, Andy flashed a triumphant smile. A moment later, we heard footsteps on the stairs, and Andy returned with a man in tow. He was young, probably not more than 20, with dark hair and startlingly blue eyes. He nodded at Jack and me. "Hi," he said, standing with his hands shoved into the back pockets of his jeans. "I'm Dan."

"Well, Dan," Andy said, sitting in an armchair and spreading his legs seductively, "want a hit?" He held out the joint. Dan took it and inhaled, looking at each of us nervously.

Andy rubbed his chest idly, letting his hand slide lower until it was resting on his stomach, his fingertips tucked beneath the waistband of his Levi's. Dan's gaze followed, fixing on the bulge between Andy's legs. I could tell by the hungry look on his face that he was ready for anything Andy suggested he do.

"Think you can handle all three of us?" Andy asked. "We're having kind of a birthday party here."

Dan nodded, dropping to his knees in front of Andy and reaching for his zipper. Andy looked at Jack and me. "You guys joining in? You're the birthday boys."

"Not me," said Jack, standing up quickly and heading for the hallway. "He's all yours."

"Yeah," I said, trying not to watch as Dan slid Andy's jeans down and reached for the already-hard dick that stuck up from his crotch. "I think I'm going to call it a night."

"Suit yourselves," said Andy, putting his hand on Dan's head and guiding him down. "I'll see you in the morning."

Jack was waiting for me in the hall. When I joined him, we both started to laugh. I covered my mouth so I wouldn't make too much noise.

"Can you believe him?" said Jack. "One porno magazine and already he's acting like a superstar."

"That's our boy," I told him.

From the living room the wet sucking sound of a mouth moving up and down a length of hard flesh spilled into the hallway. I heard Andy growl something in a low voice.

"You sure you don't want to stick around?" asked Jack. "Sounds like Dan knows a thing or two about blowing out a birthday candle."

"Do you?" I countered.

He rubbed his eyes with his fingers. "Yeah," he said. "But I'm not going to. That dick has caused enough problems for me already."

I knew he was referring not to the penis currently enjoying the hospitality of Dan's mouth, but to its owner. I also knew he was right. We'd managed to get past our mutual entanglements with Andy and form something new from the pieces of our friendship. As tempting as it was, getting involved with him again, even on such a casual sexual level, could break anew the fracture we'd so tenderly knit up over the past two years. Walking away was Jack's present to me, and I knew how much it was costing him, because I was paying the same price.

"Good night," I said, giving him a hug. "And happy birthday."

CHAPTER 36

"'Mary Ann Singleton was twenty-five years old when she saw San Francisco for the first time,'" Brian said as I watched a naked man spring from the diving board at the end of the pool, his impressive penis swinging like a pendulum as he rose into the air, bent, and knifed into the water. "'She came to the city alone for an eight-day vacation. On the fifth night she drank three Irish coffees at the Buena Vista, realized that her mood ring was blue, and decided to phone her mother in Cleveland.'"

"What are you reading?" I asked him.

"It's this new thing in the *Chronicle*," Brian explained, showing me the paper. "It's called 'Tales of the City,' by some guy named . . ." He peered at the page. "Mowpin?" he said doubtfully. "Moppin? I don't know how you say it."

I leaned across the space between our lounge chairs to look. "I think it's pronounced Maw-pin," I said. "Armistead Maupin."

"Sounds made up," said Brian. "Anyway, it's really funny."

"I'll read it later," I said. "There are too many other things to look at right now."

Brian folded the top of the newspaper down and peered over it at the men in the pool. The diver had swum to the side, where he was talking to an equally handsome man who was sitting with his legs in the water while a third man sucked his dick. The receiver of the blow job paid little attention to what was going on below his waist, laughing and talking with the diver as if he was having his hair trimmed or his nails buffed.

"This is why I hate porn stars," Brian remarked, putting his paper back up. "They can make anything look boring."

"I guess when it's what you do for work, it gets sort of routine," I said. "Like working at an ice cream parlor. The first two weeks you eat everything in sight, and for the rest of your life just looking at a bowl of rocky road makes you sick to your stomach."

"Then that boy's going to have quite the tummy ache," Brian said.

"Who's the guy in the pool?" I asked. "He looks kind of familiar."

"That's Jack Wrangler," Brian answered. "Star of such fine films as *New York Construction Company* and *Navy Blue*."

"Can't say that I know his work," I said. "I must have seen him at some party or other."

"Did you ever see that Eleanor Powell show *The Faith of Our Children* on Sunday mornings when you were a kid?" Brian asked me. "You were probably only four or five when it was on, so you might have missed it."

"Was that the one with the kid who always had some problem and solved it by praying?" I asked, reaching far back into my memory bank. "I kind of remember it. I saw it a couple of times when I wasn't in the mood for *Winky-Dink and You*."

"Well, that kid is the fellow in the pool," Brian said. "Only then his name was John Stillman. And he was much smaller," he added dryly.

"He's sure grown up," I said as Jack Wrangler put his hands on the pool deck and pushed himself out of the water. He walked toward the house, his muscular backside glistening and his feet leaving wet prints on the concrete.

Andy emerged from the sliding-glass doors, greeting Jack Wrangler as they passed one another and walking over to where Brian and I had positioned ourselves in the shade. He was wearing a small red bathing suit that only barely covered him and showed off nicely the tan he'd gotten during his two weeks in Palm Springs. He didn't even glance at the two men making love as he passed them.

"You boys having a good morning?" he asked as he pulled up a chair and sat next to me.

"It's been very educational," I said. "Brian has been filling me in on who everybody is."

"He should know," Andy said. "He's been in the business longer than almost anyone."

Brian lowered his sunglasses and gave Andy a withering glance. "You make it sound like I *invented* it," he said.

"Didn't you?" Andy teased.

Brian sighed in mock exasperation. "Keep it up, darling, and I'll make sure to only film you from your bad side."

"I don't have a bad side," said Andy.

Brian looked at me. "The sad thing is, he's right. He looks great on film."

I had yet to see one of Andy's films. He'd made three of them since his debut in *Blueboy* the year before. His scarred leg, far from being a detriment to his career, had been an asset, as the studio let it be known that he was a former soldier who had been injured in combat, turning him into an instant object of sexual longing. Now he was in Palm Springs to shoot another. He'd invited me and Jack along, but only I had accepted. Jack was too busy studying for finals of his first year of graduate school, where he was getting his master's in psychology. I still couldn't believe he'd found something he was good at besides sports or being popular, but he'd blossomed into quite the student. He was taking his classes very seriously, and had started to talk about becoming a therapist.

I, meanwhile, continued to push papers for the VA. Although the work was easy and it paid reasonably well, it was wearing on me. The problems many of the Vietnam vets were experiencing had been linked to the use of Agent Orange as a defoliant in Southeast Asia, but the government was denying that the herbicide had any harmful effects. I was caught in the middle, between seeing for myself the various conditions the soldiers had and having to stand behind the military's official position. This was made even more difficult by the fact that Quan Loi had been among the areas most heavily sprayed with Agent Orange. Already I'd seen on the claims I processed the names of some of the men Andy and I had served with. Although neither myself nor Andy were experiencing any ill health, I'd begun to worry that, sooner or later, we might.

A trip to Palm Springs was exactly what I needed to relax. The mansion we were staying in belonged to the owner of the company Andy was making films for. It was used as a location for many of the films, and was always overrun with well-built and well-hung men. Andy was the newest addition to the stable, and his position as the new stud in the barn made him the subject of both desire and jealousy, both of which served to fuel his confidence.

"What time do we film this afternoon?" Andy asked Brian.

"Two," Brian said. "Which should be when most of your co-stars are waking up."

Brian Sugarman was the principal director for Kestrel Studios, one of the many companies producing gay porn in the 1970s. Unlike most of his contemporaries, however, Brian had actually gone to film school at UCLA. Since graduating in 1967, he'd made a handful of small pictures which had earned him critical notice but failed to land him larger, more commercial projects. When a friend had suggested porn as a way to make money until something better came along, Brian had reluctantly agreed. Now, at 34, he was financially well ahead of his film school peers. Porn had turned out to be a goldmine, and with his attention to detail and ability to make even the sleaziest scene look like high art, Brian was both rich and respected. The only problem was that he hated doing it.

I'd met Brian at a Christmas party thrown by the owner of Kestrel Studios. Attending with Andy, I was overawed, not to mention intimidated, by the roomful of gorgeous men. As Andy mingled, I stood by the cheese table, nervously eating crackers and watching a line of giddy revelers waiting to be photographed sitting on the lap of hunky Al Parker, who wore only a Santa hat and black leather boots. Brian, coming over for a piece of Gouda, introduced himself to me by saying, "He looks butch, but if he was one of Rudolph's reindeer pals, he'd be Prancer."

We'd spent the rest of the evening together, Brian dishing the dirt on all the porn stars and their assorted hangers-on. It wasn't until he'd asked me to dinner and I'd accepted that I found out he worked for the studio, and only when we were in bed afterward that I'd found out he knew so much about the actors because he directed them. We began dating, and within a month were a couple. Brian was eight years my senior, which I found exciting in the way that only a soon-to-be-26-year-old with a 34-year-old boyfriend can. Although I had been to war, he seemed to me to be much more experienced. I loved to listen to him talk about film, describing the movies he wanted to make. At night, in bed, he sketched them out for me, filling my head with images and weaving stories that held me spellbound with their beauty and daring. When I asked why he didn't try to interest a real studio in them, though, he always said no one in Hollywood would ever let him make films his way.

The Palm Springs shoot, in May of 1976, was the first one I attended. Brian hadn't been keen on the idea of me watching him direct, but Andy had worked on him, and finally he'd relented and said I could come. I could tell he still wasn't completely thrilled about it, though I didn't understand why.

"I'm going to go get ready," Andy said, standing up. "I'll see you in half an hour."

"Don't come before then!" Brian ordered as Andy walked away. "I mean it. I want you to have a full load for the money shot. So hands—and mouths—off."

When Andy was gone I decided to bring up the topic of Brian's reluctance to let me watch him. "Is it that I'll be in the way?" I asked.

Brian shook his head. "It's just embarrassing," he said. "Telling a guy where to stick his cock and how hard to pump it isn't exactly directing Dustin Hoffman to emote."

"That's what you're worried about?" I said. "You shouldn't be embarrassed. You make great movies."

Brian laughed. "Well, *Mandate* did give *The Harder They Ride* four stars," he said. "I guess that's as good as having an Oscar on my mantel."

"You'll get your Oscar," I told him.

"Sure I will," he said. "But first I have to go make *Sticky Fingers*. Are you sure you want to see this?"

"And miss the chance to see a master in action?" I said. "No way."

We went into the house. The crew, busy since early morning, had set up in an upstairs bedroom. Lights were rigged around the bed, and the camera situated at the foot of it to catch all the action that would soon be taking place on top of the sheets. The set bustled with activity as the dozen or so people needed to film the scene went about their jobs.

"Are the guys ready?" Brian asked a young man who was running around with a jar of baby oil in his hand.

"They're getting fluffed," he said. "I'll go get them."

"Good," Brian said. "We should be ready to shoot as soon as they get here." He turned to me. "Stand over there," he said, pointing to an area between the room's doorway and its closet. "That way you'll see everything but you won't be in the way."

I did as he suggested, leaning against the wall while everyone attended to their tasks. A few minutes later, Andy and another man walked into the room. Andy was dressed in black pants and a black turtleneck. The other man, a well-built blond, was wearing a white bathrobe.

"Okay," Brian said. "Let's make a movie. Here's the scene. Andy's a thief. Hence the name *Sticky Fingers*. Scotty, you're the owner of this place. You walk in and find Andy robbing you. You have a confrontation, you fuck. You guys know your lines?"

Andy and Scotty nodded.

"Good. Scotty, is your ass lubed?"

"Yep," Scotty answered. "I'm all set."

"All right then," Brian said, clapping his hands together. "Let's have some action."

Andy went to the dresser situated on the wall across from me. He pulled open a drawer and began riffling through it, as if he was searching for valuables hidden among the socks and underwear. After thirty seconds or so, Scotty entered the room from the hallway. He looked at Andy, as yet unaware of his presence, and called out, "What do you think you're doing?"

Andy turned, a jockstrap in his hand. "Hey, man," he said. "It's not what it looks like."

"Don't move," Scotty said, trying to convey authority but sounding wooden. "I'm calling the cops."

"No," Andy said. "Come on. Isn't there some other way we can handle this?"

Scotty walked over to him and put his hand on his crotch. "Maybe there is," he said.

From there the scene progressed predictably. Andy opened Scotty's robe and stroked him with his gloved hand. After Scotty dropped to his knees and worked Andy to hardness with his mouth, the two of them moved to the bed, where they proceeded to fuck. As Andy was bucking his hips against Scotty's ass, Brian turned and motioned for me to come to him.

"Want to see what I see?" he whispered, nodding at the camera.

I bent and looked. In the small rectangle of the camera's viewfinder, Scotty's ass was in close-up. Andy's cock moved in and out of it, every hair on his balls visible in detail. I could see the slickness of the lube on his shaft, and the red lips of Scotty's asshole as they were repeatedly pushed in and pulled back again. It was like they were making love under a microscope, and watching it felt just as clinical as observing a sperm work its way through the zona of the egg it wants to fertilize.

"Okay, Andy," Brian directed as he pulled me back and took my place. "I want you to pull out and shoot all over his balls and asshole."

Andy did it, jerking himself off and spraying Scotty with thick ropes of cum. Scotty tried to respond in kind, furiously pulling on his own dick, but after a minute went by without ejaculation, Brian motioned at a man standing behind us. The man went to the bed and stood out of camera range holding a plastic bag from which a tube extended.

"Okay, Scotty," Brian said. "Let's see your O-face."

Scotty, who had stopped playing with himself, mimed orgasm, closing his eyes, baring his teeth, and moaning repeatedly. As he did, the man off camera squeezed the bag in his hand. A burst of fluid flew from the end of the tube and spattered all over Scotty's chest and neck. It was followed by another, then a third, until Scotty's torso was dripping with what looked like the world's biggest load.

"And cut," Brian called out.

Someone ran over and began toweling Scotty off while Andy hopped off the bed and came over to us. "What was that stuff?" I asked him, nodding at Scotty.

Andy ran a finger over his abdomen, which was also covered in some of the fake jism. He lifted it to my lips and inserted it before I could stop him. The taste was sickly sweet.

"Pina colada mix," he said.

"We used to use hand lotion for the pop shots," Brian said. "But it looked fake. Plus, this tastes better."

Andy went to get cleaned up while I stayed with Brian. The crew was already moving equipment out of the room to set up in another location. Scotty, finally wiped down, was putting on his bathrobe.

"Scotty," Brian said. "What's with the shooting blanks?"

"Sorry," Scotty said. "I guess I just wasn't that into it."

"Are you doing coke?" asked Brian.

Scotty shook his head.

"All right," Brian said doubtfully. "Next time you give me a load or I'll have to replace you. Guys don't like it when I don't show the spunk coming straight from the source."

Scotty nodded and left. When he was gone, Brian said, "Like hell he's not on coke. Andy almost drilled him a new asshole and he didn't blink an eye. That shit's going to kill this industry. Make sure Andy doesn't get into it."

"I don't know," I said. "If there's something to try, Andy's pretty much guaranteed to try it."

"Then he won't be around long," said Brian. "Guys who get fucked up can't fuck. He's a nice kid. I'd like to see him live through this."

"You make it sound like the war," I joked.

"I'm sorry," Brian said. "Sometimes I just get overprotective. Look, why don't you go hang out by the pool and we'll have dinner in town tonight, just the two of us. We'll go to Melvyn's at the Ingleside. It's unbelievable. The waiters wear white jackets and they make a steak Diane right at your table."

"Sounds great," I said, kissing him. "It's a date."

I went back to the pool and stretched out in a lounge chair. Picking up the newspaper Brian had left behind, I started reading the piece he'd raved about. Armistead Maupin's tale about a 25-year-old girl moving to San Francisco and starting a new life reminded me of my own, and when he introduced her friend Connie, a man-hungry stewardess who promised to shake up Mary Ann's world, I couldn't help but think of Andy. By the end of that first installment, I couldn't wait to see what life had in store for Mary Ann Singleton. If her life was anything like what mine was turning out to be, I thought, Maupin's story was going to be one wild ride.

CHAPTER 37

"I can't believe you made me come," Jack said testily. "For Christ's sake, it's only a *movie*."

"Yeah," said Andy. "But it's the best fucking movie *ever*."

"He's right," I agreed. "Trust me, you'll thank us when it's over."

The line outside the Coronet Theatre stretched down Geary Boulevard for nearly five blocks. Fortunately, we'd arrived early, and were sure to get in to the seven-fifteen showing of what was fast turning into not just the biggest movie of the summer, but the biggest movie ever. Since its opening on the Wednesday before Labor Day, *Star Wars* had become a phenomenon, with sold-out shows and enthusiastic fans coming back over and over. Just two weeks later, some of the people in line with us were dressed as their favorite characters.

"You love movies," I reminded Jack.

"I like passing my finals more," he said.

"You'll be fine," I said. "You've been studying for weeks. Think of this as an end-of-school celebration."

"Sorry I'm late." Brian joined us in line, eliciting disapproving frowns and a few audible protests from people behind us, all of which he ignored. "The dubbing session ran late."

"They roped you into this, too, huh?" said Jack.

"Hell no," replied Brian. "This is the third time I've seen it. I'm already thinking of doing a porn version. I want to call it *Stud Wars*. Or maybe *Star Whores* is better, but that sounds like a straight flick."

"I want to play Darth Vader," Andy said. "We can do a really hot leather scene between him and Luke."

"How about between Darth and Chewbacca," I suggested. "You can get some bear to play him and you won't even need a costume."

The line began to move, to applause from those in the front, and we filed slowly into the theater. We were close enough to the front that we were able to find four seats together with no problem. Jack sat between me and Andy, and Brian sat to my left. Jack continued to bitch about the fact that we'd dragged him away from his books until the lights dimmed and the movie began. As the opening text scrolled up the screen, he shut up and settled into grudging silence.

Two hours later, he walked out a believer, mostly in the inherent humpiness of Harrison Ford. "Did you see the way he handled the *Millennium Falcon?*" he raved. "That man is *hot*. If I was Leah, I'd stop playing hard to get and let those buns down."

"Looks like someone will be seeing it again," Brian remarked as we walked to his car.

Twenty minutes later, we were in the Elephant Walk, waiting for the bartender to get our drinks. Even on a Tuesday night it was busy, and we recognized many of the men out enjoying the unseasonably warm weather. One of them, a dark-haired man with large ears and big, dark eyes that made him look both sad and kind at the same time, detached himself from a group and came over to us.

"Hey, Harvey," Brian said. "How's the Mayor of Castro Street tonight?"

"Did you hear what happened in Miami today?" Harvey asked. "They overturned the gay rights ordinance. And it's all thanks to Anita Bryant. You know what she said?" He pulled a piece of paper from his pocket and read from it. "'In victory, we shall not be vindictive. We shall continue to seek help and change for homosexuals, whose sick and sad values belie the word *gay* which they pathetically use to cover their unhappy lives.'" He folded the paper up and tucked it away. "I saw it on the news and wrote it down so I'd be sure to get it right."

"I'm not surprised," I said. "Isn't this the same woman who said that if they gave rights to gays they'd have to give them to prostitutes and people who sleep with St. Bernards?"

"And nail biters," Harvey added. "The woman's a menace. We have to do something about her."

"Like what?" Andy asked him.

"Like this, for a start," Harvey answered, reaching into his pocket and pulling out a handful of buttons. He handed us each one. The front was orange and featured the words NO MORE ORANGE JUICE FROM THE UN-SHINE STATE, a reference to Bryant's job as a spokesperson for Florida's juice industry. "A friend of mine is making these," Harvey said. "We're going to boycott the orange juice guys like we boycotted Coors."

"Do you ever stop thinking about politics?" Brian said.

"Only when I'm having sex," replied Harvey. "And even then, I'm thinking about how Jimmy Carter is screwing us. Do you know he has a policy of never being photographed with a homosexual?"

"We know," Brian said. "You told us last year after you got him to shake hands with you at the Hilton when he was campaigning for president and your friend Donald snapped a picture of it."

"That's right," Harvey said. "And when I'm on the Board of Supervisors, I'm going to hang that photo in my office so everyone knows that this is one homosexual Jimmy Carter can't ignore."

"Well, we're all voting for you in November, Harvey, so maybe you'll get in this time," Brian said.

Harvey, seeing some new faces entering the bar, said his good nights to us and went to say hello. Watching him begin another impassioned lecture, Brian sipped his gin and tonic and smiled. "That guy is going to run this city one of these days," he said. "He's unstoppable."

"Do we really have to stop drinking orange juice?" Andy asked, looking at the button in his hand. Jack, Brian, and I had already pinned ours to our shirts.

"Only by itself," Jack told him. "It's all right if it's in a screwdriver."

Andy nodded while the rest of us laughed. Harvey was right that something needed to be done about the Anita Bryants of the world. Her Save Our Children campaign, which she'd been waging for months in an apparently successful attempt at turning voters against the burgeoning gay rights movement, was only part of the growing anti-gay backlash. During the past eight years we'd become more and more visible in American society, and we were starting to find out that not all of America was happy about it.

But Florida was far away, and social activism didn't really fit into the carefree world in which we lived in 1977. Despite his alleged aversion to homosexuals, Jimmy Carter had won the White House back from Nixon, Ford, and the Republicans. The unrest caused by Vietnam was fading. Life in San Francisco was pretty much near perfect for gay men, and we saw no reason to stir things up. We would wear the buttons

Harvey had given us, but only because it required so little effort on our part.

Personally, things were going well for me. Brian and I were 18 months into our relationship, and I was still as crazy about him as ever. Jack was about to receive his master's degree. And Andy, well, Andy was Andy. Or, rather, he was Brad Majors. His films had been huge successes, and he was now appearing regularly in magazines and on the screen. We couldn't go anywhere in the Castro without someone recognizing him, and frequently we found notes and love offerings left for him on the steps of our building.

After a couple more drinks, Jack went home to study and Brian and I decided to spend the night at his place. We left Andy talking to an admiring fan who had asked if he could buy him a beer and drove up Market Street to Brian's house on Lower Terrace. There we sat on the roof deck looking out on Twin Peaks and the lights of the city. Brian lit a joint, and we passed it between us as we wound down before bed.

"I think you have the best view in San Francisco," I told Brian. "I could do this every night."

"Why don't you?" he asked.

"Why don't I what?"

"Do this every night. If you lived here, you could."

I laughed. "I can't afford to live up here," I said.

"I meant if you moved in with me," said Brian.

I looked at him. "You're serious."

He nodded. "Why not?" he said. "We've been together a while now. I've got this big place with just me in it. You wouldn't have to pay rent."

"What about Jack and Andy?" I said.

"What about them? They're big boys. I think they can handle the place on their own."

"Well, yeah," I said. "But . . ."

"But what?" said Brian. "You think you'd get tired of me if we lived together?"

"No, it's not that," I told him. "It's just that, well, I guess it's not anything. Not anything important anyway."

"Great," Brian said. "Then you'll move in. Why don't we go to our bedroom and celebrate?"

I allowed him to take my hand and lead me back inside to the bedroom. To *our* bedroom, as he'd put it. As he pulled my shirt over my head and bent his mouth to gently bite a nipple, I closed my eyes and thought about telling Jack and Andy that I was moving out. The three of us had been together for so long in various permutations that I couldn't quite imagine what life would be without them.

Brian tugged on the buckle of my belt, pulling it open and unbuttoning my jeans. Kneeling in front of me, he took me into his mouth and began to coax forth an erection. Determined not to let my worries about the future spoil the night, I put my hands on his head and let myself slip into a dreamy state where all that mattered was he and I. I banished Andy and Jack from my thoughts, and when Brian pushed me gently onto the bed and climbed on top of me, pressing the warm center of his ass against the head of my cock, I was thinking only of him as I slipped inside.

Telling Jack and Andy turned out to be far less painful than I'd expected, which both relieved and annoyed me. I was hoping that they would be more disappointed than they were, but as Jack kept reminding me, I was only moving five minutes away. "It's not like you're going to Wyoming," he said. "You're just going up the hill."

The move itself was equally easy, as I owned almost nothing and Brian's house was fully stocked. I basically packed all of my clothes, records, and books into a couple of bags and boxes and moved them in one trip. By the following Saturday afternoon, I was out of one place and into another.

Brian was gone a lot that summer, shooting films in LA, Palm Springs, and Catalina. The first VCRs had recently been made available to the public, and although they were prohibitively expensive, the porn industry had taken note. As a result, Brian and his crew were making a record number of new films, in the expectation that if men could one day watch movies in the privacy of their own homes instead of having to go to theaters, they might soon have a larger and more widespread audience for their work. I was left at home to feed Brian's 12-year-old cat, Ginger, and water the plants.

Things settled down in the fall, and Brian and I fell naturally into a comfortable pattern. I liked being partnered. Domesticity suited me, and I spent a lot of time cooking dinner for our friends and throwing weekend parties that began on Friday afternoon and didn't end until dawn on Monday. Brian's work with Kestrel brought him into contact with a surprising number of interesting people, including some of San

Francisco's brightest social, cultural, and political lights. Many were the evenings when our living room played host to conversations between novelists and residents of City Hall, newspapermen, and the gay sons of prominent San Francisco families. And the meetings of these minds were not always strictly cerebral. Once, opening the door to the second-floor bathroom, I interrupted a tryst between one of Kestrel's most celebrated tops and a cellist from the San Francisco Symphony, and on several occasions a noted—and married—weatherman well-known to viewers of the local CBS affiliate was discovered in the guest bedroom pinned at each end by obliging young men.

It all seems unreal now, but at the time it was just how we lived our lives. "Everybody was doing it," is never a good excuse, but in this instance it was largely true. Brian, myself, and our friends were not the exception to the rule; we were the rule itself. We enjoyed life because it was meant to be enjoyed. We didn't know yet that there might be consequences later on. Drugs and sex were harmless diversions. In the light of what happened later, it's easy to look back and assign blame. But I would argue that we were blameless. We were, in a sense, children who had finally reached the age of freedom. We believed that love could save us, and that our only responsibility was to live well. We didn't know that we might be killing ourselves and each other.

In November of 1977, Harvey Milk finally won his long-sought seat on San Francisco's Board of Supervisors, beating out sixteen challengers and becoming the first openly-gay man elected to public office in America. Brian and I threw a victory party, attended by seemingly every gay man in the city, where we marked the historic occasion by partying in the street to ABBA's "Dancing Queen" and serving banana cream pie, in honor of gay activist Tom Higgins, who had hit Anita Bryant in the face with one during an appearance in Des Moines in October. Following the success of the boycott which had resulted in Bryant losing not only her juice-hawking job with the Florida Citrus Commission but a proposed television show as well, we were feeling victorious, and hoped for great things in 1978.

Later that month, Andy and I flew back to Pennsylvania for Thanksgiving. In the nearly four years since my father's death, both my mother and Jack's parents had accepted the fact that we were not going to be marrying and producing grandchildren for them. Although we rarely discussed anything intimate during our weekly cross-country telephone calls, they understood that we were part of San Francisco's gay world, and they did their best to display an interest in our lives without asking for too many details.

In my mother's case, this meant talking endlessly about the sit-com *Soap*, which had begun airing earlier in the year amidst much controversy surrounding its risque subject matter, which included a gay character, Jodie, played by the then unknown Billy Crystal. Jodie had quickly become a favorite with my mother, and she discussed him as if he—and his life—were a substitute for me and mine. It was, I understood, her way of being able to talk about things she wasn't comfortable talking about directly. Unfortunately, she believed that Jodie was emblematic of all homosexuals, and that his trials and tribulations must also be ones I had or would experience.

"Did you see last night's episode?" she asked as we drove home from the airport.

"No," I said. "I was busy packing."

"Dennis broke up with Jodie," she informed me, referring to the hyper-masculine football player boyfriend *Soap*'s writers had given Crystal's character. In order to make life easier for his closeted lover, Jodie had offered to have a sex-change operation, and had checked himself into the hospital in the previous week's episode.

"That's too bad," I said. Although I found Jodie amusing, I hated that he was depicted as a man who liked men because he was effeminate and therefore must be wired more like a woman.

"He tried to kill himself," my mother said. "I don't know if he'll live."

She began to cry, loudly and violently. I was startled. "What?" I asked. "It's just a television show."

"Promise me you won't kill yourself," she sobbed.

"I'm not going to kill myself," I reassured her. "Why would you think that?"

Her crying subsided as she wiped her eyes. "I read in *Time* that a lot of gay people do," she said.

I gritted my teeth and tried not to say anything too sarcastic. She was clearly upset, and although I knew she had nothing to worry about, I needed to calm her down. Later, we could discuss her misconceptions in more detail.

"I'm happy, Mom," I said gently. "Brian and I are happy. I love San Francisco. I'm fine. You don't have to worry."

She nodded silently, reaching over and patting my leg. "That's all I want," she said. "I want you to be happy."

"And I want *you* to be happy," I told her. "So stop worrying. Let's just have a nice Thanksgiving."

"That reminds me," she said, tucking her tissue back into her purse. "There will be someone else joining us tomorrow."

"Besides the Graces?"

She nodded. "His name is Walter Jacobsen," she said. "He's a landscaper. Patricia and I hired him to do the gardens this past summer."

"And he's coming to Thanksgiving?" I said.

"Well, he's more than just a landscaper," my mother said. "He's sort of, well, the man I'm seeing."

"You have a boyfriend?" I said, totally taken by surprise. "When did this happen?"

"He's not my boyfriend," she said. "Honestly, Ned, I'm forty-seven years old. You don't have boyfriends at my age. And we've been seeing each other for a few months now."

"That's a boyfriend," I said. "Good for you."

"It's not like we're getting married," she said.

"But would you?" I asked. "Marry him, I mean. If he asked you?"

"Oh, I don't know," she replied.

"Come on, Mom," I said. "You're still young. It's okay to think about things like sex and getting married."

"Who said anything about sex?" she said sharply.

"Well, if you're not having sex with the guy, then what *are* you doing? You can't watch television and play canasta all the time."

She didn't respond, looking out the window as if something completely engrossing had caught her eye.

"So, you are having sex," I said, needling her. "Is he any good?"

She slapped me lightly on the arm. "Don't say such things," she said. "Do I ask you about your sex life?"

"No," I said. "But I'm happy to tell you. Last night, for instance, Brian wanted to—"

"Not another word," she demanded. "Just let me think that all you do is hold hands and kiss."

"Fine," I told her. "But you're missing out on a great opportunity here. I could teach old Walt a few things you might really like."

She smiled, trying not to laugh but letting out a girlish giggle. As we pulled into the driveway, she gathered herself together. "Thank you," she said.

"For what?" I asked as I turned the car off.

"For showing me that I can have my own life," she said.

It was my turn to get teary. I leaned over and hugged her for a long moment. "You're welcome," I said. "But I'm still going to have that talk with Walt."

CHAPTER 38

The two huge flags fluttering from the poles at U.N. Plaza were the talk of the 1978 Gay Freedom Day Parade. Everyone passing through the plaza on the way to the green outside City Hall stopped to look at them waving in the June breeze. Staring up at them, we felt as if we were citizens of our own country with our very own banner.

"Gilbert outdid himself," Jack remarked. "Those are beautiful."

"Thank you," said a voice behind us.

We turned to see Gilbert Baker standing there. Famous in San Francisco for the banners he sewed for various groups and causes, Gilbert's most recent project, done at the behest of Harvey Milk, was designing something to represent the gay community in the annual Freedom Day parade. The result, an eight-striped flag with rows of fuchsia, red, orange, yellow, green, turquoise, blue, and purple, was breathtaking in its beauty and simplicity.

"The colors represent sex, life, healing, sunlight, nature, magic, serenity, and spirit," Gilbert explained.

"Can you make us one to fly at the house?" Brian asked him.

Gilbert nodded. "Can you imagine if every gay person in San Francisco had one?" he said.

"We really would be over the rainbow," I told him, earning a chorus of groans from my friends.

"We'll see you later, Gilbert," Brian said, then to us he added, "Let's go hear the speeches."

"As long as it's not some old dyke talking about pussy," Andy remarked.

"Those old dykes and their pussies fought like hell to get this parade going," I reminded him.

"I'd still rather see naked guys," said Andy.

"You see naked guys every time you go to work," Brian said. "How many of them can you see?"

"Never enough," said Andy. "Never enough."

We walked through the plaza and past the Federal Building and the library to the Civic Center green. The entire area was thronged with people, and in the center of it all stood Harvey Milk on a platform, addressing the crowd.

"Let me tell you exactly what Senator Briggs wants to do," Harvey was saying. "Let me read to you from the text of Proposition 6." He picked up a paper and began quoting from it. "'One of the most fundamental interests of the State is the establishment and the preservation of the family unit. Consistent with this interest is the State's duty to protect its impressionable youth from influences which are antithetical to this vital interest.'"

A chorus of boos met the reading. Harvey nodded. "It goes on," he said. "'For these reasons, the State finds a compelling interest in refusing to employ and terminating the employment of a schoolteacher, a teacher's aide, a school administrator or a counselor, subject to reasonable restrictions and qualifications, who engages in public homosexual activity and/or public homosexual conduct directed at, or likely to come to the attention of, schoolchildren or other school employees.'"

"What the fuck is pubic homosexual conduct?" Jack asked.

As if hearing him, Harvey read, "'Public homosexual conduct means the advocating, soliciting, imposing, encouraging, or promoting of private or public homosexual activity directed at, or likely to come to the attention of, schoolchildren and/or employees.'"

Harvey set down the papers he was reading from and looked at the crowd. "How many schoolteachers do we have here today?" he asked.

Only a couple of hands were raised. Harvey scanned the group, counting. "Seven," he said. "Only seven who felt safe raising their hands. I'm sure there are many more of you out there who are afraid to raise your hands." He paused. "And you should be afraid," he said. "Those of you who raised your hands, you should be especially afraid, because you just participated in public homosexual conduct. You're participating in it just by being here today. And if Proposition 6 passes this fall, you could very well be out of your jobs."

There were murmurs from the crowd, as if this information was new to them. Harvey let them grumble for a minute before continuing. "I have more bad news," he said. "Proposition 6 *is* going to pass. It's going to pass unless we do something now to change the minds of the people of California. Right now the so-called Briggs Initiative has the approval of sixty-one percent of the voters. Sixty-one percent," he said again, letting the number sink in. "That's a lot of people who think people like you and me shouldn't be teaching their children."

He took a drink of water from a glass on the podium. "So," he said when he began speaking again. "What can we do? Gay brothers and sisters, you must come out. Come out to your parents. I know that it is hard and will hurt them, but think about how they will hurt you in the voting booth! Come out to your relatives. Come out to your friends, if indeed they are your friends. Come out to your neighbors, to your fellow workers, to the people who work where you eat and shop. Once and for all, break down the myths, destroy the lies and distortions. For your sake. For their sake. For the sake of the youngsters who are becoming scared by the votes from Dade to Eugene."

His speech was met with thunderous applause. Brian turned to me. "Want to stick around for the rest?" he asked.

"Let's find a party," Andy suggested. "I want to have some *fun* today."

"Are you even registered to vote?" I asked him as we started pressing our way back through the crowd. He ignored me, smiling at a handsome man walking past wearing cut-off shorts and a T-shirt that read FREE PARKING IN REAR. I made a mental note to discuss the importance of civic duty with him later on, although I had a feeling it would do little good.

At Market Street we walked back toward the Castro through the remnants of the parade that had passed through earlier in the day. We'd watched the entire thing, admiring the floats and cheering the groups of marchers, which ranged from gay Asians to leathermen, a baton-twirling contingent to the requisite drag queens. Seeing them all pass by as we stood on the corner of Market and 14th Street, I was reminded of what a strange family we all were. Now there are groups for everything, from gay firemen to lesbian lawyers. But back then we all banded together because we needed one another. We understood that there was strength in numbers, and our Freedom Day celebrations were all about celebrating our San Francisco community in all its diversity.

They were also, naturally, about having a good time. Even in 1978, with the Briggs Initiative occupying our minds, we were in the mood to party, and the Castro was the scene of an all-out festival. Every bar was packed, and the crowds spilled into the streets. Everywhere you looked there were gay men and women openly expressing themselves, some more flamboyantly than others. I remember, in particular, three drag queens standing on the balcony of an apartment overlooking Castro Street and singing along to Linda Clifford's "If My Friends Could See Me Now" while an appreciative audience danced away beneath them.

Brian, Jack, and I headed to the Elephant Walk, where the crowd was so thick that drink orders and money were passed along man-to-man until they reached the bar, with the drinks coming back the same way. The music, played at deafening levels, was all disco. I remember dancing to Lipstique's "At the Discotheque," A Taste of Honey's "Boogie Oogie Oogie," and, of course, the Village People's "San Francisco," which was played every hour on the hour. We drank and danced well into the night, until finally I was exhausted. But when I told Andy I thought it might be time to head home, he took me by the hand and led me into the bathroom.

"Here," he said, taking a small bottle from his jeans pocket. "Have some of this. It will keep you going."

"Poppers?" I said.

"No," said Andy, tipping the bottle and pouring a line of white powder onto the edge of the sink. "Coke."

"I thought Brian told you not to use that stuff," I said as Andy bent down and inhaled the cocaine through a rolled-up dollar bill, first through one nostril and then the other.

"He did," Andy said, pouring another line. "But he's got the wrong idea about it. You just have to know when to stop."

I eyed the line of coke warily. I certainly wasn't against drugs, but Brian had made cocaine sound like something to be avoided at all costs. I looked at Andy. He was nodding his head to the music audible through the bathroom door.

"You're sure it's safe?" I asked.

"Safe as sugar," Andy assured me.

I bent and imitated his sniffing maneuver. As the cocaine hit my sinuses, I wanted to sneeze. The feeling quickly dulled, becoming a warmth that trickled uncomfortably down the back of my throat. The taste was awful, and I gagged.

"Hold on," Andy said, patting me on the back. "It'll stop."

For a few seconds, all I wanted to do was rinse my throat. Then, as if by magic, the cocaine cast its spell on my neurotransmitters and the world opened up. My weariness fled, and I felt as if I could dance forever. I looked at Andy, who was watching me with a knowing expression. "Holy shit," I said.

"It only lasts for about an hour," he told me, pressing the bottle into my hand. "Maybe less. Then you need to do another line."

"What about you?" I asked.

"I know where to get more," he answered. "That's all yours."

We returned to the bar, where suddenly the music sounded as if it was coming from inside my head, transmitted through some internal wiring buried deep in my brain. I heard Donna Summer cooing "I Feel Love," and I wrapped myself in her voice. I barely noticed when Brian tapped me on the shoulder. He had to grab my arm before I stopped dancing and acknowledged him.

"Hey, baby," I said, putting my hands around his waist and trying to get him to dance.

"Hey, yourself," he said. "What got into you? Five minutes ago you wanted to go home."

"I got my second wind," I told him.

"Well, I'm beat," he said. "This old man has had enough gay freedom for one weekend. I'm going to head home, okay?"

I nodded. "Okay," I told him. "I'll stay with Jack and Andy."

"Jack left already," Brian informed me. "He said to say good-bye. But Andy's here somewhere." He kissed me. "You boys try to stay out of trouble," he said.

I nodded and waved as he turned to go. A moment later, I was swept back into the song. All around me, men moved with the music and with each other. In the flashing glitter-ball light of the cocaine, they were all beautiful. I wanted to touch them, taste them, smell them. They were my brothers, and we were celebrating together. Nobody could stop us. I felt certain of that now. We were too powerful.

I don't know what time it was when Andy finally pulled me out of the bar. I know I had used up all the cocaine in the bottle. When Andy saw that it was empty, he laughed. "Christ," he said, "you sucked that stuff up like a vacuum."

"I feel fantastic," I said as we walked up 18th Street.

"Yeah, well, lay off for a while," he said. "You're new to it."

As we passed the Pendulum, we saw that there was a large crowd standing on the sidewalk, all looking west toward the corner of 18th and Diamond. There the sky was lit up by red and white flashes. With the cocaine still playing billiards with the dopamine in my brain, to me it looked like fireworks, and for a moment I thought we were witnessing some spectacular display. As Andy and I pressed through the sea of onlookers, I expected to see someone juggling flaming torches or eating fire.

"Some queen probably built a bonfire in the middle of the street," I joked to Andy.

"It's an ambulance," someone said.

"Then some queen probably fell off her high heels," Andy joked, and we laughed.

A big leatherman turned and glared at us. "It's not funny," he said, the lights glinting off the metal rings of the harness he wore. "A couple of fag bashers got some guy."

We kept walking, weaving through the maze of men who were watching the proceedings. At Collingwood, a police officer stopped us. "Where are you going?" he asked.

"Diamond," Andy answered. "I live there."

The cop waved us through and we drew nearer to the ambulance. On the sidewalk, two EMTs were bent over a body. Blood was spattered on the concrete, and there seemed to be a lot of it.

"Poor guy," Andy said as we started to walk around the ambulance. "That looks bad."

I looked again at the apparently unconscious victim. Beside one of the EMTs' feet a baseball cap lay on the sidewalk. The crown was crumpled, but I could see the letters stitched on it—HCHS—in cream thread against a maroon background. HCHS. Herndon Central High School. Home of the Herndon Wildcats.

My first reaction was surprise that someone else might have attended Herndon. I hadn't seen a cap like that since high school, except for the one Jack continued to wear ten years after he'd last played for the Wildcats baseball team. I always teased him about holding on to it, but he insisted on keeping it.

Fighting the cocaine coursing through my blood, I struggled to re-member whether Jack had worn his cap that day. I closed my eyes and tried to picture him standing at the parade. I saw the work boots, the jeans, the T-shirt featuring an image of Mighty Mouse with his fist in the air and a raised eyebrow. I saw his face with the moustache and beard he'd recently started to let grow. And on his head, the cap, pulled low over his eyes, the material worn and the lettering starting to fray slightly.

Just like the cap on the ground. I stared at it, hoping that I was wrong, that I'd misread the lettering. Crossing the street, I knelt and picked it up.

"Hey," a police officer called out, running over to me. "Don't touch anything."

"I know him," I said, looking over the shoulders of the EMTs to the figure on the ground. Beneath the blood that covered his features, I recognized the face instantly. "He's my friend."

"What's his name?" one of the EMTs asked me.

"Jack," I said.

The EMT shook Jack's shoulder gently. "Jack," he called out. "Jack. Can you hear me?"

Jack's eyelids fluttered but remained closed.

"Let's get him into the ambulance," one EMT said to the other.

By this time, Andy had joined me. When he saw that it was Jack being transferred to a stretcher, he put his hand on my shoulder. "Is he . . ."

"He's alive," I said. "Can we go with you?" I asked the EMTs.

"Not in the ambulance," one of them told me, shutting the door. "But you can meet us at the hospital. We're taking him to UCSF Medical."

I nodded as they got into the ambulance and turned on the siren, the noise piercing through the sound of Bionic Boogie's "Dance Little Dreamer," which spilled out of the Pendulum's two doors. As they pulled away, I turned to Andy, my heart pounding in my chest and my mind spinning. "We need to get a cab," I said dully.

As Andy ran to try and flag down a ride, I looked back at where Jack had been lying. I saw once again the blood. What had happened to him? I wondered. Who had wanted to hurt him so badly? I couldn't even begin to imagine.

"Ned!" Andy called out to me from the corner, where he'd managed to get a taxi. I started to move, then noticed that Jack's baseball cap was still on the ground. I picked it up and held it in my hand as I ran toward Andy and the waiting cab.

Two hours later, we still didn't know the extent of Jack's injuries. He'd been rushed from the ambulance into an operating room, where doctors were working on his battered body. As Andy and I sat waiting for news of his condition, I looked up every time a door opened or I heard a voice.

"What's taking so long?" I asked Andy, knowing he couldn't answer my question, but needing to voice my concern, if only to keep the thought from repeating itself over and over inside my head. I was still holding Jack's baseball cap in my hands, and I couldn't stop rubbing it with my fingers, as if somehow he would be able to feel it and be comforted.

"Oh, God," I said. "What if he dies?"

"He's not going to die," Andy said.

"How do you know?" I said angrily. "How the fuck do you know what's going to happen to him. You're not a goddamned doctor."

Andy crossed his arms over his chest and leaned back in his chair, ignoring me. Part of me wanted to slap him for assuming that Jack would be okay, but another part wanted him to say it again. I needed that reassurance, as I had none of my own. But Andy remained silent, looking at the floor.

"You can't die," I said softly, when it became clear that Andy wasn't going to comfort me. "You can't die."

I closed my eyes and repeated the phrase like a mantra, rocking gently and running my fingers around the edge of Jack's hat, as if saying a rosary. "You can't die. You can't die. You can't die."

The cocaine high I'd been riding earlier in the evening had become a downward slide, and now I felt as if I were sitting in a black room, looking for an exit but finding none. My head hurt, I felt sick, and I couldn't stop telling myself that what had happened to Jack was my fault.

"I should have walked with him," I said. "I shouldn't have stayed. Why was I so stupid?"

"You should call Brian," Andy suggested.

"I can't," I said. "I can't even remember the number. Can you call him?"

Andy nodded. "I'll be back in a minute," he said before heading down the hall toward the pay phone. I knew he was probably relieved to be away from my anxiety, and I couldn't blame him. But I also resented what I saw as his lack of real concern for Jack. *He* wasn't Jack's best friend, though, I told myself. He was just someone Jack had slept with a few times. A trick, really. Nothing special.

That wasn't true, and I knew it. Andy was Jack's friend, too. In some ways, he'd treated Jack better than I had. I began to enumerate my sins against the man who had been my friend and lover: Jealousy, anger, infidelity. Why had I been so spiteful, so ready to turn my back on him? All the excuses I'd used to justify my actions now seemed petty and insubstantial. I loved Jack, and he couldn't die. He just couldn't.

I held his hat to my face and wept into it. I was so wrapped in grief that when I felt a hand on my shoulder, I cried out. I stared at the person in front of me, a tall, bearded man whose face registered concern and weariness.

"Mr. Brummel?" he asked.

"Is he dead?" I blurted out.

"I'm Dr. Stanislaus," the man said. "And, no, he isn't dead."

I burst into tears again, this time from relief. Dr. Stanislaus waited until I'd calmed down a little before continuing.

"He's going to be fine, but his injuries are extensive," he said. "In addition to a broken nose, he has a punctured lung, several cracked ribs, a shattered tibia, and numerous contusions. We've stitched him up and fixed everything we can. Now it's up to his body to do the rest."

"But you're sure he's not going to die?"

The doctor nodded. "None of his injuries is life-threatening. The cuts and bruises make him look a lot worse than he really is, so keep that in mind when you see him."

"When can I do that?" I asked.

"Not now," he answered. "He's heavily sedated anyway, so he wouldn't even know you were there. But I'm sure he'll be happy to see a friendly face when he wakes up. Come by around eleven. He should be up by then."

"I will," I said. "And thank you."

Dr. Stanislaus walked off, leaving me alone. I looked at my watch. It was almost five-thirty. The whole night had slipped by, and suddenly I felt the accumulated weight of worry and lack of sleep. I closed my eyes as exhaustion washed over me. Where was Andy? Then I remembered. He was calling Brian. Well, I thought, he'd be back soon. Then I would tell him that Jack was going to be okay. Jack was going to be okay. He was. The doctor had promised. I would tell Andy when he came back. I just needed to rest for a minute. Then we could go home. I sighed deeply, and a moment later, I was asleep.

CHAPTER 39

Giving your mother away at her wedding is, I think, one of the odder experiences a son can have. As I walked mine down the aisle and handed her off to Walter Jacobsen, I wondered what my father would think of the man my mother was marrying. Walter was a quiet man, and from what I could tell, he treated my mother well. Most of all, she was happy. When she'd called a few weeks earlier to tell me she was getting married, I'd been surprised. It had only been eight months since I'd met Walter at Thanksgiving, and I'd barely gotten used to the idea of my mother dating, let alone marrying. Now I was sitting in the front pew at Ebenezer Lutheran Church watching her exchange vows with a man I barely knew.

"You did very well." My grandmother, seated beside me, patted my arm. "Your father and grandfather would be proud."

My mother's mother, Violet Renard O'Reilly, was a tiny woman, almost elfin, with the dark eyes of her French-Canadian ancestors and the personality of her maiden surname. She'd met my grandfather, Seamus O'Reilly, at the age of 19 while working for Canadian National Railways in 1926. My grandfather, seven years her senior and a doctor with an appointment at Cook County Hospital in Chicago, was on his way to a conference at McGill University in Montreal when he realized, to his dismay, that he had left the notes for his lecture on the train, which had already left the station on its way to Trois-Rivières.

Rushing to the ticket window, he came face-to-face with a raven-haired beauty who took pity on his miserable attempts at explaining in grade-school French what had happened. In perfect English, my grandmother told him not to worry and radioed the station at Drummondville to request that the young doctor's notes be returned on the next westbound train. As thanks, my grandfather offered to take her to supper, an invitation she refused on the grounds that it would hardly be proper. But he could not forget the lovely young woman, and after giving his lecture the next day, he'd returned to the station and asked her again if she would dine with him. This time she agreed, later saying that during the night she'd made a deal with the Virgin Mary that if the handsome American came to her a second time, she would consider it a sign.

Their courtship was conducted largely by letter, with my grandfather making a handful of visits to Montreal over the next six months to try to gain the acceptance of my grandmother's family, who were deeply suspicious of his Irish heritage but liked the idea of Violet marrying a physician. Ultimately, my grandfather's medical degree trumped his ancestry, and in October of 1927, the eldest of the three Renard daughters became the first member of her family in three hundred years to leave Quebec when she was brought to Chicago and ensconced in a house on Aldine Avenue in the city's Lake View neighborhood. A son was born a year later, and my mother two years after that.

Violet and Seamus's marriage was a happy one, but the male O'Reillys were unlucky. My mother's brother, called Killian, died at the age of six from rheumatic fever. My grandfather followed him in 1946, four years before my birth, felled by a heart attack while lunching with colleagues visiting from New York's Bellevue Hospital. Violet, having lost her son and husband by the age of 39 (and her soldier brother to suicide the year before), decided that she would not invite further heartbreak, and vowed never to remarry. She also discouraged my mother from taking a husband, and when a few years later my mother met and fell in love with my father, Violet did her best to talk her daughter out of it. Failing in this, a week after the wedding she moved back to Montreal, claiming that despite her bargain with the Blessed Mother, her bad luck was due to having left the city of her birth in the first place.

For the duration of my parents' marriage, she had not crossed the border into the United States, fearing disaster if she did. As a result, I knew her mostly through letters, phone calls, and anecdotes told to me by my mother. I had seen her only a few times in person, when my parents took me to see her in Canada. The last time had been more than ten years before. My mother, recalling the tragedy of her uncle's death, had not informed Violet of my time in the army, and so she remained ignorant of my experiences in Vietnam, believing me to have been too busy at college to correspond.

When my father died, Violet had been forced to reexamine her theory about the nature of the curse she believed to be upon her. As she'd not placed one toe over the line between her country and ours in thirty years, she felt she could hardly be held responsible for her son-in-law's early demise. Although some of her family suggested that the legacy of her youthful indiscretion might very well have been transferred to her daughter, she rejected that as unfair and mean-spirited on the part of the fates. At any rate, she said, if it *was* the case, there was nothing she could do about it now, and as her subsequent behavior would apparently have no effect on the outcome anyway, she declared her exile over.

Seated beside me, she watched, sharp-eyed, as Walter and my mother exchanged vows. Oddly, the fact that my mother had abandoned Catholicism early on, and was marrying for the second time in a Protestant church, didn't seem to bother her in the slightest. I suspect now that she might have considered it deserved retribution against Mary for misleading her all those years ago, but if so, she kept her feelings to herself.

As the only guests were myself, my grandmother, the Graces, and Walter's daughter from his previous marriage (a fat, sour girl named Candace who still resented her father for divorcing her mother twenty years earlier), after the ceremony we had dinner at a nearby restaurant in lieu of a reception. I found myself seated between Candace and Patricia Grace. Since Candace apparently felt I shared some of the blame for her father's remarrying, she ignored me, concentrating fully on stabbing the peas on her plate with obvious hostility and drinking far too much wine. That left me to converse with Jack's mother, a situation I found almost as uncomfortable as having to sit beside my new stepsister.

"It's really too bad Jack couldn't come," Mrs. Grace said, immediately launching into the one topic I wanted to avoid.

"He really wanted to be here," I said. "But he couldn't get the time off from school. He's really busy with his internship at the hospital."

This was all a lie. Jack didn't have an internship anywhere. He was in the guest bedroom on Lower Terrace, where he'd been for the past six weeks, ever since the night of his attack. We'd brought him there after a week in the hospital, where he'd needed to stay while the doctors made sure there was no lasting damage from his injuries. When he was able to talk, we'd learned that while walking home he had been approached by three men who asked him for directions to the nearest gay bar. Finding it suspicious that they should be standing only a block away from an obviously busy one and not know it, Jack had ignored their question. Enraged by his silence, the men had encircled him and, before he could call for help, begun beating him. It had all been over in a matter of a minute, and no one had heard anything. The men had vanished into the night, apparently satisfied with claiming one victim.

Such violence was not unheard of, even in unusually tolerant San Francisco. And it had increased since March, when the city's Board of Supervisors voted 10 to 1 to pass an historic anti-gay discrimination measure. The lone dissenter in that vote was Dan White, a former police officer and fireman who represented a heavily-Catholic and mostly conservative district. White frequently clashed with the more liberal supervisors, particularly Harvey Milk, and it was rumored that some of White's more ardent supporters were taking revenge for what they saw as a slight against their values by roughing up gay men.

Whatever the reasons for his attack, Jack needed time to mend. With Andy going on film shoots and generally being at best a reluctant caregiver, Brian and I had decided to let Jack recuperate at our house. The arrangement had worked out well. While I was at work, Brian was often home, and when he had to attend to business for Kestrel, I was able to be with Jack. And once Jack was able to attend to basic needs for himself and didn't require full-time care, it was almost like having a house guest instead of a patient. I was enjoying having him around, although I wished the circumstances were different.

Jack didn't want his parents to know what had happened to him, and so had avoided an appearance at my mother's wedding by telling them that he was doing a summer internship in counseling at a local hospital and couldn't get away. While it was an easy masquerade to maintain, I didn't like lying to his mother, and wanted to avoid talking about Jack as much as possible. In a desperate attempt at extricating myself from such a conversation, I found myself trying to make small talk with Candace.

"How's the chicken?" I asked her.

She glared at me. "Dry," she snarled.

I excused myself and went to the bathroom, where I did a line of coke. Since Andy had introduced me to it, I'd been doing it fairly regularly. I liked the way it took the edge off and made me worry less about things. I also liked how it gave everything a crystalline sharpness, as if I was looking at the world through a lens that brought every detail into focus. Mostly I liked how it made me feel invincible, especially in the aftermath of Jack's attack.

I went back to the table and managed to hold conversations without fear of spilling Jack's secret. Even Candace's glowering didn't dampen my spirits as I toasted my mother and Walter and told stories that had everyone laughing. Later, as we walked out to our cars, my grandmother took me by the arm and said, "You remind me of your grandfather. He was full of life, too."

"It's living in San Francisco," I told her. "There's something in the water."

"Well, you'll have to bottle some and send it to me," she said. "It seems to have done you a world of good."

The next day, flying home, I thought about my grandmother and her imagined curse. If there truly was some cosmic whammy hanging over the heads of the men of her bloodstock, I was next in line to be crushed beneath its heel. I pictured my grandfather, grand uncle, uncle, and father looking down on me and taking bets on how and when I would go. Or maybe, I thought, as the only member of the latest generation, I played another role in the ongoing tragedy. If my mother had inherited the curse from her mother, couldn't I then be a carrier as well? Instead of facing death, maybe I was the one who brought death to others. Maybe it was my lovers who should be concerned for their well-being. It was an interesting possibility, but one I was loath to consider, particularly considering Jack's recent misfortune. The idea that the men I opened my heart to might die as a result was far too disturbing.

But, I argued, was there not something to the idea? I had loved Andy, and he had nearly died in Vietnam. Now Jack, too, had come close. I was reminded suddenly of the dream I'd had years ago, in which I'd seen Jack lying in a hospital bed and been told he was dying of love. Is this what the centerfold-cum-angel had been trying to warn me about? Despite the ridiculousness of it, I felt myself shiver.

I couldn't wait to see Brian again, to hold him and know that everything was all right. When the plane landed at SFO, I hurried off, weaving through the less-anxious passengers and running to the gate. I looked for Brian's smiling face, and found nothing. He wasn't there to meet me. Nor was he at baggage claim, where I waited what seemed like an eternity for my sole bag to appear, tumbling down the ramp long after most of the other suitcases had been picked up and whisked away.

The cab seemed to take forever to make its way down the 280 and into the city, even longer to work its way through rush hour traffic and into the Castro. By the time we reached the house, I was beside myself with worry. I overtipped the driver and fumbled for my keys as I raced to the door. I saw Brian's car in the driveway, which only made me more concerned.

Leaving my bag at the foot of the stairs, I raced up to the second floor. The guest room was the first room I came to, and I looked in, hoping Jack was there and would tell me that everything was okay.

Jack *was* there. He was on his back, the leg with its cast stuck out at an angle. Sitting astride him, Brian was moving up and down, his hand wrapped around his own cock while Jack's filled him from underneath. Neither noticed me standing there. I watched, unable to speak, as Brian came, his cum shooting into the air and raining down on Jack's chest. Jack groaned and lifted his ass in a response with which I was well-acquainted. I waited until they had both ridden out their orgasms, then said, "I guess you forgot I was coming back today."

Brian nearly fell off the bed as he scrambled to get up and cover himself. "Shit," he said. "I thought you were coming back on Monday."

"Sorry to disappoint you," I told him. I looked at Jack. "Your mom says to tell you she loves you," I said before turning and going back downstairs. As Brian came after me, I picked up my suitcase, opened the front door, and walked out. "I'll be back for the rest tomorrow," I said.

CHAPTER 40

The stage was filled with gladiolas. The sign hanging across the back of the War Memorial Opera House said FLOWERS WHILE YOU LIVE. Thick clouds of pot smoke rose up from the orchestra section to our seats in the balcony. Not that we needed it. We were already high, soaring on the hits of coke we'd done not twenty minutes before. When the tall, skinny black man took the stage to the sound of disco music, accompanied by his two large female backup singers, we rose to our feet along with everyone else and cheered as Sylvester welcomed us to his show.

It seemed that every gay man in San Francisco was at that show on March 11, 1979. Sylvester had been our resident diva for more than a decade, first as a member of the brilliant but doomed performance group the Cockettes, then as a solo singer whose hits, including "You Make Me Feel (Mighty Real)" and "Dance (Disco Heat)," were staples in discos around the world. With his striking looks and unforgettable falsetto, Sylvester was an out gay man who had made it big. He often performed on Sunday afternoons at the Elephant Walk. We loved him, and he loved us back.

Sylvester was at his best that night, moving from the dance energy of "Body Strong" to the lyric tenderness of the Beatles' "Blackbird," taking us on an emotional journey as he sang the songs that mattered most to him. The stage that was normally reserved for the grand spectacle of the world's greatest operas could barely contain the personality of one ferocious queen as she poured out her soul, accompanied by tuxedoed members of the symphony orchestra.

Midway through the show, the music stopped and Mayor Dianne Feinstein came on stage to present Sylvester with the key to the city and declare it officially "Sylvester Day" in San Francisco. Seeing her congratulate Sylvester was bittersweet for most of us. Feinstein had assumed the position of mayor the previous November, when former supervisor Dan White, who had resigned his position weeks before, snuck into City Hall through a basement window and shot and killed first Mayor George Moscone and then Supervisor Harvey Milk. It was a stunning blow to the city, and particularly to the gay community. Earlier in November the Briggs Initiative that Harvey had fought so hard against had failed by more than a million votes, thanks in large part to the help of former California Governor Ronald Reagan, who urged voters to reject Proposition 6. While we were celebrating that victory, Dan White took it away from us by emptying five bullets into our hero at point-blank range.

The pain of losing Harvey Milk was still fresh almost four months later. Watching Mayor Feinstein (whom Harvey had infamously referred to as the "Wicked Witch of the West"), I couldn't help but wish that it was Harvey up there with Sylvester. I'd lost so much in those last few months of 1978, and I wanted some small part of it back. Harvey was gone. Brian was gone. Jack was gone. Gone, too, was Burt, one of the 913 victims of the cyanide-laced Flavor Aid drunk by the followers of Jim Jones at his compound in Guyana. Burt had joined the Peoples Temple at the insistence of a new boyfriend. I'd teased him about what I called his conversion-for-cock, but I'd never seen him happier. I learned of his death only days before Dan White murdered Milk and Moscone.

It seemed that the curse my grandmother believed had been lifted had in fact returned three times as strong, ripping from me everything I'd held close to my heart. Brian and Jack weren't dead, but I sometimes wished they were. After discovering them in bed together, I'd run to the first person I thought of. Andy convinced me to at least talk to Brian and Jack about what had happened, which I did during a tense meeting over coffee at Orphan Andy's. Brian said he'd grown bored with our sexual relationship and needed the freedom to sleep with other men. I understood that. Monogamy was the exception in those days, not the rule. (I suppose it may be now as well, but I don't think non-monogamy is currently practiced with quite the same level of enthusiasm as it was by us in those days.) I didn't begrudge him orgasms with other people; I only asked that he not have them with my best friend.

He refused. He accused me of jealousy and insecurity. I accused him of cruelty and faithlessness. I moved out and back into the Diamond Street apartment, while Jack remained on Lower Terrace and moved from the guest bedroom into the master. Once again, he had taken something that belonged to me. We only spoke about it once, at his request. He said that he was sorry but he had fallen in love with Brian. I laughed and told him he didn't know what love was. I told him he would never know. I told him that this time I would never forgive him.

San Francisco is a small city. It was impossible to avoid Brian and Jack, particularly as Andy was still making films for Kestrel, although fewer and fewer of them. I think he made two in all of 1978. How he made up the difference in his income, I didn't know. But he always had money for rent, for going out, for drugs. Especially for drugs. Our use of cocaine, pot, and various other mood-enhancers skyrocketed. I went to work stoned, stayed stoned most of the day, and came home hungry for more. I slept little. My nose began to bleed from time to time when I snorted coke, but I ignored it as I ignored Jack and Brian whenever I saw them on the street.

It felt like the magic of the '70s was wearing thin. The ever-present smiley face that symbolized the decade began to annoy me with its relentless cheerfulness. I was tired of long hair on men and bell bottom jeans on anyone. Even disco had lost its charm, as bands who came late to the party raced to capitalize on the dying fad (even KISS released a dance single in "I Was Made for Lovin' You") or rebelled against the sound and turned out what DJs were calling New Wave. With bands like the Police and the Cars pushing '70s fixtures like Fleetwood Mac and Heart off the charts, it was as if the last crumbs of the decade were being swept under the rug in a giant cultural housecleaning.

After it was all over, I would come to see the Sylvester concert as a farewell, both to the '70s and to San Francisco's innocence. The deflowering had begun with Harvey Milk's assassination. It ended in May, when Dan White went on trial. We all expected a quick and decisive conviction. White had confessed to the crimes, there was more than enough evidence against him, and there seemed to be no question that we would receive justice. The defense's argument that White had been mentally unstable at the time of the killings, as evidenced by his poor diet consisting largely of junk food, had resulted in the coining of the infamous "Twinkie Defense," the viability of which even the most lenient court observers found hard to swallow.

On May 21 the verdict in the White case was handed down, and finally I waited for some good news. Instead, it was announced that White had been found guilty of the lesser charge of voluntary manslaughter and sentenced to only seven years in prison. I was stunned. Outside the apartment I could hear the sounds of people shouting angrily, and I knew that word was spreading quickly through the Castro. I went outside, looking for some way to vent the anger that was rising inside me.

I found it in a group that had formed on Castro Street. There were perhaps only a hundred of us, but we were all furious and looking for an outlet. "Let's march to City Hall!" someone called out, and it sounded like a good idea to the rest of us. We began walking down Market Street, spreading out between the sidewalks and blocking traffic. As we marched, people joined our ranks, and within only a few blocks we had swelled to almost three hundred. Some marchers carried hastily-made signs proclaiming the injustice of the verdict. Others chanted, "All straight jury. No surprise. Dan White lives, and Harvey Milk dies," while some of us just walked, stone-faced and seething, toward the symbol of our betrayal.

When we reached City Hall, the green was filled with more than a thousand protesters. Although police had been sent to keep an eye on us, they remained quietly in the background while we stood staring at the big glass eyes of the building where Harvey Milk had fought for our rights, and where he had died a martyr to the cause he'd spent his life representing. San Francisco's City Hall is a beautiful building, but that night we hated it. When some people at the front of the crowd began pulling at the metal grillwork covering the doors, a cheer went up. Soon the glass panes were shattered. Then someone slipped inside through a broken window and started a fire.

Sensing blood, the crowd erupted. In the ensuing turmoil, police cars parked along the street were set on fire. Finally, unable to remain silent bystanders, the police attacked. They met fierce resistance, as angry protesters fought back using whatever weapons they could find. Many of us fled back down Market Street, where glass covered the sidewalks as escaping marchers smashed store windows. But our fury had been slaked somewhat, and mostly we just wanted to get back to our own neighborhood and mourn in peace.

The police, however, had only begun. Angered at our refusal to back down, they came after us, waiting until we had gathered once more in the bars on Castro Street to talk about what had happened. Then, shortly after midnight on what would have been Harvey Milk's 49th birthday, they swarmed down the street. I was sitting in the Elephant Walk when the doors burst open and police ran in, swinging their batons at anything that moved. We had no time to react as they swept through the bar, smashing the bottles of liquor and smashing the heads of the patrons.

I tried to push my way through the oncoming stream, but took only a step before a baton crashed against the side of my face and sent me reeling. I collapsed on the floor, where the last thing I saw before I blacked out was the sneering face of a San Francisco police officer as he loomed over me.

When I woke up, it was over. The Elephant Walk was a shambles, its beautiful etched-glass doors shattered and the tables overturned. Those who weren't too badly bloodied were helping those who were, and for a moment I thought I was back at Quan Loi as choppers unloaded the wounded and the dead. Then I remembered where I was, and I sat up, my head screaming in protest.

"Are you okay?"

I looked up to see the bartender kneeling beside me. I nodded, sending new bolts of pain through my body. "I think so," I said.

He helped me up and I leaned against the bar, avoiding the pieces of glass and pools of alcohol. Through the broken doors I could see people picking their way through wreckage strewn across the sidewalk. It looked like a bomb had gone off or a tornado had torn through. Looking at it all, I couldn't help but remember that on the night of Harvey's murder, the Elephant Walk had been decorated to celebrate its fourth anniversary. The owner had instead closed the bar in honor of the Mayor of Castro Street. Now the bar that had paid homage to our fallen hero had become another victim of his killer. Our city had betrayed us twice in one day, and I'd had enough.

I left the bar and walked home, the pain in my head subsiding enough for me to walk without stumbling. I knew I would have bruises for some time. The deeper wounds would take much longer to heal, if they ever did. I realized as I looked around me that I had fallen out of love with the city that had enchanted me as a 19-year-old seeing it for the very first time.

When I got to the house, I called out to Andy. When he didn't respond, I went to his bedroom and looked in. He was asleep, snoring loudly. Beside his bed was a mirror with just the faintest dusting of powder on it. An empty bottle of wine lay on the floor beside it. He'd slept through everything.

Instead of waking him up, I went to the kitchen and found a fifth of Jack Daniels. I took it to the living room, where I sat in the armchair and drank it straight from the bottle until the pain inside of me became a dull thud, as if my heart had slowed down to the point where it beat only once a minute. I listened to myself breathe and thought unexpectedly of Dylan Thomas, the poet who had downed eighteen shots of whiskey at the White Horse Tavern in New York and died not long after. We had read some of Thomas's poetry in my English Literature class at Penn. I had found it dense, but wonderful, and had purchased a volume of his work, which I took with me to Vietnam, where I read it from time to time to remind myself that humans were capable of great beauty.

I went to the bookcase on the far side of the room and found the book. Battered and dog-eared, it was falling apart. I returned to the chair and held it in my hands, looking for one of my favorite poems. Titled "Ceremony After a Fire Raid," it was written about the death of a child during a bomb raid on London in World War II. A meditation on grief and incomprehensible loss, I'd read it often when the strain of preparing bodies in the GR had become too much. I read it again now, stopping when I came to the third stanza.

> *Forgive*
> *Us forgive*
> *Us*
> *Your death that myselves the believers*
> *May hold it in a great flood*
> *Till the blood shall spurt,*
> *And the dust shall sing like a bird*
> *As the grains blow, as your death grows, through our*
> *heart.*

Reading those words, my heart broke open. Although written about a child, I saw that Thomas's poem could have been written about Harvey Milk, or the city of San Francisco, or about anything that has been loved and lost to great disaster. I wept for all such losses, and for the holes they left in the souls of those of us who survived them.

I knew then what I had to do. As if a star had come out to guide me to safety through a storm, I saw where my course lay. The revelation frightened me, but I knew it to be true. Even through the fog of whiskey I knew it. And now that I understood what I had to do, I felt a strange peace come over me. Closing my eyes, I surrendered to it, and fell asleep with the sound of dust singing like a bird in my ears.

CHAPTER 41

On the night of December 8, 1980, the radio was playing Bruce Springsteen's "Jungleland" when the song suddenly faded and DJ Vin Scelsa cut through. "This is WNEW-FM in New York," he said, his voice halting. "I have the extremely sad task of informing you that John Lennon died tonight." There was a pause as Scelsa drew an audible breath and fought back tears before continuing. "I am at a loss for words. I think for the first time in my career on the radio I don't have anything to say."

As the music returned, I looked at the Christmas ornament in my hand. I'd been just about to place it on the tree I'd bought earlier in the evening from a man selling them outside the West 4th Street subway station. He'd set up shop there just after Thanksgiving, and every night when I exited the station on my way home from work, I was met with his call to fill my home with a little holiday cheer. Finally I'd relented, handing over five bucks and walking to my apartment on Bleeker Street dragging the tree behind me. I'd set it up in a corner, then gone out and purchased several boxes of cheap ornaments and lights to decorate it with.

It was my first Christmas in New York, and I wanted to make it memorable. Now, hearing about John Lennon's murder, I knew I would forever associate the season with yet another loss. Searching for more information, I turned on the television and learned that Lennon had been shot in front of his apartment building, the historic Dakota at 72nd Street and Central Park West. Already a crowd of mourners was gathering, their empty faces turned to the windows of the huge stone building that had now become a mausoleum.

I realized that I was still holding the ornament. I put it down, pulled on my jacket, and left the apartment. Acting on instinct, I headed for the subway and traveled uptown. When I emerged at 72nd Street, I found myself in a crowd of hundreds. Across the street, police stood near the entrance to the Dakota, preventing anyone from disturbing the crime scene. Many of the building's windows were lit with flickering candles, and someone was passing out candles to the mourners as well. Several different Beatles songs played from half a dozen radios and tape recorders scattered throughout the crowd, and more than one person made their own music on guitars.

It was unseasonably warm that week, but I felt as cold as if I were standing in the middle of a frozen field. Like everyone else there, I had found in the music of John Lennon something that spoke to me. I thought back to the Beatles concert I'd attended with Jack all those years before. How was it possible, I wondered, that the joyful, wise-cracking John had been killed? Who would do such a thing, and why? All I knew then was that a suspect had been apprehended. In the meantime, a beautiful man was dead.

The irony of the moment was not lost on me. I'd left San Francisco the year before because of one murder. Now I was about to celebrate my first year in New York mourning another. Wherever I went, it seemed, death followed me. Was there any place I could go where I could be free of it?

I was thinking that perhaps I'd made a mistake in coming to New York. But everything had pointed me in that direction. I'd been able to transfer to the VA center there, and leaving San Francisco had simply been a matter of packing a few suitcases and getting on an airplane. I loved my apartment in the Village, and I especially loved the excitement of New York. A world away from the laid-back atmosphere of San Francisco, it was a nonstop parade, always on the move and always demanding attention. It had been easy to forget about what I'd left behind, if only because I had so little time to think about anything at all.

I'd arrived in September, just in time for fall. Although it's easy to fall in love with New York in any season, fall is particularly suited to it. The crisp weather chases away the lingering smells of the hot summer, and the streets take on a cozy feel as the whole city begins to settle in for its long winter's nap. I spent much of my time just walking around, taking in the towering buildings and the people who scurried in and out of them as if their constant movement was necessary to sustain the city's pulse. On weekends, I walked from Greenwich Village to the Upper West Side, sometimes stopping in at the Metropolitan Museum of Art or strolling through Central Park, but generally just getting to know my new home.

Several times, I'd stopped to look up at the Dakota. Familiar to me as the setting for *Rosemary's Baby*, I found its style fascinating. The building's high gables, steeply-pitched roofs, and *port cochère* main entrance built for horse-drawn carriages to pass through gave it a castlelike appearance, which was enhanced by the profusion of balconies and balustrades adorning its exterior. With gargoyles tucked into its many niches, spandrels filled with elaborate carvings, and the statue of a Dakota Indian perched high above the entrance on 72nd Street, it was like something out of a European fairytale. The fact that some of the most famous names in New York lived in its rooms only added to its mystique.

I wondered what those famous people thought about the death of their neighbor. Were they fearful that they, too, might be the target of a madman's gun? Did they mourn the loss of the poet who had asked the world to give peace a chance? Or did they simply find the police and the crowds a nuisance, an intrusion into their privacy that had been purchased at a price none of us standing outside the walls of their fortress could possibly afford? Were they standing now in their living rooms, looking out at us from behind drawn curtains and wishing we would all go home?

I was thinking these thoughts when a young man came up and offered me a candle. Dressed in a blue peacoat with a red scarf wrapped around his neck, he looked at me with sad eyes. He wore a black knit hat pulled low over his forehead, and straggles of light-colored hair stuck out from around the edge. He held the candle out to me and waited for me to take it. When I did, he smiled sadly.

"I know," he said. "It's all a little '*Dona nobis pacem*,' but it makes me feel better."

"A little what?" I asked, not understanding.

"Sorry," he said. "It's a chorus fag reference. '*Dona nobis pacem*'? It's this round we used to sing every year at the school Christmas concert. You sing that one line over and over while you pass the light from your candle to the candle of the person next to you. By the time you've sung it a billion times, the whole auditorium is filled with light. It's corny, but it's really pretty, too." He looked at me and ducked his head. "Anyway, it means 'give us peace.' That's why I thought of it. I guess maybe you had to be there."

"No," I said. "It sounds pretty."

He looked up. "It was," he said. "It was really pretty."

He began to cry, tears running down his cheeks as his face crumpled and his lips trembled. I reached out and hugged him to me, feeling him shake. His arms stayed at his sides, then slowly wrapped around me, holding me close. I had no idea who he was, but I understood completely what he was feeling.

After a couple of minutes, he pulled away slowly and wiped his eyes. "You must think I'm totally nuts," he said. "I was what, like, nine, when everyone was getting excited about the Beatles? The truth is, I never even liked them all that much. But his solo stuff, it just blew me away."

"I don't think you're nuts," I told him.

"It's okay if you do," he said. "I'm used to it. Oh, here," he added as a woman beside us turned to him with a lit candle. He lit his from hers, then touched the flame to my candle. As it bloomed, his face was illuminated by the glow. His tears shone, and I felt myself wanting to kiss them away.

"I'm Ned," I said, fearing that if I didn't keep him talking he would move on.

"Alan," he replied.

He didn't move on. He stayed as more people came and our impromptu memorial stretched into the night. As our candles burned, we sang the songs of John Lennon, the words floating heavenward. Despite our sorrow, a sense of calm and love surrounded us, much as it had the night we'd all gathered in the Castro's bars to mourn the loss of Harvey Milk. When we grew tired of standing, Alan and I sat on the sidewalk, our backs against the wall bordering Central Park. We sang until our voices grew hoarse and dawn began to trickle down the darkened streets.

As it grew light, people began to leave, returning to their everyday lives as the city prepared for another Tuesday morning. Many of them were replaced by new arrivals who, awaking to the news of Lennon's murder, had hurried to the site of his death to express their shock and sadness. This fresh grief tore away the thin scab that had begun to form over my heart during the night, and I decided it was time to go.

"Would you like to get some coffee?" I asked Alan, whose weary eyes were threatening to close.

"I would," he said, and I offered him my hand to help him up.

We found a coffee shop and went inside. As we slipped into a booth, Alan removed his hat and vainly tried to flatten his messy hair. It stuck up at odd angles, making him look as if he'd just rolled out of bed. I found it charming, and resisted an urge to reach across the table and pat it down for him.

Over coffee, I found out more about him. He was 24, originally from Indiana, the youngest of five boys. When I asked him what he did for a living, he told me that he was an actor, although, he added, his most well-known role was that of a waiter at one of New York's better restaurants. Like so many actors in New York, he was waiting for his big break. Until then, he said, he was sharing an apartment in Hell's Kitchen with two other Broadway hopefuls and trying to convince his worried parents that he wasn't going to starve.

"I told my mother I can just steal food from the restaurant when I need to, but that only made it worse," he said, downing his third cup of coffee. "So, what about you? You haven't told me anything. All I know is that you like John Lennon."

I told him the basics, about Pennsylvania, the army, Vietnam, San Francisco. I left out the less-pleasant details. I told him I was working for the VA, but wanted to find a different job. "I'm tired of living in the past," I said, surprised to hear myself state so simply what had been bothering me for some time about my job.

Alan looked at his watch. "I've got to go," he said. "But do you want to get together tonight? A friend of mine is in Albert Innaurato's play, *Gemini*, and he gave me two tickets. If you want to see it, we could do that."

I had no idea who Albert Innaurato was, but I did want to see Alan again, so I said yes. We agreed to meet at the theater at seven-thirty, and he left. I drank another cup of coffee before I realized that I, too, was going to be late for work if I didn't hurry. I left some coins on the table, left the coffee shop, and headed for the subway.

That night I stood in front of the Little Theater on West 44th Street waiting for Alan to arrive. I'd been nervous all day, my anxiety growing as the hours ticked by. Finally, I'd done a little coke. Despite promising myself that when I moved to New York I would leave that habit behind in San Francisco, I had found the drug so readily available that I'd taken to using it again from time to time. It had worn off hours before, and now I was fidgety again.

My anxiousness only increased when Alan arrived. He'd cleaned up nicely since the morning, his hair tamed and his face shaved. He still wore the peacoat, but his jeans and T-shirt had been replaced by khaki pants and a dark V-neck sweater. He looked even more handsome than I remembered, and I found myself turning unusually shy.

"Sorry I'm late," he said. "I had to switch shifts with another guy to get the night off, and everything ran late. I just got out about half an hour ago, and I had to run home to change. I probably look awful. I grabbed the first things I saw."

"No," I said. "No, you look fine."

"Thanks," he said as we walked toward the theater doors. "Oh, and just for the record, this *is* a date. Just in case you weren't sure."

"I was sort of wondering," I admitted. "I mean, we never really . . ."

"Come on," said Alan, taking me by the hand. "But I should tell you, I don't kiss on the first date."

I don't remember much about the play, which concerned two days in the life of a young man who might or might not be gay (he never quite figured it out). I do remember that it was very funny, and that I laughed a lot. But mostly I remember that Alan held my hand through most of it and the heat from his fingers warmed me more than any fire. When the curtain went down, I was reluctant to let go of him, and tried to think of a way to extend the evening. Alan did that for me, suggesting a drink at Mickey's Cabaret, which turned into two and then three drinks as we sat and listened to a not-very-good singer tackle Gershwin while he played the piano equally poorly.

As midnight rolled around and I started to feel the loss of sleep from the night before, I suggested to Alan that we take our conversation back to my apartment. He shook his head. "What did I tell you?" he said. "No kissing on the first date."

"Who said anything about kissing?" I replied.

"No," he said firmly. "But how about we go out again on Friday?"

"Friday?" I said, disappointed. "That's three days away."

"I have to work the next few nights," Alan told me. "But Friday I'm doing a show. I want you to come."

"You didn't tell me you were in a show," I said.

He waved his hand. "It's just this little thing I do on Friday nights," he said. "A little singing, a little acting. It's no big deal. So, you'll come?"

"Of course I will," I told him. "Just tell me when and where."

He wrote down the address for me and tucked the paper into my shirt pocket. "I'll see you Friday," he said. "Now be a gentleman and walk me home."

I did, and at the stoop of his building he said good night with a hug. I watched him go through the door, where he turned and waved. As I walked to the subway to go downtown, I asked myself what I was getting into. I was 30. He was six years my junior. It wasn't that much of a difference in years, but at the same time I had the impression that we'd lived very different lives. I wondered if the boy from Indiana who seemed to have had a pretty good life would be able to accept me with all of my emotional scars.

As the days passed, I worried about it more and more, until I convinced myself that I might as well forget about Alan. I was sure that when he got to know me and saw how beaten up I was, he would run to someone far less screwed up. I told myself I was stupid for even thinking that someone like him would be interested in someone like me, especially in a city like New York, where every next man was better-looking than the last. But, I kept reminding myself, I had moved here to start a new life, and this was a chance to try doing just that.

On Friday I went to the Duplex, the club in the Village where Alan was performing, arriving a few minutes before the time he'd told me to be there. I was pleased to see that the place was crowded, although given its size, that was accomplished with a few dozen people. I also found that Alan had reserved a small table for me, where I sat and waited for his show to begin, hoping I would like it and wouldn't have to feign enthusiasm afterward.

A few minutes later, a man stepped to the microphone at the front of the room. "Ladies and gentlemen," he said, "and I use both terms *very* loosely, please join me in welcoming those delicious sisters of sweetness, Miss Taffy Chu and Miss Bitta Honey."

The crowd applauded and whistled as two drag queens came out. One, clearly Asian, wore a pink minidress, white go-go boots, and an enormous beehive hairdo. The other was dressed in a Catholic school-girl uniform complete with long blond braids and a *Charlie's Angels* lunch box. It took me a minute to realize that beneath the wig and makeup was Alan's face. When I did, I could only sit and stare as he and Taffy Chu launched into a riotous dialogue.

"How was school today, Bitta?" Taffy asked her friend, the whole time chewing gum with exaggerated motions of her very red lips.

"It was okay," Bitta replied. "Sister Mary Fred spanked me again though."

"What for?" asked Taffy.

"She asked us to name the seven deadly sins," Bitta explained.

"Well, that's easy," Taffy said. "What did you say?"

Bitta answered, "Sneezy, Sleepy, Happy, Grumpy, Dopey, Bashful, and Doc."

Taffy rolled her eyes as Bitta chewed on one of her braids and the audience howled. As the two continued the show, I forgot that I was watching Alan perform. He played his part perfectly, and his singing was delightful. When the show was over, he and Taffy curtsied and scampered offstage, waving to the audience and promising to come back again soon. I joined in the applause, wishing the show could go on even longer.

Fifteen minutes later, Alan appeared at my table looking like the man I'd been with on Tuesday night. He sat down and looked at me, his demeanor shy and not at all like that of his alter ego. "Well," he said. "What did you think?"

"I think you deserve another spanking," I said. "That was some trick."

"Yeah, I'm sorry about that," he said. "It's just that it's easier to let guys see what I do than to tell them about it. I don't know why. I guess when I'm Bitta I don't care what they think of me, but when I'm me, well, I'm afraid of the rejection."

"I loved it," I told him.

"Really?" he said.

"Really," I answered. "I thought you were funny and great and, and, and I don't know what else. It was just fantastic."

"So there might be a second date?" he asked.

"I think there just was," I told him, leaning across the table and waiting for the kiss I'd been thinking about for three days.

CHAPTER 42

"Oh, my God, look at those shoulder pads."

Hearing Alan's remark, I glanced at the television as I passed behind the couch on my way to the kitchen. "Who is that?" I asked him.

"Linda Evans," he said. "Have you ever seen such big hair? Taffy's probably having a fit right now."

"And what is it you're watching?"

"This new nighttime soap," he told me. "*Dynasty*. This is the first episode. John Forsythe is this oil tycoon, Blake Carrington, and he's about to marry his secretary, Krystle. Only she might still be in love with her ex, who just got back from working on one of Blake's oil rigs in the Middle East. And she's all freaked out because she's never had money and the servants are all being mean to her."

"It sounds ridiculous," I told him.

"It's totally ridiculous," said Alan. "That's why it's so brilliant. Come watch it with me."

"I've got to go over those files," I said.

"Come on," Alan pleaded. "It's only got two more hours."

"I can get through twenty folders in two hours," I argued.

"Maybe," said Alan, "but you'll miss some awesome shoulder pads."

I was about to decline his offer again when a handsome man appeared on the screen. "Oh, and you'll miss him, too," Alan said, noting my sudden interest. "That's Steven, Blake's son. He came in from New York for his daddy's wedding, and guess what? He's a big H-O-M-O."

"Really?" I said, sitting down next to Alan.

"Blake is none too happy about it either," Alan informed me.

We watched as Steven and his father confronted one another. Blake was offering Steven a job on one of his oil rigs, with one condition. He had to leave New York, and his lover.

"I can find a little homosexual experimentation acceptable as long as you don't bring it home with you," Blake told Steven. "But don't you see, son, I'm offering you the chance to straighten yourself out."

"He didn't just say that," I said as Alan smacked me.

"Shh," he hissed. "I want to hear this."

Steven looked at his father as the camera moved in on his rugged face. "I don't know if I want to," he said.

The show cut to a commercial. A few seconds later, the phone rang. I picked it up and heard Taffy's excited babbling on the other end. I handed the phone to Alan. "It's Miss Chu," I said.

Taffy, a.k.a. Lawrence Wong, apparently *was* watching *Dynasty*, because for the next three minutes Alan just sat and listened, occasionally throwing in an "I know" or "We really do." When the show came back on, he handed me back the phone. "She's done," he said.

"For now," I corrected him. "I take it she approves?"

"She thinks we should start dressing like Krystle," said Alan. "I knew the big hair would be too much for her to resist."

I laughed. In the month that we'd been dating, I'd come to appreciate Taffy's eccentricities. Unlike Alan, who only donned drag when he was performing as Bitta Honey, Lawrence was almost constantly in character, unless he was working at his job as a securities analyst on Wall Street or visiting his very traditional Chinese family in Queens. Where Alan did it for fun, Lawrence wanted to *be* Taffy, to the point where he'd begun saving up for what he disturbingly referred to as his "snip-and-rip" operation, which he planned on completing by New Year's Eve of 1985. The fact that his parents were still actively looking for a suitable wife for him was only a minor roadblock, one he assured his friends he would deal with soon.

It felt like Alan and I had been together far longer than just four weeks. Being with him was easy. My worries about his being able to deal with all of my baggage had been unfounded, mostly because he'd been equally afraid that I would be put off by the fact that he sometimes dressed up as a woman. Once both of us realized that what we saw as potential problems weren't problems at all to the other, we'd quickly settled into a relationship. Now Alan spent most nights of the week at my apartment, an arrangement I was happy to encourage. I liked having someone to come home to, and on the nights when Alan worked late at the restaurant, I liked it when he crawled into bed beside me in the early morning hours and put his arm around me, holding me while we slept.

We watched the rest of *Dynasty* together, Alan marveling at the clothes and me marveling at the convoluted and only-barely-believable plots. When Steven decided to take Blake up on his offer, sacrificing his lover in the process, we booed him. But we both knew we'd be tuning in the next week to see what happened. At eleven, the news came on and we watched as the day's events were replayed for us. In Iran, American hostages were entering their 437th day of captivity, although negotiators were hopeful that an end was in sight. The Defense Department had issued an order that, commencing immediately, soldiers' boots would no longer be shiny, as the polished surface could give away their presence to enemies. And in Washington, preparations for the inauguration of Ronald Reagan were nearly complete.

"I still can't believe he won," Alan said as Reagan was shown laughing jovially with reporters. "The man made movies with a chimp."

"I voted for him," I said.

"You did?" said Alan, sounding more than a little surprised. "But he's a Republican."

"So," I argued. "He's also one of the big reasons why that anti-gay proposition lost in California."

"That was, what, two years ago?" said Alan.

"That's right," I said. "Only two years. And everyone's forgotten it already. He's not as bad as you think. Did you know he spoke out against Prop 6 after one of his aides came out to him? David Mixner. He sat Reagan down and explained to him why Briggs was wrong, and Ronnie listened to him. I'd rather have a guy who listens than one like Carter who can't get our hostages home."

"I didn't know that about Reagan," Alan admitted.

"Most people don't," I said. "That's the problem—people forget everything that happened more than a few days ago."

"Those who forget the past are doomed to repeat it," said Alan. "I know. I know."

"That's a perfect example," I told him. "The actual quote is, 'Those who cannot remember the past are condemned to repeat it.' That's how Santayana wrote it. But everybody gets it wrong."

"It's the same thing, sweetie," said Alan.

"No, it isn't," I said. "And that's why history gets all fucked up.

Someone makes a little change here, someone else makes one there, and pretty soon you've got the South winning the Civil War and Ronald Reagan setting kittens on fire for fun."

"I didn't say he set kittens on fire," Alan objected. "And if you're so worried about people knowing history, why don't you teach it to them?"

"What do you mean?" I asked him.

"Teach," he said again. "As in stand in front of a class and teach. You'd be good at it."

"I'm too old," I said.

"You're thirty," countered Alan.

"I don't even have a college degree," I said. "It would take forever. I'd be, like, thirty-five before I even got my B.A. And that's going full-time."

"You're still eligible for GI Bill benefits," Alan said. "That would pay for most of it. And it wouldn't take that long. Besides, you're going to be thirty-five anyway, so you can be thirty-five doing something you like with your life or you can be thirty-five still talking about how you wish you'd done something with your life. Seems like a no-brainer to me."

I started to argue some more, but I realized that he was right. For years I had been working at a job I despised, simply because it was something to do. It wasn't what I wanted for my life, but could I really go back to college at my age? I'd be around kids 18 and 19 years old, kids who had been in elementary school while I was in Vietnam. I'd be completely out of place.

Jack did it, I reminded myself. Granted, he'd done it at the usual age, but he'd still faced a lot of obstacles. He'd never been a good student, and nobody expected him to succeed academically. I knew that many times he'd doubted his ability to learn. But he'd done it. By now, I thought, he had his master's degree. Maybe he'd even kept going. And if he could, I reasoned, then so could I.

"Maybe I'll look into it," I told Alan, shutting off the television.

And I did look into it. Although I'd tried not to appear too excited about the idea in front of Alan, in reality I had taken his words to heart. I did love history, and the idea of teaching it to other people was something I knew I could really get into. Hadn't I spent most of my life as a witness to some of the most important events in American history? When I thought about it, it seemed I'd been born at the perfect moment to watch the life of my country unfold. Now, perhaps, it was time to share those experiences with others.

I made some calls to government offices and student centers. I ordered college catalogs and read them at work, becoming dizzy at the range of options available to someone who wanted to learn. Things had changed a lot since I'd gone to Penn twelve years earlier. Now there were courses in just about everything, and I found myself interested in all of them. But first, I needed to get in, and that meant filling out forms, writing essays, and getting transcripts from my one semester at Penn State. I did all of this without telling Alan, or anyone else, of my plans. I still felt that I might fail, and I didn't want to embarrass myself.

In February, I sent off applications to NYU and Columbia, then began the long wait for a response. I distracted myself with work and with Alan. He had recently landed an understudy role in a new musical, *March of the Falsettos*, and despite there being only a slim chance that he would get to perform on stage, he was delighted with the opportunity to rehearse with the cast.

The show premiered Off-Broadway in April. Two weeks into its run the actor playing Whizzer, the lover of Marvin, the play's central character, became ill with bronchitis, and for six performances Alan got to perform. I sat in the audience for all six, standing at the end of each one to clap as he took his bow. And I wasn't the only one to take note of his excellent performance. After his final show, he returned to the dressing room to find a note from none other than Stephen Sondheim inviting him to audition for a role in his new show. (The result, *Merrily We Roll Along*, would close after only sixteen performances later that year, but it would earn Alan more critical praise.)

I'd almost, but not quite, forgotten about my applications when on a beautiful July afternoon I received in the mail three envelopes. The first was a rejection, with their regrets, from Columbia. The second was an acceptance, with their congratulations, from NYU. And the third was a letter from Andy. Actually, there was very little in the way of a letter, just a note that said, "Jack asked me to send you this. I guess Brian has it. How are you?" Also enclosed were two newspaper clippings from the *Bay Area Reporter*. The first one, dated July 2, was headlined GAY MEN'S PNEUMONIA. The second was from two weeks later, and was titled GAY MEN AND KS.

I sat at the kitchen table and read the articles. The contents were confusing and frightening. A handful of gay men in San Francisco had developed an unusual form of pneumonia. Some also had been diagnosed with Kaposi's sarcoma, a type of skin cancer normally seen in elderly men and generally found only in two out of every three million people. Yet young gay men were now coming down with it in small but statistically improbable numbers. Even more worrisome, more than half of them had died within months. Researchers were unsure why the two diseases were suddenly cropping up in homosexuals, but feared that it may be linked to drug use or sexual activity.

I put the articles down and looked again at Andy's note. "I guess Brian has it," he'd written. Had what? Pneumonia? Cancer? In typical Andy fashion, he'd simply dumped something in my lap with little explanation.

It had been eighteen months since I'd left California. I'd heard from Andy only a couple of times, and sometimes forgot about him for long stretches. My life was in New York now, and San Francisco seemed far away. When I thought about Jack or Brian, which was seldom, it was in an abstract way, as if they were characters in a book I'd read long ago and the plot of which I could now only sort of remember. Good things were happening for me, and I didn't want to look back.

I crumpled up Andy's note and the articles and was about to throw them into the trash when I looked at the acceptance letter from NYU. How could I lecture Alan, let alone students, about the importance of remembering history if I myself was so quick to shut the door on my past? Brian and Jack had hurt me, Jack more than once, but they were still important players in my life. If Brian was really sick, I asked myself, what would I prove by ignoring him? Jack clearly wanted me to know something was wrong, or he wouldn't have asked Andy to send me the clippings.

I picked up the phone and dialed Brian's number, surprised that my fingers remembered the sequence after so long. As the phone rang at the other end, I fought the urge to simply hang up. And when I heard Jack say hello, I fought even harder, saying simply, "It's Ned."

There was a long silence. Then Jack said, "You got the articles."

"Is Brian really sick?" I asked him.

Jack started to cry softly.

"How bad is it?" I asked.

"Bad," Jack whispered, trying to control his shaking voice. "He's dying, Ned. They think he has a few days, maybe a week."

I swallowed hard as a lump formed in my throat. As angry as I was at Brian, the idea of him dying was too much. I couldn't imagine the vibrant man I'd loved being struck down by some invisible parasite eating away at his lungs or burrowing into his skin.

"What can I do?" I asked when I was able to speak again.

"Nothing," Jack answered. "There's nothing anyone can do. I just wanted you to know." He hesitated a moment before adding, "He loves you, Ned. Maybe not the way he should have, but he loves you. So do I."

"Not now, Jack," I said. "Don't do this now. I just wanted to see how he's doing."

"I'm sorry," he said. "It's just that I miss you."

"Tell him I called," I said, hanging up before Jack could say anything more.

I looked at the pieces of paper I still held in my hand. Was there really a sickness stalking gay men, or was it just a coincidence that so many of us were coming down with these things? And why only in San Francisco? Was there something poisonous in the air, the water, the fog? I knew that wasn't likely, but still I was afraid. Brian was sick. Would Andy, Jack, or I be next? Jack and I, in particular, had cause for worry. We'd both slept with Brian. For all I knew, so had Andy. If whatever was taking down gay men in California was indeed passed along through sex, it was likely we had all been exposed to it.

I told myself to calm down. I felt fine. I hadn't been sick with anything more serious than a cold in years. I had nothing to worry about. Besides, I chided myself, the person I should be worried about was Brian. He was the one dying. Part of me wanted to get on a plane and fly to his side, but another still hated him for what he'd done.

And then there was Jack. Did I hate him? No. Despite everything, I couldn't. Our relationship went back too far, and the roots were too deep, for me to hate him. But I wasn't ready to forgive him.

I heard the front door open. "I'm home," Alan called out. He appeared in the doorway a moment later. "Hey there," he said. "What's going on?"

I hid the articles and Andy's letter beneath some junk mail and held up the acceptance from NYU. "Put on your dancing shoes, baby," I told Alan. "I've got some great news."

CHAPTER 43

The white-painted face that peered out at me from behind the door of apartment 4A looked like it belonged to a china doll. The eyes, rimmed in black, peered down demurely at the floor. The cherry-red lips, were pursed slightly. Jet black hair was done up in an elaborate chignon pierced by ivory chopsticks. Somewhere in the room, a woman's voice soared in a moment of operatic exuberance.

"I'm sorry," I said, looking again at the number written on the paper in my hand. "I think I have the wrong number. I'm looking for John Fink."

"That's right," the woman said in a decidedly male voice. "Come in."

The door opened wider and I stepped inside. The geishalike figure, clad in a red-embroidered kimono, shuffled to the stereo and turned down the volume before addressing me again. "I'm John Fink. You must be my buddy from GMHC."

I nodded. "Ned," I told him.

John clapped his hands together, and I saw that despite the delicate kimono and makeup, his body was very much that of a man. Hairy wrists extended from the sleeves of his outfit, and the hands were much too large to be those of a woman. It was one of the signs Alan had taught me to look for when trying to determine the gender of someone who might be in drag.

"I've got lunch," I said, holding up the bag I'd picked up at the Gay Men's Health Crisis office on West 22nd Street and brought to John's apartment four blocks away.

"I'm sure it's delicious," John said as he accepted the bag from me and walked into the apartment's tiny kitchen.

I wasn't sure what I was supposed to do next. My training to be an AIDS buddy had been minimal, consisting mainly of an introduction to how they believed it could and could not be transmitted and some suggestions for handling the sometimes shocking appearance of people suffering from what until recently the medical community had called "gay cancer." In 1982, a year after the first cases had been diagnosed, there were still few definite answers about how or why so many gay men were becoming infected with this new ailment. But they were, and we were growing increasingly worried. A recent *New York Times* article—which still referred to the disease by the homo-specific acronym GRID, for gay-related immunodeficiency disease—had reported that since the first appearance of the disorder in San Francisco, at least 335 people had been diagnosed, out of which a terrifying 136 had died.

Those of us in the gay community believed that the numbers were actually much higher. In New York, we had already seen a steep rise in the number of men developing debilitating pneumonia and the telltale purple lesions of Kaposi's sarcoma. Foreseeing a health issue of epic proportions, a small group of friends had founded Gay Men's Health Crisis to gather and disseminate information as it became available. Housed in a building owned by Mel Cheren, known to most of us as the "Godfather of Disco" and partner in the famous Paradise Garage nightclub, GMHC was spearheading the movement to make gay men aware of what was happening.

In April, Alan and I had braved a freak spring snowstorm to attend the first benefit for the fledgling organization, a night of entertainment by the likes of Evelyn "Champagne" King and the New York City Gay Men's Chorus, as well as impassioned speeches asking for donations and volunteers. Moved by the occasion, and by the fact that already Alan and I knew half a dozen people from the theater community who were ill, I'd signed up to be a buddy to a person with AIDS. Now, a month later, I was making my first visit.

"Would you like me to leave you to your lunch?" I asked John as he took a plate from a cupboard and opened the containers of food I'd brought.

"I'd rather you stayed," he answered. "If you don't mind. I don't get a lot of visitors."

He sat down at the table tucked into one corner of the room. I sat across from him as he picked up a fork and began to pick at the macaroni and cheese that had been made that morning by other volunteers. I noticed that he swallowed gingerly, as if it hurt him to eat. He coughed, and the front of his kimono opened. I saw that his chest was covered with dark purple spots the size of quarters.

"The music is pretty," I said, trying not to stare.

John pulled his robe closed. "*Madama Butterfly*," he said. "Do you like opera?"

"I've never really listened to it," I told him. "I'm afraid I wouldn't really understand it if it's not in English."

"You don't need to understand the words," John said as he poked at a carrot. "The music tells you everything you need to know. Just listen."

He was quiet, closing his eyes as the music played. "Cio-Cio-San is a beautiful fifteen-year-old geisha," he said. "They call her 'Butterfly.' She falls in love with Pinkerton, a handsome navy lieutenant. He marries her, but he knows he can never make a life with her. They have a child. Then he leaves, promising to come back for her. She waits three years for him to return, turning down an offer of marriage from a prince who finds her beauty irresistible. When Pinkerton does come back, he brings a new wife with him. They go to Butterfly to request that she let them take her child."

John stopped speaking, sitting silently and listening to the voice coming from the speakers. I couldn't understand the words, but I could feel in the singing an intense sadness.

"Butterfly agrees to let them have the boy," said John, his voice soft beneath the singing, as if he was translating for me. "She tells them to come back later for him. When they're gone, she blindfolds her son. Then she goes behind a screen and stabs herself. When Pinkerton comes for their child, he finds her and she dies in his arms."

He was quiet again, this time for a long period during which the music swelled and filled the room. When he opened his eyes, they were wet with tears. "She loved him even when he betrayed her," he said. "And he didn't see how much he loved her until she was dying."

"Are all operas that cheerful?" I asked him.

"No," he answered. "Some are actually sad."

I laughed at his joke. He reached up and pulled the wig from his head, revealing a scalp covered in thin tufts of hair. He set the wig on the table, where it rested like a shiny cat beside his plate. John scratched his head lightly, avoiding the purple blotches that stained the skin.

"Excuse my poor manners," he said. "I realize that subjecting you to my affliction is a poor way of repaying your kindness."

"It's okay," I told him.

"May I ask why you do it?" he said.

"Do what?" I asked.

"Come here," he answered. "Visiting the dying is hardly something most people would undertake voluntarily. Usually it's done out of a sense of guilt, and I don't see that you have anything to be guilty for, at least as far as I'm concerned. We never tricked, did we? You don't look familiar, but then the lighting at the baths is not particularly illuminating."

I chuckled. "I don't think so," I said. "I guess I do it because it makes me less afraid."

"How so?" John said. "Doesn't seeing this"—he indicated his lesions—"make you fear what might happen?"

"Maybe it helps me get used to it," I suggested. "In case it does happen."

"Very practical," said John. "I commend you. And please, don't think I'm trying to scare you off. So far you are most welcome company."

"You haven't," I assured him as he resumed eating his lunch. He spilled some food on his chin, and when he wiped it away, the napkin took some of his makeup with it, revealing more lesions beneath the smooth white surface. His entire costume, I realized, was hiding the ravaged body beneath.

"What did you do?" I asked him. "Before you got . . . before." I didn't know how to phrase the question in a way that wouldn't be offensive.

"Before I became one of the damned?" he said for me. "I was a dresser. At the Metropolitan Opera. I helped people with beautiful voices get into beautiful clothes." He lifted his arm and wagged the sleeve of his kimono. "This, for instance, was worn by none other than Renata Scotto for a New Year's Eve performance in 1974. Barry Morell was Pinkerton to her Cio-Cio-San. It was divine."

"You must have seen some amazing things," I remarked.

"I have," he said. "I worked there for twenty years. It was a wonderful life. And now," he added, shrugging, "now I have the memories and the recordings."

"And the costumes," I said.

"Just a few," John said, smiling. "I don't think they'll be missed."

He finished his lunch and I cleared away the dishes for him. After that he was tired, and announced that he was going to take a nap. "But you will come back, won't you?" he asked.

"Every Tuesday and Thursday," I said.

"I look forward to it," he told me as he stretched out on the sofa in the living room. I covered him with a blanket and left him alone with his music, returning to the sunny afternoon. As I walked home, I found myself wondering if Brian had ended up looking like John at the end. I hated the idea of his handsome face being stolen from him by the cancer. I hated this disease that was feeding on the beauty of men, consuming them for some unknown reason, as if a plague had been loosed upon us. I hoped it would run its course, and soon, before too many more were taken.

That night, Alan, Taffy, and I went to Michael's Pub to hear Margaret Whiting perform. She was a favorite of Alan's, and he was particularly excited because she was singing songs made famous by Ethel Merman, whose ill-fated disco album he and Taffy sometimes performed to. As we sat at our table, waiting for the show to start, I was looking around the room when a man sitting a few tables over caught my attention. Something about him was familiar, although I couldn't place his face. Before I could ask Alan and Taffy if they knew him, Margaret Whiting came out and began singing.

Throughout the show I kept stealing glances at the man, trying to figure out where I'd seen him. It was making me crazy, because I was sure I knew him. Then, during a break between numbers, Margaret Whiting walked to his table and said, "I want to thank my husband, Jack, for encouraging me to do this show."

Instantly, I knew who he was. Jack Wrangler. I leaned over to Alan. "Did she just say her 'husband'?" I asked him.

He nodded. "I'm not sure if they're really married, but they might as well be," he answered. "They've been together a long time now."

"Does she know he's a gay porn star?" I asked.

"He doesn't do that anymore," said Alan, as if this was old news. "He makes straight ones now."

The music began again, making further discussion impossible. But I couldn't stop looking from Wrangler to Whiting. She had to be at least twenty years older than he was. And although she sang beautifully, I had a hard time understanding what the horse-hung star of *Raunch Ranch* saw in the plump, matronly songbird. When the show ended, I watched as he stood to kiss her, trying to reconcile the image of the doting lover with that of the man I'd last seen sticking it to a beefy, hairy-chested stud wearing nothing but construction boots on the set of one of Brian's films.

As I was watching them, Jack turned and looked right at me. For a moment he seemed to be thinking, then his face lit up with recognition. I was surprised to see him walk toward me, and even more surprised when he reached out to shake my hand and said, "Ned, it's been a long time. How are you?"

"I'm doing well," I answered as Taffy and Alan looked on, their mouths hanging open.

"How's Brian?" Jack asked. "I haven't talked to him in a while."

"He passed away," I told him, not sure how else to say it. "Last summer."

"Oh, God," said Jack. "I'm so sorry. I didn't know."

"It was unexpected," I said. "He had AIDS."

Jack flinched visibly. I'd heard that men from the adult film industry were running scared since the discovery that sex was a primary means of transmission of the disease, and I wondered if that had played any part in his move from gay films to heterosexual life. "What are you doing in New York?" he asked, not pressing me for details of Brian's death.

"I live here now," I answered. "I'm actually in school."

"That's great," Jack said. He took a business card out of his pocket and handed it to me. "Here's my number. You'll have to have dinner with me and Margaret one of these nights."

"I'd like that," I lied. "It's good to see you."

"You, too," said Jack. "Now don't forget to call me."

When he was out of earshot, Taffy grabbed the card from me. "I can't believe you know him," she said.

"I don't really know him," I said. "I met him a few times."

"Did you ever . . ." Taffy began to ask, looking at me and raising her overly-manicured eyebrows.

"No," I said. "I didn't."

"Too bad," said Taffy.

"You don't seem very excited about seeing him again," Alan said.

"It just reminds me of another time," I told him.

"Well, can we still go to dinner with them?" Taffy asked.

I ignored her, taking out money to pay for our drinks as Alan got up. "Come on," he said. "Let's get out of here before she asks to be in his next film."

"Oh," Taffy said, excited. "Do you think he likes Asian girls?"

We took a cab home. As Taffy talked excitedly about having seen a real live porn star, I looked out the window at the passing city. Seeing Jack Wrangler again had unnerved me, reminding me not only of Brian's death, but making me think about the unfairness of it all. Why, I wondered, were some of us dying terrible deaths while others were unscathed? Not that anyone deserved it more or less than others. Nobody deserved what was happening to us. But still, I couldn't help but question why certain men were chosen. Were we just unlucky? Had Brian's death simply been a random event? Was John's sickness merely the result of an accident? It bothered me to think so, but it bothered me even more to think that we had somehow brought this on ourselves through some action we'd believed to be harmless. All we'd ever wanted was to love one another. Now we were dying, possibly as a result.

I didn't know if I would ever have the answers to my questions or, if I did, if I would be able to live with them. I needed to believe that some things could last forever, that there was hope. I reached for Alan's hand. In the darkness, it was a lifeline to hope, and I held it, afraid to let go.

CHAPTER 44

The granite was cool beneath my fingers, the polished surface broken by the thin curves and lines of the letters carved into it. As I ran my hand down the panel, I imagined cutting each of the 57,939 names recorded on the monument's skin. The names of the dead, written in stone as a testament to the toll of the war in Vietnam. They were arranged in the order in which they had died, beginning with Dale R. Buis, age 37, killed on July 8, 1959, and ending with 27-year-old Richard Vande Geer, killed on May 15, 1975.

Washington is a city of monuments, famous for its obelisks and tombs, its statues and temples built to honor the heros of years past. It is probably the only city in America where history is immortalized in bronze and marble even as it is being made. To walk its streets is to tour the land of the dead.

On November 13, 1982, a blustery Saturday marked by wind and rain, it was the veterans of Vietnam who were being remembered. We were given a parade, something none of us had received upon our original homecomings. Even now, though, feelings of ambivalence and occasional outright condemnation remained concerning the actions of those of us who had fought. The crowd along Constitution Avenue had been sparse, with some blocks of the parade route nearly empty of observers. While those who did attend were mostly supportive, a handful of protesters greeted veterans with cries of "Shame!"

I myself did not march, electing to go directly to the site of the memorial. I felt no need to be either celebrated or forgiven by people I didn't even know. I had come to Washington because I wanted to remember the friends I'd lost, and perhaps to see some concrete evidence that the war was really, finally over. Also, I wanted to see the monument that had given rise to such debate over the past year and a half. Since the winning design had been announced in May of 1981, public opinion had been strongly divided regarding the design proposed by 21-year-old Yale architecture student Maya Lin. Some found the stark black vee cut into a low hillside as ugly and violent as a scar, while others saw it as a simple, powerful statement that encouraged reflection.

I saw it as a role call of the dead. I found the design neither offensive nor uplifting. It was simply a scroll of black rock on which the names of men who should still be alive had been cut with mechanical precision, as if they had been species of lilies or items put into storage. I was glad that they would be remembered, and that the people who had loved them would have a place to come and think about them, but to me it was still a list of victims.

Alan had offered to come with me, but I had said no. I loved him dearly, but Vietnam had been my experience, not his. Besides, I wasn't going there to indulge in memories. I didn't want to play tour guide to my time in Southeast Asia, telling him stories about this person and that occasion, reliving the battles and recounting the long stretches of boredom. I just wanted to see for myself what the lives of nearly 60,000 soldiers amounted to, how America had chosen to symbolize our sweat and blood, our broken bodies and shattered hearts.

It's interesting how we choose to remember. In 1965, North Vietnam had issued a postage stamp featuring the image of Norman Morrison, a 31-year-old Quaker father of three who had set himself on fire in front of Secretary of Defense Robert McNamara's office at the Pentagon to protest U.S. involvement in Vietnam. The government of the United States had subsequently made it illegal to own stamps (as well as coins) from North Vietnam, but I had acquired one, and I carried it in my wallet (I still do), not because I necessarily agreed with Morrison's position, but because I respected his conviction. The stamp, which depicts the hovering, smiling face of Morrison surrounded by flames as beneath him protesters carry signs decrying the American presence in Vietnam, is a fascinating piece of political propaganda, but it is also a moving memorial to the sacrifice made by one man doing what he thought was right.

In contrast, nearly a quarter of a century would pass before the United States postal service finally issued, in 1999, a stamp commemorating the Vietnam War. And on that day in 1982 when the Vietnam Veterans Memorial was dedicated, the man whose attention Morrison had been trying to get in 1965 did not even make an appearance. Now the chairman of the Overseas Development Council, and one of the few Vietnam–era figures still active in Washington, McNamara spent the day in his office catching up on paperwork instead of honoring the men he'd been instrumental in sending to their deaths. For all the speeches that went on that day, Americans were still mostly ashamed of the only war we ever lost, and those of us who fought it were still paying the price.

On the train ride from Penn Station to Union Station the night before, I'd compiled a list of the men whose names I wanted to search for the next day. Now that I was at the wall, I found that I didn't want to look for any of them. The list was in my pocket, but I left it there untouched. While all around me others scanned the rows of names until they found the brother, son, uncle, father, husband, lover, friend, or cousin they had come to honor, I stared at the names until they became a blur, running together in one long, continuous ribbon: ORVAL A BALDWIN JACKSON BARNES SAMUEL BOSENBARK WILLARD CLEMMONS JAMES H DUNN III BENJAMIN W HAIRE DUANE K HIESER JOHN C REILLY RUSSELL E HUPE VAN J JOYCE STEVEN L MARTIN DOUGLAS F MOORE. They became to me one man, one sacrifice, one offering made to the gods of war in a deal gone bad. I mourned them all, not just the men whose names I held in my pocket, but every one of them. In the way that Harvey Milk had died for all of gay San Francisco, the names on the wall stood for those who had died for the promise of freedom. But where Harvey had helped us fulfill our dreams, the people of Vietnam were still suffering.

There was another reason that I found the wall disquieting. Seeing the names stretching out on either side of me, I thought of those who were currently dying from the mysterious illness ravaging the cities of San Francisco and New York. Would we, I wondered, one day have to build a monument to those it took? Would their names fill a wall five-hundred-feet long? So far the source of the plague had not been discovered, and every week we heard about someone else who had been touched by it. I'd found myself waiting to hear who the latest casualty was, much as I'd waited to learn the fates of the men I knew in Vietnam each time they went out on another mission.

I decided I'd had enough of death. My return train to New York didn't depart until early evening, and so I decided to spend my remaining hours in Washington at the museums of the Smithsonian. Jack and I had visited the Natural History museum several times on school trips, and had been some of the first visitors to the American History addition when it was opened in 1964. I had not, however, yet seen the relatively new Air and Space museum, and I was anxious to do so.

I left the wall and began walking toward the Washington Monument, following the northern edge of the Reflecting Pool and keeping my head bowed against the wind. I was halfway along it when I heard someone call my name and turned to see Andy and Jack. We had just passed within a foot of one another, but I had not seen them. I stood, my hands deep in the pockets of my coat, and looked at them. In the three years since I'd seen them, they had changed little. Jack's hair was shorter, and his moustache was gone, but I would have known him anywhere. Andy, dressed in his fatigues from Vietnam, could have just walked off a plane in Quan Loi.

The three of us stood, not moving, for a long moment, until Andy broke the uncomfortable silence and came over to hug me. Jack hung back as the two of us embraced, and I made no move to include him when Andy released me.

"You came to see the wall?" Andy asked.

"Yeah," I said, glancing at Jack, who was watching us with an unreadable expression.

"Me, too," he said. "What do you think?"

Confronted with the question, I found I had no way to answer it adequately. I shrugged. "It's strange," I found myself saying. "I sort of can't believe it's for us."

Andy nodded. "We're just heading over there now," he said. "I met up with some of the Cocks at the parade, and we're going to find the guys we lost."

"Great," I said.

"Can we meet up later?" Andy asked me.

"I can't," I told him. "I'm catching a train at six. I'm just going to head over to the museums for a while."

"I'm sorry I didn't call or anything," Andy apologized. "We just sort of decided at the last minute, and . . ."

"It's okay," I told him. "Really. It's good to see you."

"Hey," Andy said, as if something had just occurred to him. "Why don't you and Jack go to the museum while I see the guys?" He turned to Jack. "You don't want to hear a bunch of old war stories anyway, right?"

Jack looked at me. "That's fine with me," he said. "If it's okay with Ned."

Before I could answer, Andy said, "Of course it is. You guys go on. I'll catch up with you at the hotel later." He clapped me on the shoulder. "Take care, Ned. I'll come see you in New York one of these days."

Then he was gone, leaving Jack and me to deal with one another. Jack was the first to speak. "He's kind of like a tornado, isn't he?" he said. "He just tears through and leaves everyone else to clean up the mess."

I smiled. "How are you, Jack?" I replied, still not ready to hug him, but willing to try talking.

"Pretty well," he said as we started to walk. "I'm finally done with school, and I have my own practice. Mostly gay men."

"Dr. Grace," I said, shaking my head. "Who would have thought you'd be the one to do it?"

Jack laughed. "Not me," he said. "I still don't quite believe the diploma isn't fake."

"And you like it?" I asked.

"Yeah," he said. "I do. A lot of guys in the community are running scared right now. I do what I can to help them sort out how they feel about everything."

"You're okay?" I said.

"So far, so good," he answered. "You?"

"I feel okay," I told him. "But who knows? Without a test, how do we know we won't just wake up one day with something? Fuck, they don't even know what's causing it yet."

"There's talk that it might have something to do with poppers," said Jack.

"If that's true, then we're all pretty much screwed," I said. "What gay man hasn't used poppers?"

"Brian thought he might have gotten it from inhaling all that fake smoke at City Disco," Jack said, laughing a little.

I couldn't laugh. Hearing Brian's name only reminded me of how I'd been unable to forgive him before he died. I didn't even know the details of his death. "How long did he live?" I asked Jack. "After we talked."

"Not long," Jack said. "A few days."

I nodded, not knowing how to apologize to Jack for what I'd said that day, not knowing how to forgive myself for letting those last days slip away without calling back.

"I told him you said good-bye," Jack said. "He was happy to hear that."

I stopped and looked at him. "I'm such a shit," I said.

He shook his head. "No, you're not," he told me. "We're *all* shits. The whole situation was shit."

I sighed. "We keep doing this," I said. "You're the therapist. Tell me why."

Jack slipped his arm around mine and began walking again. "Let's start with your childhood," he said. "What was your relationship like with your best friend?"

"I'm serious," I said as we walked up the steps of the Air and Space museum. "Why can't we just stop fucking up each other's lives?"

The conversation paused as we entered the building and stopped, looking around in awe. "Is that the Wright brothers' plane?" Jack asked, staring up at one of the many aircraft suspended from the ceiling.

"It's like someone built a museum of our bedrooms," I said. "Only these are real."

I totally forgot our earlier discussion as Jack and I roamed the galleries, our difficulties put aside as we became the 13-year-old boys we'd once been, marveling at the treasures contained in the museum's cases. Every turn of a corner revealed a new surprise, from a ticket for a German Zeppelin to a V-2 missile, real Spitfires and Messerschmitts to an actual slice of moon rock, which we touched with the reverence of pilgrims handling the relics of St. Bernadette at Lourdes. The hours passed swiftly, and when I finally looked at my watch, I saw that I had less than an hour before my train departed.

"I've got to go," I told Jack as we stood before the capsule from *Freedom 7*, which we'd so long ago recreated from cardboard boxes and flown on our own space missions.

"We were going to fly to Mars together," Jack said, reading my thoughts. "Remember?"

"It's not too late," I said.

"I don't know," said Jack. "I get kind of woozy on the cable cars these days. I don't think I could handle outer space."

"You're probably right," I said. "Anyway, I think we've gone some pretty strange places right here on Earth."

Jack faced me. "Yeah," he agreed. "It's been quite a ride so far. Do you really have to go?"

I nodded. "I've got a paper due on Monday," I said. "For school," I added, noting Jack's puzzled expression. "I'm back in school. I'm a thirty-two-year-old sophomore."

"That's fantastic," Jack exclaimed. "What are you studying?"

"History," I told him. "I guess I'm trying to figure out the world."

"Remember how Chaz used to say all history was lies?" said Jack.

"I'm not sure he wasn't right," I said. "We tend to only remember what we want to."

Jack looked around at the exhibits. "I wish we had more time," he said, and I knew he didn't mean for sightseeing.

"We'll talk," I told him. "I promise."

He reached out and drew me to him. We held each other for a long moment. Then I let him go and walked away, leaving him standing in front of Alan B. Shepard's spaceship. As I slipped out the door, I felt the weight of history on my shoulders, and I hurried toward Union Station and freedom.

CHAPTER 45

"And who are you today?" I asked John as I entered his apartment with lunch. He was dressed in what appeared to be a toga, tied around the middle with a gold cord.

"Norma," he informed me. "High priestess of Irminsul, god of the Druids, and lover of Pollione, the Roman proconsul and enemy of my people."

"Let me guess," I said as I took his food to the kitchen. "Something tragic happens and you die."

"Not just I," John said, sweeping along behind me. "Pollione also joins me in the fire."

"Fire?" I said, taking out the containers of beef stew, salad, and cherry pie and setting them on the table. "That's a new one."

"Pollione has betrayed me," said John. "Fallen in love with a young priestess. To avenge my honor, I plan to slay our two children."

"Nice," I said. "Why do they always take it out on the kids?"

"But I don't," John said, holding up his hand. "Instead, I reveal my sins to my father and go to my death, as demanded by our laws."

"Your father burns you to death?" I asked.

"He has no choice," said John sadly. "It is the law. But as I walk into the flames," he added, "Pollione admits his love for me and joins me."

"Well, all right then," I said. "As long as everyone's happy."

John sighed and glared at me. "It's *beautiful*," he said. "Just listen to this."

He jumped up and went to the stereo, turning the sound up until the whole apartment was filled with singing. He came back to the kitchen and stood in the doorway, eyes closed as he swayed gently.

"'Chaste goddess who doth bathe in silver light these ancient, hal-lowed trees,'" he said. "'Turn thy fair face upon us, unclouded and un-veiled.'" He spoke slowly, translating each line from Italian as it was sung. "'Temper thou the burning hearts, the excessive zeal of thy peo-ple. Enfold the Earth in that sweet peace which, through thee, reigns in heaven.'"

When it was over, he looked at me. "'Casta diva,' Norma's prayer to the goddess to stop the impending war. Have you ever heard anything so lovely?"

"No," I said. "Not since the last time I was here. What was that opera again?"

"*Pelléas et Mélisande*," he answered. "Debussy. They're doing it this month at the Met. You should go. Jeannette Pilou is singing Mélisande."

"We'll see," I said. "Now come eat this before it gets cold."

John sat across from me and spooned some stew into his mouth. I noticed him wince as he ate.

"Are you all right?" I asked.

"It's the lesions," he said. "I have a few in my mouth now." He leaned over. "Frankly, it makes fellatio almost *unbearable*," he said, as if sharing a secret.

I pretended to be horrified. I was always amazed at how he could maintain his sense of humor in the face of such devastation. In the seven months that I'd been bringing him lunch, he had yet to com-plain about his condition, even as it steadily worsened. Always he greeted me warmly, his beloved opera playing in the background as he embodied one of the characters. I'd seen him as *La Traviata*'s Violetta, *The Queen of Spades*' Lisa, as Carmen, Aida, Elcktra, the Queen of the Night, and many others. For each one he had a costume, either pinched from the collection at the Met or sewn by his own hand. He was, I'd discovered, not just a dresser, but an accomplished costumer.

"How's that boyfriend of yours?" he asked me. "I see his last show didn't get such fabulous reviews. But what did they expect, *roller skat-ing* on stage."

"That was a little strange," I agreed. "But he had fun. And now he's rehearsing for *La Cage aux Folles*."

"The Jerry Herman-Harvey Fierstein show!" John exclaimed. "How thrilling. When does it open?"

"August," I told him.

"I hope I can hold out until then," said John.

I hoped so, too, although I had my doubts. John was looking worse and worse. His lesions covered a large potion of his body, and he'd lost so much weight that the costumes he loved to wear hung on him like rags on a scarecrow. Every time I came to see him, I feared there would be no answer at the door.

"Would you be a love and help me into something warmer?" John said. "I'm afraid this shift isn't quite appropriate for the weather."

He was right about that. January had arrived with bitter cold, and the snow was piled a foot deep on the sidewalks, as a string of snowstorms had left the plows nowhere else to put it. New York had been turned into the Snow Queen's castle, but as the holidays had all passed and we were tired of winter, it was more of an annoyance than anything else.

John stood and I walked with him down the hall to his second bedroom, which I'd never entered. When I stepped inside, I looked around in awe. The room was filled with costumes. They were hung on racks, piled on the floor, and thrown over the pink velvet chaise longue that sat against one wall. A dressing table piled with makeup occupied one corner, and one entire wall was lined with heads, each one wearing a wig.

"Now you know my secret," said John. "I'm really Princess Langwidere."

"Who?" I asked.

"From the Oz books," he explained, clearing room on the chaise so that I could sit down. "She had thirty heads, which she kept in a cupboard and changed as her mood suited her. I always thought it was a most practical idea."

"It's like a museum in here," I commented. "Don't tell me you stole all of these from the Met."

"No," John said as he removed the wig he'd been wearing and slowly pulled the robe over his head. "Only some of them. The rest I made."

I turned away as he undressed, not wanting to see the emaciated body beneath his clothes. His bones protruded like those of a bird, and his skin was sickly pale, the plum-colored lesions spotting him like bruises. I was relieved when he reached for a thick bathrobe and slipped his arms into the sleeves.

"My mother taught me to sew," he said, sitting at the chair in front of the dressing table. He looked at his face in the mirror. "I don't think she had any idea what it would lead to."

"Has she seen any of these?" I asked him.

He picked up a powder puff and gently dabbed at his cheeks. "She has not," he said. "She ceased speaking to me when she realized that no grandchildren would be forthcoming from my loins."

"What about the rest of your family?"

"My father died when I was young," said John. "I have a brother and sister somewhere in the world, but like my mother, they find my preference for the charms of other men distasteful. It's one of the peculiarities of the Mormon faith, I'm afraid."

"I didn't know you were Mormon," I said.

"I'm not," he corrected me. "They are. I long ago discarded the garment of the Holy Priesthood in favor of something more stylish."

"It must be difficult," I said. "Not having any family."

"But I have an enormous family," said John. "I have my friends, my lovers, my singers." He gestured around the room. "I have all of this."

"I guess you do," I said, trying to sound as if I agreed with him. In reality, I felt deep sadness. Where were his friends? Where were his lovers? I'd seen no evidence of either in all the time that I'd been John's buddy. He rarely spoke about any real person, preferring the stories of his operas. Not once had his telephone rung in my presence, and the mail I collected for him from the box in the downstairs foyer was never anything but circulars and magazines.

"I think it's time for me to nap," John announced, standing up.

I took his cue that I should leave him alone, returning to the living room and putting on my coat. John removed the record from the turntable and put on a new one. I recognized it from another visit— *Die Fledermaus*.

"I'll see you on Thursday," I said to John as he lay down on the sofa and covered himself with the blanket he kept folded at the foot of it.

"I'll be waiting," he said, as he always did.

When I got outside, I saw that it had begun to snow again. As I walked home, I thought about what would become of me if, like John, I got sick. Would Alan stay with me? Would I have to go live with my mother and Walter? I'd never really considered the matter before. Now that I did, I found I was a little afraid, not of getting sick (although that prospect was not a welcome one) but of being alone. I was 32 years old. Most people my age, at least the ones who weren't homosexual, were married, with a child or two. My own father had been 26 when I was born, and had seemed impossibly old to me when he was the age I was now. But what did I have? I was a sophomore in college. I had a boyfriend, true, but one who still spent several nights a week at his own apartment.

I wanted more than that. I wanted a home, a husband, a life that was more than studying and evenings in front of the television. I wanted what I'd had in San Francisco when I lived with Brian. I had it to some degree in New York, yet something was missing. I hadn't developed the same kind of friendships. Partly I knew that this was because I was afraid of getting hurt again, and now that the longevity of any relationship was in doubt because of AIDS, I knew that I was holding back on forming new ones. Even my volunteer work was designed to be short-term, a situation that allowed the illusion of friendship but with a guaranteed expiry at some point in the not-far-off future.

I had, I saw, become adept at temporary relationships. But was it my fault, or was it a trait common to most gay men? The more I thought about it, the more I became convinced that maybe it was. We were, after all, masters of the limited partnership. A few months. A year. How long did most gay relationships endure? How often had Alan and I said of a friend whose latest paramour we disapproved of, "Don't worry, it won't last long"? We were casual in our certainty that the situation would change before long because it always did. Our confidence was based on historical precedence.

In San Francisco, I had known men who had been coupled for many years. I'd always imagined that someday I would be one of them myself. Now I was no longer so sure. I loved Alan, but sometimes I felt we were on different paths. I wanted to believe that forty years from now we would still be together, old and content, looking back on a life filled with happiness and ahead to the comfort of one another's love and caring as we wound down our days. But there was no guarantee that we would have that, no guarantee that we would even live long enough to consider ourselves old.

I reached my street in a dour mood. Stomping up the stairs to my apartment, in my mind I had already broken up with Alan and consigned myself to a life alone, surrounded by books and too many small dogs. So when I opened the door to find him standing there, it took a moment of adjustment before I could respond appropriately to his enthusiastic greeting and kiss.

"Hey, lover," he said. "Sorry to kiss and run, but I've got rehearsal. Jerry rewrote one of the numbers, and I think I'm going to get to sing it. I'll be back around ten."

He darted past me and was halfway down the stairs before he called up, "I almost forgot. Your friend Andy called. He says he has something to tell you. 'Bye!"

I shut the door and took off my coat. Andy calling me was unusual, and the fact that he had something to tell me didn't make me feel any less apprehensive, especially since he hadn't felt he could give Alan the message. I was sure something bad had happened, either to him or to Jack. But I'd just spoken with Jack a few days earlier, and everything was fine. Still, people were forever getting killed or discovering they had life-threatening illnesses right after assuring someone that everything was all right, so why should Jack be an exception?

I picked up the phone and dialed Andy's number before I could work myself up even more. Whatever terrible thing he had to tell me, it was best to get it over with quickly. I waited impatiently as the phone rang three, four, five times.

"Hello?"

"It's Ned," I said. "What's wrong?"

"What makes you think something's wrong?" Andy replied.

"Well, first of all, you didn't leave a message," I said. "And second, you never call."

"Yeah," Andy said. "I've been bad about that. But listen, I didn't leave a message because I wanted to tell you the news myself."

"So tell me," I said, steeling myself for the worst.

"I'm moving to New York," Andy announced.

CHAPTER 46

"So, is Boy George a drag queen or what?" asked Andy as the unmistakable opening chords of "Do You Really Want to Hurt Me?" came from the radio.

Taffy put down the feather duster she was using to clean the bookshelves on either side of the fireplace and faced Andy, who was unloading a box of video tapes.

"I think she's a what," she said. "Because if she thinks she's a drag queen, she better lose twenty pounds and get rid of those damn braids. Ruby Rims looks more like a woman than that thing does."

"I think he looks great," I said, opening another box and looking inside. "It's time America saw a big queen on television anyway."

"You mean besides that guy on *Hill Street Blues*?" said Andy.

"Which guy?" asked Taffy. "Not the one who played the prostitute who narked on his own lover?"

"Yeah," Andy said. "That guy."

"That's just what we need more of on TV," said Taffy. "Gay hookers who can't be trusted. No wonder straight people think we're freaks."

"Who's a freak?" asked Alan, walking in with yet another carton.

"Boy George," I told him. "According to Taffy, anyway."

"The other day my mother told me that my father has a crush on him," said Alan. "He saw Culture Club on *Solid Gold* last week and wanted to know who the pretty girl was."

"Did she tell him?" asked Taffy.

"No," said Alan. "She thought she'd wait until he told all the guys at work about his new fantasy woman."

"I take it you want this in the bedroom," I said, holding up an enormous dildo that I'd found in the box I was unpacking.

Taffy looked at it and whistled. "And I thought you were one hundred percent a pitcher," she said to Andy. "It just proves what I always say, the butcher they are at the bar, the faster their legs go up when you get them home."

"Speaking from personal experience?" Alan teased.

"Please," Taffy said. "You know I'm all girl. Or I will be soon enough."

"I don't use that on myself," said Andy, indicating the dildo, which I was shaking so that the enormous dong flopped grotesquely. "It's for other guys."

"Why?" Taffy asked. "Aren't you big enough for them?"

I was about to say that he was plenty big enough, but realized that I hadn't told Alan the extent of my relationship with Andy. He thought Andy was an old friend; he didn't know that we had a more complicated history. As for why I didn't tell him, well, I wasn't really sure. I knew he wouldn't care, so it wasn't that I thought he would be jealous. I guess it just seemed—and this will sound strange—but too personal. Getting into what Andy had meant to me would mean talking about a lot of things I was uncomfortable talking about, namely my own behavior when it came to falling in love with men who didn't love me as much as I needed them to. Since things with Alan were going well, I didn't want him to think he was another mistake.

Fortunately, Andy answered Taffy's question by tossing her one of the videos he'd just unpacked. She looked at the cover. "*Piledriver*," she read. "'These construction workers put the jack in jackhammer.' Who writes this stuff?"

"Don't look at that," said Andy. "Look at the picture."

Taffy examined the box more closely. She looked at Andy, then back at the box. She turned it over, and her eyebrows rose. "Is that you?" she asked.

"It is," said Andy. "Or at least, it was. I don't make those anymore."

Taffy was still staring at the pictures on the video box. Alan went over and took it from her. "Wow," he said. "That's quite a . . . tool belt you have there."

"Brad Majors," Taffy said. "Isn't that the name of the guy in *Rocky Horror*?"

"Yeah, well, we didn't know that when we thought of it," Andy said, taking the video back from her and putting it on one of the shelves Taffy had dusted. "But I still get letters for him."

"I wonder if Barry Bostwick gets ones for you," I mused. "He must wonder why all these gay guys want him to fuck them."

"I'd let Barry Bostwick fuck me anytime," Taffy said. "Brad Majors, too," she added, blowing Andy a kiss.

Andy winked at her. I knew he would never sleep with Taffy. He was just charming her, as he did everyone. What I really wanted to know was who he *was* sleeping with. He'd said he was moving to New York because of a "friend," but when I pressed him for more information, he changed the subject. He was equally vague about what he would be doing for work, telling me only that he knew somebody who was going to give him a job. Jack didn't know any more than I did. Andy had told him that an old friend was helping him out with an affordable apartment, but that was it.

Whoever the friend was, the apartment was a beauty. Located on the Upper West Side, it was on the top floor of one of the castlelike prewar buildings that lined the streets of that neighborhood, covering whole blocks like giant squatting dinosaurs. The enormous living room had floor-to-ceiling windows, and the master bedroom was large enough that it could easily double as a ballroom if necessary. Already furnished, it looked as if the decorators from *Architectural Digest* had been hired to appoint it. The carpets and furnishings were straight from the city's finest stores, and I'd already been assured by Alan, who knew such things, that the Warhol hanging in the hallway was an original.

I was dying to know the name of Andy's benefactor, and what the exact nature of their relationship was. Knowing that he wouldn't tell me, I'd engaged Taffy's help in trying to find out. She was nosy by nature, and I knew that after spending some time with her, Andy wouldn't find her questions out of the ordinary. Now that she'd warmed him up, I thought it was time. Using our prearranged signal, I said, "This view is really amazing, Andy."

"Andy," said Taffy. "If you're not making movies now, what is it you're going to do in New York?"

Andy rocked back on his heels and scratched his head. "A buddy of mine runs this company," he said. "I thought I might do some sales for him."

"Sales," Taffy said. "That sounds interesting. What will you be selling?"

"Insurance," Andy answered.

"Insurance?" I said, despite myself. "That's what my father did."

"Really?" said Andy. "Huh."

"Insurance sounds kind of boring," Taffy said.

"Yeah, I know," Andy replied. "But I'm getting older. I've got to start thinking about the future."

Something about the way he was talking made me suspicious. For one thing, Andy had never had an office job in his life. I couldn't see him in a suit-and-tie kind of business, especially insurance. Plus, the way he was answering the questions, he was giving Taffy a story that sounded plausible but didn't invite further questions. I wasn't buying it, but I didn't know how to get to the real story without just asking him outright, which I knew wouldn't yield any answers.

"Well, it must pay pretty well to have this place," said Taffy, trying a different tack.

"It belongs to a friend," Andy said. "He's living in Florida right now, so he's letting me have it."

Again we were being stonewalled. There was no way to ask who this friend was without it sounding like an interrogation. I looked at Taffy and shook my head. The game was over for now.

"Here's something else I don't get," Andy said as the song on the radio changed. "Why would you write a song about coming on some chick named Eileen?"

"It's not about coming on Eileen," Taffy said. "It's about . . . oh, never mind."

"I'm just saying," said Andy. "It's kind of rude."

"Are you up for going out tonight?" I asked Andy. "We thought we'd introduce you to the scene."

"Sure," he said. "Where are we going?"

"I thought the Monster," I told him.

"The Monster?" Alan and Taffy said in unison, clearly horrified by my suggestion.

"It's famous," I told them. "And it's not that bad."

"If you're over sixty-five," Taffy remarked.

"Don't listen to them," I said to Andy. "They're just upset because the owners won't let them do their drag act there."

"Like we'd want to," Taffy sniffed.

"Is it really an old guys' bar?" Andy asked me.

"Please, you can't get served there if you don't have your AARP membership card," said Taffy. "It's the only bar in New York with an Early Bird Special."

"You're pretty sassy for a girl with a dick," I shot back, earning a glare from Taffy and a roar of approval from Alan and Andy.

"She kind of reminds me of a certain girl we met in Vung Tau a bunch of years ago, eh, Ned?"

"Now that you mention it, she does kind of look like her," I said. "Taffy, I don't suppose your mother was a Vietnamese whore, was she?"

Taffy threw a video at me, just barely missing my head.

"Careful with that," Andy chided her. "*Pole Position* is a classic. I got to fuck Billy Studd on the hood of Mario Andretti's backup car in that one. We had to position ourselves over his sponsor's logo so nobody would know one of his crew guys was a fag."

After a minute or so, Taffy calmed down and we finished unloading the boxes Andy had shipped to New York from San Francisco. Then we left him to shower and take a nap before meeting us at the Monster.

He showed up just after nine, entering the bar and causing heads to turn as the regulars smelled the scent of fresh meat. Walking through the crowd as if he'd been coming to the bar every night of his life, Andy made his way to the rear of the room, where we'd positioned ourselves next to the piano, close enough to the bar to get a good look at everyone there, but far enough out of the way that we could talk.

"Nice place," Andy said when he reached us. "Lots of ferns."

"I told you," Taffy said.

"Come on," said Alan, taking her by the arm. "Let's get you another drink. Andy, what can we bring you?"

"Gin and tonic," he answered. "Thanks."

"What do you think?" I asked him when they were gone.

"It's sort of like Twin Peaks, but bigger," he said. "And I don't see all that many old guys," he added.

I laughed. "New York is different from San Francisco," I said. "Here you're over the hill when you're thirty."

"Christ, they're going to think I'm ancient," he said.

"I have a feeling you'll do just fine," I told him. "Look, you've already got guys checking you out." I nodded in the direction of the bar, where a couple of men were giving Andy appreciative glances.

Andy gave them a quick once-over. "Not really my type," he said. "I'm looking for something a little different these days."

"Oh?" I said. "Different how?"

He shrugged. "I don't know how to explain it," he said. "I'm just getting tired of running around so much, you know?"

"I do know," I said. "That's why I'm glad I have Alan."

"He seems like a nice guy," said Andy.

"He is. He's good for me."

"Unlike me and Jack," Andy replied.

"I didn't say that," I said, surprised that he would include himself in the same category as someone who had been my lover.

"But it's true," Andy said. "You always seemed kind of, I don't know, tense around us. You're calmer now."

"Maybe," I said. "Getting out of San Francisco was something I needed to do, for a lot of reasons."

At that point, Alan and Taffy returned with our drinks, and the conversation turned to the things gay men talk about when they're out in public in groups. Jack used to call it the Three C's—clothes, celebrities, and cock. Generally, each subject received individual attention, but occasionally we'd enjoy times where two of them would merge, those generally being clothes and cock (as in, "What do you think he's got under those jeans?"), or celebrities and clothes (a combo particularly common when discussing people such as Cher and/or Liza Minnelli). The Gay Trifecta, where all three could be applied to a single person, was the ultimate in bar chatter, but it happened so seldom that normally we didn't dare get our hopes up.

That night, however, we hit the jackpot. As Taffy and Alan were having a heated debate over who had made more guest appearances on *The Love Boat*, Marion Ross or Audrey Landers, conversation in the bar suddenly stopped for a full five seconds. When it resumed again, we still hadn't figured out what had caused the interruption. Then Taffy gave a little shriek. "Oh, my God," she said. "It's really him."

"Who?" I asked her.

She jerked her head toward the bar. "Him," she hissed.

"That narrows it down," said Alan.

"From the TV," she said. "That show about the detective."

I looked again, and this time I saw exactly who she meant. Standing at the bar, seemingly alone, was the star of a currently-hot police drama. Propriety, not to mention the possibility of legal unpleasantries, prevents me from divulging his name, but I will say that he looked even better in person than he did on the television screen. Tall, dark-haired, and well-built, it was easy to imagine him wielding a gun and pursuing criminals in real life.

"What do you think he's doing here?" Alan asked. "He's not exactly keeping a low profile."

"He can always say he's researching a role, I guess," I suggested. "Do you think he's really gay?"

"There's one way to find out," Andy said. "Ask him."

"I'm sure the last thing he wants is people bothering him," said Alan.

"You think he came here just to have a drink?" said Andy. "He could do that anywhere. He came here looking for dick, just like the rest of us."

"Twenty bucks says he'd run screaming if anybody talked to him," said Taffy.

"You're on, mama-san," Andy said, downing his drink and turning around.

"Where's he going?" Taffy asked as Andy made a beeline for the star.

As we watched, Andy went up to the guy and said something. We saw the actor smile, and he shook Andy's hand. The two began a conversation that lasted several minutes, during which Alan, Taffy, and I didn't say a word. When the two men left the bar and started walking toward us, I couldn't believe it.

"How do I look?" Taffy asked, playing with her hair.

Before I could answer, Andy and the actor were standing in front of me, and Andy was introducing us. I remember saying something stupid about really liking his show, and him being very polite in the face of my obvious nervousness.

"I love your shirt," Taffy said, touching the man's arm. "It's so much nicer than that flowered one you wore on the show last week."

"I'm sorry you didn't like it," he said. "I'll mention it to wardrobe."

Taffy giggled. Andy lifted his drink, which he'd refilled at the bar. "Here's to New York," he said. "The greatest city in the world."

"You've only been here one day," I reminded him as I toasted along with the others.

"This is your first day here?" the actor said.

Andy nodded. "Just got in this morning."

"Well, you've got a lot to see then. It's a beautiful place. I grew up here, you know."

"Really?" said Andy. "I was hoping maybe someone who knows the place would show me around."

"I could do that, if you like," the man we watched every week said, as if the two of them were acting out a scene.

Playing his part, Andy waited a moment before answering. "Sure," he said. "If it's not too much trouble."

"It's not," said the actor. He looked at his watch. "In fact, we could start now. The view of the city from the Empire State Building is phenomenal at night. If we leave now we can just make it before they close."

"Sounds good," said Andy, handing me his unfinished drink. "I'll call you tomorrow," he said.

The actor handed his drink to Taffy, who held the glass in her hand as if it was an Academy Award. "It was nice meeting all of you," he said.

We said our good-byes and the two of them left. As they reached the bar, Andy excused himself and came back to us. "I almost forgot," he said to a still-stunned Taffy as he held out his hand. "You owe me twenty."

CHAPTER 47

"Ned, it's Jerry from GMHC."

"Hey, Jerry," I said. "I was just about to come by and pick up John's lunch."

"That's why I'm calling," said Jerry, and my heart sank. A call from him could mean only one thing.

"When did he die?" I asked.

"He hasn't," Jerry answered. "Not yet, anyway. But it doesn't look good. He won't go to the hospital, but we have someone with him."

"Can I go see him?"

"I think he'd like that," said Jerry. "He really looks forward to your visits. He missed you while you were gone."

"I'll go over there now," I told him. "Thanks for calling."

I hung up and got ready to go out into the cold. I'd just gotten back from spending Christmas with my mother and Walter. I was in Pennsylvania for five days, and was glad to be back in New York. Alan was still with his family in Indiana, and was due to return on the afternoon of New Year's Eve, when we planned on ringing in 1984 in Times Square.

I hurried to John's apartment, more than a little afraid that he might die before I could see him. In the year and a half that I'd been his buddy, I'd come to be very fond of him. He'd lasted so much longer than most men with AIDS that I'd even begun to hope that he might be the one to beat the disease. Now, it seemed, he was losing the battle.

I let myself into the apartment, which felt overly warm and stuffy. As always, there was music playing. For Christmas John had bought himself a CD player, which were relatively new then and of which many people were still suspicious. But John had wanted one, and he'd given me the outrageous amount of $800 to go to Crazy Eddie's on 8th Street to get it for him. I'd subsequently made more trips to look for opera recordings on CD, horrified by the prices, which at twenty to thirty bucks were three to five times the cost of an album. But every time I commented on how expensive the new technology was, John would roll his eyes and say, "What am I supposed to do with my money, Neddie, invest in twenty-year bonds?"

I'd become familiar with many of John's favorite operas, but I'd never heard the one that was playing when I arrived that afternoon. Not that I was thinking all that much about it. I didn't even take my coat off as I rushed down the hall to his bedroom. I stopped in the doorway, looking in on a horrific scene. John, looking even more skeletal than when I'd seen him the week before, was propped up against a bank of pillows. Dark circles ringed his eyes, and an oxygen cannula affixed to his nose was connected to a small tank standing beside the bed. Even with that added assistance, he was breathing raggedly. His hands, dead birds in his lap, looked like claws. A young man was bending over him, a stethoscope pressed to his chest.

"How is he?" I asked.

"You can talk to me," John said, his words faint and labored. "I'm not dead yet, you insensitive prick."

"As you can see, he's doing as well as can be expected," the attendant said. "I'm going to leave you boys alone to chat. If you need me, I'll be in the living room watching *All My Children*. I want to see if Devon and Dr. Carson finally get together."

"Imagine," John said as I sat down. "That nice girl from *Angie* is television's first dyke character."

"Yeah, well, she sort of looks like one," I said.

"How's your family?" John asked.

"Fine," I answered. "My mother's redecorating the bedroom and Walter is spending the winter reading every book James Michener ever wrote. I think he's up to *Chesapeake*."

John tried to laugh, but ended up choking. I patted him on the back, recoiling from the feel of his bones beneath the flannel pajamas he was wearing. It sounded as if his lungs were filled with water. A wet, strangling sound came from his throat, and I could see him struggling for each breath. I was about to call for the attendant when he stopped, falling back against the pillows.

"Are you trying to kill me?" he joked.

I didn't answer. Instead, I smoothed down his hair, which had gotten tousled during his coughing fit. Thin and limp, it barely covered the top of his head now. Looking at him, I had an uncomfortable memory of Jack and I watching Lon Chaney in *The Phantom of the Opera* years before. I'd been as startled as Mary Philbin's Christine when she unmasked the Phantom and revealed Chaney's disfigured face. Looking at John now, I understood how she was also able to feel compassion for him.

"I have something for you," John said. "On top of the dresser. The envelope."

I turned and looked at the dresser. The top was crowded with old perfume bottles, hairbrushes, and other dressing items from a hundred years earlier, more of John's set pieces that allowed him to live in his fantasy world. Leaning against one of the bottles was a red envelope with my name on it. I picked it up and turned back to John.

"I wasn't sure I'd be here when you got back," he said. "So I put your name on it. Open it."

I ran my finger under the back flap, separating it from the rest of the envelope. Inside was a card. I pulled it out and something slipped out and fluttered into my lap. I picked it up and saw that it was a ticket to the Metropolitan Opera for a performance on January 6.

"It's *La Bohème*," John said. "My favorite. Ileana Cotrubas is singing Mimi. I dressed her for her Met debut in that role in 1977 with José Carreras and Renata Scotto. I have the costume she wore in her death scene. I'm going to be buried in it."

"Thank you," I said. "I don't know what to say. I . . ." I stopped as I found myself beginning to cry.

I felt John's hand, dry as dust, on mine. "You'll go, and then you'll come back and tell me all about it," he said. "I want to hear how she sounds, what she looks like, how the hall echos when the crowd stands and gives her an ovation."

He closed his eyes, and for a horrible moment I thought he had gone. Then he opened them again, staring up at the ceiling as if looking at something only he could see. "You'll come and tell me everything," he whispered.

"Sure I will," I said, squeezing his hand gently. "It will be just like you were there."

He smiled, his cracked lips turning up at the corners. He sighed deeply. "Thank you," he said. "For coming here."

I tried to answer, but couldn't. I knew we were saying good-bye, but I couldn't speak the words. I needed to believe that he would really be there in a week for me to talk to. I needed to believe it for myself as much as for him. I wanted to say something to reassure him, but nothing came.

"I think I'll sleep now," he said, turning and looking at me. "I'm tired."

I nodded. "Okay," I said. "I'll come see you tomorrow." I leaned forward and kissed him on the forehead, like you would a child you were tucking into bed for the night. When I pulled back, his eyes were closed and his chest was rising and falling slowly.

I left him there and went into the living room, where I sat down beside John's attendant, whose name I never knew. He glanced at my face and patted my knee. "I know," he said.

I started to shake as the tears came out. I sobbed silently, not wanting John to hear me. My throat ached from holding the sound in, and my breath came in short bursts as I tried to breathe without wailing. My nose began to run, and I sniffled, feeling completely helpless.

"Is he your first one?" the attendant asked.

I nodded.

"I know this won't help, at least not right away, but you did something special for him," he said. "You let him go knowing somebody cared about him, and that's really all any of us can hope for."

I sat next to him for a long time, until I calmed down enough to speak. When I could, I said, "You'll stay with him, right? Until the end."

"I'll be here," he said. "And someone will call you to let you know."

"Has anyone contacted his family?" I asked.

"They tried, but no one called back."

I leaned my head back and took a deep breath. "I can't believe that they don't want to be here," I said.

"We see it a lot," he told me. "The families don't want to know."

"What will happen to him?"

"He was smart. He left a will and instructions for his funeral. It's all set. The Met is getting his money and everything else is going to GMHC to sell off."

"Him and that damn opera," I said. "I think it's what's kept him alive this long."

"Have you seen the wigs?" the man asked.

"Oh, yeah," I said.

We both laughed. It made me feel better, being able to do that. I looked at the television, where Devon McFadden was sitting in her psychiatrist's office. "So, is she a dyke now?"

"Nah," he said. "Dr. Carson admitted to her that *she's* a lesbian, but she told Devon that she's not. She says she's just projecting or something."

"Too bad," I said. "They would have made a nice couple."

I left him to the rest of his soap and went home. The next day, I received the call I'd been dreading. John had died during the night. Hearing that he was actually gone, I found that I was relieved. All his pain, all the waiting for the end he knew was coming, was over. Although I missed him already, I was glad that he didn't have to suffer any longer.

"He wanted you to have some stuff," the man from GMHC told me. "Some stereo equipment and a lot of records. You can pick them up next week when we finish boxing up the apartment."

Alan returned on Saturday, and I met him at the airport, giving him a big hug when he walked out of the gate. He was surprised and happy to see me.

"I thought you were going to wait at your place for me," he said as we walked to baggage claim.

"I was," I said. "But I couldn't wait to see you. There's something I want to talk to you about."

"What's his name?" Alan said, stopping in his tracks. "I'll kill him."

"What?" I said. "No, it's nothing like that. It's something good."

"Good how?" asked Alan, still regarding me suspiciously.

"I want you to move in with me," I said.

"Is that all?" he said. "I thought it was something major. Yes, I'll move in with you."

"You will?" I said, not sure if he knew I was serious.

"Yes," he repeated. "I'll move in. I think it's time. And Peter and Fred have been talking about getting their own place anyway, so the timing is good."

I was so happy that I didn't know what to say. I hugged him again, lifting him up and twirling him around like Robert Redford spinning Barbra Streisand in *The Way We Were*.

"Okay, Hubbell, you can put me down now," he said in his best Streisand imitation.

"I love you," I said as people walked around us to get to their bags.

"And I love you," said Alan, kissing me. "Now can I get my bag? It's gone around three times already."

We decided that New Year's Eve was the perfect day to begin our life together as a cohabitating couple, so when we got back to my apartment, I cleared out space in the dresser and closet for Alan's clothes. Then we toasted ourselves with the bottle of champagne I'd bought for later. We ended up making love, and by the time we finished and got dressed, we were almost late for meeting up with Taffy in Times Square. We got there in time to see the ball drop, though, and afterward we celebrated the arrival of 1984 by singing show tunes at Don't Tell Mama, where Taffy's rendition of "The Boy from Ipanema" brought down the house.

As for Andy, I didn't know where he was that night. Since arriving in New York, he'd been elusive. We saw him once or twice a week for dinner or drinks, but his activities remained a mystery. He spoke of friends we never met, always using only first names, and rarely provided details about anything. But he seemed happy, and I attributed his circumspection to his familiar self-centeredness. We'd invited him to join us on New Year's, but he'd declined, saying he had some business function to attend.

The Friday after New Year's, I found myself at the Metropolitan Opera House for the first time. Seated in a box in the center parterre, I felt out of place among the grandly-dressed people surrounding me. But I was so entranced by the beauty of the hall that I soon forgot about that and fell under the spell of the building itself. Waiting for the opera to begin, I began to understand what John found so magical about it. I felt as if I'd stepped back in time, to an era when things were simpler, when men didn't die because of unnamed viruses and life's greatest tragedies were reserved for the stage.

The mood was deepened when the orchestra began to play the overture. I'd tried listening to a recording of *La Bohème* that had been among the records left to me by John, but had abandoned it when I discovered that it was the one that had been playing the day I saw him for the last time. Listening to it, I realized that he'd known his death was imminent, and I'd been unable to bear it. But hearing it live now, the musicians visible as they played their instruments, I felt only the music. I tried to listen the way I thought that John would, letting the sounds carry me to Paris of 1830, where Marcello the painter and Rodolfo the poet lived in their tiny Latin Quarter garret, burning pages from one of Rodolfo's manuscripts to keep warm.

When the curtain rose, revealing the stunning set designed by Franco Zeffirelli, I believed immediately that I was peering through a window into the shabby house. I felt the cold of winter, the wind that blew through the cracks in the walls. I grasped immediately the poverty in which these men lived, and my heart ached for them.

The singing only intensified the feelings. Although I understood nothing (the Met would be the last of the great American opera houses to employ the use of supertitles, dragging its feet until 1995), it didn't matter. The passion and sadness of Giuseppe Giacosa and Luigi Illica's libretto rang through every note of Puccini's music. When Rodolfo and Mimi, their candles extinguished by the drafts blowing through the miserable room, sang in the darkness to one another of their dreams of spring and the return of warmth, I sensed their loneliness and isolation. When in Act II Rodolfo and the other bohemians left the wealthy Alcindoro to pay their tab at a café, I rejoiced at their cleverness. And when in Act III Rodolfo and Mimi had their lovers' quarrel, I prayed that they would reconcile. When they did, I felt my spirits lift.

By Act IV, I was so engrossed in the lives of the characters on the stage that I forgot they were actors in costume. They had become real to me, and although I knew things couldn't possibly end well, I held out hope that they would. When Mimi, dying of consumption, came to Rodolfo's garret, I knew it was too late for her. Yet when Musetta went to pawn her earrings and Colline his overcoat to buy her medicine, I silently urged her to hold on until they returned. As she sang her final aria, telling Rodolfo of her love for him, I cried, and when she died and his heart broke, so did mine. I wept for Mimi, and for John, but mostly I wept for the death of love.

I have attended many operas since that first one, and every time I think about John and the wonderful gift he gave me. Now I know the libretto of *La Bohème* by heart, and when Mimi sings I hear her telling Rodolfo that her love for him is as huge as the ocean, as deep and infinite as the sea. I hear her tell him not to be worried about her little cough, because she's used to it now. I hear her ask him if he still finds her beautiful, even in her ruined state, and I weep every time he tells her that she is more lovely than the dawn.

I've heard many people say they don't like opera because the stories are silly, depressing, overblown. Yes, they are. But then so is life. What I've come to understand about opera is that it takes the most basic human emotions and magnifies them a thousandfold. In opera, love isn't just love, it's the most wonderful and terrible thing in the world. Because that's how we feel it when it happens to us. Opera is nothing less than the heart singing, and its song is as raw and violent as the fiercest storm, as soft and soothing as the gentlest kiss.

That night, I didn't know what Mimi and Rodolfo were saying to one another, but I understood them perfectly. And as I stood with the rest of the audience to give Cotrubas and the rest of the cast the ovation they more than deserved, I saw John standing beside them on the stage, taking his bow and basking in the love of the audience. In that moment, I was able to say good-bye to him, and I knew that wherever he was, he was happy.

CHAPTER 48

"Is that who I think it is talking to Bernadette Peters?"

I followed Alan's gaze to the piano in the corner of the living room. There I saw the unmistakable hair and heard the unmistakable voice of the woman who after a ten-year absence was about to make her return to Broadway in the new Stephen Sondheim musical, *Sunday in the Park with George*. And she was talking to the equally unmistakable Andy Kowalski.

It was the second week of 1984, and we had just arrived at a party hosted by *Back Stage* critic and cabaret scene fixture Marty Schaeffer. The apartment was filled with a who's who of faces from the theater world, any one of whom I would have been more interested in under ordinary circumstances. But at the moment I was concerned only with finding out why Andy was in Marty's apartment and how he'd gotten there. Dragging Alan along, I headed straight for the piano.

"Hey," I said, patting Andy on the back. "I hope we're not interrupting anything."

"No," Andy said, showing no sign of surprise at my presence. "We were just talking about Bernadette's show."

"Hi, Alan," Bernadette said, giving Alan a kiss. "I saw the show last week. Fourth time. It's amazing."

"Thanks," Alan said. "I hear yours is fantastic, too."

"I hope so," she said. "Previews are in April."

"You'll be great," Alan assured her. I nudged him and, remembering his manners, he added, "This is my boyfriend, Ned."

I shook Bernadette's hand. "We loved you in *Sally and Marsha*," I told her. "That line 'I love being touched by babies' was amazing."

"I just said it," she answered with a smile. "Sybille Pearson gets all the credit for writing it."

"So, Andy," I said, turning to my old friend, "what brings you here?"

"I'm here with Crosley," he answered cryptically.

"Crosley?" I repeated, never having heard the name before.

"Do I hear someone talking about me?"

I turned to see a tall, thin man coming toward us with a martini glass in each hand. His dark hair was thinning on top, and he wore a close-trimmed beard and moustache. Round, gold-framed glasses perched on his nose, and he wore a black turtleneck sweater covered by a black jacket. He handed Andy one of the martini glasses, then extended his hand to me.

"Peter Crosley," he said. "But everyone calls me Crosley."

"Ned Brummel," I replied, taking his hand. When I released it, Peter slipped it around Andy's waist in a clear gesture of ownership.

"Crosley's a producer," Alan said to me. "He's responsible for a lot of the big shows that are going on right now."

"Well, my money is," said Crosley, laughing. "I'm afraid I don't have an artistic bone in my body, just a talent for the stock market and an interest in the theater. Fortunately, there are a lot of people willing to help me spend what I have."

"Ned is an old friend of mine," Andy said. "We went to college together." I noticed Crosley relax a little at hearing this. His hand remained on Andy's waist, but he didn't seem quite as territorial as he had a moment before.

"And what do you do, Ned?" Crosley asked.

"I'm getting my degree," I said. "In history."

"That's a long time to be in college," Crosley joked.

"Well, there was a war in between," I said, annoyed by his mocking tone. "That tends to interrupt things."

"Bernadette," Crosley said, ignoring the remark, "do you have a minute? I want to introduce you to someone." To Andy, he said, "I'll be back in a few minutes."

"I'll be here," said Andy.

Bernadette excused herself, and she and Crosley walked off, leaving Alan and me with Andy. As soon as they were swallowed by the crowd, I turned to Andy. "Well," I said. "When did this happen?"

"When did what happen?" he asked.

"You," I said. "And him."

"Oh," said Andy, taking a sip of his martini. "That. The end of December, I guess."

"And you just forgot to mention it?" I said.

"I didn't know if it would go anywhere," said Andy. "Why bring up a trick if he's not going to be around more than a night or two?"

"He looks like more than a trick to me," I countered. "He seems to think you're his personal property."

"That's just Crosley," said Andy. "He gets a little possessive is all."

"So he *is* your boyfriend," I said.

Andy nodded. "I guess you could call him that," he admitted.

"You could do a lot worse than Peter Crosley," Alan said. "The guy's loaded."

"Is he?" Andy said, as if this was news to him.

"Where'd you meet him?" I asked.

"I forget," Andy answered. "A party, a bar, something like that."

I could tell he was lying, hoping I would drop the subject. But I was annoyed, both at Andy for playing dumb and at his apparent boyfriend for talking down to me. I decided I wasn't leaving until I knew exactly what was going on between them.

"Are you guys serious?" I pressed. "I mean, is he the one?"

"The one?" said Andy. "Christ, you sound like some high school girl. Yeah, I've got my hope chest filled with dish towels and silverware. I'm just waiting for him to pop the question."

"Hey, I'm just trying to figure out what the situation is," I said.

"There's no situation," Andy said, clearly irritated. "We're just dating."

"I think I'm going to go get some drinks," Alan said. "What do you want?"

"Scotch and soda," I told him, knowing that he was leaving to give me time alone with Andy.

"Andy?" he asked. "Another one?"

"Thanks," said Andy, handing him the empty glass.

"Okay," I said when Alan was gone. "I know you. And I know that guy isn't your type. Now what's going on?"

"What do you mean 'my type'?" said Andy. "What's my type?"

"Not that queen," I answered. "Since when are you into theater?"

"Since he started paying me," Andy said.

"Paying you? What, you work for him now? Doing what?"

"Being his boyfriend," said Andy.

I looked at him, speechless. "He pays you to be his boyfriend?" I said. "You mean you're an escort?"

"No," Andy said. "It's not like that. He doesn't pay me, exactly. It's more like I'm his executor."

"You lost me," I told him.

"He's going to leave everything to me," Andy explained. "Not everything, but a lot. When he dies. Until then, I'm his boyfriend."

I was dumbfounded. "He *bought* you?" I said.

Andy shook his head. "You don't understand," he said.

"You're right about that," I told him. "So, enlighten me."

Andy looked around, as if to make sure no one was listening. "He has AIDS," he said, speaking quietly. "Nobody knows. He's not sick yet, but he will be. He knows no one will want to be with him when he is. I will. Then, when he dies, I get some money and his apartment."

"You're joking," I said. "You've got to be. Why would anyone do that?"

"He doesn't want to be alone," said Andy.

"I can't believe he's buying a boyfriend," I said. "Do you even like him?"

"He's all right," Andy said. "Like you said, maybe he's not my type. But I'm not fucking him, so who cares?"

"He's not even getting sex out of this deal?" I said.

"I jack him off," Andy said. "Sometimes I let him suck my dick. But that's it. He doesn't really like getting fucked anyway, so he doesn't care."

I shook my head. "How much are you getting?" I asked.

Andy shrugged. "A couple of million, I guess."

I couldn't help but laugh. "This is insane," I told him. "Totally insane."

"How's it any different from making porn?" Andy asked me. "It's a fantasy. I let him live out his fantasy, he pays me. What's so weird about that? It's not like I know how to do anything else, Ned."

"No," I said. "I guess you don't."

Alan reappeared at that point, balancing three glasses in his hands. I took my scotch and Andy retrieved his martini.

"So," Alan said. "Are all four of us having dinner soon?"

"I don't think so," I told him as Andy drained his glass.

We left soon after that and went home. As we got ready for bed, I told Alan what Andy was doing with Crosley. He was as shocked as I'd been.

"He has AIDS?" he said. "You can't even tell."

"He's not that sick yet," I reminded him, squeezing toothpaste onto my brush.

"And Andy's getting all his money?" Alan asked.

"Not all of it," I said through a mouthful of suds as I scrubbed. "But enough. And the apartment."

"I guess I should be nice to him," said Alan from the other room, where he was taking off his clothes. "He might be producing my next show."

I spit into the sink. "I just don't get it," I said as I rinsed my toothbrush. "Why would a guy like Peter Crosley need to *pay* someone to be his boyfriend?"

"Well, I sort of understand it," Alan said. "If he just had a normal boyfriend, I mean one who wasn't like Andy, he might not know if the guy was sticking around because he loved him or because he wanted his money. With Andy, he knows, so he doesn't have to worry about it."

"That's totally fucked up," I said, turning out the bathroom light and coming into the bedroom.

"Maybe," Alan said. "But it kind of makes sense. You've seen how these guys look when it gets bad. How many boyfriends do you think would stick around if they weren't getting something for it?"

"They should stick around because they *love* them," I argued.

"They should, yes," Alan agreed. "But you know a lot of them don't. They can't handle it and they leave. With Andy, Crosley has insurance. Andy won't leave because he won't get anything if he does."

I pulled back the comforter on the bed. "But Andy doesn't love him!" I said.

"Sometimes pretend love is enough," said Alan. "What do you think theater is anyway?"

"But he could do so many other things with all that money," I said as I slipped between the sheets.

"Right," said Alan. "He could give it all to the Met, like John did. Who also gave *you* something for coming around twice a week, I might add."

"A box of opera records is a little different than a couple million dollars," I said.

"It's the same thing," said Alan as he squirted hand lotion onto his palm and began rubbing it into his skin. "My great aunt Charlotte left my mother a diamond necklace when she died, all because when my mother was twelve she told her that she made the best lemon cake in the world. John left you opera records. Crosley is leaving Andy a couple million dollars and an apartment."

"It's more sad than anything else," I said. "What does it say about us as people that we abandon each other when things get hard?" I looked at Alan. "What would you do if I got sick?"

Alan put the lotion away and got into bed. "You're not going to get sick," he said.

"That's not an answer," I told him. "What if I did?"

"I'd bring you chicken noodle soup and read you bedtime stories," he said, kissing me.

"You're avoiding talking about it," I said.

"Because we don't need to talk about it."

"Would you leave me?" I asked him.

"Are you going to give me a million dollars?" he asked.

"Alan, I'm serious. Would it scare you away if I was sick?"

"I don't think so," he said after a moment. "I hope it wouldn't."

"That wasn't the answer I wanted to hear," I told him.

"I love you, Ned," he said. "And I want to believe that I wouldn't be the kind of person who would run away if you got sick. But we're not talking about regular sick here. We're talking about *sick* sick. You know what happens. Shit, I freak out when I have to pop a zit."

I nodded. "I do know what happens," I said. "I know what happened to John, and I know what's happening now to Ike and Bart and the other guys I take food to. And I know that if it ever happened to me and you couldn't handle it, I'd probably die."

"Then you understand why Crosley's willing to give Andy everything he has for not leaving him," he said.

"We're not talking about Crosley and Andy," I told him. "We're talking about you and me."

He took my hand, running his thumb along mine as we sat for a while in silence. "I'm not leaving," he said finally.

"Even if I lose my hair and end up covered in purple spots?" I asked. "Like Mad Madam Mim in *The Sword in the Stone*?"

"Even then," he said. "Disney queen."

"Promise?"

"I promise," he said. "Now can we go to sleep?"

I nodded. Alan reached over and turned off the light. Then he turned onto his side and put his arm around me, pulling me close.

"You worry too much," he said.

"And you don't worry enough," I answered.

"Which is why we're perfect for each other," he said. "Between the two of us, we're a normal person."

I closed my eyes and tried to sleep, but my brain was still wide awake, unwilling to settle down and go to bed. It jumped up and down like an unruly child, demanding attention and ignoring my pleas to stop. I couldn't stop thinking about Andy and Crosley. I did see Alan's point. But I also couldn't ignore the fact that Andy was taking advantage of the situation, like a vulture hovering a few feet above a cowboy slowly dying of thirst. I knew there were men in apartments and hospital rooms all over the city who were dying alone, with only people like me and other volunteers to hold their hands and care what happened to them. Why should men like Peter Crosley be using their money to buy an illusion when it could be used for so many better things? And why should a man like Andy be getting it?

It was an unfair question, and I knew it. Crosley had just as much right to buy Andy's affection as someone else had to buy drugs, or chocolate, or a pet to sit on his lap and provide comfort. That Crosley's need required an obscene amount of money to meet was simply a measure of its enormity. If anything, it was Andy who should be considering using some of the wealth he would acquire to help those who had less. Would he? I was afraid that I knew the answer to that question all too well.

Behind me I felt and heard Alan breathing. Would he, I wondered, really stay if I discovered spots on my skin or found it difficult to draw air into my lungs? He became a baby when he had so much as a stubbed toe or a sore throat. Could he handle a wasting body and everything that came with it? I hoped he was right, and that we would never have to find out. For now, I could only trust in his promise.

CHAPTER 49

"Who controls the past controls the future: who controls the present controls the past." So wrote George Orwell in 1949, when his novel *1984* looked ahead to a time when life was dictated by the will of the authoritarian Party and individuality was a crime. And certainly history, both prior to and following the publication of Orwell's most famous work, has proven him correct. What we know as history has been written and rewritten so many times that what is really true has been lost in a thicket of conjecture, mistake, and deliberate lie. Following his rise to power, for example, Josef Stalin employed what Trotsky referred to as his "School of Falsification" to cover up his bloody crimes and erase all mention of his enemies' contributions to the rise of the Bolsheviks and the success of the October Revolution. More recently, after assuming power from the secularist government in 1998, India's Hindu Nationalist Party rewrote the country's history books, removing, among other things, all references to the assassination of Gandhi by a Hindu fanatic.

This is what we do. We revise history, whether personal, familial, or global, to our advantage. Is it surprising that Henry VII would want to wipe the name Plantagenet from the record books? Is it shocking that the people of Japan don't want to acknowledge the massacre of an estimated 300,000 Chinese by Japanese soldiers during the Rape of Nanking? Does anyone really question why, time and again, criminals declare themselves innocent in the face of overwhelming proof, or why juries often do likewise?

Vladimir Lenin famously asserted that "a lie, told often enough, becomes truth." It's not that easy, of course. The transition from falsehood to fact requires active participation on the part of those being deceived, either a failure to question the "truth" in question, or a willful disregard of any evidence that contradicts the so-called facts as they are presented. Fortunately for those who would seek to rewrite history, the human mind seems to have a limitless capacity for rearranging events to render them more satisfying or less wounding, as befits the situation.

In 1984—the year, not the novel—things were not quite as bad off as Orwell supposed they might be. They were, however, not good, especially for gay men in America. We'd hoped that AIDS would be a temporary inconvenience, a frightening but curable one that scientists would quickly corner and subdue. But things hadn't worked out that way. The plague continued to spread, and like the residents of 14th century Europe, we examined ourselves and one another for the telltale signs of infection. (In a grotesque homage to the red-ringed "roseys" that indicated the bite of the Black Death, the first signs that AIDS had taken hold were the purplish-red spots of Kaposi's sarcoma.)

On Sunday, April 22, I walked to the corner bodega for coffee and the *New York Times*, bringing both back to Alan, who was still asleep but woke up as soon as he smelled the cup of French roast I set on his bedside table. Never a morning person, he struggled to accept the arrival of a new day while I settled in next to him to see what was going on in the world. Removing the circulars, magazines, and TV guide that were the paper's innards, I opened the first section to see, on the front page, an article announcing that the head of the Centers for Disease Control was confident that the cause of AIDS had been found by a team of French researchers.

"Listen to this," I said to Alan, reading him the first part of the article.

"It's about time," he said. "What's it been, three years? Maybe we'll finally get a vaccine and life can get back to normal."

"Not for a while," I told him, reading further. "They say it will take at least a year to manufacture one. But they should have a test for it soon."

Alan yawned and stretched. "Fantastic," he said. "So you can know sooner that you're going to die. No thanks. I'd rather not know."

"Really?" I said. "You wouldn't want to know if you were sick?"

"Why would I?" he replied. "There's not much I could do about it. It's not like they've found anything to fight it with or really know how to prevent spreading it, so, personally, I'd rather not be all freaked out about it." He leaned over and kissed me on the cheek. "Besides, we're both fine."

"How do we know that?" I said. "We could be infected and not know it."

"We've been through this a hundred times," he said, drinking his coffee. "We're *not sick*. Now, give me the arts and entertainment section. I want to read about something I actually care about."

As Alan turned his attention to less depressing topics, I read the rest of the article. Looking back on it more than twenty years later, when AIDS has claimed a reported 25 million lives (the same, incidentally, as the Black Plague took between 1347 and 1352), I'm struck by how hopeful we were then. We really did believe that once the culprit was discovered, a cure would be close behind. Although AIDS had first been called "gay cancer," none of us, I think, thought that it would turn out to be a disease whose eradication would, like its nominal sibling breast cancer, be a battle seemingly without end. But we needed that hope. If we'd known then that decades would pass without either a vaccine or a cure, I think maybe we would have given up. We were already scared; the idea that our entire way of life might need to change was something we were not ready to face.

If, like Stalin, I were to rewrite the history of that time, specifically my own history, I would make myself less certain that "the government" or any other faceless entity actually cared about my personal well-being. Again, though, to even begin to believe that we might survive the virus, I had to believe that someone was looking out for me other than myself. Like the responsibility for ensuring the safety of air travel, the purity of my drinking water, and the worth of the currency in my wallet, I placed in the hands of the United States government the duty of making sure that I and all of my friends made it through alive.

The first sign that this might not be the case came the day after I read Alan the *Times* article. Apparently annoyed that the U.S. had been beaten to the punch by rival France, Secretary of Health and Human Services Margaret Heckler called a news conference to announce that an American team at the National Cancer Institute had discovered their own virus, which they believed would be proven to be the cause of AIDS. A beaming Heckler told reporters, "Today we add another miracle to the long honor roll of American medicine and science."

Ultimately the two viruses would turn out to be the same one, but the scuffle over who deserved credit for the "miracle" of its discovery, and even which name would be used to describe it, would rage for some time. In the meantime, we continued to sicken and die. Ronald Reagan, the man who had helped us defeat the Briggs Initiative six years before, had not even uttered the word *AIDS* in public, and public health officials were treating the disease as something affecting primarily homosexuals. Still, we continued to believe that they would help us.

Alan was right about one thing, though. We were both fine. Neither of us had experienced so much as a cold in months, which was something of a miracle considering how busy we were. *La Cage* was a smash hit, and despite having a small role, Alan was getting all kinds of offers for new productions. I was finishing my junior year at NYU and spending all of my time studying and writing. We were constantly on the go, sometimes seeing each other only for an hour or two between Alan's return from the theater and my departure for my first class. It was a crazy life, but we were both doing what we loved, and so we were happy.

Since learning of Andy's relationship with Crosley, I'd seen him only a handful of times, mostly at theater community events. I'd tried to make peace with what he was doing, and had largely succeeded, mainly by reminding myself repeatedly that Peter Crosley had as much right to be happy as anyone else did, and that my judging him for how he chose to live his life was just as bad as someone judging me for how I chose to live mine. Which a lot of people were, by the way. Not me personally, but gay men in general. Since AIDS was still largely thought of as a gay disease, our popularity among other segments of society had plummeted. Like the mice and rats who were discovered to be the primary carriers of the plague and were summarily dispatched, we were viewed with suspicion, as if every last one of us housed within us the seeds of death. A poll taken at the time showed that 15% of the American public believed that people with AIDS should be visibly tattooed for the protection of everyone else.

And so I tried not to judge Crosley too harshly, particularly as his health declined precipitously during the spring. Each time I saw him, it was as if he had faded a little more. He lost weight, and his eyes took on the haunted look of someone who saw his own ghost when he peered in the mirror. Word quickly spread that he was the latest to be stricken, and a deathwatch commenced as people gossiped about what would become of his fortune and worried producers wondered if they should look elsewhere for funding.

Through it all, Andy remained at Crosley's side. He was recognized openly as Peter's boyfriend, and more than once someone unaware of our friendship commented upon his loyalty. I never revealed his secret, seeing no point, and I never discussed it again with Andy. He pretended as if we had never quarreled, and in this way we maintained a cordial social relationship, even if, in private, I still found what he was doing disturbing.

In May, the Tony Award nominations were announced, and *La Cage* received nine of them, including ones in all the important categories. I completed the school year on the first day of June, and two days later attended the Tonys at the Gershwin Theatre, where I watched Alan and the rest of the company perform "We Are What We Are" as the show went on to win six awards, including Best Musical.

At the party afterward I saw Andy standing alone and went up to him. "Where's Crosley?" I asked.

"Getting another drink," said Andy. "He's not taking his loss to the drag queens well."

"He'll have other shows," I said. "How's he feeling otherwise?"

"Not great," said Andy.

"Your investment might pay off sooner than expected, you mean?" I said, surprised at the harshness in my voice. I held my hand up. "I'm sorry," I said. "I didn't mean that."

"Sure you did," said Andy. "And you're right, it is an investment, of time and energy and lots of other things."

I was angry again. "Did it ever occur to you that he might not die?" I asked Andy. "If they find a cure, or even a treatment, you could be looking at years with him."

Andy took a drink. "I hadn't thought about that," he said. "I suppose it could happen."

"How many years is he worth?" I said. "Two? Five? Ten? Have you already worked out the per-hour rate? At what point would you have to just cut your losses and leave?"

"I don't think I have to worry about that," Andy said evenly. "Have you seen him lately?"

Before I could answer that I hadn't, Crosley appeared. In just the few weeks since I'd last had a glimpse of him, he'd aged noticeably. His face, heavily made up, was thinner, although his blue eyes still sparkled when he smiled at me. His voice, when he spoke, was raspy.

"Trying to steal my boyfriend, Ned?" he asked. "Isn't one enough for you?"

Even sick, he was officious. For a moment, my sympathy for him drained from me, and I readied a comeback. Then I noticed his hands, and the spots on them, faintly visible beneath the stage makeup he'd applied, but which was failing him after a long night of wear. Seeing the sigil of AIDS stamped upon him, I relented. I raised my glass to him instead.

"If you'd been *one* minute later, I would have had him," I said.

Crosley touched his withered lips to Andy's cheek. "I can stand losing a Tony," he said. "But not this prize."

"I should be getting back to Alan anyway," I said. "It's nice seeing you two."

I left them standing together and returned to the table occupied by the *La Cage* group. Already in good spirits because of their win, they were now completely out of control, laughing and passing their Tonys around so that everyone could have a turn giving an acceptance speech. When I arrived, Alan was in the middle of his.

"And, of course, I'd like to thank all the little people," he said. "Especially my not-so-little boyfriend, Ned Brummel," he added, holding his hands a considerable distance apart. "Ned, thanks for teaching me how to take it like a man."

The rest of the table let out a roar at his joke. I bowed, earning more applause, and took my seat. As the partying continued, I looked over at Andy and Crosley. They'd sat down, but they were alone at their table, everyone else in their contingent having gravitated elsewhere. Crosley was watching us, his face a mask of resentment. Beside him, Andy sat oblivious, his eyes fixed on the ass of a waiter passing by with a tray of glasses brimming with champagne.

CHAPTER 50

"Rock Hudson has AIDS," Alan announced.

"What?" I said, pouring myself another cup of coffee.

"AIDS," Alan repeated. "Rock Hudson has AIDS." He waved the issue of *Variety* he was reading at me. "It's in Army Archerd's column."

"Please," I said as I added some milk to my mug and swirled it around. "You're going to believe a gossip column?"

"It's not a gossip column," said Alan. "It's industry news."

"Having AIDS is news now?" I said, leaning against the counter and drinking my coffee. "Where would that fall, in between who's dating Heather Locklear and which supermodel is in rehab?"

"Don't be a jerk," Alan said. "If this is true, it could really change the way people in America look at the disease."

"Sure," I replied. "Now they'll think that gay *actors* get it."

"Why are you being such a prick?" asked Alan.

"Because," I answered. "People aren't going to start caring about AIDS just because Rock Hudson has it. If he even does. They won't start caring until someone they really like gets it."

"Like who?" Alan asked.

"I don't know," I said. "Mary Tyler Moore. Michael Jackson. Jane Pauley. Someone . . . wholesome."

"What's more wholesome than Rock Hudson?" said Alan. "He and Doris Day are the poster children for wholesome."

"Not if he got it by taking it up the butt," I said. "People will turn against him like that." I snapped my fingers to emphasize my point.

"We'll see," Alan said.

"Twenty bucks says he denies it," I suggested.

"You're on," answered Alan.

I looked at my watch. "I've got to go," I said. "I'm meeting Jack and Andy in ten minutes."

"I'm glad Jack moved here," said Alan. "Especially now that you're done with school. He gives you something to do when I'm working."

"Hopefully I'll have a job myself in September," I said. "I've had three interviews at Stuyvesant and two at Bergtraum. One of them better hire me. Leave it to the New York City public school system to let you know at the last minute."

"You're a brand-new baby teacher," Alan reminded me. "All those grizzled old spinster schoolmarms have to say no to the jobs first."

"That makes me feel so much better," I told him.

"You'll hear next week," said Alan. "I'll bet you another twenty. Now go have fun at dinner."

"You have fun at rehearsal," I countered. "Tell Bernadette hello for me. I'll see you when you get home."

"I might be late," said Alan. "So don't wait up."

I kissed him good-bye and headed a few blocks over to Christopher Street and David's Pot Belly, a narrow sliver of a restaurant that had been there for ages and which served, as far as I'm concerned, the best hamburgers on the planet. On a summer night, it was the perfect place to eat and watch the constant parade down what might be, with the possible exception of San Francisco's Castro Street, the gayest thoroughfare in the world. Jack was already there when I arrived, seated right up front by the big picture window.

"How'd you score such a prime spot?" I asked him as I sat down.

"I had to wrestle a dyke bowling team for it," he said, indicating a table of four very large, mulleted women wearing jerseys with their team name—The Split Lickers—stitched in pink across the backs.

"I see Andy's late as usual," I remarked, opening the enormous menu and flipping through it.

"He's in the bathroom," said Jack.

"Alone?" I asked.

"Be nice," said Jack. "You promised me you wouldn't give him a hard time."

I shut the menu. "Come on," I said. "Crosley died last August. It was what, Labor Day, when he had the next one?"

Jack held up his hands in mock surrender. "Don't get mad at me," he said. "I'm not his pimp."

"How's Luke doing, anyway?" I asked him.

"Ask Andy," said Jack. "Here he comes."

When Andy joined us, I greeted him as warmly as I could make myself. He patted me on the back. "How's tricks?" he said.

"I was just about to ask you that," I answered as Jack scowled at me over his menu.

"Things are good," he said. "They're still working on the apartment, so it's kind of a mess, but it should be great when it's all done. I'll have a party so everyone can see it."

I concentrated on my menu to avoid saying anything bitchy. Since Peter Crosley's death, Andy had moved into the spacious Central Park West apartment that had been one of his consolation prizes as the AIDS widow. He was currently spending a substantial portion of the money he'd gotten fixing it up, which to Andy meant tearing out all of the original fixtures and woodwork and turning the place into a showroom of modern design. Many of his neighbors, not to mention Crosley's friends, were horrified, but there was nothing they could do about it.

"I was talking about Luke," I said finally.

"Oh," said Andy. "He's okay. He got into this test for a new drug. AZT, I think it's called. I guess they originally made it to fight cancer, and they think it might work on AIDS."

"One of my patients told me about that," Jack said. "Apparently the trials are almost impossible to get into."

"Yeah, well, he got in," said Andy, shutting his menu. "You guys want to get some buffalo wings?"

Luke—if I may intrude upon the story for a moment—was Luke Matthias. Unlike Peter Crosley, Luke was not well known in New York society. In fact, he was not well known at all. He was not handsome or powerful, did not occupy a fashionable address, and was possessed of neither a sculpted body nor a large penis. What he was was a mid-level accountant at Macy's, a man whose job consisted primarily of auditing payments made to foreign suppliers of women's wear. While earning his business degree at Fordham University he had, on a whim, enrolled in a course in Mandarin, and to the surprise of everyone involved had turned out to be very good at it. He'd stuck with it, and by graduation was fluent not only in Mandarin, but also in Cantonese.

This had gotten him his job with the fine firm founded by Rowland Hussey Macy, where he spent most of his time arguing with other accountants in Beijing and Taipei. Because of the time difference between New York and these cities, Luke worked from three in the afternoon 'til eleven at night. When he got off, he went straight to the Anvil, one of the city's more notorious gay watering holes, where he unwound by letting men insert their Crisco-slicked fists into his rectum and urinate on his face, often while forcing him to look up at them by pulling on his Geoffrey Beene tie.

Luke's willingness to accommodate some of the more rarified sexual proclivities of his partners ensured that he never wanted for erotic fulfillment. But at finding someone he could have dinner and take in a movie with, he had been less fortunate. The passivity that served him so well in his nighttime pursuits manifested itself as pathological shyness during daylight hours, and the men in whom he was interested seldom even knew he was there. Coupled with his overall averageness, this was not a recipe for romantic success in the competitive world of gay New York.

The upside was that Luke had, during his seventeen years at Macy's, managed to amass an impressive amount of both stock and savings. And because he was afraid of having nothing when he retired, he had managed to hang on to most of it. His expenses were few, and the rent on his one-bedroom apartment on East 78th Street was impossibly low due to his having taken over the lease from an elderly aunt who had lived there for some fifty-two years before her death.

In August of 1984, while trying on a pair of loafers in the Macy's men's department and considering whether his employee discount made the $135 shoes an acceptable purchase, he noticed a small spot on his ankle. Unable to rub it away or pick it off, he had at first thought it a bruise, possibly sustained the previous evening during an encounter with a gentleman who had traveled to the Anvil from the Bronx solely for the purpose of forcing someone to lick his scuffed motorcycle boots while he spat on them from above. But when it did not vanish after a few days, and in fact seemed to divide and multiply into a tiny cluster of spots, Luke had gone to his doctor and sought his opinion on the matter.

The diagnosis, when it came, had changed his life in unexpected ways. Understandably believing that he'd been handed a death sentence, he had decided that since fate hadn't seen fit to provide him with the life that he wanted, he would now purchase it for himself. With the determination of someone who has long been deprived, he undertook a campaign of retail therapy, the culmination of which was a two-week stay at a beach house on Fire Island. He stocked the house with every vice that might appeal to the handsome men he hoped to attract: drugs, alcohol, food, music, and several well-appointed bedrooms that he put at their disposal. He then opened his doors to all who would come.

The results were glorious. For two weeks he was the center of attention, getting anyone he wanted simply by setting out a bowl mounded with powder or uncorking a bottle of Krug 1976. He danced all night to the Communards, Frankie Goes to Hollywood, and Baltimora, taking breaks every half hour to get fucked in the hot tub by yet another big-dicked boy who wouldn't have given him a second glance back in New York.

The party climaxed on the Saturday of Labor Day weekend with an all-out orgy that would end with the house trashed and a young man from Hackensack dead on the beach from an overdose of some unnamed drug. In the midst of it, while snorting a line of cocaine that he'd sprinkled the length of the erection belonging to a porn star who called himself Jet Rocket, Luke had looked up to see Andy standing in the doorway of his house. With the lights from the deck limning Andy's body in gold, Luke for a moment believed that an angel had come to carry him to heaven. He'd stood and walked toward Andy with his hands outstretched, only to trip on the living room's shag carpeting and fall, landing at Andy's feet.

Andy, who had gone to Fire Island to mourn the recent loss of Crosley, had rented a house some distance from Luke's. Attracted by the noise (and the rumors of free drugs), he'd taken a walk over there to meet the man he'd heard so many stories about. Seeing him in person, he'd recognized a potential partner in his new enterprise, and had stayed around long enough to get a fairly good estimate of Luke's net worth, which, even after the expenses of his Fire Island binge were deducted, was not insignificant. Even more attractive was the substantial life insurance policy he'd taken out some years earlier on the advice of his father, who at the time had been thinking ahead to the welfare of his unborn grandchildren.

A deal was quickly struck, and the two men returned to New York on Monday afternoon with the understanding that until Luke's death, Andy would treat him in almost every way as he would an actual lover. This included moving Luke into Andy's apartment, which was nicer, although they maintained separate bedrooms. The sex, when it took place, occurred in Luke's room, so that Andy always went to sleep in clean sheets.

On the night that I met Jack and Andy at David's, Luke and Andy were approaching their one-year anniversary. The engagement had gone on longer than Andy had expected, which I knew was irritating to him. I, however, was pleased, and not just because it gave me some small measure of satisfaction to see Andy uncomfortable. I liked Luke. Unlike Crosley, he was someone I felt deserved better. His only sin was being not quite marketable enough, and since I'd felt that way myself many times in my life, I sympathized. The several times I'd met him (on one of which he'd told me the story I've just related), Luke had struck me as someone who had much to offer the right man. In choosing Andy for that position, I suppose he had gotten what he wanted, but I had a feeling he sometimes regretted the Faustian pact he'd made that night.

Hearing that Luke might be going on a new medication, I couldn't help but press Andy for more details. "When does he start taking the drug?" I asked him.

"I don't know," he said irritably. "He just found out this week that he got into the trial."

"That's great," I said. "Maybe he'll beat the virus then."

"I guess he could," said Andy. "Where's the waiter?"

"Stop it," Jack mouthed at me from across the table.

I reluctantly dropped the subject as Andy located our waiter and we ordered. As we waited for the food to come, Jack prevented any further goading of Andy on my part by turning the conversation to me. "What's the name of the show Alan's in now?" he asked.

"*Song & Dance*," I said. "Bernadette Peters remembered him from *La Cage* and suggested him for the role."

"That's the one by the guy who did *Cats*, right?" Andy said.

"Andrew Lloyd Webber," I said. "Right."

"I remember Crosley saying he heard some of it and it was terrible," said Andy.

"Alan says it's fantastic," I said, ignoring him and speaking to Jack. "You've got front row seats when it opens in September." I looked over at Andy. "I'll get some for you and Luke, too. He loves musicals, as I recall."

"Did I tell you guys about the nut job who was assigned to me this week?" asked Jack as the waiter appeared with our buffalo wings.

"I thought you weren't supposed to call them nut jobs," said Andy.

"Yeah, well, there's no other word for this one," Jack replied. "He thinks the ghost of Judy Garland gave him AIDS."

"How'd she give it to him?" I said. "In a box?"

Jack stripped a chicken wing of its meat. "She appeared to him," he said. "He was at the St. Mark's Baths, giving some guy a blow job, and he looked up and it was Judy Garland's face looking down at him."

"He was blowing Judy Garland?" said Andy, licking blue cheese dressing from his fingers.

"I told you," Jack said. "Nut job. Anyway, he says she just smiled at him and he felt something inside of him change."

"Why would Judy Garland give him AIDS?" Andy said.

"Revenge?" I suggested. "Maybe she hates all gay men because we made her sing 'Over the Rainbow' so many times."

"Judy Garland is the cause of AIDS," said Jack. "What a great theory. We should send that to the *Times*."

"Was it old Judy or Judy from *The Wizard of Oz*?" asked Andy.

"Good question," Jack said. "I'll ask him when I see him next week."

"So," I said, "was it worth moving to New York?"

Jack nodded. "I like working for the hospice," he said. "It feels like I'm really helping instead of just watching or reading about what's going on."

Much to my delight, Jack had decided to come to New York in March, when he was offered a job as a counselor at Hope House, a hospice for people with AIDS. The move allowed him to escape what he said felt like a ghost town back in San Francisco, as well as put him nearer to his parents, whom he missed. Now that he was in the city, our strange little family was back together, which made me happy. Despite my feelings about Andy's recent behavior, I still cared about him, and it was nice to have Jack around as a buffer on the occasions when we butted heads.

Our dinners came, and as we ate we fell into more relaxed conversation. "Did you hear about Rock Hudson?" I asked in between bites of my bacon, wine sauce, and blue-cheese burger.

"The AIDS thing?" said Jack. "Someone at work mentioned it. Do you think it's true?"

"I don't know if he has AIDS," Andy said. "But he's definitely a fag."

"How do you know that?" I asked him.

Andy grinned, dipping his French fries in ketchup and popping them into his mouth.

"You did not," I said.

"Did, too," he said. "Twice. At the house in Palm Springs."

I looked across the table at Jack, who in turn looked at Andy. "Well," he said, "how was he?"

Andy shrugged. "Not bad," he answered. "Nice ass. Liked to talk dirty."

"He didn't ask you to pretend you were Tab Hunter, did he?" I asked hopefully.

We tried to get Andy to give us more dirt on what Rock was like in bed, but he claimed not to remember much. Giving up on that, we began teasing Jack about not having found a boyfriend yet. That conversation continued as we finished up and walked out into the beautiful summer evening.

"Where to now?" I said. "Ty's? Boots & Saddles?" I listed two of the street's more popular bars.

"Bras & Girdles?" Andy said. "No thanks."

"Ty's it is, then," I said, steering them toward the small, dark bar favored by locals.

We spent the next two hours drinking and trying to find a guy for Jack, to no avail. By the time we left, we were laughing the way we used to, and all our disagreements—both old and new—were forgotten. Jack decided to walk up 7th Avenue to his apartment in Chelsea, and I said good night to Andy at the subway. Then I went home. Alan wasn't back yet, so I turned on the television in the bedroom and watched *Remington Steele*, fantasizing about Pierce Brosnan's hairy chest, then *Charlie Chan at the Olympics*. I fell asleep halfway through, waking with a start when I heard the front door open.

"Hey," Alan said as he came into the bedroom and sat on the edge of the bed. "How was dinner?"

"Fun," I said as sleep claimed me again. "Remind me to tell you a funny Rock Hudson story tomorrow."

Rock's story turned out to be not so funny. I won my bet with Alan when Hudson's camp vocally denied that he had AIDS, saying that he was in Paris for treatment of liver cancer. But the jig was up not long after, and finally almost all of America knew someone with AIDS. And as Hudson's Hollywood friends, including Elizabeth Taylor, began speaking publicly about the need to find a cure for the disease, it seemed his illness might provide the push needed to end the epidemic.

Alan won his twenty dollars back the following week when I received a call from Stuyvesant High School asking me if I'd like to teach ninth-grade history. With my immediate future set, I spent the last few weeks of summer preparing for class and looking forward to my first day as a teacher.

CHAPTER 51

1986 was a year of anger.

It shouldn't have been. In the beginning, things seemed to be just about perfect. My second semester at Stuyvesant was proceeding nicely as I tried to get four classes a day of teenagers to care about the Civil War. Alan's show, despite receiving a withering review from *Times* critic Frank Rich, was doing well, and looked to be another contender come Tony time. Jack had even managed to find himself a boyfriend, a crackling firebrand of a lawyer named Todd who handled discrimination cases against people with AIDS. They'd met at a holiday party hosted by Hope House, and had been going out ever since.

The first indication that the initial happy forecast for the year might have been premature was the death of Luke in the second week of January. Although the AZT had at first seemed to be reversing the progress of the AIDS virus, the effects had been temporary, and finally his immune system had been unable to fight the infections that ravaged his body. Death was attributed to pneumonia, and his insurance company sent Andy a check not long after the sparsely-attended funeral. His paycheck for the seventeen months he spent as Luke's lover was $750,000.

On Valentine's Day, Alan and I celebrated with Jack and Todd at Café Loup, our favorite Village restaurant. Jack, nervous about his first romantic holiday with his new boyfriend, had begged us to double date. Having had few opportunities to get to know Todd, we were only too happy to oblige, if only because it gave us an opportunity to subject him to the Best Friends' Inquisition. He, however, was the one to begin the questioning.

"How long have you two been together?" he asked Alan and me not long after we'd been seated.

I looked at Alan. "Five years?" I said, trying to count backward.

"We've been together a little over five, but this is our sixth Valentine's Day," he said. "Remember, we met in December of eighty."

"Five years," Todd said. "That's a lifetime in gay years, especially now."

"I guess it is a pretty long time," I agreed.

"Sometimes it seems a lot longer," said Alan.

"What's that supposed to mean?" I said, feigning indignance.

"See, I told you," Jack said to Todd. "They even act like old married people."

"I think it's great," Todd replied. "I don't know a lot of couples who have been together for a long time."

"Hopefully you'll find out what it's like," said Alan, winking at Jack, who blushed.

"Jack tells us you work with some of the Hope House clients," I said.

"I work with a lot of the AIDS agencies," Todd said. "GMHC, the People with AIDS Coalition, places like that. AIDS legislation is all brand new, so this is a total gray area as far as the law is concerned. We've got people losing their jobs, their apartments, everything. I'm representing a waiter who was fired because some customers complained they could get AIDS from eating off of plates he carried. It's terrible what's happening."

"It doesn't help any when Reagan tells people that AIDS only affects fags and drug users," Jack added. "Middle America thinks this is a good thing because it will wipe out the undesirables."

Todd drank some of his wine. "I'm sorry," he said. "We're supposed to be having fun. I promised myself I'd start leaving work at the office."

"It's all right," I told him. "This is important stuff. It's changing everything."

"Did you know this place used to be a gay bar?" Todd asked. "In the seventies. It was called the Turnover."

"It's funny how quickly things change or disappear," I said. "I bet the Village won't look anything like this in twenty years. It will probably be all straights with kids."

"If AIDS keeps spreading like it is, it won't matter," Todd remarked. "There won't be any gay people around to notice."

"We have to think positively," Alan reprimanded him. "They'll find a cure. It just takes time."

"Speaking of that," said Jack. "Did you hear they're doing an AIDS Walk in New York this year?"

"I went to the first one in LA last year," Todd said. "It was amazing. They raised something like $650,000."

"I saw a brochure about it at GMHC the other day," I said. "It looks fun. I'm in."

"Me, too," added Andy. "I'll hit the cast up for donations."

Three months later, on a sunny May Sunday afternoon that also saw New York hosting the Martin Luther King, Jr. Memorial Parade, two conventions, a bicycle tour, two circuses, a game between the Yankees and the Seattle Mariners, and the final performance of *Singin' in the Rain* at the Gershwin Theatre, we fulfilled our promises. Gathering with 4,500 others at Lincoln Center, we listened as Mayor Ed Koch welcomed us before we started our walk. Then, en masse, we took to the streets.

I hadn't marched for anything since the ill-fated White Night rally eight years before. For the first mile of the walk, I kept waiting for police to come at us with their batons, or for someone to throw a homemade bomb. But when nothing happened, I relaxed and began to enjoy myself.

"This is almost better than Pride," Alan remarked. "Except we don't get to hear Alicia Bridges sing 'I Love the Nightlife.'"

"But we do have Peter Allen," Todd reminded him. He and Jack were holding hands as they walked.

"I'd rather have Liza," I said.

"I've had Peter Allen," said Andy, who was walking with us reluctantly after being tricked into it by an invitation to brunch.

"You've had everybody," Jack teased.

"Twice," I added.

Andy, his eyes hidden behind sunglasses, scanned the crowd. I couldn't help but wonder if he was looking for his next boyfriend. Where better to find someone with AIDS than at a fund-raiser for its eradication? But he'd donated one-thousand dollars to each of us, so I couldn't be too angry at him.

We were halfway through the walk when Alan shook his head.

"What's wrong?" I asked him.

"My vision just got blurry for a second," he said. "It's this sun. It's so bright."

"Are you all right now?"

He nodded. "Yeah, it's gone. I've got a little bit of a headache, though."

I handed him the bottle of water I was carrying. "Drink this," I told him.

"You probably need to get out of the sun," Todd suggested. "Why don't you guys go sit down for a while and meet us back at Damrosch Park?"

That seemed like a good idea, so Alan and I made our way against the stream of walkers until we found an empty bench. We sat down and Alan drank some water.

"Feeling better?" I asked him.

"Feeling stupid," he said. "I didn't need to stop walking."

"It's better than getting heatstroke," I told him.

He rubbed his eyes. "I've been having trouble with my vision for a while," he said. "I need to go get some new glasses."

"Getting old sucks, doesn't it?" I teased. His thirtieth birthday was coming up in October, and for months I'd been reminding him of it.

"You're the one who's almost forty," he said.

"In four years!" I said.

"I'm rounding up," he said, laughing.

We sat for another ten minutes, then walked back to Lincoln Center, where we waited for Alan, Todd, and Andy to return. I thought we would never see them in the sea of people gathered to celebrate the walk's success (it raised over $700,000), but Alan spotted Todd's New York Rangers hat and we flagged them down.

"Are you going to live?" Jack asked Alan when we'd regrouped.

"For now," said Alan. "How was the rest of the walk?"

"Hot," Andy said, pulling his sweaty T-shirt away from his chest. "But a lot of the boys took their shirts off, so it was worth it."

"That's why we're here," I said as Jack shook his head.

"Is he always like this?" Todd asked me.

"Yes," Jack and I answered in unison while Andy gave us the finger.

Two weeks later, during a matinee performance of Song & Dance, Alan collapsed and couldn't get back up. Called by the stage manager, I rushed to St. Vincent's Hospital, where I found Alan sitting up in bed.

When I entered, he turned his head toward me, but looked over my shoulder, not at my face.

"What happened?" I asked him.

Again he looked in the direction of my voice, but not quite at me. "I can't see," he said.

"What?"

"I'm blind," he said, choking on the last word as he started to cry.

I held him, not understanding. I assumed that if his eyes could produce tears, then they must be working. I was sure I'd misunderstood.

"I was standing on stage," Alan said between hiccupy breaths. "Then the audience started to get fuzzy. Then everything went black."

"Have you seen a doctor?" I asked him.

"They ran some tests," he answered. "They haven't told me anything."

"You'll be okay," I said, patting his back. "You'll be okay."

"Mr. Corduner," a voice behind me said. I turned to see a doctor standing in the doorway. She was looking at some papers in her hand.

"Dr. Veasey," Alan said. "Did you find anything?"

The doctor walked over to the bed. A small, thin woman, she had a kind face and long, red hair that she wore in a thick braid down her back. She looked at me. "You're his partner?" she asked.

"Yes," I said. "Ned Brummel. What happened to him?"

"Right now my best guess is CMV," she said. "Cytomegalovirus," she elaborated when neither Alan nor I reacted. "It's a common virus. Most of us have it in our systems at one point or another and our immune systems fight it off with no problems. But in people with compromised immune systems it can cause serious damage, including retinitis."

"He's been having blurry vision for a few weeks," I said.

"That's how it starts," Dr. Veasey said. "As the retina deteriorates, the vision worsens, eventually causing blindness. We see it a lot in people infected with HIV."

"But Alan isn't infected," I said. "He's fine."

Dr. Veasey looked at her charts again. "I'm sorry," she said slowly. "I assumed you already knew."

"Knew what?" asked Alan.

Dr. Veasey looked at me, her eyes suddenly very sad. "According to the blood tests they ran, you're positive for HIV," she said.

I heard Alan gasp. When I turned, he was shaking. Tears had begun to run down his cheeks again, and his mouth was open in a silent cry. I took his hand and he gripped my fingers so tightly I almost yelped. I looked at the doctor. "You're sure?" I asked.

"I'll run the tests again," she said. "But we usually don't get a different response on multiple tests."

Alan had turned his head away from us and was sobbing. I took him in my arms, but he was a rag doll, flopping against me as if the ability to hold himself up had evaporated with the news of his infection. All I could do was hold him as he repeated one word—*why*—over and over again.

I want to say that my thoughts were entirely with Alan at that moment, but they weren't. As he cried and asked *why*, I couldn't help but wonder *how*. How had he become infected? We'd been together for more than five years. The chances of his being positive before we met were almost impossible, which meant that he had acquired the virus during our relationship. That meant one of two things: Either I was infected as well, or he had been involved with someone else. Neither option would make the situation better, but at that moment I would have preferred that it be the first one.

"Mr. Brummel, have you been tested?" Dr. Veasey's voice interrupted the storm of my thoughts.

"No," I answered, helping Alan settle back into the pillows. "I never have."

"You might want to," she suggested. "We can do that for you if you like."

I nodded. "It's probably a good idea," I said.

"I'm going to leave you two alone for a few minutes," she said. "But I'll be back. I'm sure you'll have questions for me."

She walked from the room. I hesitated a moment, then got up. "I'll be right back," I told Alan.

Dr. Veasey was halfway down the hall. Hearing my footsteps, she stopped and waited. "What can you do for Alan?" I asked her when I reached her.

"We can probably start him on AZT," she said. "There are some others that have been helpful in fighting CMV."

I then asked her the question I'd been dreading. "Will he get his sight back?"

She waited a moment before answering. "The effects are irreversible," she said.

"So he's blind," I said, more to myself than to her. "Is he going to die?"

"Advanced CMV damage is usually an indication of late-stage AIDS," she said. "Based on his white blood cell count, I think Alan is very sick."

"But he looks fine," I said. "Could you be wrong?"

"I wish I was," she answered. "But I don't think so. Not everyone with AIDS gets KS. He could look like he always has and still have the virus. That's why it's important for you to find out if you're infected as well."

"I'll take care of that tomorrow," I said.

"I have to go see another patient," she said, touching my arm. "I'll see you shortly, though."

"Thank you," I said as she walked away. I returned to Alan's room. He had stopped crying and was simply staring at the wall, his eyes open and unseeing.

"I'm never going to see again, am I?" he asked.

I sat on the bed, stretching out alongside him and leaning my head against his. I took his hand and held it in mine. I didn't answer his question.

"If you're sick, I won't be able to live with myself," he said.

"If I am, it's not your fault," I said. "For all we know, I infected you."

Alan said nothing. We sat in silence for several minutes before he spoke again.

"I have to tell you something," he said.

CHAPTER 52

When Alan died, I was reading him page 367 of Stephen King's *It*. We'd been working our way through it for nearly a week, and had reached the part where two of the boys, Bill and Richie, were escaping from a werewolf (actually *the* Werewolf of horror movie fame) by riding as fast as they could on Bill's bike, named Silver after the Lone Ranger's horse. After a close call, they had finally outrun him, and were now collapsed on the ground in relief.

" 'D-Don't, R-Richie' Bill said, 'duh-duh-duh-h-h-'" I read, trying to duplicate the boy's stutter. "'Then he burst into tears himself and they only hugged each other on their knees in the street beside Bill's spilled bike, and their tears made clean streaks down their cheeks, which were sooted with coal dust.'"

I looked over at Alan, lying in his hospital bed, and was about to ask him if he wanted me to go on to the next chapter. Then I saw that his chest had ceased rising and falling. Dropping the book, I went to him and placed my hand on his chest. Feeling nothing, I lifted his wrist, which felt heavy and lifeless in my hand, and searched for a pulse. When I found none, I gently placed his hand on his stomach, kissed him once on the mouth, and rang for the nurse.

They let me sit with him for an hour alone before taking his body away. I sat in the chair I'd sat in every night during his stay at the hospital and watched him. At first, I tried to pretend that he was asleep, but already the coldness of death was filling the room, as if his soul, when it left his body and flew skyward, had drawn all the warmth with it in its wake. I was left with the shell, empty and decaying even as I gazed upon it. But I couldn't bring myself to leave him.

There will be a last time for everything. For eating your favorite cookie, for hearing your favorite song, for making love to your lover. There will come a moment when you will have done those things for the final time in your life. But even when you know that time is coming, even if you can identify the event before it happens, how can you ever be prepared for that last taste of chocolate, that last swallow of bourbon, that last rush of pleasure before it's gone forever? You can linger, and savor, but eventually you will have used up every last particle and there will be no more.

I had three weeks with Alan after that first visit to the hospital. During the first, I had to go to school each day and try to forget about him while I administered final exams and graded last-minute papers. For the final two, I'd spent every day with him, reluctantly going home only when the nurses threw me out for my own good, telling me to get some food, a shower, some sleep. Even then I slept badly, afraid that Alan would leave while I was dreaming. In the morning, I was at the hospital before the sun rose.

From the moment of his diagnosis, I'd tried to see every moment we had together as the last one. I'd memorized Alan's face, his words, my feelings about him and us and his sickness. I exhausted myself with documenting what I saw as our tragedy. Then one day, as I imagined repeating his last words at some distant juncture in my life, I realized that I was attempting to construct a scrapbook of our last moments together, something I could leaf through later when I was grieving. But the effort was too great, and eventually I'd given up and just accepted every hour he remained alive as a blessing.

I had, however, made love to him one final time. That I allowed myself and him. One rainy Thursday afternoon, after trying to recall our last time together and coming up with a hazy memory of a hurried morning fuck before I ran off to school and he to a dentist appointment, I'd shut the door to his room, pulled the curtain around his bed, and removed first my clothes and then his. Alan had laughed like a nervous teenager afraid of being caught, warning me that the nurses would be shocked if they came in to take his temperature or administer medication. I'd ignored him, slipping into the bed beside him and sliding my hand into his pajamas while I kissed his neck.

I'd stroked him slowly, trying to prolong the moment. Holding his cock in my hand, I'd brought him to the edge and stopped, waiting for his breathing to slow before repeating the process over and over, each time taking him a little farther. Finally I'd let him come, catching him in my hand and using his warm jism to jerk myself off. Afterward, he'd cried, telling me repeatedly how much he loved me.

I knew that he loved me. I knew that he'd loved me even when he'd allowed someone else to fuck him while watching a porn movie at the Adonis Theatre, where he'd stopped on an impulse one night in November while walking to the subway following a show. Just one time. One other man. One encounter that had been fueled purely by lust and meant nothing. But it had taken everything from us.

I wasn't able to be angry at him while he was alive. All of my energy went into caring for him. Now that he was dead, though, I felt the anger rising inside of me. I heard it humming in my head like approaching bees, growing louder and louder until I wanted to rip the sheet from Alan's body and hit him with my clenched fists. I knew then that it was time to leave him forever.

I called his mother first. A lovely woman, she had accepted her son's gayness long ago, as had her husband. They'd even been willing to come to New York to see Alan, but he had asked them to wait until he felt better, knowing full well that he never would. He'd thought it a kindness on his part, sparing them from having to see him as he was, but I wasn't sure. As I relayed the news of his death, I was certain that it had been a well-intentioned but cruel deception. His mother, reduced to incoherent sobs, had to hand the phone over to Alan's father. More stoic than his wife, but with a trembling voice, Mr. Corduner had given me the address to which Alan's body should be sent and thanked me for calling.

I next dialed Jack, who picked up right away.

"I thought you were Todd," he said when he recognized my voice. "I'm supposed to meet him for a movie tonight."

"What are you seeing?" I asked out of habit.

"We're arguing about that," said Jack. "I want to see *Hannah and Her Sisters* and he wants to see *Poltergeist II*. Do you want to come? You can be the deciding vote."

"I can't," I said. "Alan died."

"Oh, shit," said Jack. "Fuck, Ned. I'm sorry. And here I am talking about going to the movies."

"It's okay," I told him. "Actually, it's nice to hear someone talk about having a normal life. It makes me think things might be okay."

"Do you want me to meet you somewhere?" Jack asked.

I started to say no, then changed my mind. "How about Uncle Charlie's?" I suggested. "I could use a drink."

"I'll be there in half an hour," he said.

It took me half that time to walk from St. Vincent's to the bar, and I was well into my first vodka tonic when Jack arrived. He came over to me and gave me a big hug, which I accepted reluctantly. I appreciated his kindness, but I didn't want pity. I just wanted someone to talk to.

"How are you doing?" Jack asked after ordering his drink.

"Why do people always ask that?" I said.

"Probably because anything else sounds strange," Jack answered. "It's not like you can say, 'Did you see the hot ass on that guy with the blue shirt over there?' or 'So, what kind of flowers are you going to have at the memorial service?'"

"I guess," I said. "And, yes, I did see the hot ass on that guy. But he has a butter face."

Jack laughed at our old joke, used to describe a man with a nice body but who was otherwise unattractive. "You know what I mean," he said.

"But it's a stupid question," I said. "No offense. It's just that how do people think you are? My lover just died. Am I okay? No. Am I managing not to drink myself into a stupor? Yes. But I'm not okay. How can you be okay?"

"I remember when Brian died," Jack said. "Everyone kept telling me it would be all right, and I kept wondering how it could ever be all right when men were dying everywhere and nobody was doing anything to stop it. Now that seems so long ago."

"It's only been five years," I said.

"That's what I mean," said Jack. "You think it's going to hurt forever, then one day you wake up and realize it's not quite as bad as it was the week before. You know, sometimes I look at Todd and I think about what he was doing when I was living in San Francisco. I had no idea then that I would meet him, and he didn't know anything about me. But we did meet, and now we're together."

"You're making me sick," I said. "Seriously, if you say another word I'm going to throw up on your shoes."

"It's not like I'm telling you to start looking for someone new," he said cautiously, as if I might be serious. "I'm just saying that good things happen when you let them. Look at you, for example. What were the odds that you wouldn't be positive? But you aren't."

"Not yet," I said grimly. "They don't know how long it takes for the virus to show up."

"Still," said Jack. "You're probably not."

"That's supposed to make me feel better?" I said. "Alan has sex *once* with someone else and he gets sick, but I have sex with him a hundred times since then and I don't? That just shows you how fucked up this disease is."

"Are you sure it was just once?" Jack said.

"He just *died*, Jack," I said a little too loudly. "And you want to know if I think he cheated on me more than once?"

"I just meant that maybe it wasn't as random as you think it was," he said. "It just came out wrong."

"Please," I said. "Try again. Tell me how you could possibly say it right? I'd love to hear that one."

I stood looking at him, waiting for him to say something else. He hung his head. "Ned, I'm sorry," he said. "I'm just trying to help."

"Like you *helped* Brian while I was gone?" I said.

His head snapped up. "That's not fair," he said.

"Life isn't fair," I shot back.

"We both lost him," said Jack.

"But you stole him," I said. "That's the difference."

Jack put his unfinished drink on the bar. "Maybe I should go," he said. "I think you need to be alone."

I reached out and grabbed his arm. "Stay," I said. "I'm just talking."

He didn't move. "You're right, though," he said. "I did."

"It wasn't like he wasn't willing," I told him. "Besides, it probably would have ended anyway. He wanted to see other people, and I wasn't into that."

"I think that's what probably killed him," Jack said.

"I doubt it," I said. "There were a lot of guys before us. It could have been anyone."

"Then why aren't you or I sick?" he asked.

"Hey, I'm bulletproof, remember?" I said. "I've dodged it twice, apparently. For all I know, I'm immune to the goddamned thing. I don't know about you."

"Maybe I haven't," he said. "Maybe it's inside, waiting, like one of those things from *Alien*."

"You need another drink," I said, signaling for the bartender.

We had several more drinks, until we were so stoned we had to get a cab to drive the four blocks to my apartment, where Jack was dropping me off before heading uptown. Before I got out, he leaned over and kissed me on the mouth.

"I love you," he said drunkenly. "I don't think I've ever told you that before."

"You tried once," I said, remembering the time I'd called when Brian was sick. "But I wouldn't let you."

"Well, I do," he said. "You're my best friend."

For a brief moment, looking at his sleepy-eyed smile, I almost asked him to come in and spend the night with me. Then I noticed the driver's impatient stare in the rearview mirror, and I gave Jack's leg a pat. "Thanks for staying with me," I said.

"I'll call you tomorrow," Jack said as I got out.

I managed to find my key in my pocket and let myself into my building. Navigating the three flights of stairs was another matter. It took me a while, and even then I had to think hard about which door led to my apartment. Fortunately, I picked the right one and eventually got the lock to open.

Sometimes your body knows what it needs better than you do, and that night my body wisely demanded the numbing effects of alcohol. I think had I walked into the apartment sober, Alan's absence would have struck me like a hurricane. As it was, I had only to stumble to the bedroom, remove my shoes, and collapse on the bed. Before I had time to register that I was alone for the first time in more than five years, I was asleep.

I dreamt that I was riding a bicycle, the kind every 10-year-old boy has, with a bell on the handlebar, and playing cards tucked into the spokes. Alan was seated behind me, his hands wrapped around my waist. I was pedaling furiously, and at first I thought we were trying to gather enough speed to fly. Then I realized that something was chasing us, something big and bad that wanted to tear us to pieces.

"Faster, Ned!" Alan screamed in my ear. "It's almost on us!"

"I c-can't go any f-f-f-aster!" I shouted back, the words choking me as I tried to get them out.

"You have to," Alan said, his voice filled with terror. "I can feel it coming."

I tried to pump my legs harder, but they wouldn't move. It was like we were riding through tar. No matter how much I pushed, the bike went slower and slower.

"It's got me!" Alan screamed.

I felt Alan's grip begin to slip as something dragged him backward. I heard a ripping sound, and Alan clawed frantically at my shirt.

"L-l-let him g-g-go!" I shouted at the invisible monster.

"Ned!" Alan yelled. "Ned! Help me!"

Whatever was behind us gave a terrific pull, and Alan was yanked from the seat. Without his weight, the bicycle lurched forward, and I found myself speeding away. I turned, trying to see over my shoulder. All I saw was darkness, and in it, something huge and shapeless. Alan's voice emerged from the center of the darkness, high and strained as he called my name, and then it was cut off.

"Alan!" I shouted.

I woke up confused, not knowing where I was or what was happening. It took me several minutes to remember that I was in my bed and that Alan was not with me. There was no bike, no Silver to take us away from danger. But there was a monster. Oh, there was a monster. It was very real, and very hungry. And I had been unable to save Alan from its ravenous maw.

CHAPTER 53

Ronald Reagan was laughing at us. His enormous head was rocking back and forth, his mouth open in a mocking grin and his shiny, perfectly-combed hair making him look like a Satanic version of the Bob's Big Boy mascot. As we booed him, he pointed his finger at us, shaking it from side to side, as if we were naughty children in need of a reprimand.

Behind him a phalanx of guards wearing gas masks marched, carrying machine guns in their yellow-latex-glove-covered hands. They surrounded a group of prisoners, men and women who had been cowed into a pen formed from barbed wire. Some of the captured wore black-and-white striped uniforms with pink triangles sewn to the fronts. Others looked as if they'd just been picked from the crowd and forced to join the others.

"Silence equals death!" the prisoners shouted. "Silence equals death!"

As the float passed by us, I couldn't stop staring at it. The sight of the people trapped behind the wire, their frightened, angry faces looking out at us as they called for help, made me want to jump on the truck and tear down the fence that held them in. I felt myself shaking as I beheld the grim tableau. When a man wearing a white T-shirt emblazoned with SILENCE = DEATH appeared before me, offering me a button with the same logo on it, for a moment I thought that he had come to drag me into that horrible prison.

"Act up!" he chanted as he pressed the button into my hand. "Fight AIDS!"

It was June of 1987. Gay Pride weekend. Alan had been dead a year, and I was still mourning. I'd planned on skipping Pride altogether, but

Jack, Todd, and Andy had insisted that I come. I knew they were tired of the brooding person I'd become. I was tired of myself. But nothing had been able to rid me of the rage and sadness that had planted itself deep within me following Alan's death. It had bloomed and thrived, nourished by a steady stream of alcohol and drugs, which I'd returned to following an absence of several years. Fed by the cocaine and, more recently, Ecstasy that I used to help me get through, my garden of pain had turned into a jungle, its vines and creepers twining themselves around my heart, slowly strangling it.

I looked at the button in my hand. ACT UP. The AIDS Coalition to Unleash Power. I'd never heard of it. Then again, I had run as far away from AIDS as I possibly could. I'd stopped volunteering as a buddy. I no longer read the newspaper articles. I pretended that AIDS was over, that it had all been a hellish nightmare from which I'd now awakened. When Todd and Jack talked about their work, I tuned them out, nodding politely and never asking questions.

Oddly, Andy had been my greatest comfort. Ironically, given how he was making his living, for him it was as if AIDS had never existed. He never spoke of it, despite the fact that it had made him a very wealthy man. He was now on his fourth paid lover, a New York politician whose deep personal homophobia kept him from ever acknowledging his desires for men. He had, in fact, been the driving force behind some of the most virulent anti-gay legislation ever passed in the city, including the decision that shut down the gay bathhouses in 1995 under the guise of protecting the health of the public.

Now he was dying, and in an attempt to have the life he'd long resented others having, he was paying Andy handsomely to reprise his role as Brad Majors, whose movies he was obsessed with. Because KS had ravaged his face, he refused to leave his apartment, and so Andy's time with him consisted primarily of sitting in the man's living room while the two of them watched tapes of the films Andy had starred in and the politician tried to bring himself to orgasm. It was, as Andy said, a part with a limited run, as the man refused treatment for the disease he denied he had and was not expected to live much longer.

Because he didn't like to talk about AIDS, Andy made a perfect companion for me. We spent a lot of time together, using the money Andy made to attend whatever events we wanted to. We also spent it on drugs, which we consumed with even greater relish than we did the food we ordered at the city's best restaurants. When Andy discovered Ecstasy, we'd begun to spend our nights at the clubs, dancing into the early morning hours while the tablets we placed under our tongues dissolved their sweet poison into our blood.

I'd stopped having sex, except with myself, and even that was done more out of routine than desire. Jacking off was about as exciting to me as brushing my teeth or spraying antiperspirant beneath my arms. When I did do it, I didn't fantasize about having sex with another man. I didn't really think about anything. I just kept applying friction, relying on my body's mechanics to do their job and eventually set the process of ejaculation in motion.

Surprisingly, my work had not suffered. Teaching was an escape, eight or nine hours a day when I didn't have to be with myself. The facts and stories I shared with my students crowded out anything I didn't care to think about. I distracted myself with elaborate lesson plans and dreaming up novel ways to get the kids interested in history. And it worked. I had quickly become one of the most popular teachers at Stuyvesant. My reviews were exceptional, and having just completed my second full year in the classroom, I'd been assured that tenure was forthcoming.

"There's Taffy!" Jack exclaimed, jarring me from my focus on the ACT UP button. I stuffed it into my pocket and looked at the float headed our way. It was sponsored by Wigstock, the annual drag extravaganza that had begun two years before as an impromptu performance in the East Village's Tompkins Square Park, and was now a Labor Day tradition for the city's fairest and freakiest faux femmes.

The float looked like some kind of crazed birthday cake, with three tiers draped in yellow silk and flowers everywhere. Drag queens decorated it like candles, dancing and lip syncing to Ohio Express's "Yummy, Yummy, Yummy." Taffy was on the second tier, wearing high heels, a hot-pink beaded dress, and a wig so high it swayed as she shook her hips. Her impossibly long eyelashes fluttered madly as she pouted and threw handfuls of SweeTarts to the spectators.

"Taffy!" I called out, getting her attention. She beamed and waved, then held her hand up with the thumb pointed toward her ear and the pinky touching her lips, the universal sign for "Call me."

I nodded, knowing full well I probably wouldn't. I loved Taffy, and she'd been a great help to me after Alan died, but seeing her made me think too much about him. The two of them had performed at the first Wigstock, dueting on "These Boots are Made for Walking," and they'd been planning a big production number for the 1986 show. It was to be Taffy's first public appearance following her long-awaited sex change surgery, and they were going to perform "I Enjoy Being a Girl" from *Flower Drum Song*. Alan's death had also been the death of Bitta Honey, but Taffy had gone on with the show alone, dedicating her performance to Alan's memory and holding a minute of silence in his honor. I'd left halfway through the song, overcome with sadness, and had spoken with Taffy only a few times since.

Suddenly it felt like the entire parade was a parade of memories. I turned to Andy, Jack, and Todd. "I think I'm going to go," I said.

"Stay," Todd protested. "The parade's only half over. We've still got the guys from Splash coming."

"And then there's the pier dance," Jack said. "We got you a ticket."

"Thanks," I told them. "Not this year."

"You're sure?" Jack asked.

I nodded. "I'm just a little gayed out," I said.

"Okay," he said. "I'll call you later, though."

I left them and started to walk home. As I did, I stuck my hands into my pockets and felt something prick my palm. I'd forgotten all about the button I'd stashed there. I took it out and was about to toss it into a nearby garbage can. Then I stopped and looked at it. SILENCE = DEATH. The words struck me with their simplicity and truthfulness. I looked at the tiny hole the pin on the back of the button had made on my hand. A little drop of blood was welling up from the center of my palm, like a miniature stigmata.

I returned the button to my pocket and continued home, thinking about the ACT UP float and how I'd felt seeing it. I thought about the clownlike Ronald Reagan jeering at me, and about how he represented the feelings of so many Americans. It angered me, the indifference and blame. It angered me that so many people were dying for nothing, while instead of looking for answers, politicians and pundits were looking for someone to blame.

As I walked past the various booths that lined the streets offering everything from overpriced bottles of water to Pride stickers, I saw a young woman with an ACT UP T-shirt handing out flyers. I took one from her and read it as I walked. It was a call for volunteers. "Don't wait for someone else to do something!" it said in bold letters. "ACT UP! FIGHT AIDS!"

The following Tuesday, I arrived at the Lesbian and Gay Community

Center on 13th Street to find the main meeting hall packed with people there for the ACT UP meeting. Taking a seat in the back, I looked around at the other faces. Most of them were young, white, and male. They were the faces I saw in the clubs and on the streets, handsome and untouchable. They seemed to me too young even to know who they were, let alone to be interested in political action, but they seemed determined to do something.

The meeting began when a young man with a body built by hours in the gym stood up to speak. "I'm guessing that for a lot of you, this is your first ACT UP meeting," he said. "Can I have a show of hands from the first-timers?"

A full third of the room raised their hands, myself included.

"Great," the young man said. "We want to thank you for coming out tonight. My name is Max, and as our name says, we're the AIDS Coalition to Unleash Power. We're fighting in the streets to get people to give a fuck about this disease."

His remark was met with applause and clapping. He continued. "We're fighting because nobody is fighting for us. The government doesn't give a shit. The churches don't give a shit. Well, we're going to make them give a shit!"

The passion behind Max's words reminded me of Harvey Milk. I hadn't heard such intense dedication to a cause in many years, and I found myself believing what the young man said, that we could change things by taking action. When he asked us to break into smaller groups for more discussion, I gravitated toward the group of which he was the facilitator.

"What we're looking for," Max said once we were gathered around, "is people who are willing to hit the streets to protest. This isn't an organization that writes letters. We put ourselves right in the middle of things. You might have heard about our Wall Street protest in March, where we demanded that the pharmaceutical companies stop making such huge profits from AIDS drugs. That was our very first action. Seventeen of us were arrested at that. We've also protested at the White House and the International Conference on AIDS, and we got Northwest Orient to reverse their policy on banning people with AIDS from their flights. Two weeks ago, we held a four-day, nonstop protest at Sloan-Kettering to demand clinical tests on more AIDS drugs. Those are the kinds of things we need to do more of. But this isn't easy. You could get arrested. You'll *probably* get arrested. So make sure this is something you're willing to get involved with, because we only need people who are really committed."

Max spent an hour with us, answering questions about what ACT UP was planning and how we could help. At the end of the meeting, I signed up to be part of the next action. I half hoped nobody would actually call me, and when the phone rang a few nights later, I was surprised to hear Max's voice.

"Hey, Ned," he said, as if we were old friends. "We're planning a protest for Friday in front of the Health Department. We want to snarl traffic at rush hour and get maximum exposure. Can you come?"

"School gets out at three-fifteen," I said. "I could be there by four."

"That's perfect," said Max. "Do you have an ACT UP shirt?"

"Not yet," I told him.

"Pick one up over at A Different Light bookstore on Hudson," he said. "They're selling them for us. Wear that. We're making signs, so you can get one at the protest. I'll see you Friday."

On Friday afternoon, I rode the subway downtown, my ACT UP T-shirt hidden beneath my button-down blue Oxford. When I arrived at the protest site, I removed the outer shirt and stuffed it into my backpack. Max was there, along with five or six other volunteers, stapling posters to wooden handles to make our signs. When he saw me, he shook my hand. "Thanks for coming," he said.

"What do we do?" I asked him.

"Take a sign and get ready to block traffic," he answered. "That's all there is to it."

I chose a sign at random. It was the generic ACT UP logo printed over a large pink triangle. I considered exchanging it for an image of Reagan with devil horns added to his head, but a part of me still felt kindly toward him for his work defeating the Briggs Initiative, so I stuck with the one I had. As more and more people showed up, our group swelled, until there were almost eighty of us.

Right at five, Max shouted for our attention. When we quieted down, he said, "Just walk into the streets. Stop traffic. Don't move, even when they start blasting their horns. I give us about twenty minutes before the police show up. Let's go!"

We followed him into the street. As we swarmed around the cars stopped for a red light, the surprised drivers looked at us with a mixture of bemusement and irritation. We ignored them, scattering ourselves among the vehicles.

"Act up! Fight AIDS!" I shouted as someone began the chanting.

The honking began as soon as the light turned green. We stood our ground, continuing to shout and wave our signs. A few feet away from me, a skinny Puerto Rican man waved a sign proclaiming YOU THINK THIS IS INCONVENIENT? TRY DYING. Behind me, a woman shouted, "More trials, fewer deaths!"

It was bedlam. Cars honked. Drivers shouted obscenities. We shouted back. And as Max had predicted, all too soon the police showed up. At first, they tried to reason with us, asking us politely to come out of the street. When we ignored them, they began taking us one by one and dragging us to the sidewalk. But because there were only a handful of them, the process was ineffective, and as soon as they turned their backs to go after another protester, the one they'd just dragged away would return to the street.

We lasted maybe forty-five minutes. Then, on Max's signal, we emptied the street. The police watched us go, but didn't follow as we made our way back toward the subway. I looked back at the traffic, hopelessly backed up, and felt a rush of excitement.

On the train home I wore my ACT UP shirt for all to see and held my sign face out. The suit-and-tie commuters eyed me warily, as if I might at any moment begin to rail about the end of the world, or ask them for change. A few riders, mostly men, nodded at me approvingly.

When I got home, I was still feeling the adrenaline pumping through my veins. I hadn't felt so alive in a very long time. Every part of me was trembling with forgotten excitement, and to my surprise, I realized I was unbearably horny. Afraid the sensation might fade if I hesitated, I stripped and lay down on the bed. With a sense of urgency, I jacked off, thinking the whole time of Max.

CHAPTER 54

By the end of 1987, ACT UP had become the main focus of my life. I was not unique in this. Many of the group's members spent the majority of their time planning, protesting, or meeting. When we weren't actively doing these things, we were thinking about them, and when we weren't thinking about them, we were feeling guilty about applying our resources elsewhere.

I did nothing about my attraction to Max. He was, I told myself, too young, too beautiful, too focused on our work to be interested in me. Instead, I threw myself into being the implementor of his plans. I made posters. I leafleted. I made calls and wrung donations out of the people who signed up for our mailing list, which seemed to double every time we made appearances at community events. I did whatever I could to ensure that Max's ideas were made flesh. Because I could not have him, I turned him into a reason to keep going.

At first, Jack and Todd found my interest in activism a relief. I was getting out. I was happy. I wasn't moping. They supported my efforts, and listened to my stories over dinner. They themselves were slightly wary of ACT UP's tactics, finding them too confrontational.

"I understand their anger," Todd said one night while we ate at Clare's in Chelsea. "The problem is, all people see is a bunch of angry queers getting in their faces. That's not likely to make them feel more kindly toward us."

"They need to know what's going on," I argued. "Until they know, they're not going to do anything."

"That's true," said Jack. "But don't you think there are less offensive ways of educating them?"

"Offensive?" I said. "What's offensive is that we still don't have a vaccine, we still don't have enough money for AIDS research, and we still don't have enough drugs. That makes me angry, and if someone doesn't like that I'm angry, then tough shit."

I'd gotten very good at being angry. Fueled by the message of ACT UP, I'd started to see the world as Us *vs.* Them. "Us" was anyone whose life had been affected by AIDS and who had decided to do something about it. "Them" was everyone else, including the apathetic gay men who did nothing while their brothers died. Them I despised most, because I believed them to be cowards. Hiding their heads in the sand, they waited for AIDS to go away so that they could get back to fucking and sucking without worry.

In early 1988, we began preaching the message of safe sex. Suddenly, rubbers were hot, or at least we tried to convince people that they were. Latex barriers were eroticized, and we proved it by holding demonstrations in which we rolled condoms onto bananas using only our mouths and donned examination gloves and simulated fisting. We let people know that sex was once more an option, although we knew that most of them had never stopped having it in the first place.

It was Max's idea to promote kissing as an intimate act. Where before many of us had regarded it merely as foreplay, now it became one of the safer forms of physical connection. We decided to hold a kiss-in, where pairs or groups would make out for the edification of the masses, demonstrating both that mouth-to-mouth contact was not a means of transmitting HIV, and that it was one alternative to riskier activities. The first one was planned for the Friday before Valentine's Day, with groups gathering at strategic locations throughout the city.

I was assigned to Grand Central Station, where I went with Max and two dozen others. Spacing ourselves beneath the dome of the great hall, we prepared to shock the commuters who would soon be passing through on the way to their trains. It was dusk, and the lights that covered the ceiling above us glowed faintly, forming the astrological constellations for which the hall is famed.

"Who's your partner?" Max asked me as people paired up.

"I don't have one," I said.

"You're with me, then," he said, counting heads to make sure everyone was accounted for.

I started to protest, but it was too late. As five o'clock neared and the streams of passersby grew noticeably heavier, we began our demonstration. Facing me, Max put his arms around me and pressed his mouth to mine. I stiffened, and he pulled back.

"You can do better than that," he said. "Just pretend I'm some guy you have the hots for."

We tried again, and this time I gave in, kissing Max passionately. He responded, slipping his tongue into my mouth and moving his hands lower on my back so that he could press himself into me. Oblivious to the stares of the people heading home to Westchester, Croton-on-Hudson, and Mahopac, we kissed without stopping for what seemed an eternity. When we finally stopped, Max cleared his throat and said, "Do you want to take this back to my place?"

Few things spark passion as easily as revolution. In Max's bedroom, we explored lovemaking with an energy born out of our shared convictions. When his mouth moved down my chest toward my belly, I reminded him to beware the stickiness already seeping from my aroused cock, and when later on he entered me, it was with the protection of not one, but two, rubbers. Our ejaculate remained a safe distance from any vulnerable tissues, and afterward we cleaned ourselves separately and well.

I expected our exchange to be a onetime event, and was surprised when Max suggested we do it again. I agreed, and soon we were regularly spending time in one another's beds. We became known as a couple within ACT UP, and it pleased me to watch Max lead an action or invigorate a group and know that he was my boyfriend.

Because it was an election year, our attention was on the race for president. Vice President George Bush (we had only the father to worry about then, and so did not feel the need to use either his initials or "Sr." to distinguish him) had proven to be as ineffective and uncompassionate as his mentor when it came to AIDS, and we were dearly hoping for a changing of the guard in November. Encouraged by early polls that showed Democratic challenger Michael Dukakis leading Bush by a margin of ten points, we dared to hope that perhaps the tide was going to change.

Throughout the summer, we continued our campaign for safer sex and improved resources for PWAs. Max and I also added Dukakis to our list of pet projects, organizing several events within the gay community to raise both money and awareness for the beetle-browed governor of Massachusetts. We were constantly on the go, running from meeting to meeting, from march to rally. I had little time for anything or anyone else, and consequently saw little of Jack, Todd, or Andy during the first half of the year.

In August, the tide began to turn. We watched, dumbfounded, as Dukakis slipped in the polls, his margin narrowing point by point until, by July, it had been halved. In August, we sat glued to the television in Max's living room during the four days of the Republican National Convention. On the final night we watched as Bush officially won his party's nomination and took the podium for his now-famous speech.

Standing before a crowd of adoring fans, he spoke in his familiar nasal twang. "This has been called the American Century," he declared, "because in it we were the dominant force for good in the world. We saved Europe, cured polio, we went to the moon, and lit the world with our culture. And now we are on the verge of a new century, and what country's name will it bear? I say it will be another American century."

"I don't think I can stand it," Max said, burying his head in my chest. I put my arm around him and held him while the former head of the CIA continued.

"This is America: the Knights of Columbus, the Grange, Hadassah, the Disabled American Veterans, the Order of Ahepa, the Business and Professional Women of America, the union hall, the Bible study group, LULAC, 'Holy Name'—a brilliant diversity spread like stars, like a thousand points of light in a broad and peaceful sky."

"LULAC?" I said. "The Order of Ahepa?"

"Latin Americans and Greeks," Max said, sitting up. "He's just throwing everything in there."

"Except gays and lesbians," I said.

"It doesn't matter," said Max. "He's saying just what America wants to hear."

He was right. Following the convention, Bush's numbers soared. His "Thousand Points of Light" speech was quoted everywhere. Dukakis and the Democrats attempted to bring the focus of the election back to the state of the union, but they had nothing to counter with.

On election night, Todd and Jack threw a party, although since we expected defeat, the mood was more somber than celebratory. As we watched the numbers come in and saw the states on the graphic map of America turn red one by one, with only a handful of states going blue for Dukakis, we knew we had lost.

"Even California voted for that dickhead," Max raged. "What is wrong with people?"

"They're afraid of change," Todd said.

"They're just afraid," said Jack.

In the end, Bush only won 53% of the popular vote, but it was enough to get him 79% of the electoral votes, making it a landslide victory. And that's exactly how we felt waking up on November 9, as if we'd been buried in a landslide. I remember Max and I turned on the television, hoping against hope that some miracle had occurred between our going to bed and the sun coming up. But Bryant Gumbel informed us that it had not, and we reluctantly got up and prepared for life under George Bush.

The election changed us. Overnight, we went from being filled with enthusiasm to feeling tired and worn out. While I expected the threat of another four years under Republican control to energize our movement, it seemed to have the opposite effect. The ACT UP meetings started to feel repetitive to me, as if we were saying the same things over and over and over (which, of course, we were, since most of the problems we were fighting had yet to be solved). I continued going, however, and in December participated in a mass protest at St. Patrick's Cathedral to voice opposition to the Catholic Church's homophobia and views on safe sex education. The action resulted in widespread media coverage, but resulted in a black eye for ACT UP when the public decried the behavior of a single protester who grabbed a communion wafer and threw it to the floor.

Not only the public was angry at us. Noted AIDS activist Randy Shilts published a scathing diatribe against the St. Patrick's action, calling ACT UP irresponsible, morally wrong, and strategically stupid. While Max fumed over the article and vented his frustrations at everything from the Church to "gay conservatives," I couldn't help but think that maybe Shilts was right. Maybe we had gone too far. And maybe I had gone far enough.

I told Max that I was going to cut back on the amount of time I spent with the group. I had planned on going to visit my mother and Walter for Christmas anyway, and now I looked forward to the trip as a chance to get away from the responsibility of being a professional AIDS warrior. New York had begun to feel like an inescapable island to me, and when Jack (who brought Todd with him) and I boarded an

Amtrak train for the trip to Philadelphia, I had the discomforting feeling that I was on a lifeboat leaving a sinking ship.

I returned a few days before New Year's. The night I arrived back in New York, I had dinner with Max, who picked nervously at his spaghetti carbonara until I demanded to know what was bothering him.

"I can't see you anymore," he said.

"Why?" I asked him. "Because I don't want to spend so much time with ACT UP stuff?"

"No," Max said. "Because you're not positive."

I stared at him from across the table. "You're kidding," I said.

He shook his head. "It's been bothering me for a while now," he said.

I put my fork down. "What difference does it make if you're positive and I'm not?" I asked. "We talked about that when we started sleeping together, and I told you that it's not a problem for me."

"See," he said. "That's it right there. My being HIV-positive is a 'problem' that you have to accept."

"I didn't say it was—" I began.

"Not you," Max interrupted. "I didn't mean you specifically. Anyone. Us positive guys, we're the ones who have something that negative guys have to deal with. When you sleep with us, it's like you're doing us a favor. Do you know how that feels?"

"Have I ever made you feel like I was doing you a favor?" I asked him.

"No," he admitted. "But it's how *I* feel."

"Then isn't it something *you* have to learn to deal with?" I suggested.

"I shouldn't have to deal with it," said Max. "And if I was with a poz guy, I wouldn't have to. I wouldn't worry that if the condom broke, I might be infecting him. I wouldn't have to worry if we got carried away and he swallowed my cum."

"So this is about the sex?" I said.

"Yes and no," Max said. "That's part of it. But it's more about poz guys sticking together."

"What," I said. "Now you're a club? Are you going to start having bars only for positive guys? No negative guys allowed?"

"Some people are talking about that," he told me. "I'm not sure it isn't a good idea."

"This is crazy," I said. "You can't divide the world up that way."

"You don't understand," said Max. "You can't. You don't have to live with this inside of you. You don't know what it's like to think that you might die before they find something to stop it, or that you might make someone else sick."

"I've lost two lovers and a whole bunch of friends to this disease," I said, getting angry. "Don't tell me that I don't understand."

"It's not your fault," he said.

"I know it's not," I said. "I'm not going to apologize for not being sick. I'm not going to apologize for being lucky while a lot of other guys weren't."

"I didn't ask for an apology," Max said.

"What if I was positive?" I asked him. "What if I found out tomorrow that I have the virus? Then could you be with me?"

He nodded. "Then I wouldn't feel so weird about it, yes."

I laughed. "So take off the rubber and fuck me," I said. "Get it over with. Then we can move on."

"I couldn't be responsible for giving it to you," he said.

"But it would be okay if someone else did?" I said. "Then you wouldn't have to feel guilty? That's fucked up, Max."

"I don't want you to be positive," Max replied.

"But you can't be with me if I'm not," I said.

He hesitated before answering. "Right," he said.

I stood up and took some bills out of my wallet. "Here," I said, dropping them on the table. "I'll see you around."

I left him sitting at the table and walked home. It had snowed heavily during the week, and the Village was filled with dirty gray drifts. As I made my way through them, I felt as though I was walking through a ruined landscape, a place that had once been beautiful but was now locked in never-ending winter. It felt cursed, hostile, and forbidding. I was a stranger there, looking for companions who had been lost and would never be found, even when spring came to melt away the snow.

CHAPTER 55

"Happy birthday, dear Jeffrey, happy birthday to you!"
As the subject of our congratulations leaned over to blow out
the candles on the cake set before him, I resisted an urge to reach over
and push his face into the rose-tinted frosting. Instead, I turned to Jack
and said, "I need more champagne if I'm going to keep this up. Want
to come with me?"

He followed me to the table where nine bottles of Veuve Clicquot
1985, three bowls of caviar, and several dozen oysters nestled in beds
of crushed ice were tastefully arranged for our enjoyment and, more
important, appreciation. It was a display of wealth more than it was of
edibles, and the message was clear: Our host could afford to indulge
himself.

I poured champagne into two of the flutes arranged like armies on
either side of the bottles, handing one to Jack and keeping the other
for myself. As I sipped from it, I eyed the caviar warily. The tiny black
roe glistened wetly, and although I knew it was a delicacy, I couldn't
bring myself to take a spoonful. Instead, I selected one of the oysters
and tipped it into my mouth, enjoying the way the brininess con-
trasted with the smooth ripeness of the Veuve Clicquot.

"I'll say this for him," I told Jack. "He knows how to throw a party."

"What do you think this is?" asked Jack, poking one of the bowls of
caviar with the tiny spoon that had been tucked into it.

"Fish eggs," I said.

"I know that," he said. "But why's it white?"

"It's albino Osetra," said a voice behind us. "You almost never find
it. I paid a fortune for it at this shop on Madison."

Jeffrey Benton-Jones, the birthday boy and latest boyfriend to Andy, proudly scooped some of the pale roe onto a cracker and popped it into his mouth. As he chewed, he closed his eyes and held his hand over his heart, as if savoring the pulse-quickening properties of the eggs in his mouth. Jack and I exchanged glances and fought back the laughter that threatened to erupt from our throats.

"Heaven," Jeffrey said, swallowing and opening his eyes. "Absolute heaven. And this one," he added, indicating a bowl of impossibly small, golden roe, "is the rarest. Sterlet. It used to be reserved for the czars of Russia and the shahs of Iran. The fish are practically extinct now. You can only get this through, shall we say, underground channels." He gave us a knowing smile, as if we'd been let in on a secret the sharing of which would result in our deaths.

"We'll have to try it," I said.

Jeffrey looked past me to elsewhere in the room. "Excuse me," he said. "I need to go speak to the quartet. I distinctly asked them not to play any Mendelssohn. He's so dreary."

"How does Andy put up with him?" I asked as Jeffrey walked away.

"How has he put up with any of them?" replied Jack. "He just looks at his bank statement."

"What do you think he's worth now?"

Jack piled a large mound of the sterlet caviar on a cracker and took a bite. He chewed tentatively, once, then brought his napkin to his mouth and spit into it, making a retching noise. Then he balled up the napkin and looked around for somewhere to put it. Finding nowhere suitable, he stuffed it into his pocket.

"I can't believe people eat that," he said, taking a long swallow of champagne.

"You're not a czar or a shah," I reminded him. "You have plebeian taste buds. And you didn't answer my question. How much do you think Andy's made off of this little business of his?"

"Well, he's had how many of them now?" said Jack. "Seven?"

"Six and a half," I said. "There was the one whose ex-wife sued. He had to split it with her."

"Then I'd say he's got a cool five or six million stashed away," said Jack. "Plus the two apartments and the Fire Island house."

"But he keeps doing it," I pointed out. "And you've got to admit, even for Andy, this latest one's a real pill."

"I don't think it's about the money anymore," Jack said. "I think he gets off on it. It's like people who get a new car every year. They do it because they're bored. They need excitement. I think Andy sees this as a game."

"More like the lottery," I said. "And he keeps winning."

"Yeah, well, he's good at it," said Jack. "Look at him."

I searched the room for Andy, and found him standing beside Jeffrey, his arm around his waist as the two of them chatted with an arts critic from the *Times* and his portly lover. In his dark blue Armani suit and Italian leather shoes, Andy looked nothing like the soldier in worn fatigues and muddy combat boots who remained in my memory. He was still beautiful, and watching him, I knew he would always be beautiful. He had one of those faces that only gets better with time, like Paul Newman's or Lauren Bacall's. The gray that had crept into his hair only heightened his beauty, and even the extra weight he'd put on in recent years suited him, making him look fuller and more robust.

"Do you think he's happy?" I asked Jack.

"I think he's happy the way a little kid is when you give him candy," Jack said. "He's happy until it's gone. Then he wants more."

"Tell me again why we're friends with him?" I said.

"Because he has the best caviar," said Jack.

"Seriously," I said. "Why are we friends with him?"

It took Jack a moment to answer. "I guess because he changed our lives," he said.

I couldn't argue with that. Andy had changed our lives completely. Because of him, I'd gone to Vietnam. Because of him, Jack and I had broken up. Because of him, at least in big part, we had become who we were. It was hard to believe that someone so self-centered and so thoughtless had wrought the kind of changes Andy had in our lives, but he had.

"Do you think he even cares about us?" I said.

"In his way, I think he does," said Jack. "I don't expect he thinks much about it."

"What are you two so engrossed in?" asked Todd, walking up with a piece of birthday cake.

"We're dissecting our friendship with Andy," Jack said. "How's the cake?"

"Try it," Todd told him, holding out the plate. "It's vanilla with some kind of caramel-cream filling."

Jack accepted the cake, taking a forkful and sampling it.

"Why try to figure out why you're friends with him?" said Todd as Jack took another bite. "Either you like him or you don't."

"Andy's a little more complicated than that," I said.

"Only if you make him more complicated," said Todd. "It's not like you *have* to be friends with him, right?" He looked from me to Jack. "Or is he paying you guys to do it?" he joked.

"I never thought of that," said Jack. "Maybe we should start charging him."

Todd and Jack continued to talk about the cake, Andy, and the other people at the party. I only half listened. Todd's comment had made me think. He was right, we didn't have to be friends with Andy. But we kept him in our lives. Why? Was it out of habit? Was it out of some weird sentimentality? I tried to come up with an answer, and I couldn't.

"Hey, Todd, take a picture of the three of us."

Andy had come over. He handed Todd a camera, then stood between Jack and me. I was turning my head when the flash went off.

"I don't think I got it," Todd said. "But that was the last shot."

"Don't worry about it," Andy said, taking the camera from him. "I just wanted to use up the roll."

Andy rejoined the party, and shortly afterward I excused myself and left. Jeffrey's apartment was on 76th Street, near Central Park. It was a warm spring evening, one of the first after the harshness of winter, and still light, so I decided to walk home rather than endure a ride in the noisy, stuffy subway.

At the corner of 72nd Street I stopped in front of the Dakota. Following the death of John Lennon, a portion of Central Park had been renamed Strawberry Fields in his honor (despite disapproving Republican members of the City Council arguing that it should be named after Bing Crosby instead). Lennon's widow, Yoko Ono, had further inflamed the situation by taking out a newspaper ad requesting that all the countries of the world send plants and rocks to be used in the creation of the garden. Many wonderful items were delivered to New York, including such lavish gifts as a totem pole from the Aleutian Indians and an enormous amethyst from the government of Paraguay, but ultimately the Landmarks Preservation Commission told Ono that she could include only one of them in the final design.

She'd chosen a mosaic, a round, black-and-white sunburst design created by the Italians after a similar one at Pompeii. In the center of the circle was one word: IMAGINE. The mosaic was placed at the entrance to the park at 72nd Street, just across the street from where Lennon had lain dying from the four bullets in his back. Since its installation, the mosaic had been the site of yearly memorials on the anniversary of the assassination. Throughout the year, flowers, notes, candles, and gifts were routinely left there by fans and mourners of the late Beatle.

As I stood in the circle, I looked back at the Dakota and thought about the night nine years before when I'd met Alan. I'd had almost six years with him. Already he'd been gone nearly three. It hardly seemed possible. I could still remember as if it were yesterday the sadness in his eyes on that winter night when his hero had died. I remembered, too, the emptiness of those eyes when he himself died, his sight stolen by a virus too small to see. A gulf as wide as the sea seemed to separate those two Alans, a space so impossibly wide I couldn't fathom how he'd gotten from one side to the other. But somehow, he'd crossed over, and now he was gone.

I kept walking, cutting over to Columbus Avenue, then Amsterdam. I passed Lincoln Center, site of the AIDS Walk, and the Metropolitan Opera House, where Ileana Cotrubas had broken my heart. Somewhere in the 50s I reversed direction and went east, toward the Avenue of the Americas, which I followed to Rockefeller Center. Alan and I had come there one year for the lighting of the enormous Christmas tree, gazing in childlike wonder as it burst into color. Afterward, we had gone skating, fumbling and laughing as we circled the rink on unsteady legs. A few blocks away, the spires of St. Patrick's Cathedral pierced the sky, a reminder of my last ACT UP demonstration. I thought of Max, defiant and achingly beautiful in his anger, being dragged from the steps by police.

Continuing toward home, I once again headed west, to Broadway, and walked diagonally across Manhattan as I descended south. When I came to Times Square, the memories seeped from every storefront. There was the theater where I'd had my first real date with Alan, and others where, later, I'd watched him perform. There was Don't Tell Mama, where we'd spent so many hours with friends. And there was the Adonis, where Alan had unknowingly invited AIDS into our world. It was boarded up now, the latest casualty in the city's campaign to rid the tourist area of the sex merchants who were bringing down the property values. Its marquee was dark, the men who had frequented the theater driven elsewhere.

Everywhere there were remnants of the past nine years. I could walk only a few blocks before I was reminded of someone or something. Grand Central Station and the taste of Max's mouth. Jack's apartment on 24th Street. The Center on 13th. Restaurants. Movie theaters. Bookstores. They all held memories, like a living scrapbook I could wander through, touching, seeing, remembering. That's what New York had become, a place of memories.

I'd hoped that the passing of winter would lift my black mood. Now I saw that it was with me for good. Too much had been taken from me, and what remained was no longer enough. Only Jack was left. Jack, my first friend and lover. As everything else was torn away, he stayed.

I thought once again of the dream I'd had of Jack's death. He'd been dying from love. I hadn't understood the angel's words then. Now, I thought, I might. How many times had I seen that dream played out in my life with other men? Brian. John. Alan. My AIDS buddies. My friends. Most likely Max. They had all died from love, and thousands more besides.

Was Jack next? Was that the angel's message, delivered years before we even knew AIDS was coming for us? Had she been telling me to keep vigilant, to keep Jack out of harm's way? Suddenly, it made sense. Everything made sense. Andy. Vietnam. Brian. Alan. Max. AIDS. Everything.

My strength renewed by my revelation, I walked the rest of the way to my apartment buoyed by a rising sense of hope. Everything was going to be okay. It was going to be okay.

CHAPTER 56

"Where are we going?" Jack asked as we walked up the stairs from the subway at 81st Street.

"Just come with me," I said, walking toward Central Park.

"I don't know why you can't just tell me what's going on," he said.

"It's a surprise," I told him. "Just trust me."

When we came to the monumental building at Central Park West, Jack stopped. "The Natural History Museum?" he said.

"Come on," I said, starting up the wide front steps to the doors.

Jack followed me as I entered the museum and purchased two tickets. I handed him one and we passed into the huge front hall.

"Are you going to tell what's going on now?" Jack asked.

I ignored him, looking for the elevator to the upper floors. Finding it, I pressed the button and waited for the doors to open. When they did, I got in. Jack stood outside, looking in at me. I reached out and pulled him in.

"I've been to the museum," Jack said testily as the doors closed.

"Remember when we were kids?" I said as we rose.

"What does that have to do with this?" he asked.

"We used to love looking at the stars," I said. "Remember? We'd lie outside in the summer and try to find the different constellations. We even got our Scout badges for astronomy."

The elevator doors opened on the third floor and we got out. The entrance to the Hayden Planetarium was ahead of us.

"Yes," Jack said. "I remember looking at the stars."

"And remember how we promised we'd go to space together? And how we went to the museum in Washington after not speaking for so long?"

"I remember all that," Jack said as we walked into the planetarium. Above us, the map of the universe was projected onto the dome. Looking up at it, I felt as if we were 10 years old and in the backyard. "What does it have to do with right now?" Jack asked.

I tried to calm my nerves before I spoke. "I figured it out," I told him. "The other night, while I was walking home."

"You figured what out?" he said.

"What it all means," I said. "The dream. Everything that's happened. All of it."

"What dream?" said Jack. "Ned, I don't know what you're talking about."

"I had a dream," I explained. "Years ago, when we were kids. You were dying, and I asked the angel why—"

"Back up," Jack said, interrupting. "What angel?"

"The angel in my dream," I said. "It doesn't matter. What matters is that she showed me that you were dying, and it was because of love."

"Love?" Jack repeated.

"Yes," I said. "I didn't know what she meant, but now I do. AIDS. Love. Dying. Don't you get it?"

"No," Jack answered. "I don't."

I ran my fingers through my hair. What I wanted to say wasn't coming out the way it had in my head. Jack wasn't understanding me. I tried again.

"You were dying of love," I said. "In my dream. But it wasn't really love, it was AIDS."

"You think you dreamed of me dying from AIDS when we were kids?" said Jack. "Ned, that's nuts."

"Why?" I said. "Why is it any more nuts than people really dying from AIDS? Why is it any more nuts than people who dream about talking to their dead parents, or about finding something they've lost, or anything at all, really?"

"Okay, so maybe you had this dream," said Jack. "What about it?"

"She was telling me that I'm supposed to save you," I told him. "I'm supposed to save you from dying."

"And how are you supposed to do that?" Jack asked. "By bringing me to the museum?"

"By loving you," I said. "By loving you and making sure you never get sick."

I took Jack's hands and held them while he stared at me, not speaking. I could see that he thought I was crazy, and I desperately wanted him to understand how terribly serious I was.

"I love you, Jack," I said. "I always have, since that very first time. Even through everything else—Andy, Brian, all of it—I've loved you. But it took all that for me to see it."

"I love you, too, Ned," he said.

"That's why we need to be together," I said.

"Together?" said Jack. "What do you mean together?"

"Lovers," I explained. "Partners. Like we were before."

Jack took his hands away from mine and put them in his pockets. "That's not possible, Ned," he said. "I'm with Todd."

I shook my head. "You can't stay with him," I said. "If you do, you'll get sick."

"We're both negative," Jack said. "And we're going to stay that way."

"That's what Alan and I thought," I said. "And look what happened to us. That's what the angel was saying. We're only going to be safe if we're together, you and me."

"People don't die from love, Ned," Jack said. "They die because they make bad decisions. They decide to have unsafe sex. They decide to shoot drugs. They decide to put themselves at risk."

"Brian didn't know," I countered. "None of us knew then."

"But we do now," said Jack. "We can't use that excuse anymore."

"So it's Alan's fault he died?" I asked. "Is that what you're saying?"

"I'm saying he made a choice," Jack answered. "He made a choice to go into that theater. He made a choice to have unsafe sex with a stranger. I'm sorry about what happened to him. I'm sorry about what happened to you. But he made a choice, and it's a choice I'm never going to make."

I was stunned. I didn't know what to think, and certainly not what to say. All I could do was stare at Jack, waiting for him to take back what he'd said. A long time went by before he spoke.

"AIDS isn't about love," he said finally. "I'm not sure it ever was, but it's certainly not now. It's about a virus. And staying alive is about keeping that virus out of our bodies. Love doesn't do that."

"Then what does?" I asked him. "Rubbers? Dental dams? Covering our cocks and protecting our assholes even when we're fucking our own lovers?" My voice was tense with anger. "Is this what you've learned from your work? To blame people with AIDS?"

"I know what you're feeling," Jack said, ignoring the question. "I see it in my patients all the time. They want to go back. They want to live in a time when things were easier, when we didn't have to worry about all of this shit."

"I'm not one of your patients," I said.

"I feel it myself sometimes," he continued. "It would be great to be ten years old again. Christ, we didn't worry about anything then."

"You mean *you* didn't," I said. "I worried enough for the both of us. You just never noticed."

"People change," said Jack. "We grow up. I grew up. But I don't think you have, Ned. I think you're still that same ten-year-old boy, thinking you can make everything okay if you just try hard enough."

"Fuck you," I said, resorting to the basest of insults. "You don't know what I feel. I'm trying to *help* you, Jack."

"By telling me to leave my boyfriend and become yours?" he said. "Because some angel told you that you need to save me? Do you know how this sounds?"

The thing was, I didn't know how it sounded. At least not to him. To me it made perfect sense. But I couldn't get Jack to see that. I sat down on a low wall that ran around the hall and stared at the floor.

Jack sat down next to me. "Have you been taking anything?" he asked. "Pot? Coke? X?"

I didn't answer. I had smoked some pot earlier in the day, but I knew that had nothing to do with how I was feeling. The dizziness I was experiencing was purely the result of realizing that Jack was telling me no. My stomach was churning, and I was afraid I might vomit.

I stood up. "Good-bye, Jack," I said.

He stood and reached for my arm, but I pulled away. "Please don't follow me," I said.

"Where are you going?" he asked.

"Home," I told him.

"We'll talk later?"

"Sure," I answered. "I'm sorry," I added. "About everything."

I walked quickly out of the planetarium. An elevator had just emptied a group of schoolchildren into the hallway, and I waded through them, getting in and sighing with relief as the doors closed without anyone else joining me.

I didn't go home. Not right away. First I went to a bar—the Works on Columbus Avenue—where I drank four Seven & Sevens. Then I went home with a man who looked to me like he could conjure up the Devil. I made him fuck me without a rubber, hard and fast, and when he came inside of me, I prayed that what I hoped he carried would find its way into my blood.

I made one final stop before going home, walking through Washington Square Park and pausing long enough to purchase an eight-ball from a skinny skateboard punk whose hooded sweatshirt hid his face as one nimble hand quickly shoved my money down the front of his jeans and emerged with my bag of coke. He was gone a second later, disappearing into the shadows beneath the trees, the drugs in my pocket and the raspy sound of his board's wheels on the asphalt the only proof that he hadn't been a mirage. I left him to his nightly wanderings and returned to my apartment, my journey completed.

I did half of the coke while watching a tape of *Pee-Wee's Playhouse Christmas Special*, numbing my brain until I forgot all about the disastrous meeting with Jack. I howled when Pee-Wee opened a gift box to find Grace Jones inside, and sang along with the crazy Del Rubio Triplets and Dinah Shore. The manic energy of Pee-Wee Herman and his wild holiday extravaganza matched the twirling of my brain. It all seemed perfectly normal and ordinary to me, and I imagined myself living forever in that world, where Miss Yvonnne would be my neighbor and nothing would happen that couldn't be fixed.

I can laugh now about how insane I was, but the truth is, I came very close to dying that night. I snorted cocaine until I couldn't feel anything, washing it down with old reliable Jack Daniels. My heart was probably close to stopping, or exploding, as the cocaine and alcohol were distilled by my liver, releasing cocaethylene into my system and increasing the effects of the blow until I heard Pee-Wee tell me to go find the skateboard punk and invite him home for a three-way.

I must have gotten up and tried to pull on my jacket. When I woke up hours later, I was facedown on the floor, one arm through the jacket sleeve and the other trapped beneath my body. I tried to move it, but it had gone numb and was useless. I managed to roll myself over, only to find that my face had been stuck to the carpet by a combination of blood and spit. My nose had bled profusely, leaving a large red stain on the beige carpeting, and I couldn't breathe through my nostrils. I raised my hand to wipe away some of the blood, and only succeeded in banging myself with my dead hand.

I lay on the floor for a long time, first fearing that I had done irreparable harm to my arm, and then wondering if I'd had some kind of aneurysm from the coke. I felt strange, and I was a little concerned that if I tried to move, I might do further damage to my brain, which still didn't feel quite right. Then my arm began to tingle painfully as the blood flowed back into it, and one worry was crossed off my list.

As I waited for the tingling to stop, the phone rang. I let the machine take it, groaning when I heard the chirpy voice of the school secretary leaving a message asking if I was all right. I had no idea what time it was, but I'd clearly missed getting to work. I would have to invent some plausible excuse for my absence, and my failure to alert anyone to it.

Finally, I sat up, then slowly got to my feet. Everything seemed to be moving correctly, and I made it to the bathroom without further mishap. The mirror, however, revealed the extent of the damage I'd done to myself. Besides the bleeding nose, both of my eyes were black, a consequence of falling on my face. My lips, too, were puffy and bruised. Amidst all the swelling and discoloration, I congratulated myself that I'd at least managed not to break my nose.

I got a washcloth, soaked it in warm water under the tap, and began to gently erase the marks of my binge. Every touch made me flinch, and even without the blood covering my skin, my face looked worn and defeated. I hurt everywhere, both inside and out. My asshole ached, and I remembered the man from the night before and what we'd done. I'd wanted him to fuck me so hard that I split open. I'd told him that, and he'd done his best to oblige. I saw myself on my back, his hands gripping my thighs painfully while he pumped in and out. I'd wished that I'd feel something inside of me burst, and that I would die on his bed, my heart failing as he emptied himself.

But I was still alive, although I felt more dead than ever before. The man staring back at me in the mirror was no one I recognized, and no one that I wanted to know. I wanted to get away from him, leave him alone in his apartment with his sadness and anger while I ran far, far away. He wanted me dead, and I feared that if I stayed with him, I would let him have his wish.

CHAPTER 57

"And so I left," I tell Thayer. "Again. I probably should have expected it, since it was the end of another decade."

"You didn't even tell Jack you were going?" Thayer asks me as he gets up for another cup of coffee. By now it's closer to lunch than it is to breakfast, but we're still sitting in the kitchen in our robes. Only Sam has moved, reluctantly, to investigate the bowl of food Thayer set out for him earlier. Having eaten, he's back to napping, sprawled across the floor, dreaming, his paws twitching as he chases rabbits. I lean down and scratch him behind the ear, reminding him that he is a good boy, and that he's safe.

"No," I say, answering Thayer's question. "I didn't tell him. I didn't tell anyone. Except for school," I add. "I told them my mother had died unexpectedly and I needed to go take care of my stepfather. They had no reason not to believe me. There were only a few months left in the year anyway."

He knows the rest of the story. I returned to San Francisco. I don't know why, really, except that I remembered how beautiful it was and had some notion that it would revive me. But when I got there, I found that its beauty had faded, at least for me. The friends I'd had were mostly gone, dead or left to escape the memories. I spent a year there, living in a house on Army Street, trying to bring the past back to life. It was to that house that Jack mailed the Christmas card with the photos. He got the address from my mother, one of the few times I ever regretted the closeness of our families. I never replied.

In the spring of 1990, my mother found a lump in her breast, and by summer she was dead. Walter, unable to live with the ghosts of both his wife and her husband, sold the house and moved to Florida to be closer to Candace, who was pleased to finally have all of his attention. I received a sum of money in my mother's will, and decided to use it to start my life anew. I chose Maine because I had never been there, and therefore had no memories to face, and because I wanted to live in a place that had not been devastated by the plague.

I arrived here the day of my 40th birthday, moving into a house that I'd bought sight unseen, reassured by the no-nonsense voice of a real estate agent whose thick accent convinced me that I was getting the place for a *bah-gin*. At first I was frightened by the large, empty rooms and the smell of the ocean, so much stronger here than in San Francisco, where the sea's aroma is overpowered by the scent of the eucalyptus trees first planted in 1853 by W.C. Walker of the Golden Gate Nursery from Australian seeds. Where those foreign invaders had quickly made Northern California their home and waged a battle for control of the native landscape, the pine forests of Maine are happy to play second fiddle to the mighty Atlantic, keeping a respectful distance from the lapping waves and confining their redolence to the space beneath their branches.

Soon, though, I filled the house with furniture and came to love the ocean's wildness. As the days passed, I breathed more easily as, bit by bit, I let go of the past. I threw out the last of the cocaine I'd brought with me from San Francisco, pouring it into the sea from the deck of a whale-watching boat while the other passengers were distracted by the appearance of a pair of minke whales, and I began to think about a return to teaching. When I read about an opening at a local school, I applied and was accepted.

In the summer of 1991, I was walking through town and stopped to admire a painting in the window of an art gallery. It was an abstract, bursts of indigo and lemon against a cherry-red background. Curious, I entered the shop and met the artist, who was there delivering some new work. Thayer and I had dinner that evening, and when he moved into the house after a six-month courtship, we hung that painting over our bed.

It was Thayer who encouraged me to return to school, Thayer who applied gentle pressure when progress on my master's thesis stalled, and Thayer who convinced me that, at 45, I was not too old to become the junior instructor in the history department of the University of New England. I owe a great deal of my current happiness to him, although I like to think that I have been equally supportive of his painting.

I fear perhaps Thayer will be angry at me for never telling him the roles Jack and Andy have played in my history. If he is, though, he doesn't show it. He asks only, "You haven't spoken to either of them in fifteen years?"

"Not until yesterday," I tell him. "Jack called."

"After all this time?" says Thayer. "Why?"

This is where I begin to feel the weight of the past pressing down on me. "Andy's dying," I tell Thayer. "Jack thinks I should see him."

"In New York?" Thayer asks.

"Chicago," I answer. "I guess he moved there a few years ago. Jack really didn't say much, and I didn't ask for details."

Thayer is quiet, drinking his coffee as I look out the window. The rain has slowed, and again I think about finding the ladder and cleaning the gutters. It will be a good way to distract myself from the thoughts in my head.

"You should go," Thayer says, and I look at him. "You should go," he repeats. "It's been too long."

"But—" I begin to argue.

"Ned, they're your family," says Thayer. "Like it or not."

I fold my hands and tap my fingers against the backs of my hands, a habit I don't remember having when I was younger, but which I find myself engaging in more and more. Thayer puts his hand on top of mine, stilling the wiggling spider of my fingers. I look into his face, and he leans forward, his forehead resting against mine.

"Go," he says.

He makes the calls, arranges the flight while I pack. I will be in Chicago in less than nine hours. Jack has agreed to pick me up at the airport. His voice when I told him I was coming was filled with happiness, but I feel only dread.

When Thayer drops me off, he kisses me and says, "I love you." I don't want to leave him, but he assures me that we will both be fine. "Call me when you're settled in," he says as I take my suitcase from the backseat. When he drives away, I consider hailing a cab and following him. Instead, I face the glass doors and force myself through them.

The flight itself is uneventful. We stop in New York, where I sit in the American Airlines waiting area at LaGuardia and try not to think about the fact that I'm once again moving backwards through my life.

Thankfully, the city is far enough away from the airport that I can pretend I am somewhere else—Amsterdam, maybe, or Berlin. When the call to board the next flight crackles from the terminal's intercom, I am relieved that we are going.

On the second and final leg of the journey, I find that the passenger before me has left a paperback tucked into the seat pocket. When I take it out, I am unnerved to discover that I am holding a copy of *It*, undoubtedly picked up at the last minute by someone desperate for something to read and forced to choose between either Stephen King or Patricia Cornwell, who seem to have a monopoly on airport bookstores. I have not opened the book since Alan's death, and therefore have never gotten beyond page 367.

I'm tempted to put the novel back, but its appearance seems far too unlikely (the popularity of Stephen King as in-flight reading notwithstanding) to be accidental, and so I open it and begin reading where I left off twenty years before. I'm surprised that after only a few pages I can recall the plot with very few holes in my memory of it. As the story of seven friends who face a monster as children and return twenty-eight years later to do battle with it again unfolds, I can't help but feel a kinship with them. I, too, am returning to my past, to face a monster I believed to be dead and gone until a phone call drew me back.

I am sixty pages from the end when the captain's voice announces that we are making our final descent into Chicago. I leave the six surviving characters (one, unable to face his fears again, has killed himself) as they enter the sewers in search of the evil, hoping that King will let them survive. I do not take the book with me when we reach the gate and disembark, feeling it belongs somehow to the world within the plane.

The passengers ahead of me are in no hurry to leave. They take what seems an inordinate amount of time putting on coats and taking down carry-ons from the overhead compartments. They chat easily with one another, and I am growing increasingly impatient. I want them to be quiet and move. I am anxious to be off the aircraft, both because I want to get the reunion with Jack over with and because I badly need to get to the men's room. I have never liked using the bathrooms on airplanes, and my bladder has been demanding release for the past hour. Now that I'm standing, the need to go is urgent, and I shift back and forth like a nervous child.

Finally, we begin to file off. As I clear the doorway and enter the gangway, I step around the woman in front of me, cursing the inventor of roller bags, and walk quickly to the end. I look for Jack, then remember that in the new age of increased security, he is not allowed to meet me at the gate. Instead, I head for the nearest bathroom. Emerging a few minutes later, I begin the long walk through Terminal 3, passing the Great American Pretzel Company, Cinnabon, and no fewer than three Starbucks before arriving, finally, at the exit. There I join the stream of travelers going out to meet loved ones and limo drivers.

I recognize Jack at once. He is standing apart from the crowd, his hands folded across his chest. When he sees me, he waves and calls my name. For a moment I hesitate, until the force of the people behind me urges me forward and I go to him. When I get there, Jack embraces me and kisses my cheek, as if only a day or two has passed since we last saw one another.

"You look great," he says.

"So do you," I tell him. And he does. His hair is still golden, his face still handsome. He resembles his father now, but with the added grace of his mother's beauty.

As we walk to the parking garage, Jack fills me in on Andy's condition. "The heart attack has really weakened him," he tells me. "Normally, a guy his age would be able to recover from it. But his heart is so damaged from all the cocaine that they can't operate. They've loaded him up with medication, but that's all they can do."

"When did it happen?" I ask him.

"Three days ago," says Jack. "A friend found him on the floor of his apartment."

"Friend?" I say.

"Just a friend," says Jack, understanding my meaning. "He hasn't had a lover in seven or eight years. Not since the last one died."

"How did he end up in Chicago?"

"Reuben, his last partner, lived here," Jack informs me. "He was an architect. Really nice guy."

"Nicer than Jeffrey?" I say.

Jack laughs. "I think Mussolini was nicer than Jeffrey," he replies. "I have to say, I didn't miss him when he died."

We haven't discussed our own lives, and I wonder if Jack is avoiding it on purpose. I told him nothing about my life during our phone call, and asked him nothing about his. We have many years to catch up on, but we seem to be in no hurry to do it. There are many possible reasons why, and I wonder which is closest to the truth.

In the garage, Jack stops at a Ford Explorer and opens the back with the electronic fob. As I place my bag inside, he apologizes for the size of the vehicle. "I never get to drive in New York," he explains as we get in. "I thought I'd see what it's like to be a soccer mom."

The drive from the airport into the city proper is surprisingly long, and finally Jack begins to poke tenderly at the edges of our severed friendship. "Do you have a partner?" he asks me.

I tell him about Thayer, speaking more about his art than the man himself. I'm still not comfortable with the situation, and want to be able to retreat with my secrets intact if need be. Jack listens politely, asking questions and congratulating me on my domestic arrangement. When I've said all I can about the subject, I return the favor and inquire about his relationship.

"I'm still with Todd," he says. "Can you believe it? Twenty years. We're like the poster boys for long-term gay relationships in our circle."

"What about work?" I ask.

"Hope House closed in ninety-two," he tells me. "It turns out the executive director was skimming money to pay for his condo. I worked for a couple of different agencies for a year, then Todd convinced me to open my own practice again. I've been doing that ever since."

"Do you still like New York?" I say.

"You know how it is," he answers. "The longer you stay there, the harder it is to get out. Sometimes we talk about moving somewhere else, though. Todd thinks we should go to Toronto so we can get married. We flew to San Francisco and did it when Gavin Newsom made it legal for all of ten minutes, but it would be nice to do it for real."

"Listen to us," I say. "We sound like old married people."

"We *are* old married people," says Jack. "And there's nothing wrong with that." He looks over at me. "I was sorry to hear about your mom," he says.

I nod. "She went fast," I say. "How are your parents?"

"Dad died two years ago," he tells me. "Mom is still there. A couple of gay guys bought your old house a few years back, and she spends a lot of time helping them with their garden. They're like her best friends. All she talks about is how Sean and Christopher throw the best dinner parties, and how they take her to the ballet and go shopping with her. She loves Todd, but I think she still wishes you and I were a couple and living next door to her."

I laugh at the image of Patricia Grace as a fag hag. It's easy to picture, and I'm glad she has people in her life now that my mother and her husband are gone. But she's also the last of our parents alive, which reminds me that Jack and I are the last of our generation as well. We have no siblings, no children to continue our lines. I have never much cared about the extension of my family name, but faced with the fact of its eventual demise, I can't help but be a little wistful.

"We're staying at Andy's apartment," Jack says as we exit the freeway and head downtown. It's been a long time since I've been in such a large city, and although Chicago's streets are wider than most, for a moment I feel claustrophobic. The buildings rising up on either side of us create high walls, like the sides of a maze. As Jack turns the Explorer right, then left, then right again, I feel like we're searching for a way out, trying to find our way to the lump of cheese at the end.

I close my eyes and focus on my breathing, a trick Thayer claims works for him in times of stress. I count to a hundred, slowly, and when I open my eyes, I am indeed more relaxed. Either Thayer's exercise has worked, or I've simply tapped into the remnants of the urbanite in me, the one who learned to live penned up like a barnyard animal whose grassy field had been replaced by acres of concrete. Although the busy-ness around me is distracting—the lights and horns and people crossing the street in front of us—I can feel myself adapting. Living in Maine, it seems, hasn't quite killed the city dweller in me.

Jack pulls into the garage of a modern, glass-fronted building, navigating the Explorer into a spot marked RESERVED. We get out and walk to an elevator, which at the turn of a key inserted by Jack takes us to the penthouse and opens directly into a living room whose windows provide a panoramic view of Chicago.

"Here we are," Jack says.

"Leave it to Andy," I remark as I look around at the beautiful room.

"That's just what Reuben did," says Jack, tossing his jacket onto a leather couch that looks as if it cost more than the entire contents of my house. "Do you want a drink?"

"Just water," I tell him, not adding that it's been more than eight years since I last tasted alcohol. I'd held on to drinking for a while after giving up coke, but eventually I'd realized that I needed to abandon it as well. Luckily, I'd also found that I didn't miss it, and the transition to tea, water, and fruit juice had been fairly painless.

Jack goes somewhere, presumably into the kitchen, and returns with two bottles of water. He hands me one and sits on the couch. I sit in a chair across from him, the two of us separated by a glass-top coffee table on which an orchid sits in a beautiful glazed pot.

"We can see Andy in the morning," Jack says. "Visiting hours are over for tonight."

"Okay," I say, drinking some water and relishing its cool touch on my dry throat.

"Are you hungry?" Jack asks. He looks at his watch. "I think we can find someplace open late. There's not much here. I've mostly been eating at the hospital."

"No," I tell him. "I'm fine."

"I'm glad you're here," he says.

I'm not sure if I'm glad to be here or not, so I say nothing.

"The place has three guest bedrooms," Jack tells me. "I'm in the first one on the right down the hall. You can use either of the other ones."

"I'm pretty tired," I say. "I think I'll turn in."

I stand up, and so does Jack. We walk down the hall and he shows me the two rooms. I choose the one farthest from his, on the opposite side of the hall. "I'll see you in the morning," I tell him, and go inside. I shut the door behind me and lock it.

CHAPTER 58

Even dying, Andy commands attention. The nurses who attend to him, both male and female, treat him like a child. They smooth the blanket covering his body and push his hair away from his eyes. They speak gently to him and smile when he answers. His face and hands are puffy, a common result of congestive heart failure, and Jack has warned me, so I'm not shocked when I see him for the first time. Still, seeing him so weak is disturbing.

"Hey, soldier," I say, pulling a chair next to his bed and sitting down. "How's it going?"

Andy looks at me and flashes a pale imitation of his cocky grin. "Hi," he says, his voice hoarse.

I can tell he's tired, so I don't ask any more questions. I know everything anyway. I've come to see him, not to interrogate. Jack takes a chair on Andy's other side and we sit watching as he fades in and out of sleep. Sometimes he recognizes us and tries to smile, as if entire days have passed and he's seeing us for the first time since our last visit. Other times, he looks around the room in confusion, and draws his hands away from our touch.

He's 56 years old, and yet when I look at him, I see a 19-year-old boy. I look over at Jack. "Remember when we met him for the first time?" I ask.

"He wanted to know if we were brothers," Jack says.

"Those stupid matching towels," I say, and we both laugh.

Hearing us, Andy wakes up, and for a moment his expression is lucid. "Ned," he says. "Jack. I knew you guys would be here. I knew you wouldn't let me go without saying good-bye."

It's as if he's been possessed. His voice is clear, and he looks from me to Jack with eyes unclouded by pain.

"No," Jack says. "We wouldn't let you go without saying good-bye."

Andy looks at me. "What happened?" he asks. "You got old."

"I'm sorry," I tell him. "I didn't mean to."

He coughs and closes his eyes. His chest rattles as he tries to breathe. I wonder if we should call a nurse, and start to stand up, when Andy opens his eyes again.

"Fuck," he says. "This really sucks."

I can't help laughing, although the sound that comes out of me is mixed with muffled crying. I know he's dying, but it's such an Andy thing to say, an expression of resentment for the way his body is failing him. Even at the end, he won't take responsibility. I love him for that.

Those are his last words. Jack and I have both seen enough death to know when it's come, and we let the heart monitor's high-pitched wail alert the nurses. A doctor is called, and soon enough the verdict is in. Andy is gone.

Jack and I stay only long enough to sign over the body. In a last (and possibly his only) gesture of magnanimity, Andy has agreed to let himself be used by science. I try to imagine medical students cutting him open, peering inside at his organs, poking around in the viscera as they search for answers to the body's riddles. What would they think, I wonder, if they knew they were handling the spleen and liver of Brad Majors? Would they even recognize the name? Perhaps the gay ones would. Vintage porn is, after all, making a comeback now that audiences have tired of paying money to see cocks sealed in latex. Like a populace weary of a war that has dragged on too long without resolution, our enthusiasm for protected sex has waned as the plague remains undefeated.

Jack suggests lunch, which I agree to readily. With the exception of coffee and a bagel, I've eaten nothing since the night before. It's early afternoon, and we find a restaurant uncrowded with lunch hour diners. When we're seated, I flip through the menu.

"This feels weird," I tell Jack. "Shouldn't we be more upset?"

"That's one of the things about getting older," he says. "You've been through this before, and you know how it goes."

"It still feels like someone's crossing off names and there aren't that many more ahead of ours on the list," I say.

"We've lived longer than a lot of people we know," Jack reminds me.

This is true, I think, but only because we've been very lucky. "I guess I've seen too many movies," I say. "I sort of thought there'd be some big final deathbed scene."

"Do you remember the scene in *Terms of Endearment* when Debra Winger dies?" Jack asks. He doesn't wait for an answer before continuing, because of course I remember the scene. "Her boys have come to see her," says Jack. "She tells them she's sorry she's sick, and to not be afraid of girls, and to keep their bangs trimmed."

"But it's okay to leave the back long," I say, remembering how the scene had made me both laugh and cry.

"Right," says Jack. "They leave, and you think you've got a while before she actually dies. Then, just like that, she gives Shirley MacLaine this last little look and that's it, she's gone."

"What is it Shirley says?" I ask him, trying to remember, and coming up with the line. "'Somehow I thought that when she finally went, it would be a relief.'"

"That's it," says Jack. "She doesn't scream and fall apart. But you can tell it's hit her hard, and that it's going to take her a long time to get over it."

"Sally Field screamed in *Steel Magnolias*," I say.

"Sally Field screams in everything," says Jack.

"Do you think it will hit us later?" I ask him.

Jack sighs. "I don't know," he says. "Sometimes I think the more someone meant to you, the longer it takes. Then, one day, you realize how much you miss them."

"We're back where we started," I say. "It's just you and me."

Jack takes a long drink from his water glass. "Ned, there's something I have to tell you," he says. "I'm positive."

I wait for him to say that he's joking, attempting some deathbed humor that's fallen flat. He doesn't. "I thought you were okay," I say.

"I am okay," Jack replies. "I've got it in check, and I'll probably live as long as I would have without the virus."

"But how?" I say. "Was it Brian?"

"Maybe," he tells me. "I doubt it. I think I would have known way before I did if that was it. But it could have been anyone. I wasn't always safe."

"What about Todd?"

"He's positive, too," Jack says. "That's why we don't know who had it first. We both thought we were okay, so we weren't using rubbers."

"How long have you known?" I ask him.

"Since right after you left New York," says Jack. He straightens the silverware beside his plate. "I got tested after that day at the planetarium."

"Because of what I said?" I ask.

He nods. "It really freaked me out," he says. "That stuff about needing to save me and dying from love and all of that. I thought you were nuts, but I went and got tested because of it. That's when I found out. If I'd waited, I'd probably be dead. Todd would probably be dead. I had to make him get tested. He'd refused to do it because of privacy issues and confidentiality of patient records and all of that. But when I got my results, I told him he had to find out."

"You're sure you're okay?" I ask him.

"Yeah," he says. "We've got a great doctor. Plus, Todd has us doing yoga and acupuncture, and we're on this diet he insists will help us live forever. He made me give up red meat. At least when he's around. I'm ordering a steak, and if you tell him, I'll deny it."

"Scout's honor," I say, holding up my hand.

The waiter comes to take our order. As threatened, Jack requests a steak, and I get the chicken piccata. When he leaves, I pick up my water and drink, giving myself time to think about Jack's news. I can see him through the glass, his image distorted by the ice cubes so that he looks like a ghost, faceless and blurred. The revelation of his status isn't as unsettling to me as the irony that I, who actively sought out infection because of the same incident that has resulted in what Jack calls his salvation, am not positive. To my initial disappointment and eventual relief, my prayers that my Mephistophelian trick had poisoned me the night of my bust-up with Jack had gone unanswered. Six different tests taken obsessively over the course of a year confirmed my failure to become one of the damned, and subsequent annual tests consistently came back negative, until finally I had accepted that I was not going to die that way.

Being positive is no longer the death sentence it once was, as evidenced by the casualness with which we speak about Jack's HIV status. I know that he is more likely to expire from any of the myriad "normal" causes of death than he is from something associated with the virus in-side of him. But I also can't help feeling guilty. I know that this is a re-action common to men who have emerged unscathed from the firestorm that has claimed so many of our brothers. I know, too, that it is foolish to feel this way. We all took the same chances. Those of us without the virus are not blessed or special. We are simply lucky.

I know that Jack would never want me to feel guilty either. But I still do, if only a little. He says that I saved him. I think that I saved myself. Maybe, I tell myself as I drain the last drops from my glass and set it down, it doesn't matter.

"If anyone had told me when we were twelve that when I was fifty-six I'd be living with a man and have an incurable disease, I would have laughed," Jack says. "Then again, if anyone had told me when I was thirty-nine that I'd be HIV-positive and alive, I would have laughed, too."

"It's all about perspective," I tell him.

"Do you ever think about what it might be like if we'd stayed to-gether?" Jack asks me.

"No," I lie.

"Yes, you do," says Jack. "You answered too fast. That's how I always knew you were lying when we were kids. You were never good at it."

"Of course I've thought about it," I tell him. "Not in a long time, though."

"Same here," says Jack. "I think we would have driven each other crazy."

"We did," I remind him. "Several times."

"I used to think that's why you left New York," says Jack. "Because of me."

"You always give yourself too much credit," I say. "It's not always about you."

"Says who?" Jack teases.

"You were only part of it," I say. "I just had to get out of there. I felt like a dog chasing its own tail."

"Have you caught it yet?" Jack asks.

"I stopped trying," I tell him.

"Do you remember the fight we had over the comic books?" he says. "About Superman and Batman?"

"I'm surprised you remember," I say. "I didn't think you really no-ticed."

Jack picks at a roll. "I noticed," he says. "It was the first time you ever stood up to me. I just pretended not to care because I was afraid you might figure out you could take me." He puts the roll on his plate. "I needed you, Ned, and I was so afraid you would leave because I wasn't as smart as you were."

"Says the man with the Dr. in front of his name," I say.

"I'm serious," Jack says. "I never understood why you put up with me."

"It was because I loved you," I say. "That's all."

"When I was in seminary, I used to beg God to make me straight," Jack says. "At least until James suggested we sleep together. Even then, I hoped it was something I'd grow out of."

"Why?"

"You and Andy were off in Vietnam being heroes," says Jack. "I was the one hiding behind God. I was sure you'd end up together somehow, and I'd be stuck in some church, preaching sermons and thinking dirty thoughts about my male parishioners."

"I never did think you'd be a very good minister," I say.

"I wished I was more like you," Jack says.

"Funny," I tell him, "I always wanted to be more like you."

"Do you still?" he asks me.

I wait before answering, so he knows I'm not lying. "No," I tell him. "I like who I am."

"Same here," he says. "It took us long enough to figure it out."

Our food arrives, and we eat. Outside, the October afternoon is gray and cold. Jack and I talk some more, filling in the gaps of the past fifteen years. When Andy's name comes up, we toast him with our water glasses and take turns remembering stories about him. I forget that it's been only a few hours since his death. Already he seems a happy memory. Maybe Jack is right, and one day I'll feel his death more acutely. For now, I'm happy to put him to rest.

After lunch, we walk beside the Chicago River, not quite ready to return to Andy's apartment. It occurs to me that my grandmother may have walked here sixty years before me, contemplating the death of her husband and trying to make sense of her life. She's gone now, having passed peacefully in her sleep at 87, and I am the last of her blood. Perhaps, with Andy's death and my return to the city where Violet Renard O'Reilly believed a curse fell upon her, we have come full circle. Maybe Jack is right and I have, in my clumsy way, saved him from the tragedy shown to me by the angel all those years ago.

We walk without talking, two men who were boys together. Soon we will return to our separate lives. But we will never be far from one another, linked forever by the bond formed before our births. Our stories are inextricably bound together, and although the endings have yet to be written, the pages contain tales enough to fill a lifetime.

EPILOGUE

They say that when the last mystery is solved, the world will end. I don't suspect that will happen, or, if it does, it will be long after my own death and I won't be around to care. Unless Thayer is right and we all keep coming back until we've figured out what we did to deserve being human. Given what I know of humans, though, I have faith that we never will figure it out, and that the death of the world will be due instead to the burning out of the sun or the stupidity of George W. Bush's great-great-great-great-great-great-great grandchild.

Until that happens, there will always be friendship and love, and between the two of them, there are mysteries enough to last lifetimes. I've spent mine trying to figure them out, and have only begun to scratch the surface. If I'm lucky, in the end I'll be the tiniest bit closer to understanding why I've loved the people I've loved and where doing so has taken me.

Not that I really want answers. Sometimes the best part of a mystery is that it can never be solved to our satisfaction. Like God and death, the question of what drives the heart may be one we never fully understand. The possibilities are many and, like the true identity of Jack the Ripper or the source of creation, are a matter for endless debate. And although some will doubtless be disappointed when no clear answer arises to give them comfort, those who look carefully will find that in the search—in the questioning and wondering and raging— there is beauty beyond reckoning.